I0611572

Praise for

A Decision of the Heart

"Donna Rhine offers the reader much more than just the surface: one receives mouth-watering bites of real life from her interesting characters. I enjoy grabbing a glass of iced tea, kicking back in my La-z-boy recliner, and entering this delightful author's wonderful world."

Alan Maki
Author of *A Choice to Cherish* and *Written on Her Heart*
Broadman and Holman Publishers

"A charming nostalgic debut! Kaleb is a hero to cheer for as he patiently woos Liz, a spunky tom-boy with bigger things than marriage on her mind. Mrs. Rhine builds a tender love story between two long-time friends who have much to learn about each other. This one's not to be missed!"

Jenna Mindel
Author of *Miss Whitlow's Turn*
2006 RITA finalist

A Decision of the Heart

Donna Rhine

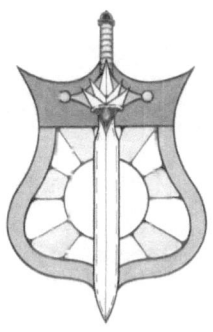

© 2007 Donna Rhine
© 2011 Donna Rhine

Published by:
Armoury House Publishing
P.O. Box 60
Carleton, MI 48117 USA

ISBN-10: 0-615455-33-6
ISBN-13: 978-0-615455-33-4

All Rights reserved. No part of this book may be reproduced or transmitted in any form or by any means including, but not limited to, electronic or mechanical, photocopying, recording, or by any information storage and retrieval system without written permission from the publisher, except for the inclusion of brief quotations in review.

All scripture quotations, unless otherwise indicated, are taken from The King James Version of the Bible.

Author: Donna Rhine
Cover: Steve Rhine, James Dunayski, Chamira Jones
Editor: Rebecca Hayward, Steve Memmer, Steve Rhine

First U.S. Edition 2007
Second U. S. Edition 2011
Third U.S. Edition 2014

Library of Congress Cataloging-in-Publication Data

Rhine, Donna, 1958-
  A decision of the heart / by Donna Rhine. -- 1st U.S. ed.
     p. cm.
  ISBN-13: 978-1-934363-01-0 (pbk. : alk. paper)
  ISBN-10: 1-934363-01-4 (pbk. : alk. paper)
  1. Marriage--Fiction. 2. Pregnant women--Fiction. 3. Frontier and pioneer life--Michigan--Fiction. 4. Michigan--Fiction. 5. Domestic fiction. I. Title.
  PS3618.H56D43 2007
  813'.6--dc22

                          2007003764

  A decision of the heart / by Donna Rhine. -- 2nd U.S. ed.
     p. cm.
  ISBN-13: 978-0-615455-33-4 (pbk. : alk. paper)
  ISBN-10: 0-615455-33-6 (pbk. : alk. paper)

For current information about releases by Donna Rhine or other releases from Armoury House Publishing, visit the author's Web site: http://www.daisytales.com

Printed in the United States of America
tv5 04JUN20
cv3 2B 11

Acknowledgments

My life without God in it would be but dust in the wind. My heart ever rejoices in His goodness! And, oh, how my spirit dances on!

Writing my first novel has taken me on a journey that has stretched my heart and mind like nothing else ever has. Tears and laughter filled my soul as life experiences became intertwined in the characters' lives and the story unfolded before my eyes. This venture has been one I will always cherish ....

So, it is with great pleasure that I share this historical adventure with you—enjoy!

For all who have been encouraging me and praying for me along the way, I am truly thankful. May God bless you abundantly for the way you have blessed me.

Oh, Stephen! You are not only the love of my life, my treasured friend and husband, you are so much more than words could ever convey. Thank you for believing in me and giving me the endless hours I needed to fan the flames of the gift He has given.

To my parents, Donald and Carolyn Williams; my in-laws, Lauren and Geraldine Rhine; and the rest of the Rhine and Williams families, thanks for the many ways you have touched my life.

To my children and grandchildren: Anthony and Toviah Washington (Tyrin, Trevon, Tovias, Tydelle and Tayeh), Jason and Joy Grzywacz (Austin, Andrew, and Alyssa), Tirus and Krista Kimani (Lauren, Mya, Isaiah, Stephen, and Olivia), and Joshua, thank you. Each and every one of you is a special gift from the Lord!

To Pastors Rocky Barra and Dave Stephens, thanks for allowing me to weave bits and pieces of your life-giving messages on Philippians four into this book. Your input was, is, and always will be invaluable.

Rebecca Hayward, my dear, sweet sister-in-law and cherished friend, your willingness to share your editing skills has blessed me beyond measure. When all the red ink on my manuscript should have made me cry, your comments had me laughing out loud. What a way to learn and grow! Rich, thanks for sharing her.

Steve Rhine, Chamira Jones, and James Dunayski, thank you for sharing your illustrating gifts with this author. Your talent amazes me!

William Chefan, thanks for being another set of eyes. Your efforts meant so much!

Alan Maki, your critiques and editing remarks have been priceless. Thank you!

To God be the glory for the great things He is doing in and through His servants.

From my heart to yours,

Donna

A Decision of the Heart

Contents

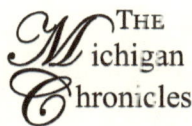

THE
Michigan
Chronicles

The Michigan Chronicles are a collection of stories from the days of yesteryear. The adventures begin in the nineteenth century, with two families farming in a small pioneer community nestled along the Huron River. The site, now known as Ypsilanti, is where the old Indian trail crossed over the Huron River. Come travel to a place in time where life was simpler ....

He Loves Me!

Prologue

Ypsilanti, Michigan Territory

August 1824

*G*LISTENING RAYS OF yellow light danced playfully in the cloudless sky, as the discontented child ran toward the ever-moving waters. Flyaway strands of golden hair clung to her delicate face as beads of sweat trickled down. The heat of the August sun was unbearable. Relief was just beneath her, but would that relief cost her more than she was willing to pay?

As Elizabeth Somers waded aimlessly along the shallow banks of the Huron River, she smiled as the cool muddied water squished between her toes. The desire to sink her sweltering frame in the soothing ripples overwhelmed her, but her pesky brother Jesse and his peskier friend Kaleb White wouldn't allow it. *No noise,* they had said, *not until we have enough fish for supper.*

Elizabeth spent the better part of her morning staring at the fishing line that lay undisturbed in the water. She couldn't understand. The guys were pulling in one fish after another, but

1

not so much as a single nibble twitched her pole. She must be doing something wrong. When she asked, her brother's kind reply was the same as always. *Fishing requires a great deal of patience, Lizzy. It's not about how many you catch—it's about the joy you find in the adventure.*

Some adventure, she mused. Her patience had run out hours ago. She was bored, sweaty, and becoming more annoyed with her big brother and his oversized friend with every passing moment. As she stood on the shore glaring at them from a distance, her impertinent mood played havoc with her young mind. *It isn't as if one puny girl in the river could scare their old fish away anyhow! Kaleb may be sixteen and five years older than me, but Jesse's only thirteen. I don't know why Dad makes me listen to those bossy boys! Doesn't he know I'm big now? I can take care of myself!*

Since Elizabeth knew better than to question her father's orders, she reached for her bucket and set off on a venture that was sure to be more productive. Her goal was to catch ten polliwogs before she'd even think about swimming again. Without so much as a single utterance, she scoured the river's edge for her first glimpse of the squirmy things.

By the time she had seven polliwogs, she became a little anxious. Jesse and Kaleb were behind the tree getting ready to take a dip. She wanted to join them in the worst way, but she couldn't stop now—only three more to go. Determined to finish what she had started, she ignored their antics and went back to the task at hand.

"You ready, Kaleb?"

"Sure. You ready, Jess?"

"Yep. Here we goooo!" Whooping and hollering, the boys latched onto the rope that hung from the limb of a big oak, and swung out over the river, dropping with a huge splash into the brisk water. They swam for a while, expecting Elizabeth to join them. When she didn't bother to look their way, they knew something was wrong. Elizabeth was either lost in her own endeavor, or her agitation had gotten out of hand.

When a playful solution crossed Kaleb's mind, he decided to share it. "I think your sister's miffed. What do you say, Jess ... is it time we end this stalemate, sneak up on her, and throw her in?"

Jesse's brow rose. "Let's do it!" he said, as he flashed Kaleb a rascally grin. "Just keep in mind we're dealing with Lizzy. She'll be madder than a wet hornet when we grab her, so expect the unexpected. Oh, one more thing. Since this was your brilliant idea, you can have her arms and I'll take her feet. I'd rather get kicked than deal with her endless threats!"

Absorbed with finding the last polliwog, Elizabeth didn't hear the scalawags approach. Before she had time to react, Kaleb grabbed her arms while Jesse, who got kicked twice in his attempt, managed to get her ankles.

Startled, though not intimidated, Elizabeth fought like a wild cat trying to get loose. "Let me go, Kaleb White!" she bellowed.

Her fierce scowl did nothing to sway him. Had this been any other little girl Kaleb might have complied—but this was Elizabeth. Every time they brought her fishing it was the same old story. She would get bored and then angry because they wouldn't let her swim. The quickest way to get her over her annoyance would be to give her a little of what her playful heart wanted— to be in the water with them. She fussed and carried on at first, trying to make them think she wanted no part of what they were offering. Only thing was, they knew better.

"Jesse," she tried again, "if you guys don't let me go, I'm gonna tell Dad—then you'll be sorry!"

"Go ahead and tell him."

When her attempts to wriggle out of their grasp became futile, her struggling subsided. As a delighted smile lit her impudent little face and a sparkle tweaked her sky blue gaze, Elizabeth's flippant declaration came as no surprise at all. "I'm glad you're throwing me in, I wanted to go swimming anyway!"

The young men exploded with laughter as they began moving her back and forth.

"Swing her high, Kaleb; we'll throw her on three. You ready, Lizzy?" The second she nodded, the count began, "one ... two ... three ...!"

Elizabeth squealed in jubilation as the momentum carried her flailing willowy frame into deeper water—landing with a big splash. Kaleb and Jesse stood there waiting for what seemed like minutes, but she didn't come up. In a near state of panic, they glanced at each other then back to the water.

"Jesse," Kaleb asked, his pulse quickening, "do you think she's all right? She's been under a long time."

Already moving into the water, Jesse's calm words belied the dreadful stirrings within. "We'd better check, Kaleb. She can be a real twit, but I love her."

The pranksters searched the river, looking frantically. They dove under the cloudy water again and again, but she was nowhere to be found.

"Where could she be, Jesse? The river's not moving fast

enough to carry her away." Taking a moment to catch their breath, they scanned the muddy banks—praying that at any second she would emerge.

The passing minutes seemed like hours. Defeat had begun to settle in like a heavy cloud when Kaleb spotted her. Smacking Jesse in the arm, he pointed up to where the rope swing hung from the limb of the big oak tree. Elizabeth was grinning like a Cheshire cat. The little imp swung out over the water and dropped in.

Infuriated, Kaleb and Jesse's angry steps took them down the bank ready to give the clever stink a piece of their minds. About halfway to her, Kaleb's pace slowed. As he reached for Jesse's arm and pulled him to a halt, a broad smile creased his tanned face. The ingenuity she displayed was remarkable.

Jesse, astounded by the change in Kaleb's countenance, asked, "Are you just going to stand there with that grin on your face? Tell me what you're thinking?"

"Maybe we should cut Liz some slack. We do pick on the poor girl an awful lot. To be honest, I'm amazed she hasn't tried to outsmart us before. Think about it. The way we tease her, we deserve whatever she dishes out. Hasn't she learned from the best?"

"Well, yeah, but I can't just let her think she can scare us like that."

"True," Kaleb said, pausing for a instant, "maybe you should let me talk to her this time."

"What?"

"I'm not sure why, Jesse, but ... she's leery of me. She might even listen to what I have to say."

"Oh, she'll listen all right ... but only if you stand your ground."

"Jesse, I know what she's like."

Relieved, he reached for Kaleb's hand, and shook it before he had time to back out. "You have my blessing, she's all yours."

The boys moseyed on down the bank, grabbed the rope, swung out over the water and joined her for a swim.

Elizabeth, having seen their exasperated faces, expected Jesse to scold her. When it didn't happen, she was puzzled, but she wasn't about to let her confusion spoil her fun.

They had been frolicking and playing in the river for close to an hour when she suddenly realized—*Kaleb's missing!* In a frenzied state, her eyes skimmed over the river, her heart ticking faster and faster. Having been subjected to their games her whole life, she had no doubts they were up to something. When Kaleb's hands slid around her waist from under the water, Elizabeth cringed.

Kaleb cradled his friend in his arms, sank into the water and rocked her as he said with the mildest intensity, "Liz, I need to talk to you about what happened earlier. It's fine if you want to get back at Jesse and me for picking on you. We certainly deserve it."

Hearing a "but" coming on she tried to look away, but Kaleb's oversized hand reached out and held her chin in place.

"Elizabeth, I'm going to hold you until you quit struggling and pay attention. I have something to say, and this time you're going to listen." Her tenacious spirit made him smile. For such a little thing, she had more spunk than ten girls her age. Her wiggles seemed to quit the very second her words flew out.

"When I grow up, I'm gonna marry a man who's not so big and strong." She paused, before adding, "Then he can't boss me around!"

Kaleb did all he could to ward off laughter. She was madder than a peeled rattler, and while it was difficult, he forced himself to go on. "I'm glad you have a plan, Liz, but the size of your future husband has nothing to do with this conversation."

"Does too! I don't stand a chance against a giant like you. If you were my size I could squiggle out of your hold. Then I wouldn't have to listen to a word you say!"

"If you weren't so stubborn I'd let you go, but we both know you'd run off. I'll ask you again, are you ready to hear me out?"

Close to tears, Elizabeth stared into Kaleb's deep brown eyes. "Do I have a choice?"

This seemed to be her standard question, so he offered his standard answer. "No, you don't."

Sighing in frustration, she resigned herself to the inevitable. "Then I might as well get it over with."

Elizabeth found his reproof insufferable, and the extent of her irritation made Kaleb chuckle. "Like I was saying, "we don't mind you getting back at us, but you will not, under any circumstances lead us to believe that you've been hurt. Do I make myself clear?" When the silence dragged on, he added, "We don't always tell you, but we like having you around, Liz. How could we live with ourselves if we let you drown?"

The tears that had been pooling in her eyes spilled slowly down her cheeks, effectively melting Kaleb's heart. He snuggled her close until she settled. As she drew in her last sob, he found her humble reply encouraging.

"I'm glad you and Jesse like me, Kaleb. I shouldn't have made you worry. Momma says if I'm really sorry I'll ask for forgiveness.

Will you?" Tucking her wet hair behind her ears, he sent her a playful wink.

"I already have."

Elizabeth turned to her brother, asking the same.

Jesse nodded as he stood there in the water, stunned by what had just transpired.

"Now, Liz," Kaleb asked, "can I toss you in the water or are you ready to call it a day?"

She threw her hands over her head in all-out surrender. "Throw me in!"

He laughed in the light of her exuberance.

The warm summer sun had begun its descent in the western skies before Jesse called Elizabeth out of the water. While she moaned and groaned as he fully expected, she did as she was told. "Grab your things, Sis. We need to head home and get the fish ready for supper."

They were well on their way when Kaleb, still in an ornery mood, sent Jesse a corroborating wink just before taunting their shivering, blue-lipped companion. "Ya know, Jesse, I could have sworn I heard Liz say she was cleaning the catch today. Was I mistaken?"

When Elizabeth's wide panicky eyes flew up at Kaleb, his heckling smile gave him away.

"Don't tease me like that, Kaleb. You two caught the smelly things, not me! You clean them!"

Kaleb's brow furrowed. "So ... you're saying that if you were the one to catch them, you'd do the deed?"

She rolled her eyes, saying, "You should know the answer to that without asking."

"I should, should I?"

"Umm-hmm ... not if my life depended on it!"

Jesse glanced at his friend and smiled as he shrugged. "Her mind's made up, Kaleb. May as well give it up!"

"I suppose ...."

"Kaleb," Elizabeth announced, "Mama told me I could make oatmeal cookies with chocolate in them for dessert. I could save ya some."

Kaleb's eyes lit with pleasure as he ran his fingers through his damp honey-blonde hair. If memory served him, and it usually did when sweets were involved, those tasty little morsels held an irresistible draw. He tweaked her little nose as a solution came to mind. "No need to do that, Liz. I'll go home for supper and be back before you even know I'm gone."

Overjoyed with Kaleb's answer, Elizabeth presented him with a great big doting smile, just before skipping off toward the house. She had stories to tell her mom about her day—good ones that simply couldn't wait!

He Loves Me!

Chapter One

Deliverance

Ypsilanti, Michigan Territory
November 30, 1828

$\mathcal{W}$ITH SLOW DELIBERATE moves, George Somers lovingly ran his fingers along the soft skin of his daughter's face. She was sleeping, and he took such pleasure in watching her. There was something so innocent, so angelic about the way all of his children appeared when they were asleep. He was sure that most fathers would agree—the hands of time pass too swiftly. Elizabeth, his oldest girl, was no longer a child, but a beautiful young woman who would always hold a special place in this daddy's heart.

"Lizzy," George softly prodded, "I need you to wake up."

Gradually opening her eyes, Elizabeth yawned, stretched, and smiled into her father's endearing gaze.

"Good morning, Sunshine!"

"Morning, Daddy." Her brow furrowed. "Did you forget it's Saturday? I thought you were going to let me sleep in?"

"I could have done that and sent your brothers, but I told

your mother you'd be willing to ride to Ann Arbor for supplies?" The delighted beam that lit her face confirmed his suspicion. "Should I assume that silly grin means you'll go?"

"Don't tease me, Daddy. You know I'd never turn down an offer like that."

"Then put your brother's clothes on and come down for breakfast."

"I won't be long." She reached for her father's calloused hand and gave it a squeeze. "Thanks for letting me go."

George stood to leave. "You're welcome. Just promise you'll be careful ...."

"You know I will."

On his way out the door, George glanced back and said, "It's cold out. Grab a pair of Joseph's warm underclothes."

She would probably never understand why her father found this necessary when no one would see them, but she wasn't about to question him—not when her freedom was at stake.

Elizabeth traipsed into the kitchen and found her mother, Jayne, frying bacon over the hot stove. She tucked her mother's stray wisps behind her ears and kissed her cheek. "Morning, Mom."

Jayne winked. "How's my Eli doing this chilly morning?"

Elizabeth rolled her playful eyes. "I'm fine, Mom, but please let me be Lizzy to you. I'm Eli when I go to town and dress like a boy clear down to my under drawers to ease my father's mind. I don't feel like a boy and I never will." She raised her hand to forestall her mother's response. "I know, Mom! No need to remind me. We don't live in a perfect world, so I should trust my father's judgment."

Jayne smiled. "Honey, as far as I'm concerned, nothing

could make me think my daughter looks like a boy, not even in that getup. But people see what they want."

"I know ...." Elizabeth poured herself a cup of tea. "I'm starving, Mom. Is anything ready? I won't make it home in time for supper if I don't get moving." Jayne handed her a plate filled with all her morning favorites: scrambled eggs, crispy bacon, and biscuits. The wild raspberry jam she added made her mouth water in anticipation.

"Thanks!" After asking the blessing, she licked the jam that was running down her fingers, and filled her rumbling stomach.

"Mom, did you write me a list?"

"It's on the bench by the back door."

Elizabeth nodded. "You haven't seen Jared's old bluchers, have ya?"

"On the bottom shelf in the pantry."

After popping the last bite of bacon in her mouth, Elizabeth went to collect the rest of her brother's paraphernalia. Jayne followed her daughter into the pantry, handed her the canteen filled with water, and a sandwich wrapped in a towel. "This should hold you if you get hungry."

"Thanks, Mom. I'll see ya later."

Elizabeth's steps quickened as she moved toward the barn to saddle Lady. Jared's bluchers were too big for her feet and although the extra socks helped, she walked like a clumsy boy in her attempt to keep them on. "Oh, well," she said to the open air, "they only add to the effect of my lovely attire." She could only hope that her skinny legs and the scent of lilacs in her hair would not give her away.

Lost in thought, she slid open the big door but started when she heard steps coming her way. Her eyes, wide with uncertainty, rose to meet her father's bewildered look.

George handed her Lady's reins. "You're kind of jumpy this morning. Are you sure you're up to going?"

"I'll be fine, Dad. Thanks for saddling my friend." Elizabeth patted Lady's thick neck in greeting. "I thought you went out to tend the flock. You know I don't like those kinds of surprises."

"As long as you're sure. The gun's loaded. If you run into problems don't panic if you have to use it—just remember what I taught you."

She grinned. "You worry too much, Daddy, but I love you for it."

As George pulled her into his arms, a sparkle lit his eyes. "It's my job to worry about you, Young Lady. You keep in mind, I wouldn't mind handing the chore over to a nice young man some day soon."

"Forget it, Dad!" Elizabeth ignored his playful words, grabbed the supply bag off the hook, looped it over the saddle horn and mounted Lady. "See ya this afternoon. Let's go, girl." With a click of her tongue they were off.

"Hey, Lizzy!" George called out to her. "Jesse and Kaleb will be coming home. Don't dilly-dally; we'll have a big supper waiting. And be sure you alter that voice. Hear me?"

Elizabeth nodded, waving as she led Lady down towards the river's edge. She thrived on these adventures, and although her father's reservations were many, about six months back he began allowing her to make occasional trips into Ann Arbor, with an unusual stipulation. She had to make herself look like a man. With her small stature and fair-soft skin, he accepted the fact that she could never look like a man, so he settled for a boy. In reality, she looked like a scrawny lad of about twelve, maybe fourteen years old. Her father had watched Ann Arbor grow from a few log homes into a flourishing town. Since many of their family friends resided there, he had few doubts about her safety once she arrived. Getting her there was where he had issues. Their homestead was nestled along the banks of the Huron, in the small neighboring community of Ypsilanti. Her father insisted that the wilds of Ypsilanti were no place for a young lady to be off gallivanting on her own so she submitted to his unusual request.

Lady followed the Huron as if it were an everyday occurrence, giving Elizabeth the opportunity to enjoy her surroundings and allowing her overactive mind to wander. If she got caught up daydreaming and went too far, she'd eventually run into Godfroy's abandoned trading post. From there, she could just shoot up the Pottawatomie Trail and find her way without any problem.

The barren trees hovering above the ever-moving waters were being decorated with light flakes. Winter had begun to make its presence known, and although the unexpected snow made for a chilly ride, she loved the way it made her feel inside. There was something majestic about the changing of the season, from harvest shades of fall to the unpredictability of a sullen Michigan winter. It stilled Elizabeth's heart in ways she found difficult to define.

Wildlife could be found, but unlike during the summer months, it had to be sought out. It wasn't just hers for the viewing. Sparse pairs of cardinals and blue jays could be seen fluttering about. Often she would spot hawks soaring across the open skies in search of their next meal. *Oh, to possess the ability to fly!*

Winter was a time for her to sit back and take notice of all the wonders in God's creation. True, like everyone else, she looked forward to the coming of spring—a chance for new life to begin. Wild flowers were always in abundance from skunk cabbage blooming in early spring with its purple shell-like covering, to milkweed, clovers, and beautiful lilies of different vibrant hues. Elizabeth's favorites, daisies and black-eyed-susans, could be found dappled along the water's edge and through the rolling fields. From the planting of new crops to the promise of fresh fruits on the trees and vegetables in the gardens, every living thing seemed to flourish in this rich land with the promise of new beginnings.

Still, Elizabeth needed winter as a time of renewal—a time to reflect on where she had been and where her life was going. For someone with her venturesome mind, it would be too easy to take up the reins and look to her own selfish yearnings. Now in her last year of school, Elizabeth prayed every day that God would give her direction. So far she had no answers.

Her parents had high hopes that she would marry and build a life with a nice man, but she didn't have the heart to tell them that marriage was the furthest thing from her mind. Besides, prospective husbands weren't exactly plentiful in these parts. Elizabeth and her best friend Amy had talked about traveling to Detroit or even as far as New York with Amy's father. Elizabeth's biggest hitch was money. Even if she could find a way to earn the funds, how would she ever convince her overprotective father to allow her to go? She did love to dream, too bad dreams were not always practical.

Elizabeth's greatest fear was that she would go through

life and somehow miss her calling—her reason for being here. Oh, she knew the important things—that she was a child of the King, called to love and serve Him and others, but she was sure there had to be more. Something special God wanted her to do, a purpose for her existence. Until she knew what that was, she could rest, knowing her life was in His all encompassing hands.

Her brother Jesse, and his good friend Kaleb White had hogs to deliver to a sweet elderly couple who owned a small farm above Ann Arbor. Jesse often said that Jacob and Anna Woods were the grandparents he never had, and treated them as such. The boys had spent last night with the Woods and planned to head back before the day got away from them. Drawn to these people, Jesse went often just to check up on them and do odd jobs that their weary bodies could no longer accomplish.

Kaleb's family had become the closest thing to relatives Elizabeth's family had ever known. They were neighbors in Detroit. Having heard about the rich farmlands in the Huron Valley, the two families migrated together. Her father said that God never blessed him with siblings until he met Samuel, who was also an only child. Her mother, Jayne, and Samuel's wife, Ruth, had been closer than two peas in a pod since they were introduced at church in Detroit. Their eight-year-old daughter, Sarah, fit right in with Elizabeth's younger sisters, Suzanne, now ten, and Louise, also eight. Whenever those three chatterboxes were together, it was difficult to get a word in edge-wise. Just the thought of them giggling and carrying on was enough to make Elizabeth laugh in delight. Her younger brothers, Jared and Joseph, were so close in age that Mom always said raising them was like having a set of twins. They didn't seem to need other friends around to make them feel complete. Elizabeth spent much of her spare time tagging along with Jesse and Kaleb.

Pulling her scarf up over Joseph's hat, she shivered as the chilling winds and icy flakes continued to make their presence known. Although the beautiful morning sky had turned to a hazy gray, she wasn't about to let a little snow ruin her day. No doubt anything was possible when it came to Michigan's fickle weather. She assured herself that blizzards didn't come this early in the season. Pushing care aside, she turned Lady away from the water and headed up the tree line to the rolling pastures. Without need for encouragement, she gave her mount full rein. Lady took off like a bolt of lightning shooting across the barren land. Elizabeth, loving the exhilaration of galloping through open fields, pointed her mare westward towards town.

The weighted clouds were darkening as she rode into Ann Arbor. Although snow had blanketed the ground, she sloughed it off as nothing more than a minor annoyance.

As Elizabeth passed the livery, she noticed the smithy standing outside. He seemed to be contemplating what the storm would do when she interrupted his thoughts.

"How ya doing, Jeff?"

He nodded. "How's the Somers family? Here for supplies?"

"Yep. Everyone's fine."

"Not sure what's brewing out here ... doesn't look nice. You be careful going home, Eli." Jeff paused for a moment before adding with a sly grin, "You be sure and tell my sweetheart, Lizzy, I said, 'hi'."

"Eli's" smile was kind, but Jeff wasn't getting any younger, and Elizabeth knew of a girl that would jump at the chance to

18

have him in her life. Throwing caution to the wind, she made a suggestion. "If you ask me, I think you'd be wise to keep your eyes open for another prospect. The way I hear it, Elizabeth has sworn off men for years."

He lowered his head and then peered back up. "I suppose it doesn't hurt for a man to dream, provided he comes to his senses sooner or later."

He sounded so depressed—she had to tell him. "Ya know, Jeff, Cindy Sue Cox has been sweet on you for some time." Elizabeth knew this information to be truth, not rumor, so when his brow flew up in wide-eyed curiosity, she was glad he knew.

"You wouldn't be playing with a lonesome man's heart ... would ya?" He didn't wait for a response. "Now that you mention it, I have noticed her looking my way from time to time. She's a pretty one, don't ya think?"

"She is at that. Quit wasting your time on a woman too young to know her own mind and call on Cindy before some other young buck jumps the gun."

Jeff nodded, thanked Eli, and she was on her way.

Elizabeth tied Lady to the hitching post, leapt onto the platform, and ambled into the store. Her father had to be kicking himself for letting her come in this weather, but here she was, and she had every intention of getting their supplies before heading home. Stepping into her role, "Eli" moseyed on back to the counter.

The proprietor, Mrs. Grant asked, "What can I do for you ... young man? You're George and Jayne's nephew, aren't you?"

"Yes Ma'am. I have a list from Aunt Jayne. If you wouldn't mind," she slid the supply bag onto the counter, "could you put the items in the bag? I have a few things to check on. Be back in just a minute."

Maybe she was wrong, but Elizabeth enjoyed coming in disguise. Whenever she would come as Elizabeth, the woman would go out of her way to remind her of what a wonderful catch a certain tall blonde distinguished-looking gentleman was. Not today. In obeying her father and coming dressed as a boy, she would not be subjected to the woman's infinite wisdom.

"Excuse me, young man," Mrs. Grant asked as "Eli" moved away. "Did you say your name is, Eli?"

"That's right."

"Well, Eli, could you do me a favor? Kaleb White ordered this hunting knife a while ago. Since he'll be around your aunt's place calling on Elizabeth, would you see that he gets it?"

It took every ounce of restraint she could muster to keep her thoughts to herself. *Does she never listen to a word I say?* Elizabeth's dead calm belied her intense emotions. "That's fine, put it in the bottom of the bag. Don't think I saw tea and sugar on that list; could you add some?"

"Be glad to."

Elizabeth, annoyed by the way Mrs. Grant's inquisitive eyes followed her every move, was unable to resist giving the busy body something to look at. A mischievous thought ran through her brain that involved a quick stop by ladies apparel. She watched the proprietor out of the corner of her eye as "Eli" held up a camisole, gave it a thorough looking over, and fingered the delicate lace, before folding it and putting it back on the shelf.

Mrs. Grant shook her head and mumbled something under her breath.

Elizabeth thought, *boys will be boys!* She did all she could to contain her laughter. That is, until her father's face came to mind. If he had any idea how she was misbehaving, his response would not be favorable. While she found this little escapade a pure delight, she scolded herself for her insensitivity, moved to the counter, and paid the bill.

As she lumbered down the stairs with the weighted bag over her shoulder, her steps slowed considerably. The amount of fallen snow was disconcerting, but she convinced herself that it had to let up soon. Plodding down Main Street on Lady, Elizabeth turned onto Huron at Bloody Corners, and headed towards home.

About an hour into the trip, she regretted not staying the night with Pastor and Carolyn. If she didn't make it home, her parents would worry, but at least she would have been safe and warm there. What started as a light covering of snow had turned into a major winter storm.

She had passed the Cox Ranch a while back. Her family farm would be the next place she'd come to, but that was a long way off.

On a good day, she loved the solitude of this sparsely inhabited land. Bad weather had a way of changing the way she looked at everything. The howling winds were setting her calm companion on edge, and the way Lady skittered about did nothing to soothe her own frazzled nerves.

Keeping a close watch on the trail in front of her, she began humming her favorite hymn. For a while she found it soothed both her and her mount. Even so, she couldn't keep it up for long. The ghastliness of the darkened sky caused the hair at the base of her neck to stand on end. She tried to pray. The snow was blinding her. She needed to pay attention or she would be lost—

for all she knew, she already was!

The fierce winds and icy flakes flailing against her raw skin made it impossible to see where she was going. Over and over again, she thought she saw the path that led to the Huron. Each time she was gravely mistaken. While fear and desolation threatened to consume her, thoughts of family urged her on.

As if things weren't bad enough, her horse started when a huge buck leapt out of the trees. With Lady standing on her hindquarters, the supply bag threw Elizabeth off balance, and she fell helplessly towards the cold wet ground. She cringed in despair as the realization hit her—her booted foot was caught in the stirrup. When Lady lunged forward, she heard her ankle snap just before it slid out of its hold—hitting the frozen earth with an excruciating thud. The intense pain made it difficult to breathe. As she regained her senses, her eyes scanned the area. Lady was gone.

Gone!

What am I going to do, Lord?

Groping in agony, and close to tears, Elizabeth cried out to the only one she knew could hear her. *Father, nothing is beyond you, but I'm scared! My life is in Your hands. Please help me ... I want to go home!*

Elizabeth crawled into a copse of pines and made her way to a fallen log. Pulling her quivering body out of the slushy snow, she sat in quiet contemplation. Making it home on her own was impossible. Having tested her ankle, she harbored no doubts; her foot would not support her. She had no choice but to wait, hope, and pray. While her strength was weak, her faith remained strong.

As the minutes turned into hours, she grew cold—so cold she

could barely feel her limbs. With no reprieve the chilling winds and billowing flakes proceeded to envelop her slender frame as she clung to her unyielding belief that God would somehow deliver her.

A verse her mother used to remind her of played over in her mind, becoming her comfort. *God is my hiding place; He will keep me from trouble, and bring me peace and deliverance. Thank you Lord, for my deliverance!*

Elizabeth's frigid draw towards slumber muddled her thoughts, sending her into a fitful sleep. Teetering between dreams and reality, she panicked when large hands grabbed at the front of her coat. In her weakened state, her arms flailed in revolt, yet her captor was unyielding. Through half-open eyes, she saw the abominable snow-covered man shake his head. The momentum of being thrown over his broad shoulder left her feeling dizzy and light-headed. Too exhausted to combat his overpowering strength, Elizabeth drifted in and out of consciousness ....

He Loves Me!

Chapter Two

My Brother's Friend

ELIZABETH AWOKE WITH a start! She was lying in a clouded haze on a hard surface with a roof over her head. While her meager surroundings held not a flicker of familiarity, the same snow-covered ruffian who had thrown her over his shoulder was removing her coat, her bluchers, her wet pants, and her wet shirt. When he reached to unbutton her long underclothes, alarm slammed though her. She came out of her stupor—fighting! Agonizingly, the intense pain in her ankle would not allow her to stand.

What does he think he's doing? her brain screamed out in revolt.

Recalling her father's warnings of despicable men's intentions, the blood now raging through her veins began to boil! *Swines, brutes, horrible degenerates, they wouldn't think twice about robbing a woman of her virtue!* Understanding the full impact of her father's warnings, she asked herself, *how does he know I'm a woman?*

No matter, no one will take anything from Elizabeth Somers—not while I have breath left in me! Curling her fingers in a tight knot, she punched him square in the nose. The scant light from the small window revealed a trail of blood, trickling from his nostrils. Her courage was renewed. His size alone should have kept her from such a brazen attempt, but if determination was indeed a powerful weapon, this could be a close match!

The vindictive glower in his deep menacing eyes strengthened her resolve. As yet he hadn't lashed out, and while this confused her, Elizabeth would not take chances. His feet were spread apart, poised and ready, waiting for her next move. She would not back down. In one fluid motion, she drew back her uninjured leg and kicked him hard in the shin. He grimaced and painfully dropped to the floor.

As he rose to his feet again, the beat of her heart thudded out of control. His scowl housed the fury of ten men. Out of sheer desperation, she lunged for the poker, but not fast enough! He nailed her to the floor with his huge bulk, bellowing as he wailed on her rump.

"You ungrateful brat! Is this the thanks? ..." The split second his thunderous words reached her ears, the tenseness in her body gave way to her weakened state. She calmed, and so did he.

Stunned by "Eli's" sudden change in behavior, he loosened his hold, but he did not let down his guard.

I know that voice, she thought. He was unrecognizable wearing all that snow; and she, dressed like a boy, he couldn't possibly know who she was. As her lips parted to speak, an impish thought touched her mind. Having been on the receiving end of his teasing so many times, how could she deny herself this one scintillating moment. As her head spun to face him, her narrowed gaze pierced right through him.

"My brothers will come after you with a vengeance when I tell them what you just did!" She could see the lights go on.

"Elizabeth ... Somers?"

At her hesitant nod, Kaleb reached for her brother's hat and watched as long golden locks tumbled down around her shoulders. His mouth dropped open in shock. Contemplating whether he should be furious with her for taking unnecessary risks or relieved that he had found her when he did, he gave her the benefit of the doubt.

"What were you doing out in this storm? Dressed like a boy no less!"

She had never seen him like this. His stern intolerance made her shudder; his revulsion unnerved her. Though she hated her weakness, she could no longer suppress the tears burning the back of her eyes.

"Your father and brother would berate me for letting you off with such ease! What were you thinking, Elizabeth?" He continued to stare.

It was more than she could bear. In fact, it shook her to the core. In that instant she knew she had better give account for her actions without further delay. "Kaleb, I'm sorry. I can't take back what I've done, but your anger over me being out in this storm is unwarranted. My father sent me to Ann Arbor for supplies."

The tenseness in his jaw eased.

"I'm surprised Jesse never told you. Dad makes me dress like a boy when I go alone. It works like a charm; no one has ever bothered me. Truth is, they seldom notice I'm there. I even confuse Mrs. Grant, and you know how hard that is." Her insides calmed when a lighthearted grin creased his icy face.

"Who does she think you are?"

"A nephew named Eli, here for an extended visit."

As the adrenaline wore off, Elizabeth began to shake from the unbearable cold. Sitting on the rough wooden floor in her brother's wet underclothes didn't help.

Kaleb, noticing her quivering frame, rushed to her side. "Liz, I'm sorry. Forgive my outburst. I'm fine, now, but look at you—you're trembling out of control. We have to get you warm."

This was the Kaleb she had grown up with, her brother's good friend. She could relax now, feeling safe in his capable hands.

Elizabeth's eyes never left him as he strode across the room and his oversized frame crouched down to start a fire in the rough stone fireplace. She often wondered how he managed to find jeans long enough to cover those legs, but she wasn't about to ask. Kaleb may be the best-looking man she had ever met. Even so, she did not want him to think she was interested in any way. Liz, as only he called her, was not in the market for a man. When he stood and turned to face her, his lips were curved in a grin that embellished his pleasure.

"I'm glad I came along when I did, Liz. Do you know how long you were stuck out there?"

"It felt like forever. This storm ... I've never seen one this bad in November?"

"Took us all by surprise."

"I would have stayed with Pastor and Carolyn if I would have known."

"Jesse and I were together until he took the turn off at the river. I had planned to go home with him, but we saw a saddled horse without a rider. We decided to cover both trails in case someone was stranded. I'm thankful we did."

"Me too!"

As the silence lengthened, a sinking sensation began in the pit of her stomach. She had to ask, "Kaleb, what's wrong?"

Her anxious words brought him back to his senses. "Oh, nothing ... we need to get you out of those wet drawers."

Filled with timidity, her eyes met his, "You know I don't have anything to put on."

"I've got something for you. First, I have to know, are you injured?"

Her distorted expression made him laugh. "My ankle's messed up." Kaleb knelt beside her to remove her sock and assess the damage. He tried to be gentle, but his touch set every nerve in her leg on edge. Her hand came to her mouth to quell her cries as a fresh wave of pain engulfed her.

"I'm sorry, Liz. I had to ...."

"I know ...."

His stomach whirled at the sight of her bruised and swollen foot. "This is horrible! What happened?"

She wasted no time filling him in.

The thought of her being in such a helpless state tore at his heart. "Try not to think about it. You're safe now. I'll take care of you."

Fighting tears, she could only nod.

Kaleb removed his outer clothes before retrieving a pair of his long underdrawers, and dry socks from his saddlebag.

She chided herself for the warm flush crawling up her face. Unfortunately, he noticed.

"Liz, I'm sorry you're embarrassed, but we need to get you dry ... this is all I have."

Her lips were sealed.

"Do I need to remind you that you're freezing?"

"No ..." He was right, but the clothes were only half of the problem—he was the other half. Why did it have to be him and not her brother who found her? "How do you propose we do this?"

His hand rose. "Give me a minute." He slung the dry things over his shoulder, gave her the socks and rearranged the room.

The scent of pinewood filled her nostrils as she took in their paltry haven. A small log bed that sat in the corner, he put in front of the warming embers. Alongside it he placed the feeble remains of a wooden chair. Everything was fine until he reached down and plucked her off the floor. Her heart beat at such a pace, she thought it might leap from her chest. She could only hope he didn't notice. She, hoping he did not notice, sagged with relief when he placed her in the dilapidated chair.

"Liz, I'll turn around while you change, but everything you're wearing has to come off before you put the dry things on."

She was a woman of small stature. He was built like the mighty Goliath, and she couldn't fathom being in this man's clothes. The thought of disrobing with him in the room—inconceivable! But what choice did she have? Kaleb, like her brother, would not think twice about changing her clothes for her if she chose to defy him. Since she refused to let that happen, she obeyed, with much reluctance.

When her movements ceased, Kaleb asked, "Are you finished, Liz?"

Her voice sounded strange—distant. "I suppose ...."

He turned and was not prepared for the picture she presented. Balanced on her good foot, she hung onto the chair. The seat of his long underdrawers dangled down past her knees, and although she had hands, they were lost somewhere in the sleeves. He burst into gut-wrenching laughter. The fierce scowl she sent his way astounded him. "I'm sorry, Liz. You look so funny! I knew you were small, but I must be huge!"

"You're a giant!" Her smile told him he was forgiven.

"I'm glad to see you smiling and not angry, but I'm cold, Kaleb. What are we going to do?" She rubbed at her arms and looked around the room. Her slender finger pointed to the thin quilt on the narrow bed. "Is that the only blanket we have?"

"I'm afraid it is. Go ahead and sit on the edge of the bed. I need to stabilize your ankle before we get you tucked in." He found an old piece of toweling, shook the worst of the dust from it, tore it in strips, and proceeded to wrap her foot as best he could. "Don't move this any more than you have to. The storm isn't letting up. It could be a while before we get you back into town to see Doc."

"It hurts too much to fight you, Kaleb. By the way, I'm sorry I gave you a hard time when we got here. I panicked. My father wanted me to be on my guard, so he told me some stories about horrible men. The way you were removing my clothes ... I thought you were one of them." Guilt washed over her. "I hope your nose and leg are all right."

He sent her a playful wink. "I'm sure they're no worse than your bum." Before she could reply, he added, "If I had known it was you, I wouldn't have hurt you, Liz."

"Sure you wouldn't have! Remember ... I was the one on the receiving end of that furious look." She started to giggle. "You really did think I was up to no good, didn't you?"

He grinned. "I suppose you're right. I'm glad I gave you the chance to explain. I would have regretted my actions."

"I would have forgiven you. After all, you did save my life."

"God's dealing with me about my temper, but you, My Dear Friend, are a fortunate woman. For me to find you asleep under that tree on a day like this is nothing short of a miracle. God must have something wonderful in store for you."

"I can only hope I won't disappoint Him."

Kaleb ran his thumb along the trim line of her jaw, "I don't believe you could be a disappointment to anyone. You're always lifting someone's spirits. You just get a little side-tracked here and there."

Although she found the compassion in his words encouraging, the tenderness in his gaze was a bit unsettling. The lowering of her eyes did nothing to dispel the odd sensation swirling inside her. "You're too kind," she said, putting an end to their awkward moment.

"Not at all. I'm hoping you won't change your mind and decide I'm one of those despicable men when you hear what I have to say."

"Why would I think that?" As hard as she tried to push down her rising panic, her wide eyes filled with doubt. Her defenses heightened.

"Elizabeth, settle down. You know I'd never do anything to bring you harm or take advantage of you, but you're freezing, and we're both exhausted. I'm going to lie next to you. While we're stuck in this cabin, we have no other alternative. There is only one bed, and one blanket." Although Kaleb was thankful for both, the anxiety on her face was hard to bear. "Liz, if it helps, pretend I'm one of your brothers."

If only I could!

Ignoring her despairing mood, Kaleb took care to settle her in, before sitting on the little chair to remove his bluchers. When he stood to unbutton his jeans, he couldn't do it. Sleeping in them would be difficult, but knowing Elizabeth's discomfort would be magnified if he removed a single stitch of clothing, he left well enough alone.

"Liz," he said as he slid down alongside of her, "If you turn toward me I should be able to get you warm."

With no end to her difficulty in sight, she did as he suggested. She buried her crimson face in his broad chest, and accepted the warmth being offered.

Kaleb was all too aware that Elizabeth would prefer to run for the hills. Since that was not an option, and he had no desire to add to her discomfort, he pulled the blanket around them and closed his eyes. Rest was not long in coming for either of them. When her tremors ceased and her breathing evened out, he drank in the irresistible scent of lilac mingling in her long golden hair and drifted into a peaceful sleep.

He Loves Me!

Chapter Three

Confinement

"KALEB, ARE YOU awake?"

"Yes." He had been for a while. Out of concern for Elizabeth's welfare, he chose not to disturb her.

Her mind reeled. Her needs were pressing in, but how could she tell ... him? The alternative would be worse. "I ... I have things ... needs to take care of."

Kaleb, noting her deepening shade, his own cheeks warmed at the thought. *My, this is awkward.* "Oh ... I ... ahh ...saw a bucket by the back door." She offered no response, so he added, "I wish I could make this easier for you, Liz. You don't have many options with that broken ankle."

Elizabeth, feeling more than a little leery of his closeness, nodded. The silence lagged on as Kaleb stuck his feet into his bluchers, laced them, and reached for his coat. She couldn't bear to look at him when he retrieved the chamber pot.

"I'm going out to check on Lightning. That should give you

enough time to take care of ... things."

"All right."

"I only have a few pieces of jerky in my saddlebag, so if the snow lets up, I'll need to do some hunting."

Her curious look caught his attention.

"Did you bring that big bag I had with me?"

"Yes, I couldn't have missed it; you were using it for a pillow."

"Kaleb, we won't starve. There's tea, sugar, oatmeal, rice and beans that I know of. I'm not sure what else Mom had on that list. Surely there's enough to hold us for a while."

"The supplies will help, but I'm not willing to bank on them being enough."

A quick peek at the window told her he could be right. It was still coming down in buckets.

"I'll bring in some snow for tea. And, if you're asking me, oatmeal sounds great. What do you think?"

"Absolutely!"

"Be careful, Liz. I'll be back soon."

"I will." Since Kaleb had given every indication that he was leaving, she froze when he had more to say.

"Can you handle this alone without putting that foot down, or should I stay and just close my eyes?"

She told him honestly, "I'll manage. I'd never survive the humiliation if you stayed." His dark, hooded stare gave her the willies! Before his over-protective tendency had time to take root, she needed to set him straight. He had a stubborn streak as long as hers, and she had no desire to start a battle of wills with him in her present condition. "Kaleb, please don't look at me that way. I'll be careful, I promise. You need to go." When her attempt to shoo him out the door didn't seem to be working, she added with all the firmness she could muster, "You're not staying, so don't give it another thought!"

Not totally satisfied, Kaleb stopped at the door to issue his absurd orders: "Use the bed for support, and stay put until I return ... do you hear me?"

Good grief, she thought, *he's worse than my dad and brother put together! What does he think I'm going to do in this condition, dance around the room?* She listened as he continued, but not enough to know his advise required a response.

"Elizabeth, did you hear me?" he repeated.

She nodded, willing to do whatever it took to get him to walk out that door. Had she known in advance how painful her movements would be, she *may* have reconsidered Kaleb's offer. Recalling his sternness brought a smile to her face and somehow helped her through her agonizing moments.

For some odd reason the men in her life insisted on treating her like a child—ordering her about as if she were incapable of making a rational decision without their input. She often wondered if her small stature contributed to their actions, though never once did it occur to her that her impetuous nature had everything to do with it.

❀ ❀ ❀

"Kaleb," Elizabeth asked, when he came back in, "where are we?"

With a baiting smile he said, "It's certainly taken you long enough to ask."

"Well, the movement snapped me out of my muddle, and I'm

asking now."

"We're in an old cabin, about halfway between Ann Arbor and my parents' homestead." After removing his coat, Kaleb hung the big pot of snow from the crane over the open flames, added a log, stoked up the burning embers and sat next to her in the rickety chair. "Jesse and I come by here when we're hunting. I've never seen anyone living here, so more than likely it's been abandoned. I'm sure you've heard about the three Frenchmen who founded Godfroy's." Elizabeth nodded, so he went on. "Rumor has it that those men built this shanty." His eyes scanned the small room. "Hardly big enough to call a cabin."

"No bigger than our chicken coop."

"There's no way to know if the rumor is true, but I'm thankful it's here. You were chilled to the bone when I found you, Liz. I don't think you would have made it home. Besides, Lightning would have been hard-pressed to carry both of us through the deep snow."

Kaleb was staring out the window with a faraway look in his eyes. Moments had passed when he glanced over at her and said, "I hate knowing that our families are sick with worry, but this is out of our control. I won't leave until we can travel safely together."

"I'm glad you feel that way. I wouldn't like being alone with this broken ankle."

Kaleb couldn't comprehend why her father allowed her to go off on her own in the first place. Didn't he know what could happen to a woman alone? Realizing it was none of his business, he instead asked, "I don't suppose there's coffee in that bag?"

Elizabeth laughed at the needy expression on his face. "Sorry, only tea. I'll admit, you're more coherent than Jesse would be without his brew."

"Boy, isn't that the truth."

"Hey, Kaleb. I just remembered something. Mrs. Grant asked me to give you the knife you ordered. It's under the food."

Curious, he went to retrieve the bag, his thoughts questioning as he looked the knife over. Clearly it was the one he ordered, but why would Mrs. Grant send it with a young cousin?

"I ordered this knife a few months ago. I'm surprised she had you bring it."

"Well, I'm not!" The second the words were out of her mouth, she regretted them. Kaleb's deep amber eyes were impossible to ignore. "Don't look at me that way. It's not my fault she is the way she is. I went into town as Eli, and that woman still went out of her way to find out when *Elizabeth* would be seeing you."

His brow furrowed on her blatant admission.

She was digging herself into the mire, with no way out. She wanted to melt into the floor—or bury herself under the covers. What good would it do? Kaleb knew her too well. He would not let this fall by the wayside.

He reclaimed his seat, and asked, "Why do you suppose that is?"

Her cheeks flamed under his scrutinizing stare. *How will I ever escape that insistent brown-eyed glare?*

"Liz," he coaxed in that deep unyielding tone, "you're the one who brought it up. Do tell." He was only inches away, waiting for a response. It was not long in coming.

"Knowing when to keep my mouth shut seems to be one of my greatest sins." She had no more averted her eyes when his large hand gently captured her jaw and brought her reluctant gaze back to his.

"Tell me, Liz—or I'll ask the woman myself." She wanted to refuse, but the thought of him discussing this with that woman was too much. Reconciling herself to her plight, she came clean—though not without adding, "I think you're cruel for making me say this."

Her pitiful expression made him smile. Having seen it so many times before, he merely said, "I think you'll get over it and be none the worse for wear."

She took a deep breath and began. "For years, the dear—sweet—pest has gone out of her way to remind me what a wonderful catch you are. Though I'm not sure why ...."

He laughed out loud at the way she shuddered in mock disgust.

"You can quit your bellowing right now, Kaleb White. You know full well what she's like. She's not happy unless she's in the middle of someone else's business. Why, I can see her right now, those little glasses sitting on the end of her upturned nose, her wide-eyed stare, just waiting for the split second she can catch me off-guard. I remind her that our families have been close for years, and that you and I are just friends. It doesn't seem to matter. She finds a way to bring you up every time I go into town. Even when I go as Eli—which was quite often, before this happened. She gives new meaning to the word 'annoying'." Elizabeth wasn't about to divulge the comment Mrs. Grant made about Kaleb being at their house for the sole purpose of calling on her. Perish the thought!

On the outside, he was smiling, yet he couldn't help wondering if he should be offended by her reaction. He watched as she rolled her eyes and went out of her way to let him know that the idea of their being a match was inconceivable—to the point of the extreme! His question might be a bit too personal considering their present circumstances, but his pride was involved. It couldn't wait.

"Am I really that repulsive to you, Liz?"

"No," she conceded without the slightest hesitation. "As men go, I think you're probably the kindest one I've ever known. But think about it! You're five years older than me. You're ready to take a wife and have a family. I'm only sixteen. I have no intentions of being tied to a man for years. Besides, I already have two men in my life that keep track of my every move. Why would I want a husband who would more than likely be worse than they are?"

He chuckled. She really did have her own way of looking at life. "I'm sure that wouldn't be the case with every man."

If only that were true! she mused. *Look in the mirror, Kaleb White, you're a prime example of the kind of man I'm talking about and trying to avoid!* "I have things I'd like to do when I finish school and a husband is simply not part of those plans."

"Are your parents aware of these *things?*"

"No! Talking to them about it is out of the question. They wouldn't understand. Dad teases me about finding a nice beau and settling down. I'm pretty sure he's only baiting me, but he is anxious to move into the next phase of his life. He can't do that unless Jesse or I marry."

Confused, Kaleb asked, "What phase is that?"

Rolling her eyes, she turned away, murmuring her response. "He wants grandchildren."

"I see."

Elizabeth was sure that if she looked back right then, she would find a smile on Kaleb's face, and for some reason the thought irritated her—immensely! After a moment, she turned back to face him, her eyes narrowing in on him. "I'm not ready. Besides, there are some things a woman would like to decide for herself. Surely even *you* can understand that."

"I think you're selling your parents short, Liz. They could give you some good advice. You confuse me. You're open with me and I'm only a friend; why not them?"

"I've often wondered that myself. I've always found it easier to open up with you and Jesse."

"Why do you suppose that is?"

"You've never given me a reason not to trust you, Kaleb. When you know I'm struggling or even wrong in a certain area, you don't run to my parents. You talk to me and help me get back on track." She looked up at him and smiled. "Like you're trying to do right now. I like that! At any rate, Jesse trusts you and his opinion goes a long way with me."

Needing to get herself out of the hot seat, Elizabeth turned the tables and decided to be a little inquisitive herself. "With all those young ladies at church looking your way, I'm sure one of them has piqued your interest—am I right?" With a slight tilt to her head and brow raised in wide-eyed curiosity, she informed her suddenly wordless friend, "You never know, Kaleb, I happen to know several available women quite well. Maybe I can set you up."

Although he offered no response, she wasn't about to let that stop her. "Since you've sealed your lips tighter than a drum, let's see if I can figure this out on my own."

He let her ramble on with obvious eccentricity. However, the more she said, the more his mind trailed off in a direction that surprised even him.

Elizabeth tried to extract information from her quiet companion, while sharing more than a little of her own. For some odd reason, he didn't seem interested—not in the least. While this concerned her, she wasn't sure why.

As his thoughts wandered, looking away from the babbling vision before him became an even greater challenge. *Maybe I'd be bored without a feisty little beauty like you, Elizabeth Somers!*

Over the last few months, Kaleb had begun to notice little things about Elizabeth—things he had never seen before. Maybe they were there all along. No longer was she the child looking for pollywogs in the river; she had become a delightful young woman. His days were so much fuller whenever she was around. Oh, she still housed a will made of iron that would challenge the most tolerant of men; but her love for others and her willingness to give of herself no matter the cost had endeared her to him.

Until she brought up the town gossip's input, Kaleb hadn't realized the attraction. When he considered the closeness of their circumstances, he attempted to put his mind onto firmer ground. *The woman just said that she had no intentions of being married for years and here I am thinking about her as a potential wife. As if she would change her mind solely because I'm interested. What's wrong with me, Lord? Thank you, Father, that you're in control of my life, not me. You know the perfect spouse for both of us and I thank you in advance for whoever that might be. Help us, Lord, to seek Your will for our lives and not our own. Help me to keep my mind on the mission you've sent me on—to get her home safe and sound.*

"You know, Liz, it's a relief to see you're feeling like your old self again, but you can drop the matchmaking. I'm not interested."

Kaleb was hiding something, but the thought of digging herself into another hole she'd have to climb back out of sealed her lips, almost completely. *Someday, Lord, Kaleb will be married and then even Mrs. Grant will have to leave me alone!*

"The water must be boiling by now. I could really use some tea, so if you help me up, I'll get breakfast started."

Kaleb scowled. Had she taken leave of her senses. "Please tell me you're not serious."

"Why wouldn't I be?"

"You're not cooking, Elizabeth." His tone dared her to dispute him.

She rose to the challenge. "And why not? I won't just sit here and do nothing. I'll do my part, Kaleb White, and you'll not stand in my way!"

He smiled at her tenacity and actually started to laugh. Then he thought better of it. "I appreciate your offer—really I do, but the last time I checked you still had a broken ankle. You're going to let it heal."

Her fierce scowl astounded him.

"Liz, you're not thinking this through."

"I have, Kaleb. You've done too much for me already." Her mellowed tone was a step in the right direction.

"Didn't you just get through telling me how bad your foot hurts?"

"Yes ..."

"Then you need to heed the warning. Until we leave this

cabin, there are only two things that I need you to do. Lie on the bed or sit in this little chair and prop your foot up on the bed. We can't chance your falling and doing more damage. Are we clear on this?" As the seconds ticked by, she seemed to be moving past irritation, and well into sulking—the sulking he could handle with little effort.

"Kaleb, it's still snowing. We could be here for weeks. I can't sit that long."

"Yes, you can—and you will."

"I'll be bored." She stated, folding her arms in resignation.

The wounded expression on her face was so adorable, he was tempted to kiss her. Since that would never do, he offered what he hoped would encourage a semi-peaceful truce.

"I'm sure you'll be quite busy helping right where you are."

Her soft blue gaze met his. "I'm listening."

"Did I see sewing needles and thread in that bag?"

Her eyes brightened. "Yes, wool and knitting needles too."

"What did you plan to do with the wool?"

Her interest peaked. "Mom was going to make Dad a scarf for Christmas." She smiled in remembrance. "The moths did a number on his old one. It's rather holey."

"If you know how to knit, you could make it for her."

"That's a great idea!"

"Those sewing needles and thread will come in handy too." Holding her inquisitive look, he teased, "When I lifted a noncompliant boy out of the snow last night, the shoulder seams on my coat gave way."

Guilty as charged, she offered, "Sorry!"

"No need to apologize, as long as you fix it."

"I'll be glad to. Thanks, Kaleb."

"You don't need to thank me!"

"Yes, I do! Think about it. Not only did you save my life, you've been the calm in the midst of this storm. I could never thank you enough for all you've done. I think my brother's blessed to have such a wonderful friend."

"I'd like to think we're friends too, Liz."

She stared at him for a moment. "We are. I can see that now more than I ever have before. It's just that you and Jesse have always been so close, I've always thought of you as his friend."

He nodded in understanding. "You have your work cut out for you. This detour from life won't be all fun and games."

She smiled, thinking he had to be exaggerating. "All right, Kaleb. I'll take the bait. What's going to keep me so busy?"

"I intend to fully test your skills as a teacher." As if on cue, Kaleb's rumbling stomach growled unmercifully. They burst into laughter. "I don't know about you, but something tells me I'm hungry. This, My Sweet Friend, is where your abilities will be challenged to the hilt. I can only pray that you're a patient woman."

Her scrunched expression was a bit too patronizing. "I'm stuck in this bed. I don't think I have any pressing engagements, so spit it out!"

"I have no cooking skills." Elizabeth did not appear convinced, so he added, "None whatsoever!"

"None?"

"Zilch! So, My Dear Lady, if you'd like to survive, I'll be counting on you to teach me how to prepare our meals."

She lowered her eyes. "You could be nice and find me a walking stick to help me get around. Then I could do the cooking, and you wouldn't have to learn a thing."

He had to laugh at the way she peeked through squinted eyes. As if they could shield her from his impending response. "Elizabeth Brenae Somers! You're a mite too sassy for your own good. I know you heard what I said!"

"I'm teasing, Kaleb Samuel White, so you can just settle your bossy self down."

He couldn't believe her boldness. "Maybe I should warn you about a little problem of mine. The lack of coffee in my diet has many negative effects. I wouldn't recommend being too plucky around me first thing in the morning."

"I'll keep that in mind."

Elizabeth's laughter became an almost constant presence in the little room as Kaleb's first cooking lesson ensued. He presented her with many scowls, but the tall man's antics over a task that came so easy to her went beyond funny and well into hilarious!

The runny substance he started with baffled his mind. He kept insisting the instructions she had given him could not possibly be right. When the spoon suddenly stood still, he retracted his many condescending remarks. After his experience with porridge, he had a little more faith in his teacher's skills. The problems came in when Elizabeth would fall asleep. The meals Kaleb prepared when she was off in dreamland were enough to make a sow turn up its nose.

❀ ❀ ❀

Elizabeth's heart leapt in delight when Kaleb announced after breakfast that the snow had receded enough for Lightning to make it through to Ann Arbor, and then home. Her wistful thoughts escalated as she readied for their journey. She missed her family, longed to see them. The turmoil they had to be in over their disappearance had plagued her throughout the week. No doubt their relief would be great.

Kaleb watched her intently.

Elizabeth had felt those big brown eyes on her several times since he came in from his morning walk. She wondered what he was thinking, but didn't ask.

Their relationship had changed; she knew that. He had become more than Jesse's friend—her's as well. While she was thankful for that, she couldn't help reflecting on situations that would arise. He did have a way of making her feel bristly at times. True, she wasn't always Miss Agreeable, but he didn't have to be so highhanded. How he managed to be comforting one minute and annoying the next baffled her. *No matter*, she thought. *Soon this awkward confinement will be over and I'll be safe at home with my family.*

She started when Kaleb burst out laughing, seemingly out of the blue. "What's so funny?"

"You!"

Puzzled, she pressed him further. "What did I do?"

"You haven't quit smiling since I mentioned leaving and now you look irritated. Is something wrong?"

She couldn't possibly reveal all her thoughts. "I can't help it, Kaleb, I miss everyone."

He nodded in understanding.

The journey was slow and arduous. As they trudged through the slushy streets of Ann Arbor, the town appeared deserted. The chilly weather had a tendency to keep most folks inside, but Kaleb expected to see someone meandering about. As he moved past the livery, Lightening sidestepped when the doors swung open. A bedraggled rider came out, spewed his chaw off to the side and headed south.

Jeff spotted Kaleb, and waved in greeting.

Kaleb returned the gesture and kept on. The one person he had hoped to avoid stepped out of her store as they neared. It was more than obvious she had come out for the sole purpose of being nosy.

"Who do you have there all bundled up in that blanket, Kaleb?" He hesitated, wondering what disastrous thing she might do with the news.

"It's Elizabeth Somers. She's injured. Is Doc's in?"

"I believe so. Too cold for a body to be out in this if you don't have to."

Inside the covering of the blanket, Elizabeth remained silent. She had no desire to allow this gossipy woman to see her in her brother's attire. Dressing like a boy, and playing the part when the woman was unaware, that she could live with. But this was different. She refused to expose her father to ridicule. He had his reasons for insisting on duplicity and she trusted his judgment.

Wisely, Kaleb moved on before Mrs. Grant's inescapable questions began to flow.

With Elizabeth in his arms, he pressed on the latch that opened the office door and called out, "Hey, Doc, you here?" Kaleb unraveled the twisted blanket just before Doc came out of the back room.

Doctor Taylor couldn't believe his eyes. "Come on back. Your fathers and Jesse have been all over looking for you two. They're worried sick. Where have you been?"

Kaleb set Elizabeth down on the table. "We were stuck in that old cabin up the way. I stumbled across Liz the day of the white-out. She was in rough shape, Doc. Would have frozen to death if I hadn't come along when I did. The storm made it impossible for us to make it home, so I took her there to try and get her warm and wait it out. Now mind you, she was dressed like a boy. I know it looks bad me taking her there, but I had no idea it was Liz until she woke up and attacked me."

Doc burst into laughter. Elizabeth had always been full of surprises. "Why would you do that, Lizzy Girl?"

"He stripped me down to my skivvies and he was about to take those. I had no choice. A woman has to defend herself." She giggled in remembrance. "You should have seen him, Doc. He looked like the abominable snowman in one of Jesse's horror stories."

Kaleb's intense stare taunted her. "Other than a sore nose, she didn't do any real damage. You'd have been amazed, Doc. For such a little thing, she packs a powerful punch. Fortunately, I stopped her before she grabbed the poker or you'd have two patients on your hands."

"He stopped me all right," Elizabeth put in, "but not before he bruised my backside!"

"Oh?" This was news to Kaleb.

When the good Doctor threw him a questioning glance, he defended his actions, "I was only trying to help *him* and all *he* could do is act like an ungrateful brat."

Kaleb breathed a sigh of relief when Elizabeth acknowledged his story, with laughter intertwined in her words. "When he hurled his threats, I recognized his voice and finally quit fighting him."

"Well, Lizzy," Doc put in, "I suppose a sore bum's a small price to pay for someone saving your life."

"I'm glad he came along when he did."

"Me too," Doc said. "All right, Kaleb, how bad is she hurt?"

She found it odd that Doc would ask him when she herself was sitting right there.

"Her foot got stuck in the stirrup ... ankle's in rough shape." Kaleb moved to her side and carefully removed the socks and makeshift splint. Her bruises had gone from shades of purple and blue to greens and yellow. The long ride probably didn't help, but her ankle was still quite swollen.

Doc asked, "Lizzy, is it any better than it was?"

"It's not as painful. Kaleb would barely let me move for the last week."

Doc chuckled inside at the scowl she sent Kaleb's way. He would love to know how Kaleb managed to keep this one down that long, but how could he ask with her present? The old doctor turned and nodded to Kaleb. "It's a good thing you listened, Lizzy Girl. You could have done more damage."

"I suppose you're right."

"I need to put a firmer splint on for a while. I'll lend you one of Martha's dresses. If you don't get out of those jeans you'll be stuck in them until the splint comes off. I have crutches in the back to help you get around. You have to stay down and let that ankle heal. Are we agreed?"

Kaleb didn't miss her reaction. He understood the extent of her frustration. The last few days she'd begun to feel like a caged animal, desperate to get out of the walls that were closing in on her. He had bundled her up and taken her outside to sit on Lightning. The deep snow made it impossible to take her far. Just getting her outside seemed to pull her out of her doldrums. There was no question in his mind: the thought of staying in bed any longer was playing havoc with her thoughts. As she often did, Elizabeth managed to get a handle on her spiraling emotions and had no trouble pressing him.

"Doctor Taylor, I can't stay in bed any longer! I'll go crazy!"

Her frantic expression melted his heart. "Honey, I don't mean you have to stay in bed. I'm only saying that you need to sit as much as possible and prop that thing up."

"Oh." Breathing a sigh of relief, she pierced Kaleb with an irate glare. He was chuckling and he needed to be stopped. "You can quit your laughing, Kaleb White, or you might just live to regret it!"

Trying to explain only dug him in deeper. "I can't help it, Liz, I don't think I've ever seen anyone look more relieved."

"Well, you try staying in bed for that long, and we'll see how you like it!"

Doc laughed at the way they sparred back and forth, but after a time he intervened. "Now stop all that fussing, you two. You've been stuck in that cabin for so long you're starting to sound like an old married couple."

Appalled by his absurd insinuation, Elizabeth was silenced.

Kaleb muttered as Doc walked out of the room, "I wonder what he'd say if he knew we've been going at it since you woke up in the cabin."

Elizabeth ignored her friend, refusing to justify his comment with a verbal response.

"Lizzy," Doc said as he came back in and handed her a dress, "Martha isn't here. Kaleb and I will make some coffee while you put this on. I have a brick of cheese and Martha made a fresh batch of muffins this morning. It's not much, but it should hold you over until you get home."

"Sounds like a taste of heaven to me. The giant standing next to you may have a few good qualities, but cooking is not one of them."

Doc chuckled. "Now I know why you've lost so much weight."

"Is it that obvious?" she asked as her head lowered to take in her appearance.

Kaleb, wishing he could have done better, admitted, "It is, Liz. Sorry."

Her eyes followed Doc and Kaleb as they left the room and closed the door behind them. She wiggled out of the jeans, and managed to get Martha's dress on. She couldn't reach the buttons in the back without standing, so she left them alone. Having women's clothes on after a week in men's felt strange. She giggled as she took in her appearance. Mrs. Taylor was a tall robust woman and Elizabeth's slight frame was lost in her attire. The dress would drag on the ground if she stood to her feet, but she had a feeling that would not be an issue. If Kaleb had anything to say about it—and he would—she wouldn't be using her new crutches until she got home. The men were talking about some new-fangled buggy Doc had ordered as they strolled in.

"Would you look at that?" Doc exclaimed as he smiled in her direction. "I think we have our young lady back. Wouldn't you say so, Kaleb?"

He nodded in agreement.

Doc turned back to Elizabeth. "I gave your Dad a piece of my mind for letting you come into town alone, dressed like a boy. Not sure what was he thinking?"

Kaleb, though he gave no verbal response, agreed with Doc.

Elizabeth wasn't about to touch that comment with a ten-foot pole. Her brother's bluchers were the cause of her injury. Still, her father was the one who insisted she put them on and she had no intentions of discussing this with anyone but him.

While Doc worked on the splint, Kaleb moved behind Elizabeth to button her dress. Seeing to her needs had become so much a part of his everyday life, she no longer flinched when he touched her. The sight of her slender frame ensconced in his long underdrawers brought a smile to his face. She would need the added warmth for the long trek home, but he couldn't help recalling how funny she looked in them.

Chapter Four

The Tongue

*A*S JESSE STOOD gazing out the picture window, his thoughts went to Kaleb and Elizabeth. He missed them terribly. The camaraderie the three of them had shared through out their lives was a rare and special gift. He knew there were no guarantees in this life. God was God and He loved them more than Jesse ever could. Every time he prayed for them a calm assurance would fill his wary heart. Unable to bear the thought of life without them, he held on to the hope that God had indeed sustained them.

In his humdrum state of mind, Jesse couldn't be sure if the figure, or figures, on horseback coming toward the farm were real or a figment of his imagination. From a distance, it appeared to be a man on a horse carrying someone, or something, wrapped in a colorful quilt. He could not look away. *Could it be?* His hopeful heart raced out of control when his good friend Kaleb came into full view. Jesse called out to his family, "Dad, Mom, come quick! Kaleb's coming up the road, and I can't be sure ... but it looks like he has ..." Jesse paused for a moment, the blanket began to move. When a golden head pushed its way out, his excitement spilled over. "Lizzy! Thank God! Kaleb has Lizzy in his arms!" Jesse didn't wait for a response. He ran out the door, the rest of the family following. Tears of joy and thankfulness flooded their eyes as they greeted one another.

Elizabeth slid her arms around her father's neck when he reached to take her from Kaleb. Hugs and kisses were shared all around. Elizabeth, overwhelmed by her family's exuberant response, tried to hear what everyone was saying. They were all speaking at once!

"We had to believe you were both alive," Jesse said and then asked, "How did you find her, Kaleb?"

George realizing that they could be standing in the yard for hours, put a halt to the inquisition. "I think we should let them get in the house before we bombard them with questions. Suzanne, Louise, come on girls. Let the man get off his horse. I'm sure his legs are numb from holding your sister."

Elizabeth gazed into the tear-stained faces of her family members and knew how much she was loved. As her father carried her across the threshold, the familiar smells that assailed her brought everything back. For the life of her, she couldn't remember a time when coming home had ever felt so good.

Kaleb stepped around George to help Elizabeth out of her wraps and fill him in on what Doc had said about her ankle.

Elizabeth smiled, thinking she was quite capable of offering her own explanations. Since Kaleb had taken over with Doc while they were in town, she could only assume that he still felt responsible for her care. She made no attempt to interfere.

George rubbed his hands together in anticipation, plopped down on the sofa next to Elizabeth, slipped his arm around her and kissed her cheek. His eyes moved back and forth between Elizabeth and Kaleb. "All right you two, who's doing the telling?"

Elizabeth glanced around the room at all the inquisitive eyes. They were anxious to hear, but she was hoping Kaleb would do the honors.

Kaleb, sensing her reserve, made a suggestion, "Why don't I start, and if Liz has anything to add she can chime in."

The room grew so quiet, a pin drop could have been heard as Kaleb retold the events of the last week. He began with how he found her. Then he explained how he thought she was a boy when he took her to the cabin, and finally reminded them of the storm that held them captive for so long. Roars of laughter erupted as he shared Elizabeth's interpretation of her abominable snow-covered captor and also her appearance in his underclothes. To his credit, Kaleb left out the embarrassing moments that seemed to come up from time to time. His reenactment had been so thorough that Elizabeth didn't have anything to add. However, she did have a question for her father.

"Dad, did Lady make it back home?" Laughing eyes turned toward her as she again asked, "Well, did she?"

"Yes, Honey, she did." Her father squeezed her, adding, "You're something else, Elizabeth. You've been through a terrible ordeal and here you are worried about that silly horse."

"There's nothing silly about Lady, Dad. She's a wonderful horse."

Elizabeth turned her twinkling eyes on Kaleb.

He could only imagine the playful thoughts going through her mind.

"With God's help, Kaleb found me. I'm on the thin side from his wonderful cooking, but other than my ankle I am fine." The wounded expression on Kaleb's face made her giggle.

"Watch it there, Liz; don't you be picking on my newly-acquired skills!"

She rolled her eyes, rebuking him without mercy. "If you're wise, you'll leave the cooking to your mother. There's nothing skillful about the meals you prepare. Frightful, yes—skillful, no!"

Kaleb's final announcement was given to her entire family, with a taunting smile well in place. "As all of you can see, Elizabeth is just as sassy now as she was before her latest adventure. You have your Lizzy back, and on that note I really should take my leave."

George stood and pulled Kaleb into his arms. "We can't thank you enough for all you've done for our girl, Kaleb. She's back in our lives because of you."

"The pleasure was all mine." Kaleb walked over to Elizabeth, leaned down, kissed her cheek, and scolded her one last time. "Be sure you follow Doc's orders and stay off that foot, or I'll be back to make sure that you do!"

She could feel a warm flush moving up her face. "You're such a worry wart, Kaleb White."

Her flippant retort did not convince him that she would comply. When his eyes narrowed and an expression covered his face that left no room for denial, she reassured him.

"Okay, I promise. There. Satisfied?" Everyone was staring

in disbelief, and to top it off, her father's mouth was hanging open. Elizabeth swatted Kaleb away, sharing a smile as he went to retrieve his coat. He had to be anxious to get home to his own family.

As George followed Kaleb to the door, the interaction that took place between his daughter and this young man ran delightfully through his mind.

"Kaleb, check with your parents and see if they'll have dinner with us tomorrow night. I think we could all use a night of celebration."

Kaleb gladly accepted his offer. "I'm sure they'll agree."

"We'll see you then."

Without Elizabeth's warm presence snuggled against him, the frigid winds ripped right through Kaleb, chilling him to the bone. As he plodded along, he began reflecting on all that had taken place over the past two weeks. It had taken Elizabeth a few days to relax and enjoy their time together, but he understood. It was awkward at times. Since Jesse had always been around whenever they were together, this was a new experience for both of them. Inasmuch as he would love to pursue a relationship with her, she had made it clear that she was not ready to have a man in her life. In some ways this knowledge saddened him. But then again, their time together was not a loss by any means. It certainly gave him hope. Their friendship had moved to a different level. That would have to be enough. Perhaps, given time, it would grow into something more. For now he would continue to pray that God would lead her and protect her as he did that day in the storm.

※ ※ ※

Pastor Williams picked up his horse at the livery and headed towards the Somers' farm. The ride would be long, but he was thankful for the time to pray. His thoughts were running in every direction, and he had no desire to enter their home feeling so unsettled.

Tying his horse to the post at the side door, he noticed the Whites' sleigh in the yard. Relief washed over him. Now he could sit down with his friends, pray, and arrive at an agreement they could all live with. As he moved up the steps, roars of laughter were coming from within.

George extended his hand in welcome, as he ushered him in. "This certainly is a nice surprise, Pastor. The Whites are here celebrating the safe return of our children. What brings you so far out of your way?" George didn't miss the grim look that crossed his good friend's face. He was about to question him, when the rest of the group noticed his presence and extended their greetings as well.

Pastor Williams waited for a comfortable amount of time to pass before pulling George aside. He mentioned that he had something of a delicate nature he needed to discuss. And, that he would like to include Jayne, Kaleb, Samuel and Ruth in this meeting. Although the topic pertained to Elizabeth, taking her age into account, he would prefer to leave her out of the conversation for the time being.

George turned to clear the other children out of the kitchen, his concerns mounting as he did.

The small group of friends joined hands at the table, and Pastor led them in prayer.

"Father God, we thank you for the wonderful blessing of friends and family. Thank you that in the midst of all the turmoil in this world, you never change—You are the peace that passes all understanding. Thank you that nothing in our lives happens without Your knowledge. Give us wisdom, Lord, and may your children come to know Your blessings in spite of the wickedness that dwells within the hearts of men. Thank you, Jesus, for all that was accomplished on the cross, and may Your spirit reside over this meeting, guarding each heart that is affected here tonight. In Your Holy Name we pray, Amen!"

Pastor, looking at all the concerned faces around the table, fixed his gaze on Kaleb. "First of all I would like to say that I'm very thankful you and Elizabeth are home safe, Kaleb."

"Thanks, Pastor. We're glad to be here."

"Carolyn wanted me to tell you that she would love to have the two of you stop by and tell us your story." Kaleb nodded and Pastor continued.

"I am certain the rumors that have begun to circulate are unwarranted, so I want you to understand right off that these are not why I'm here. Kaleb, I've asked you to join us because this concerns you and Elizabeth. Considering her age, you and George should hear me out before the two of you decide how best to remedy this rather delicate situation."

Kaleb said, "Pastor, since all of us are speculating, I'd like you to come right out with it."

"I couldn't agree more, so I'll get right to the point. I was in the store a short while ago and overheard a disturbing conversation among several prominent women in town. To make a long story short, these women are convinced that Elizabeth has not only lost her innocence as a result of your stay in the cabin, they are sure that she is in a family way. Need I say more?"

Kaleb's heart flooded with dread. He hated what this would do to Elizabeth, and not knowing what her father would say left him feeling more than a little uneasy. George's expression was completely unreadable.

"She's only sixteen!" George said and then added, "what's wrong with these people! Don't they have anything better to do with their time than sit around thinking up ways to destroy the lives of others?"

"It's a tragedy," the Pastor agreed, "but we have to live in this imperfect world. Her age doesn't seem to matter. What I need to know as your pastor is how you and Kaleb would like me to handle the rumors? You know as well as I do, it will only get worse."

"I'm all too aware of that," George said as he lowered his head for what seemed like an eternity to Kaleb. The silence unnerved him. However, in view of the circumstances, Kaleb would give him all the time he needed.

When George lifted his head, he focused on the young man whose gaze was fixed on him. "Kaleb, your life will be affected as much as Elizabeth's. I'd like to hear your thoughts." Kaleb didn't hesitate for a second, and George found this very reassuring.

"I'd marry her in a heartbeat, Mr. Somers, but she'll never agree."

George reached across the table, needing to hold his wife's hands. Her daunted expression matched how he felt inside. "This is your daughter too, Jayne. How do you think Kaleb and I should handle this?"

"She'll fight you ... but don't give her a choice, George. She could have died in that storm, and now this. I can't bear to sit back and watch her destroyed."

Jayne paused, looked at Kaleb and asked, "Kaleb?" but then faltered, trying to hold back a fresh rush of tears. After a moment she gave up trying. These people around the table were her friends. They understood why she was hurting. These tales could tarnish Kaleb's reputation as well as Elizabeth's. The Whites would only want what was best for both of their children. Reaching for Kaleb's hand, she tried again, "Could you love our Lizzy?"

"I care about her more than you know, Mrs. Somers."

"We think the world of you, Kaleb. Please don't think my tears are because I don't want the two of you together. Nothing could be further from the truth. You should keep this in mind: if we press this marriage you could be in for a bumpy ride. You've been around Lizzy enough to know, it may take her a while to accept you as her husband."

Kaleb shook his head and said, "First, she'll have to forgive me for betraying her like this." He looked to his parents, who both encouraged him.

"Follow your heart, son. We're with you, whatever you decide."

Kaleb's eyes were riveted on George when he asked, "If you're offering her hand, my answer is yes. I would love to make Liz my wife."

George looked to his wife for confirmation. When she nodded, he turned back to face Kaleb. "Could we discuss a few of my concerns in private, before I speak with Elizabeth?"

"Sure," Kaleb said. He followed him into Jesse's room and shut the door. George encouraged him to ask anything that came to mind.

"I suppose my first question is an obvious one. How soon would you want this marriage to take place?"

"Tonight."

Kaleb's eyes widened. "That's fine with me, but how will you convince Liz?" Kaleb, recalling the conversation they had in the cabin, knew what her father would be up against.

"I'm not giving her a choice. Waiting will only make this harder for her. I've watched you down through the years with my daughter. I know you care a great deal about her. She'll fight this at first, but if you're willing to give her time, I'm sure she'll eventually come around. Lizzy cares for you more than she'd be willing to admit. Jesse's comments at different times have made me wonder if the two of you would eventually end up together. As her father, I suppose my question for you is: do you think you're up to the challenges that will lie ahead? Once you're married, she'll no longer be under my authority. Lizzy's not the most predictable of my children, Kaleb. She could surprise all of us and take this in stride; more than likely she won't."

Kaleb smiled in remembrance. "There were a few times during our stay in the cabin that I thought about throwing her out into the snow. For the most part we had a good time getting to know each other, but ..." He didn't miss the smirk that crossed George's face. "I think it'll take both of us time to see each other as husband and wife. We've been friends for so long."

George knew the answer to his next question. He asked, just in case Elizabeth wanted to know. "Will you live with your family, or here?"

"With my parents, until we can build in the spring. If you don't mind, it might make the transition easier for Liz if we could come for an extended visit now and again."

"You've always been welcome here, Kaleb. That won't change."

"I kind of thought that, but I'd rather know what my options are."

"I have one favor to ask you for Elizabeth's sake." George hesitated for a moment, then forced himself to look at Kaleb and go on. "This question is awkward. Considering the circumstances, I think it's crucial. I know my daughter, Kaleb. This will be her biggest drawback. Could I tell her that you'd be willing to give her time to get used to the idea of being your wife before the physical side of marriage enters in?"

Kaleb didn't even pause. "I'll expect her to share my room, but I have no intentions of rushing her in any way."

George grimaced. "I hate to pass the buck ... if you don't mind, I'll let you deal with sleeping arrangements when you get her home. The marriage alone is bound to throw her for a loop. Until you're wed I'd rather not give her anything else to think about."

"I'm sure you're right."

"If you don't have any more questions, go ahead and tell the others that we'll proceed in just a bit. Welcome to the family, Kaleb." They shared a hug, but Kaleb, not quite as confident, reminded Mr. Somers that although he was a willing participant, the hardest part was yet to come.

"After you talk to Liz," Kaleb said, "I'd like to have a few minutes alone with her."

"I was hoping you would."

Kaleb went back to the kitchen, as George called his unsuspecting daughter to the room.

Chapter Five

Not of My Choosing

"ELIZABETH," HER FATHER began, after seeing that she was seated. "It saddens me to have to tell you this ..." he paused, trying to prepare himself for her reaction. "Rumors have begun to circulate concerning your stay in the cabin with Kaleb."

She didn't care for the direction this conversation was going, but out of respect she let him go on.

"Your mother and I have discussed this, and we agree. The only way to stop the rumors is for you and Kaleb to marry right away."

She paled instantly, horrified by her father's words. How could he even suggest such a thing? An emphatic "No!" was her enraged reply.

"Elizabeth!" he scolded. "I understand that you're upset, but you will not speak to me in that tone."

Her father would not tolerate disrespect, yet her brain was

screaming in defiance. She wasn't about to marry anyone, let alone her brother's best friend. This outrageous notion needed to be laid to rest, so she persisted, but she did so in a calmer manner.

"Dad, Kaleb is a friend, that is all. I don't love him and he doesn't love me." He nodded in understanding—or so she thought.

"Many marriages begin with far less, Elizabeth."

She took a deep breath and tried again. "You're not hearing me, Dad. I don't want a husband. I won't marry Kaleb and nothing you say will change my mind!" When he continued to stare, apparently unmoved by her words, she huffed in contempt and turned away from his insistent glare. She wanted to flee the room, this house, this town. Only knowing he would stop her before she took her first step kept her from trying.

George understood her impertinence. Even so, it did nothing to alter his resolve. Hoping for some form of compliance, he explained. "Lizzy, we don't always understand why these things happen. It's unfortunate, but these rumors are destroying your reputation as we speak. I've talked to Kaleb and he's more than willing to make you his wife."

Gasping in disbelief, she wondered when or if her father would listen. "That's all well and good, but doesn't my opinion count for something? This isn't just about Kaleb, you know. I appreciate his willingness to protect me, but marriage? Please, isn't that a bit extreme?" The steeled look in her father's eyes said it all. Her words had fallen on deaf ears. "Dad, I've told you before and nothing has changed. I have no intentions of being anyone's wife for years. I'm only sixteen!"

"I am more aware of your age than anyone. You're not thrilled with the prospect, I can see that, but this is one of those times in your life where you're going to have to trust your mother and me. We've been down this road with friends and we won't sit back and watch you destroyed."

She folded her arms and lowered her gaze. She knew better than to openly defy her father. What choice did she have? Appalled by his determination, she searched the limited resources of her mind for something, anything that would weaken his position.

"Dad, you're talking about the rest of my life. I don't care what people are saying—I know the truth. I won't be bullied into a marriage not of my own choosing." She paused for a moment. Hoping for a glimmer of understanding, she took Kaleb's advice and exposed her secret longings. "When this school year is over, I'd like to travel, do some things before I think about settling down. I have no desire to be a wife or a mother. Not yet. Please! I beg you to stop this foolishness. Things couldn't possibly be as bad as you think."

Her notion of travel was news to George, but Kaleb would see that she chased these outlandish ideas out of her head. While his heart was breaking for her, she made it clear that she was not going to cooperate.

"You'll be married tonight, Elizabeth."

His piercing stare sent rippling chills up her spine. Never in all her life had her father been so cold towards her. He was acting out of fear; that was obvious. His forceful words cut deep into her wounded heart. Her scattered thoughts whirled fantastically as the words to combat him further eluded her.

Not tonight! I can't marry him tonight! What is he thinking? Lord, please help me! Her father's tempered words interrupted her spiraling despair.

"After the nuptials, you'll go home to live with Kaleb's family until another house can be built in the spring." Her small frame shook so violently George was forced to look away. Could he find the strength to see this through? A piece of his heart was being ripped away. He wanted to take his daughter into his arms, tell her everything would be fine. As much as he loved her, he also understood the strength of her will. If she thought for a second that his resolve had waned, she would never go through with his bidding. As her father, he needed to stand firm this one last time. Perhaps after a while she would forgive his harshness and understand that he did what he had to. *Help us both, Father God. Give us the fortitude we need to move forward.*

Her father was thinking. The silence frightened her.

While her pleading words hung heavy within the hidden recesses of his mind, he was convinced this was the only way.

"Please don't ask me to do this. I can't, Daddy. You of all people should understand why. I'm not ready to give myself to a man in marriage." As she spoke the words, an all-consuming fear of Kaleb's unknown expectations assailed her. She had no idea what her father was thinking, but surely he didn't think ... did he?" Terrified, her words came out in a rush. "I won't let him touch me!"

"You're going to be married, Elizabeth. I talked to Kaleb and he is willing to give you time to get comfortable with him."

Her father talked as if the physical side of marriage was no big thing. To her it was huge! What if she never loved him? She couldn't give herself to a man she didn't love. The very thought repulsed her! "And what if I never am?"

"I can't ask for more. It's not my place."

She knew the answer to her next question. She asked it anyway. "What about my rights? I never did have a choice, did I, Father?"

His voice was calm. However, his words were written in stone. "Not this time, Elizabeth."

As tears flooded her eyes, she refused to look away. He needed to know what she thought of his scheme to salvage her reputation. "I hate this, Father; I've always tried to honor you. This time you're asking too much!"

He took a deep breath, attempting to calm the thunderous beat of his heart. "That may be, but don't take your anger out on the one person who can save you in all of this. I pray that you will come to love him. In the meantime, you will be kind—you will obey your husband .... Am I understood?"

She put her head down, refusing to look his way. Promises were not something she would make. She felt desolate—so very alone. Her life was raging out of control and she was powerless to stop it. If this were summer, she would flee this house without a second thought. With a broken ankle and all this snow she was trapped, entangled in this nightmare with no hope for escape. The desire to crawl beneath her brother's quilt and have a good cry overwhelmed her. She wanted her mother—she needed her brother—her mind was screaming out, *Jesse, where are you?* She needed time—time to plan her escape. But her father knew her well and time was not something he would give her.

"Elizabeth, I know you're hurting, but God has a purpose in all of this. Don't let your stubborn pride destroy your chance for happiness. Right now this seems harsh, but Kaleb is a good man. Give him a chance and I think you'll be surprised."

"I can tell you in all honesty, I'm surprised already!"

His inquisitive glare met her obstinate glower. "What do you mean?"

"I can't believe he would go along with this insidious plot. He knows better than anyone how I feel about marriage. I told him while we were stuck in our so-called 'den of iniquity'!"

George was at the end of his rope—exhausted from fighting her, yet understanding of her apprehension. "Lizzy, you've always been a blessing to this family. We adore you. Trust me when I say that this marriage is not a plot. It is a necessity. I need you to tell me you'll honor our wishes and wed Kaleb tonight."

She wanted to defy him with all that was in her; regardless, in the end he would force her to marry him. Experience had taught her that fighting her father was useless. Besides, God's word doesn't say to honor your parents only when you agree with them; it says to honor them always. She would do what her parents asked, but this time her heart was not in it. She wondered if it ever would be.

The fight drained out of her as she answered her father numbly? "What I want is irrelevant. You gave my consent before I ever walked into this room."

George held her chin in his work-worn hand, and gazed into the tearful eyes of his beautiful daughter. She was so much like her mother. He adored her and he had to believe that Kaleb would cherish her as well. "Kaleb wants to speak with you. I'm sorry it has to be like this. I need you to handle this well." George would have preferred the choice be left in her hands. With Elizabeth, it could take weeks, even months for her to agree—they didn't have days.

She was angry, hurt, and feeling abandoned by her parents. She wanted to scream, but knowing it would accomplish nothing, she held in her rage. Her father had no more left the room when she heard Kaleb's steps coming toward her.

Elizabeth, glowering at nothing yet everything, saw Kaleb's bluchers appear on the rug beside her. As if he wasn't close enough, the bed sank next to her. Her frantic heart beat at a dangerous pace. She had no desire to look at him, never mind converse with her father's collaborator. She watched helplessly as he gathered her hands within his own and gave them a reassuring squeeze. His touch made her tremble—his words, so softly spoken, did wonders for her shattered mind.

"Liz, I know you're hurting. You'd like me to make this all go away, but I think you know that this is out of my control. With that in mind, I would like you to hear me out." Without a trace of acknowledgement on her part, he continued, "During the time we spent together snowed in, we became good friends, wouldn't you agree?"

"I thought so ... now I'm not so sure."

"Your confusion is understandable, but I think we could have a good life together. We've only been apart a day ... I miss our lengthy discussions."

She scowled. "I find it hard to believe you miss the way we argue."

"I saw it more as bantering. I like the way you stand up for yourself." His heart wrenched as she offered her stilted response.

"It does me no good. Today's a prime example. My supposed friend and my father are both betraying me—on the same day." She raised her clouded blue eyes. "But then you're already aware of that, aren't you? You both know I don't want to be married. Apparently, my opinion doesn't matter. My father insists that I go through with this even though I don't love you." Like the walls of Jericho, the tower of strength she presented came tumbling down all around her. She hated her tears, her weakness, her despair, but time was running out. She forced herself to go on. "How can you marry me when you don't love me? We don't even get along, and you know I'll challenge your every command. You deserve an obedient wife. You know that's not me. I'm not going to change, Kaleb. Why would you even want me?"

With a tenderness that surprised her, he dried her tears with the palm of his hand and tucked her golden locks behind her ears. "In spite of what you think, we are good friends. I can only hope that, given time, you will come to accept me as your husband. If we're willing to open our hearts to one another, I have to believe we'll come to love each other."

"But what do we do for now?"

"We care about each other, Liz. For now, it'll be enough."

She was not convinced. "In all fairness, you need to understand. I'm not prepared to be a wife. Not in any way."

As silent tears continued to pour down her delicate features, Kaleb gathered her in his arms, and simply held her, letting her weep. She was trying to process so much. He wasn't blind to the fact that they would have bridges to cross. He even began to wonder if her father was asking too much of her. And yet, knowing the devastation encountered by others under similar circumstances, he stood firm. Her father had given her hand. He would marry her tonight, willing or not, and deal with the repercussions as they arose.

"I'm sorry I put you in this position, Kaleb. If I hadn't gone to town that day, none of this would be happening."

Gazing into her saddened eyes, he held her tear-drenched face in his oversized hands. Her admission surprised him. In his heart he knew that everything leading up to this marriage did not just happen. He wanted her to see this as well. "I'm not sorry, Liz. I want you for my wife, and the way I see it, God must want us together awfully bad to have gone to all this trouble. He doesn't make mistakes and we need to trust Him." His eyes held a teasing glint. "Besides, the thought of being your husband intrigues me. In the cabin you tried to convince me to marry one of the women from church. All I could see was the feisty little beauty before me. She's the only female who has ever caught my eye, and as far as I'm concerned, there's not a woman in the world that could hold a candle to my bride."

Bride! Oh, Kaleb ... I don't want to be a bride! Can't you see that? "I'm not questioning your sincerity. In truth I feel sorry for you—you haven't got a clue as to what you're getting yourself into."

He smiled in remembrance. "Oh, come now, Liz. After our stay in that cabin, I think I have a pretty good idea."

She shook her head, biting nervously on her lower lip. "I'm telling you, Kaleb, you have no idea what goes on inside my head."

"Then I suppose I'll take my chances."

Although Kaleb didn't seem to have reservations, it changed nothing for her. She had enough reservations for both of them. Having her father and brother monitor her every move was one thing. She knew what to expect from them. Kaleb was a different story. All that aside, how could she ever see Jesse's friend as her husband when he'd been like a brother her whole life? She would have to take things in stride or she wouldn't make it through the night, never mind a lifetime, with this oversized farmer.

"I wish we had more time to talk this through, but our families and Pastor Williams are waiting." Kaleb, realizing that no amount of comforting words would make this any easier, claimed her hand. Bringing it to his lips, he pressed a kiss to her palm. Their eyes joined as mere friends. Within the hour they would be husband and wife. Kaleb spoke to his bride with a tenderness that came from his heart.

"Elizabeth, I know you have doubts. I also know that if you'll give us a chance, we can have a wonderful life together. Will you come with me and be my wife?"

She nodded her consent, but in her heart she knew this decision was not hers to make. *Help me to find joy in this, Lord! The only thing holding me together is knowing You'll carry me through. Kaleb is a kind man, but right now I feel broken inside, so very alone.*

Their families were gathered in the parlor. Pastor Williams stood as Kaleb and Elizabeth made their way in. The mood in the room reminded her more of a funeral than a wedding. Not even her giggly sisters smiled when she looked their way. Jesse stood in the back. Although he nodded when she saw him, his thoughts were a mystery. Her mother and father were on her left side, she couldn't bring herself to look their way.

Here she stood in her drab navy day dress, a true depiction of how she felt inside. She was about to be married to her brother's friend. If only a glimmer of hope would lift her weighted heart, she might find the strength to make it through.

Pastor Williams asked, "Are you ready to proceed, Kaleb?"

"Yes, we are." As he glanced at the frightened woman beside him, he felt genuine concern. Like a fragile flower, she needed his tender care. Without a doubt, she was struggling to maintain her composure. He would do whatever he could to help her through. When Pastor Williams began the ceremony, Kaleb set her crutches aside, slipped his arm around her waist and reached for her quivering hand.

"Dearly beloved, we are gathered together this day in the sight of God and this company to join Kaleb Samuel White and Elizabeth Brenae Somers in the bonds of Holy matrimony ..." The ceremony went along as expected, until it was Elizabeth's turn to repeat her vows. Kaleb didn't miss the way her wary eyes connected with her father's. His look was enough to spur her on. Having declared that they were husband and wife, Pastor Williams' last words were spoken with a smile.

"Kaleb, you may kiss your bride." As he leaned down to do just that, the wide, fear-filled eyes of his new bride stopped the beat of his heart. He settled for a hug and a kiss to her brow.

Kaleb carried his somber wife up the stairs so she could pack her bag. Thinking she could use some time alone with her mother, he put her down on the bed and left the room.

Mother and daughter gathered up the scattered remnants of her life. Elizabeth didn't have much in the way of temporal things. It didn't take long. She glanced around the empty room, saying her silent goodbyes. So much of her life had been spent within these walls—so many cherished memories, now only distant dreams. No longer would her little sisters bustle in to giggle and talk with her in the morning or just to say goodnight. She wouldn't be here to help Jared and Joseph with their schoolwork, and oh, how she'd miss their constant pranks. She couldn't allow herself to consider how she would survive without her big brother. If she did, she'd never be able to hobble out the door. Jesse had always been her guardian angel, her best friend, and her endless source of comfort through everything life sent her way—until now. No longer would she flounce down the stairs to be greeted by her family. Like it or not, her life changed forever when she said *I do* to the man waiting for her downstairs. The uncertainties of the future left her feeling cold and frightened, not all that different from the way she felt that day in the storm. Somehow she would find a way to go on ... somehow. She prayed so many times that God would lead her in the way she should go. *Surely this is not part of Your plan, is it, Lord?*

If it was, she was not ready to see it as such.

As mother and daughter's solemn eyes joined, Elizabeth could no longer hold back her unspoken fears. She needed her mother's touch, her understanding, and most of all her unending love.

"Mom, I'm scared. This is all happening too fast. I don't know how to be a wife—I don't want a husband."

Jayne wrapped Elizabeth in her arms and held onto her oldest daughter with all her might. They shared a few tears, but she needed to be Elizabeth's mother right now and somehow help her to get through the challenging days ahead. Minutes passed before she released her, caressed her damp cheeks, and gazed into her daughter's disheartened face.

"Honey, you're going to make a wonderful wife. You know so much more than I did starting out."

Elizabeth appreciated her mother's words, even though she

didn't understand what Elizabeth was saying. "What I want to do is wake up in my own bed and find that this was all a bad dream—but dreams don't hurt this much, do they, Mom?"

"Honey, God can turn this into something wonderful. You have to do your part—you have to work through your anger and frustration and be willing to open your heart to your husband. If you fight him you won't find the happiness you both so richly deserve. Kaleb is a caring, godly man. He has more than proven that to you. Lasting love is not a dreamy feeling that comes and goes on a whim; it's an unwavering commitment to each other. The choice is yours. Choose to love him."

Her mother might as well have asked her to jump off a cliff and trust that she would walk away unscathed. She was asking the impossible. Elizabeth wanted no part of any of this, and she resented her father for taking the choice out of her hands.

"Honey, Kaleb is waiting. Jesse is in the hall. He'll bring you down after the two of you have a minute to talk." Jayne hugged Elizabeth again, reassuring her that they would see each other soon. Her mother reached for her bag on her way out, and Jesse walked into the room.

His strong arms enveloped her. "Come on now, Sis. It isn't going to be all that bad. If I could have chosen your husband, Kaleb would have been my only choice. I know you're hurting, and I'm sure you don't want to hear this, but I agree with Dad. He was right to have you marry."

Tilting her head upward, her wary eyes held onto his. "Oh, Jesse, I wish I understood. I don't want to be his wife."

"Lizzy, listen to me." His tone was firm, but he spoke out of love. "Kaleb is your husband, and denying that won't change

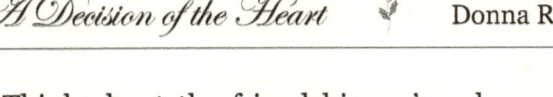

a thing. Think about the friendship we've always shared. You can trust him. You know as well as I do how much he cares. I'll be there for you as much as I can—but now you have my friend looking out for you as well."

"You're the best big brother a girl could ever ask for, Jesse. What am I going to do? I feel like my life's being ripped away, and I'll never be happy again."

"You have to try. God is leading you down a different path than you thought He would. You can't see clearly right now, but He does have a purpose in all of this. You need to trust Him."

"I won't make promises, but for you I would do almost anything. I'll even try. I don't know how to do this, Jesse, it's happening too fast. Pray that we can find a place to start."

"You know I will."

Jesse's mischievous grin tweaked her sullen eyes.

"We need to get you downstairs before Kaleb thinks I snuck you out the window." His lighthearted inflection was exactly what she needed. He chuckled, and sweet giggles bubbled up from deep within her as they recalled a few of the sneaky things they had done through the years. Jesse dried her remaining tears. The venerable look that came over her as he carried her down the narrow staircase tore at Jesse's heart. His friend adored her. He didn't doubt that for a minute. Elizabeth; however, was a different story. He could only hope that, given time, she would lay her fears aside and come to cherish Kaleb as much as he did her.

Elizabeth didn't miss the look that passed between her brother and his friend as they helped her into her coat. Doom and desolation settled over her like a cloak. She was a pawn in the game of life. Perhaps it wasn't fair to blame Kaleb for agreeing to this union, but she did. How could she not?

Jesse issued his gentle warning before releasing Elizabeth to his lifetime friend. "Take good care of my sister, Kaleb, or you'll be hearing from me."

Kaleb's brow furrowed. "You know I will."

Elizabeth's thoughts were anything but calm as she reached for her crutches, glanced back at her parents with a sick feeling in the pit of her stomach, and turned to leave. If Kaleb would have let her pass, her irritation might have been overlooked. Instead, when his hand wrapped around her arm and he murmured his orders, the hair at the base of her neck stood on end.

"Liz, I won't chance your falling. I'm going to carry you."

She wanted nothing from this man and told him as much. "Let go of me, Kaleb White, I can do this myself!" Her statement, heard by all standing in the foyer, brought a hushed silence. She flushed with embarrassment as all eyes fell on her.

Kaleb, understanding her duress and knowing he should have handled this better, ignored her remark and all the stunned faces. He simply stepped in front of her, lifted her into his arms, and walked out the door.

Elizabeth, intent on avoiding his discerning eyes, moved to the far side of the seat and turned away. As the sleigh began to move, she leaned back and her gaze rose to the heavens. The brilliant stars sparkled high in the evening sky, but the comfort she usually found in the wonder of God's design did not have its normal effect. Nothing seemed to lift the crushing weight that held her soul captive. *Why, Lord? You know my heart. You know that I'm not ready for marriage. And Kaleb—why him? He's the epitome of all I didn't want in a husband. Why would You ask this of me? Your Word tells me that You will never leave me nor forsake me. If that's so, why do I feel so alone?*

Kaleb, not knowing what to say to his silent wife, also prayed along the way.

Father, help me to be a source of comfort to my unsettled friend. Her world has been turned upside down. Give me the wisdom I need to help her through. May the life we share as man and wife somehow glorify you.

Chapter Six

Hopeful Arms

*I*N THE ARMS of the man she was bound to share her life with, Elizabeth was carried across the threshold of Kaleb's parents' home. His father, mother and little sister retired for the evening, and although she didn't care for the idea of being alone with their son, *perhaps,* she thought, *we could use a moment to adjust to this rather awkward situation.*

Kaleb helped Elizabeth remove her coat and watched as her eyes scanned the sitting room.

She had been in this house so many times as a guest, yet this night everything appeared different. Whether she liked it or not, this would be her new home until theirs could be built in the Spring. Since the thought of living alone with Kaleb terrified her, she put those thoughts out of her mind, refusing to add one more concern to her list of many. If she were ever going to find a sense of peace, and someday contentment with this man, she would have to leave tomorrow in the Lord's hands. The only thing she wanted to do was get up to Sarah's room and sleep. However, the thought had no more crossed her mind when she wondered what Kaleb would say; they hadn't discussed sleeping arrangements. Elizabeth was startled when his deep voice broke into her uneasy state. She turned to face him.

"Liz, I'm heading out to the kitchen to make some tea. Would you care to join me?"

Sounded good, but in her impertinent mood, she thought she should make her excuses and call it a night. "Kaleb, I feel numb inside. Maybe if I get some sleep things will seem clearer in the morning."

"That's fine. To be honest, I'm kind of worn out myself. If you'd like to go ahead and get settled in *our* room, I'll bring your bag in after I put the water over to boil."

So much for a reprieve! she thought. In an attempt to hide her distress, she averted her eyes, but that did nothing to calm the rapid beat of her heart. *Surely he doesn't think I have any intentions of sleeping with him. If he does, he's completely deluded!* When a sudden ray of hope crossed her mind, her tension eased. *He could have twin beds like Sarah. I suppose I could live with that if he gives me no other choice.* On the slim chance she misunderstood, she claimed ignorance and questioned him again. "Where am I supposed to sleep?"

Recalling her father's warning, and thinking it was possible that she hadn't heard him in her rather unusual frame of mind, Kaleb alleviated all doubt when he said, "Liz, I agreed to take things slow, but you are my wife. You'll sleep in my room."

Although the notion appalled her, his staunch reply told her the subject was not open for discussion. Too weary to defy him, she made her way to *his* room, wondering what she would find inside. As she turned the knob, the door swung open, revealing one large bed. Needing to get a grip on her spiraling emotions, she took a firm stance. *He can't force me I'll simply refuse!* If she was convinced that Kaleb would listen she might have been comforted. Lost in a mull of anguish, her frail tremulous frame jolted when the source of her dilemma came up behind her.

On impulse, Kaleb reached to console her, but she immediately pushed him away, appearing angry and scared all at the same time.

"Don't touch me, Kaleb White. I'm not sleeping in that bed and you can't make me!"

Her fears confused him. "Liz, we had to lie next to each other in the cabin. This is no different. The bed is bigger."

She grimaced. "No different! How do you figure? It's completely different! In the cabin you were like one of my brothers. Now—now you're my ..." she couldn't even say the word. It sounded so foreign, so unwelcome on her tongue.

He said it for her. "Husband!"

"Yes! That changes everything."

"I'm still the same man. I won't hurt you, Liz."

His words held no comfort. "You'll have to forgive me, Kaleb. I'm having a hard time trusting anyone right now—least of all you."

"Let me ask you this. Have I ever touched you in a way that made you uncomfortable?"

"No ..." *What about vulnerable? Ask me if you've ever made me feel vulnerable!*

"I'm going to the kitchen. When I come back with the tea, we'll continue this conversation. In the meantime, get ready for bed."

He walked past her into the room, lit the lamp, and placed her bag on the small table next to his bed. Mechanically, she followed him, though she berated herself upon realizing what she had done. Her wide eyes cautiously scanned the room. She was searching for something—something that had to be lurking and would surely appear if she happened to let down her guard. *Why did I allow him to do this? I didn't say that I'd sleep with him and here I am in his room.* She stood mute, waiting for him to leave.

Kaleb, counting on the possibility she would be more agreeable when he returned, overlooked her strange behavior and went to the kitchen.

When he came back with the tea, her navy dress hung from the hook, but she was nowhere to be seen. He went in search of his reluctant bride, and found her with little effort, sitting on the sofa, ensconced in a pale yellow nightgown and matching robe. Entranced by the flickering flames, she didn't seem to notice his presence, so he took a moment to gaze at her loveliness. Her hair was pulled back in a thick golden braid that streamed down around her shoulder and ended in her lap. He loved the way she was put together.

Everything happened so fast. He found it hard to believe he had a wife, and not just any wife, the very woman who of late consumed his thoughts.

Elizabeth, while she appeared soft to the touch, was untouchable. He would love nothing more than to gather her in his arms, snuggle her close, and assure her that everything would be fine. Even if she would allow it, they needed the benefit of time.

Their stay in the cabin had drawn them closer. Not close enough to court, and certainly not close enough for this. She was right. Their marriage changed everything. He was thankful that her father offered her hand, but that was all he had—a marriage contract, not a union based on mutual love. While his heart rejoiced over having her in his life, she made it clear that he was not a welcome addition to hers. If she were ever going to accept him as her husband, he would have to be patient and give her the time she needed to adjust.

"Mind if I join you, Liz?"

She turned to face him. "This is your house." *Not mine!* "Do as you please."

He chose to ignore her sarcastic comment, poured the tea, and handed her a cup. She thanked him kindly and was fine until he sat next to her on the sofa. A blind man would have noticed her reaction to his closeness. Her hands began to tremble, and the cup rattled so against the saucer that he wondered if it might topple over. Just as he was about to help, she turned and set it down on the table. It was more than obvious that his wife could use a distraction.

"Liz, I thought about something in the kitchen. Would you mind my sharing?" On her reticent nod, he continued, "Do you remember the day I went hunting?"

"How could I forget? I was bored out of my mind."

His soft chuckle brought her gaze to his. "We both had too much time on our hands. I asked myself what I would do if someone got the wrong impression about our stay in the cabin.

We had no option, but having been through a similar situation with friends from school, I had my concerns. I've seen how cruel people can be when they think others are living immorally."

She scowled. "We didn't do anything wrong. Why would they say such things?"

"God is our judge, Liz, but we have to live with these people. It's the appearance of evil that starts the gossip. We have to look at this through their eyes."

"I'm not sure I know what you mean."

"We were alone in that cabin for days. People chose to believe the worst. What I need you to understand is that I could never stand by and allow anyone to do to you what they did to Kendal and Horace."

"Was it really that bad?"

"Yes. They didn't marry, and things went from bad to worse. Their only recourse was to move away."

She didn't understand. "If you ask me, I think this union makes us look like we're trying to cover our sin."

"Some may think that. Our friends and family know the truth."

"I can appreciate your wanting to save our ..." Kaleb's fingers came to her lips, stopping the flow of words.

"I didn't marry you just to save our reputation. I adored you as a child. You've become a beautiful, kindhearted woman, and I'm blessed to have you for my wife." She seemed to be considering his words, so he took a chance, admitting, "Laying alone in my bed last night, I realized how much I missed you. I was determined to find a way to let you know I wanted to court you."

Confused, she said, "Kaleb, you knew I wasn't ready for any

of this."

"I would have waited, Liz. Something changed during our stay in the cabin. I can't explain it other than to say that my feelings for you are different. This marriage took place sooner than either of us would have anticipated, but I honestly believe we're meant to be together."

She had built up so many hopes and dreams of what the future would hold; had so many preconceived notions about marriage. Could she let go of them and find happiness with this man? She didn't know. His wanting to be with her did ease some of her despair—even if having a husband was not part of her plan. "Kaleb, you're not just saying all this to make me feel better, are you?"

"No, Liz, I'm not." He paused for a moment, contemplating his next words. "Do you think you could tell me why you're suddenly so afraid of me?"

The compassion emanating in his gaze encouraged her. "I know what you're like, Kaleb. I'm terrified that you'll expect more than I'm willing to give."

"Then we need to come to an understanding that both of us can live with. I want you to feel secure with me. I'm not saying there won't be compromises to make along the way, but I haven't changed. I'm still the friend you've known all your life—the same friend who took care of you in the cabin and brought you home."

If they could come to an agreement, maybe, just maybe, a few of her anxieties would be relieved. "What did you have in mind?"

"For now, only two things."

"Go on."

"I'd like your permission to hold you."

She did not expect this. The day had brought so many changes into her life. How could she handle one more concession? As she thought about his request, she realized that this might not be a concession at all. She would miss the affection she has always shared with her family—so maybe those big strong arms about her now and again wouldn't be horribly unbearable. "I suppose I can allow an occasional hug—as long as you don't get carried away."

In the short amount of time it took for Kaleb to turn and take a sip of his tea, Elizabeth had scooted to the far end of the couch, putting as much space between them as possible. Apparently, holding her now was not an option. His integrity was in question, so his last request might not be accepted with ease. "I'll do my best to be considerate. How about you? Is there something you want from me?"

Her uncertainties heightened. *He said two things—I know he did! Perhaps he's stalling? What if ...? You have to get a grip Elizabeth or you won't make it through the night!*

One thing did come to mind. Deep down she knew he would not agree, but she would never forgive herself if she didn't ask. Wary of his reaction, her eyes remained in her lap.

"You could take me home and annul this marriage." Had Elizabeth known what would happen next, she never would have asked. To her chagrin, he slid toward her on the couch and captured her face in his hands.

"Oh, Liz, I understand that you don't share my joy. Given time, it's my hope that you'll see this union as I do—as a blessing from the Lord. I'm sorry you feel this way. My answer is no. I could never give up such a rare treasure."

Emotions transfused her that she had never felt before.

None of them were good, and certainly not righteous. The strongest being annoyance. Boy, was she annoyed! She wanted this conversation over. And now! She had seen just about enough of this man for one night.

"What else did you have in mind?" When he didn't respond, her thoughts digressed further. *I'm tired and I want to go to bed! Since my room at home is not one of my options, I'll have to make the best of this impossible situation.*

"I need you to sleep in *our* room."

With slow measured moves, her head shook back and forth, denying his request with escalating uncertainties. "Maybe in time, Kaleb. Not yet."

He was unmoved by her denial—or so she thought—and his lack of response left her feeling terribly unsettled. She had learned much about this oversized farmer during their time of confinement. The one thing she knew above all else is that he housed a will as strong as hers—maybe stronger. While he may appear to accept her rejection, he would not give up without a fight. Not if he felt strongly about this. She needed to test the waters. With a boldness that came out of nowhere, she said, "I'll sleep out here for now." When he didn't so much as flinch, she added, "on the couch."

"That's fine," he replied with a tilt of his head and the utmost calm.

She held her breath, hoping against hope that this would be the end of his diligence.

"But, " he had the gall to add, "don't you think it'll be a little cramped for the two of us?"

I knew it! She scowled at this bold unyielding man with

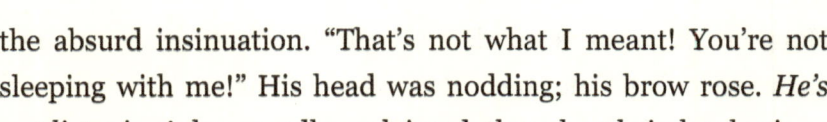

the absurd insinuation. "That's not what I meant! You're not sleeping with me!" His head was nodding; his brow rose. *He's not listening!* she soundly exclaimed, though only in her brain.

"Fine! I'll sleep in Sarah's room." Convinced this declaration would end his persistence, she folded her arms. Her chin went high in the air.

"You can tuck that stubborn chin of yours back in place, Elizabeth. We'll be just as cramped in Sarah's extra bed as we will be on the sofa."

"I'm not sleeping with you."

Ignoring her protests, he went on as if she hadn't spoken. "It makes so much more sense for us to sleep in the big bed, but I'm more than willing to move around until you're comfortable with *our* room. Of course, I'd be glad to snuggle you close in the big chair until you fall asleep—then I could carry you to *our* room."

"Kaleb White, you know full well that you're the problem, not the location."

"I kind of got that impression."

Elizabeth sighed in frustration. "Why is this so important to you?"

"You're my wife, Liz. I need you close so I can hold you. How can I do that if you're somewhere else?" She would never get beyond her fear of him if she weren't pressed to a degree. When she didn't seem moved by his response, he took a firmer approach. "If you continue to be disagreeable, I'll be forced to add something else to the list of things I'll expect from my bride."

Her new husband was pushing his luck, but she waited too long to respond. He simplified things. Completely!

"I'll ask for kisses! I'm assuming from the expression on

your face when we were wed that you'd rather not kiss me. To be honest, I wouldn't mind a bit, but I'll leave that decision completely in your hands."

She couldn't believe the audacity of this man. At the same time, his determination, now bordering on the extreme, struck her funny! In retrospect, she could not recall a single instance where Kaleb prattled so. Elizabeth hated to admit it, even to herself. He was beginning to sound like her when she was nervous or upset. She didn't know why, but suddenly the idea of sleeping next to him didn't seem quite so scary after all.

Now that she had come to this decision, she had to ponder this further. She couldn't allow him to think that she could be manipulated into doing anything he wanted. "You're not being fair, Kaleb, and you know it!"

"Shall I come and claim my first kiss or is this particular topic closed?"

When he leaned towards her, dramatically puckering up, her single word was intermixed with giggles in an attempt to push him away. "Closed!" The levity they shared over her hesitant acceptance lightened the air, and again they were able to converse as friends.

Although Elizabeth was not happy with her circumstances, the heavy cloud that had been hovering since her father called her into Jesse's room was lifting.

Feeling more like herself, she couldn't resist one more ploy and muttered in teasing revolt, "I'm not sure where, but there must be a verse somewhere in the Bible that reprimands men who manipulate their wives."

He winked. "I'd prefer to call it gentle persuasion. I'm more than willing to read any verses that would support your claim, but I'm sure we could find a few more passages that refer to wives needing to obey their husbands."

Since this was not a subject she was ready or willing to touch, she let it drop.

When Kaleb turned to pour himself more tea, she remembered that she hadn't touched her own and took a sip. "Mmm! This is good. What did you sweeten it with?"

"A touch of Mom's blueberry syrup."

She didn't appear ready to call it a night, so he waited for her to set her drink down before broaching a subject he thought should be addressed. "We're married, Liz, so what I'm going to ask you is irrelevant. Perhaps my pride is involved, but I need to know: was there another gentleman from church or school who you were interested in?"

She couldn't believe he had to ask. When she considered the way their marriage took place, she realized that he might have insecurities of his own. "If you're talking about a boyfriend, no— but I did have definite ideas about what I wanted in a husband." The words were out of her mouth before she could stop them. What was she thinking? She wanted to take them back, but a quick glance at Kaleb told her that was not feasible. Her only hope of evading the raised brow and that inquisitive brown glare would be to tell him what he wanted to know. And, she couldn't possibly do that without offending him.

"I'm assuming you're going to share these ideas."

Elizabeth, needing to flee, reached for her crutches, cringing when his large hand came up to forestall her. While his actions were not harsh in any way, she couldn't bring herself to look his way. "Kaleb, when I'm tired I say things that I shouldn't. I need to go to bed before I say anything else I'll regret."

"Come now, Liz. You brought it up, so I think it's only fair to tell me." She turned to face him. Her eyes begged him to let it drop. In his heart, he knew that if she brought it up, these ideas held more importance than she was willing to say.

She told him in all honesty, "You won't like what you hear, and besides, it's too late. We're already wed. For better or worse, isn't that what Pastor Williams said?" He only stared—the silence was her undoing. "Kaleb, please."

"Elizabeth, just tell me." His dark amber gaze, though sweetly imploring, did not fool her. "You're calling me by my full name. You're upset with me already, and I haven't even begun. Besides, it's only a few things. I hadn't planned to be married for years, remember?"

"Perhaps it's best to know up front how badly I fail."

She attempted to make light of her blunder. "They're only silly notions." For a split second, she thought he might relent.

"If that's true, then there's no reason not to tell me. Besides, this could be fun." He sat back, folded his arms and propped his ankle on his knee.

"Fun for who? Certainly not me."

"Liz," he asked as he leaned her way, "Is it time to claim that first kiss?"

Her eyes flashed blue lightning at this bold uncompromising man. "No! Is this what I can look forward to every time we don't see eye to eye?"

"You leave me no choice. You're just as stubborn as I am."

Finding no end to his persistence, she rolled her eyes and

said, "You meet my first criteria. You have a personal relationship with Jesus Christ."

"That had to be first and foremost for both of us. Now that was painless, wasn't it?"

"Yes," she said in an insipid tone. "The other two are the ones you won't like." She smiled at the tall man sitting next to her, trying to think of a way to say this without offending him. Faced with an impossible task, she wanted to be kind. In the end she just blurted it out. "You weren't supposed to be so ... well, you know ... big and strong."

He threw back his head, laughing out loud at the way her outstretched arms emphasized his broad shoulders and her hands fluttered about trying to accentuate his height. "Now I have to admit, this one has me bamboozled! Why wouldn't you want your husband to be big and strong?" While he waited for her explanation, he thought of a conversation they'd had years earlier. He was scolding her for something she did as a child. He wondered if anything had changed.

"You know what I'm like, Kaleb." She paused for a second, maybe three. "You're built like a grizzly. I don't stand a chance against someone your size. I was supposed to marry a little man. Someone passive and much more agreeable—someone that might overlook, shall we say, some of my minor indiscretions."

He leaned over, gazing straight into her wide blue eyes. "God knew what He was doing putting us together, Liz. Provided you do what's expected of you, you have nothing to worry about."

His words, though firm, did nothing to alter her response. "I suppose if you keep your expectations on the low side, I might hit the mark on occasion."

How could he respond to such a remark? After considering all she'd been through, he opted to leave it alone. Things would come up, he could be sure of that. They would cross those bridges when they came to them.

"All right, let's hear the last one."

She peeked up, and while he smiled at her reluctance, his curiosity was getting the best of him. When he pressed her, his domineering tone only served to draw her out and drive her point home. "Just tell me, Elizabeth!"

"You weren't supposed to be so overbearing—like my father!"

"What?" He was shocked.

She wasted no time defending her accusations. "I used to think you were the kindest man I've ever known."

"So, why the change of heart?"

Her eyes widened—did he really not know? "That stay in the cabin let me see the real you—you're just like him. Think about it ... I could barely move without your say-so. When we arrived at my parent's home you were wonderful, then tonight you really blew it!"

"What did I do?"

She huffed in agitation! How could he forget so soon? Without an ounce of reserve, she tweaked his forgetful mind. "You went along with my father and married me—against my will! Now you've conned me into sleeping in your bed. The only thing that remains to be seen is what I'll be up against next."

Flabbergasted, he choked out, "Liz ... I can't—I can't believe you would think this of me. I'm nothing like your dad."

"I'm sorry, Kaleb. I hate to be the bearer of bad news, but you are. Maybe worse! I suppose whether I want to or not, I'll find out the truth soon enough."

It took him a moment to process what she was saying. When the shock wore off and his mind cleared, he had to ask, "Have you ever thought that maybe your daring nature has a bit to do with how the men in your life deal with you?"

"I have. I'd be the first to admit that I can be a bit difficult at times. I do like to have my own way, but so do you."

He calmed. "Liz, let me ask you this: do you believe God's design is for me to be the head of our family?"

She lowered her gaze in thought. *Six hours ago I was laughing and carrying on with my family and friends without fear or reservation. Pastor stopped by to share his concerns and my world became a riotous mess. Life as I knew it was being devoured by a ravenous lion. I haven't even finished school! I shouldn't have to be thinking about marriage, never mind already being some man's wife! Lord, help me to get past my anger, my hurt, and despair. How can I begin to explain what I can't understand myself?* She had to try.

"I do. In my heart I know it to be true. It's my mind that's struggling. I'm angry with my father, Kaleb. I'm sure you can understand that. His reasons for insisting on this marriage may have been right, but he did so much damage to our relationship in the process. My mind keeps telling me that if I give in to you, my father wins. I know that's not fair, but your agreeing to this union doesn't exactly leave you guiltless."

"Then we need to pray that you can get past your anger. I know we did the right thing, Liz. I wish for your sake time would have been on our side."

She could appreciate his desire to help her through, and

attempted to ease his mind. "I know God is sovereign. He allowed this marriage to take place. To be honest, I'm not sure if this was God's will, or my father's and yours. I understand that we're married no matter what, but I need time. I can't think right now. Too much has happened. I'm weary."

"If your parents had given you a choice, would you have married me?"

"No. If Dad would have given me a day to think about it, I would have been gone. I'm not ready to be a wife. You know that."

While he heard what she was saying, he loved her parents and wanted her to understand their position. "Your father and mother adore you. They've seen the destruction that takes place when these women get a bee in their bonnet. We couldn't sit back and ignore this. They knew you wouldn't agree. That's why they made the decision for you."

"I understand that—but knowing doesn't make it easier to accept."

What she was saying made perfect sense. "Will you come to me if you need help working this through?"

Elizabeth couldn't promise him anything; her emotions were raw. How could she put what was left of her shattered heart in anyone's hands—let alone the hands of the one whose betrayal put her in this mess. "The trust we once shared is on shaky ground. I did tell Jesse I'd try, and right now that's the best I can offer. Submitting to your leadership would be easier if I chose to be your wife, Kaleb. I know God expects me to honor you no matter what brought us together, but I need you to be patient with me. I'm trying to come to grips with the fact that you're now my husband. Like I said, I need time."

His warm hand came up to caress the soft skin of her face. Her instincts told her she should pull away, but his touch was so comforting she could not. As their gaze held, his tender words went a long way towards easing her tattered mind.

"I'm amazed that you're doing as well as you are. If we keep talking like we are, we'll do fine. We're both exhausted emotionally and physically. Let's get some sleep, and maybe things will look clearer for both of us in the morning."

"You're not upset about my silly notions?"

"No. I'm glad you shared." She finished her tea, and Kaleb asked, "Well, Miss Elizabeth, are you ready to call it a night?" Under Kaleb's watchful eyes, a twinkle lit her soft blue gaze.

"That's Mrs. to you, Mr. White."

He chuckled softly. "You know, Liz, for a woman whose life has been drastically altered in the last week, you're incredibly high strung."

"This is your wife, for better or worse."

He shook his head, and asked, "What am I going to do with you?"

She wanted to tell him that nothing at all would suit her just fine. Instead, she shrugged only half apologetically, reached for her crutches and headed toward *their* room.

Terrified—feeling lost and so out of place, she questioned her husband who was bent down, untying his bluchers. "Kaleb, which side of the bed do you prefer?"

With a baiting smile he told her, "I like the middle, so you choose."

She should tell him that the middle was so not an option, that there was now an imaginary line down the center of his bed, and he was not to cross it for any reason. That would never do. Kaleb was her husband, not one of her brothers, and far too bullheaded to allow her to order him around. *No, she thought, it's best to stay quiet and hope against hope that he's a man of his word.* "I'd better take the outside until the splint comes off. But don't get too comfortable, I don't like sleeping by the door."

"Can I ask why?"

She got settled beneath the quilt, and watched without thought as Kaleb shed his shirt, his belt and his bluchers. "Jesse's horror stories growing up. None of us can sleep by an entrance." When Kaleb reached to unbutton his jeans, Elizabeth realized what he was about to do and buried her face in the covers.

"That sounds like something he would do just to get the side of the bed he wants." Kaleb, not missing the cause of her aversion, cracked a smile. While it was obvious they had a long road ahead, he didn't mind. He had every intention of enjoying the adventures along the way.

"That may be. To this day I can't convince myself to do otherwise."

"It's not a big deal, Liz. We'll change the room around tomorrow."

"You don't have to do that."

"Yes I do! I can't have my wife missing her sleep or I'm the one that will end up paying for it."

She smiled. She could be such a grouch when she didn't get her rest.

Kaleb blew out the lamp and joined her under the icy covers. *Their* room held a frigid chill in the winter months, and he looked forward to her added warmth. It would seem, however, that he had one minor problem that needed solving. The moonlight drifting through the window revealed her profile lying so close to the edge that he wondered if she might topple off. While he understood her reluctance, he would like them to make a habit of praying together before they found their rest. If she agreed, it would serve a dual purpose. This was their wedding night—the only one they would ever have. Although he didn't want much, he would love to hold his bride. In the stillness of the darkened room, Kaleb's soft words broke into the awkward silence. "Liz, I'd like us to make a habit of praying together. Would you mind if I held you?"

She hated to give him an inch for fear he would take a mile, but Jesse's words came to her, easing her tortured mind. *Remember the friendship we've shared—you can trust him.* She could only hope that her brother was right, as she moved into Kaleb's outstretched arms.

By the time he said *Amen,* her tremors had ceased and she drifted into a peaceful sleep.

Kaleb lay in wonder. The day had brought so much more into his life than he could have ever imagined. Last night he lay in this very bed, asking the Lord to open the door where Elizabeth was concerned. While the circumstances that had brought them together saddened his heart, he couldn't help himself: he was thrilled that she was now his wife. It wouldn't happen over night, but he would continue to pray that in time she would open her heart to him as well. His spirit soared with happiness. Exceedingly thankful, he knew without a doubt that God had blessed him beyond measure. He had to believe that the possibilities were endless with his lovely bride who was now tucked safely within the warmth of his hopeful arms.

He Loves Me!

Chapter Seven

Trapped

ELIZABETH AWOKE IN a panic. *Where am I?* she asked, as a crushing weight pinned her to the bed. Realization dawned. *I'm in Kaleb's room. I'm trapped in my husband's arms—legs. Gracious, Kaleb! I said you could hold me, not mangle me! This is ridiculous!*

Her movements disturbed him. Even so, he didn't release her as she had hoped. Instead, he wrapped himself around her, drawing her closer into his hold. She asked herself, *what does he think I am, his pillow?* Her anger flared, but she knew that wasn't fair—he was sound asleep and snoring quite loudly. No one could fake such a noise.

"Kaleb, you have to let me go." When his eyes remained shut, she tried again—louder. "Kaleb, I have to get up." His lids flipped open. His dark amber eyes, only inches away, were frightful. A shallow cough—more like a gag—escaped, as she caught a whiff of his breath—or was it her own?

"Kaleb, you're squishing me. You have to let me go." In an obvious muddle, his voice held a morning growl as he turned and sat up.

"I'm sorry, Liz. I should have warned you. I sleep like a brick in this bed. Your warm body must have made things worse."

She tried to sound angry, but wasn't very convincing, even to her own ears. "It's entirely too dangerous sleeping with you, Kaleb White! Perhaps I should sleep in your sister's room from now on."

Rubbing his wiskered chin, he grinned. "Trust me, you do not want me to claim that first kiss right now."

His reminder silenced her, though her frown proclaimed her intolerance, as did her thoughts. *Never would suit me just fine!*

Kaleb ran his fingers through his messy blonde hair, and asked, "Did you want something?"

"I have needs to take care of."

His brain was screaming for coffee when he said, "I'll get your robe and crutches."

"Kaleb, shouldn't I get dressed? I can't go out there like this, can I? Your parents ... they're probably awake. I'm not decent!"

He thought, *so many questions for so early in the morning— why did I not remember you talk so much?* Sounding more civil than he felt, he relieved her many doubts with a simple explanation. "My family is not like that. Mom doesn't get dressed until after breakfast, and you should feel free to do the same."

"You're sure?"

He chuckled softly. "Yes."

She felt more than a little clandestine walking out of this man's bedroom—in her nightclothes no less! Desperation pressed her forward.

Elizabeth heard voices in the kitchen and hobbled in to join her new family. Samuel and Ruth greeted her as always with kindness, and Sarah couldn't have been more elated to have her there. Elizabeth loved these people. Their families have been friends for years. Had circumstances been different, she might have enjoyed a visit, but not as Kaleb's wife, and certainly not sleeping in his bed. Her shoulders slumped as the reality of her new life began to take hold.

The man who confused her—terrified her—whose hugs had the power to make her melt like snow over an open flame, was sitting at the table with a cup of coffee in his hand. He now appeared more coherent than when she had awakened him. Perhaps the effects of the hot brew had kicked in.

"Liz, come and sit down."

She heard him, but his mother stood alone frying bacon and eggs over the hot stove. If she was ever going to feel like she belonged, she would have to do her part. "Mrs. White, is there something I can do to help?"

Ruth turned to her and smiled. "Lizzy, would you prefer tea or coffee?"

"Tea, please. If you tell me where things are, I'd be glad to make it. Would anyone else like some?"

"I'd love a cup. Sarah, what about you?"

"Sounds good, Mom. I'll get the honey."

"The kettle's ready, and the leaves are in the smallest canister." Ruth craned her neck around. "Kaleb, will you get Lizzy the pot?"

"Sure." Since she wouldn't be able to carry it by herself, Kaleb waited for her to finish making the tea and set it on the table.

Elizabeth took the seat next to Kaleb and leaned her crutches against the wall. Her stomach rumbled as the delicious aroma of warm apple muffins wafted past her nose. Ruth, like her own mother, was a wonderful cook, and Elizabeth looked forward to learning some of Ruth's trade secrets before—but she closed her eyes. She could not allow her mind to go there. Not yet. She would have to take this in stride.

As soon as everyone found their seat, Kaleb reached for her hand. Elizabeth took Sarah's, and when the circle was complete, Samuel asked the blessing over not only the food, but the new marriage as well.

Elizabeth's mind drifted often as she nibbled on her food and listened to the light conversation. She envisioned her own family sitting around the table at home, and couldn't help wondering if they felt the same way she did—that nothing would ever feel normal again. Did they miss her as much as she did them? If she didn't get her mind off her woes, she would burst into tears. She had no desire to expose her aching heart, so when everyone finished, Elizabeth made her way to the counter to help with clean up.

Noticing her intent, Ruth said, "Lizzy, I'll do the dishes until your ankle heals."

She could appreciate the concession, but she would go crazy sitting there with nothing to do. Her wayward mind needed to be kept busy or it would get her into a heap of trouble. "Mrs. White, I have to do something that makes me feel a part of this family. I mean no disrespect, but I'm not a guest in your home. I'm afraid you're stuck with me."

Ruth, pleased by her clear attempt to fit in, said, "I'll tell you what, Lizzy. If you'll call us Mom and Dad from now on, we won't treat you like a guest. Just promise you'll elevate that ankle often so it has time to heal."

Kaleb had been listening to the entire conversation. His eyes were glued to his new wife, so he didn't miss the taunting look she sent his way.

"I'm afraid your son won't give me a choice."

"Good!"

"No, Mom, ... it's not good." Her eyes were still riveted on Kaleb. "I'm not sure if you're aware of it or not, but he's a real tyrant when you don't follow his orders to the letter ...."

Ruth smiled. She often envied Elizabeth's ability to speak her mind. Although her overbearing son would rise to the challenge, this mother knew without a doubt that Kaleb had finally met his match. There was nothing passive about Elizabeth. She would not readily cave in to his every demand, no matter how much she was hurting.

"Now wait just a minute, Elizabeth White! That strong will of yours can be a bit of a challenge for a kind gentleman like myself!"

Hearing her new name rolling off her husband's tongue left her feeling strange—weak inside. She withdrew, responding to his baiting words with quiet resolve. "From the looks of things, you'll have to get used to it."

Elizabeth was all too close to tears. When she drooped over the counter, Kaleb jumped up from his place at the table and went to stand behind her, offering support. He informed his family that he would be helping his wife with clean up. Out of respect, they left the room.

"Kaleb, I'm sorry. I've managed to chase your family away."

His heart was breaking for her. "They're only trying to give us the privacy we need. You're my wife and part of this family, Liz. They understand."

"I felt so much better last night after we talked. I convinced myself that the worst was over. It's not over, is it?"

"Liz, please let me hold you."

As she turned in his arms and looked up, the sun seeping in the kitchen window danced in his eyes. Did he know the vulnerable state she was in? Could she trust him? She had to try. Overwhelmed, the tears that had been pooling in her eyes, spilled down her cheeks as he gathered her to him.

"You're going to be sorry you married me, Kaleb."

"I'll never be sorry. God's word tells me that finding a wife is a good thing. You didn't ask for any of this. You need time to sort everything out. I'll give you all time you need."

His kind words weakened her resolve. She gave in to her whirling emotions. Kaleb lifted his sobbing wife and carried her to their room.

He lay down on the bed beside her and pulled her up so that her cheek rested against his chest. When she offered no resistance, he removed the tie from her hair and proceeded to unravel her braid. Finger-combing her long flaxen mane, he massaged her scalp.

Nothing had ever felt so wonderful. His soothing touch eased not only her troubled mind, but her weary heart as well. Eventually even the tenseness in her slender body relaxed in the warmth of his tenderness.

He stayed with her long after she fell asleep. Kaleb thought she looked like an angel lying against the white pillow—golden hair falling like a halo surrounding her lovely face. Her soft lids and long lashes concealed her beautiful blue eyes. Overly drawn to her rosy red lips, he longed for the day that he would be free to caress their softness. *Give me the patience I need to move slowly, Lord. My feelings for her are changing at a rapid pace, and I have no desire for this to be one-sided. Open our hearts, Lord, and someday make us one.*

Hearing voices as he approached the kitchen, Kaleb found his parents finishing up. Mom hung her apron on the hook and Dad had just poured himself another cup of coffee.

"I'm sorry. I couldn't leave her."

Samuel tried to set his mind at ease. "Kaleb, don't apologize. Lizzy needs to know that you'll be there for her. The magnitude of what she's done is bound to hit her hard today. You were open to taking a wife. She wasn't looking for a husband. Her adjustment is bound to be more difficult. Show her you care, and she'll come around. She's a fighter, and that might be the very thing that helps her through."

"It's all so unbelievable, Dad—that's my wife lying on my bed."

Samuel smiled. "When it sinks in you'll come to depend on her more than you know, Son. Your mother and I didn't start out on solid ground, but by the grace of God we made it. The two of you have the advantage of Christ living in your hearts. Lean on Him. Encourage her to do the same. Be the spiritual leader she needs you to be. She may not see God's will in all of this now, but

she will."

Kaleb's eyes glistened as he asked his mother, "She showed a little of her old spunk in the kitchen. Did you notice?"

"Yes, I did."

"She confuses me. She trembles like a leaf when I come near her, but she doesn't think twice about speaking her mind."

"Since your father and I were married under similar circumstances, I can relate to what she's going through, Kaleb. You're the only one who can alleviate her fears. Show her that you only want to love her."

"Let us know if there's anything we can do to help."

"Thanks, Dad. I thought she might like to take a bath when she wakes up."

Ruth agreed and offered a few suggestions. "Pull out the big tub, Kaleb. I have some lavender salts on the second shelf in the pantry. I'm sure she'll enjoy them as much as I do."

"Thanks, Mom."

Kaleb ambled into the room an hour later to find his wife lying on her stomach, reading her Bible. Her thoughts must have been intertwined in the words, because moments passed before she sensed his presence. He flopped down beside her and reached to tuck her loose hair behind her ears.

Her husband's face held a note of pleasure. No doubt, he had something to say. She was about to question him, when he asked, "What are you reading?"

"Philippians. Dad usually goes over Pastor's sermon in our family Bible studies. I know we discussed parts of this while we were at the cabin, but I have some questions."

"If you'd like, I could borrow my father's notes on the message we missed. We could go over them together."

"You wouldn't mind?"

"Not at all."

Perhaps she was imagining it, but in some ways he seemed different to her already. "You had something on your mind when you came in. Can I ask what?"

Her insight made him smile. "I have a surprise for you in the kitchen."

"What did you do?"

"I'll give you a hint."

Her brow rose with interest.

"You begged me to let you do this in the cabin. If I remember correctly, you wouldn't speak to me for hours after I told you no."

"Is it a bath?" she asked, her eyes alight with pleasure.

Kaleb nodded. "Everything's ready."

Elizabeth didn't have to be asked twice. She scooted off the bed and reached for her bag. After collecting the items she would need, Kaleb carried them, and she followed him to the kitchen.

The changes in the room were astounding. The table had been moved and a big tin bathing tub, filled with steaming bubbles, now sat next to the stove. Curtains were pulled across the entrance for privacy, and the aroma of lavender bath salts filled the air. "Kaleb, this is wonderful!" She paused in contemplation. "That tub is really deep. How can I get in and out with this splint?" His smiling eyes set her on edge.

"I thought about that. If you bathe in your shift, I can help you. I'll even wash your hair if you promise to sit in front of the fireplace until it's dry."

All reluctance melted away. Knowing she'd finally be able to clean her dirty mop would be worth any amount of humiliation. "Kaleb, thank you for making this happen. I feel so grubby, and those salts smell splendid!"

Her smile made his effort so worthwhile. "We'd better get you in before it cools down again."

Hesitant, she admitted, "I feel funny undressing in front of you. Will you turn around?"

He did, but not without revealing his confusion. "You swim in the Huron in your shift. How is this any different?"

"I told you yesterday. Knowing that you're my husband changes everything."

"We're married, Liz. You should feel more at ease in my presence."

"Then something must have gone terribly wrong in my brain, because I don't. I'm ready; you can turn around."

"I'm confused, but since your face is a deep shade of cherry, I'll let it drop."

"Thank you."

But his thoughts continued to question as he lifted her into the tub and secured her ankle on the outside edge. *She used to be so relaxed in my presence. The extent of her apprehension is disheartening. She's afraid of me, Lord. Why?*

The warm fluid enveloping her slender frame felt like a taste of heaven. She watched Kaleb pour a cup of coffee, pick up his book, and sit down at the table to read. For at least ten minutes she floated mindlessly in the soothing liquid. She enjoyed it so much, she could only hope that her husband would become so engrossed in his book that he'd forget her for hours. He did not.

Little did she know, Kaleb never read a single word on the

page. He was too busy trying to comprehend what he had done to induce this drastic change in her. Standing up, he stretched. Without a word he ambled over to the counter, picked up the soap and turned to find his whimsical wife sliding under the water. The sight of her splinted ankle dangling in the air above her floating frame was comical, but he panicked when she didn't come back up. Sticking his arms in the bubbles, he lifted her head above water.

She, taking in his flustered appearance, said, "Kaleb, please don't look at me that way. I'm sorry if I frightened you. I like the scent of the salts in my hair."

"You were under there a long time, Elizabeth."

His use of her full name spoke volumes. "Are you angry?"

"No ... it's just that you have your own way of doing things, and sometimes they worry me."

She sighed. "Kaleb, I'm not used to having someone in the room when I bathe."

He nodded. "Just warn me next time." He knelt on the floor beside her and proceeded to wash her hair. His large hands massaging her scalp were amazingly gentle, but his silence gave her an uneasy feeling.

"Would you like to rinse or shall I?" In answer she waved as she slid under the water. When she came up with bubbles covering her face, he chuckled and pushed them aside.

"Liz," he said in a better mood, "we should get you out of there before you catch a chill."

He had a tendency to be overly cautious, but she would do nothing to deter this from happening again. She slid her wet arms around his neck as he lifted her out of the tub and wrapped her in toweling. "Thanks again for doing this, Kaleb. I enjoyed it more than you know."

"You're welcome. I'll leave so you can get dressed. I won't go far, so call if you need me."

Kaleb had the rocking chair sitting in front of the fire waiting for her when she hobbled into the sitting room to join his family. Sarah saw the brush in Elizabeth's hand and wasted no time offering to brush her hair.

"Thanks, Sarah. I know your brother could use a break. He wasn't planning on acquiring a gimpy wife, and he's done so much already."

Kaleb cast her a dark look as he came around the chair.

"It's true and you know it. You need to find something that I can do for you."

"That, My Sweet Wife, is not a problem." Kaleb left the room and returned wearing a nefarious grin. A huge stack of his clothing and his mother's sewing box filled his arms. The pile he placed in her lap came up to her chin, and she laughed out loud when he presented her with the same cheesy grin she usually bestowed upon him.

"Are you happy? And when you finish mending those, there are plenty more where they came from."

Her smile embellished her pleasure. "Thank you, Kaleb. I love to sew, and ..." her eyes fell on the pile, "this should keep me going for quiet a while."

"Kaleb," his mother asked, "why didn't you tell me you had mending that needed to be done?" She couldn't help wondering if he was overwhelming Elizabeth.

"My wife seems to have a compelling desire to do something

for me, so it all worked out for the best."

"If you need help, Lizzy, feel free to ask."

Ruth's concern made Elizabeth smile. "I appreciate the offer, but I really am glad to have something to do."

"Sarah," Elizabeth asked as she threaded her needle and began mending the first shirt in the pile, "Tell me what you've been doing since the storm hit?"

"Mom has been teaching me how to crochet, but my stitches aren't very good."

Elizabeth smiled in remembrance. "Keep at it, Sarah. I started a blanket for my favorite doll when I was your age. The pattern wavered at first, but by the time I finished my stitches were more consistent."

"After you're finished with your mending, would you mind helping me start a blanket for my doll?"

"We don't have to wait that long, silly. Kaleb won't mind if I take a break after dinner. Maybe your mom has some leftover wool she wouldn't mind us using."

Sarah glanced at her mother, who had been listening to their conversation. "Honey, that box with all the leftover wool is under my bed. Go ahead and find some colors you like. I saw your crochet hook on top of your armoire. While you're up there you should finish reading that book your teacher sent home."

Elizabeth had two of Kaleb's shirts mended, and she was looking at a huge hole in the knee of his jeans as he spoke. She set them aside to listen.

"When we head into town to do our Christmas shopping, we'll have to pick up some yard goods. Until this weather breaks, and your ankle heals, you'll need something to help pass the time.

I'm sure you could use a few new dresses, and I wouldn't mind a couple new shirts for spring."

Her father had always seen to her needs and now Kaleb offered to do the same. The thought of him spending money on her didn't sit well. How could she let him go out on a limb for her? After all, he hadn't planned to take a wife. Until she felt more secure in their relationship, she thought it was best to make due. Not knowing what to say, Elizabeth remained silent, leaving Kaleb in an odd state of confusion.

Although they were living with his parents, he would prefer to work through their struggles on their own. He let it drop, but when he noticed his wife staring blankly at the floor, his concerns began to mount.

Minutes passed before she looked at him and said, "Kaleb, it's going to be a while before I'm willing to go into town again." Samuel and Ruth, noting the expression on their son's face and understanding the newlyweds' need for privacy, went to the kitchen.

Elizabeth, so engrossed in her thoughts, did not hear them leave.

This time Kaleb knew exactly what she was thinking. If he had anything to do with it, she would face those who had wronged her and move on. While his insides were in utter turmoil, his tone remained calm. "Liz," he said from the edge of his chair. "The best way to get through this is to confront your fears head on. You can't hide away. We've done nothing wrong."

I'll stay home as long as I need to, Kaleb White, and you'll not stop me! If she could just keep her impertinent thoughts to herself and continue with her mending, maybe he would leave well enough alone. She picked up one of his shirts and tried her best. But the more she thought about it, the more unsettled she became. "Kaleb, I'm not ready to see my own father, let alone that woman."

Avoiding Mrs. Grant was bad enough. But the thought of her avoiding her father troubled him. Although confronting her on such a sensitive issue could take them weeks to recover; this could not wait. "Liz, why would you say that?"

"My father turned his back on me, Kaleb. He wouldn't listen to a word I said. He told you I'd go through with this marriage before he ever spoke to me—didn't he?" She knew the answer; she was testing him.

"Yes."

"He threw me away like an old shoe. All for the sake of pride!

"Liz, you have to know that isn't so." His hands ran precariously through his hair. He had to find a way to help her see. Her next words really knocked him for a loop.

"If my parents didn't abandon me, why do I feel so alone—so empty inside?"

In that instant his countenance changed. His actions were her father personified!

"That's it! Pack a bag. We're going to see your family."

She hated his dictatorial tone. *Why did I think for a minute that he would hear me? I allowed myself to believe that he was different. That he cares about me!* She regretted having opened her mouth, but it was to late to stop now. The words she spoke were woven in steel—no different than his own. "I'm not going!"

His deep flush startled her. Having no desire to encounter his wrath, she took a deep breath and attempted to quiet her own enflamed nerves. "I need a few days to think things through."

"We're going, Elizabeth."

She pleaded, though, just like her father, he was not swayed.

"This discussion is over. Go pack our bag. We'll be gone for at least a week."

His words may have been calm, but they were given as a command—a command that she was expected to obey. Shuddering in frustration, she wanted to go on, but she was faced with a dilemma that happened only on rare occasions. Her mind went blank. The words to combat him were no longer there. Although she sounded inane, she no longer cared. But her eyes remained in her lap. "My Father said I had to live with you. I can't go home."

"We're going, Elizabeth." Growing weary, he wondered how much longer this would go on.

"You told me I had to sit here until my hair was dry."

Like your extreme need to obey me in this area somehow excuses your outright defiance in another. He wanted to laugh—but he knew better. Her tenacity was unbelievable.

"I'll give you a half hour before I go to the barn to hitch up the sleigh." Her hands rubbed at her face; her fury knew no bounds. Her words, though spoken through her fingers, exuded a boldness that would try any man's patience.

"I'm quite sure my hair will take days to dry!"

"Elizabeth! You're pushing too far!"

Her blazing eyes flew up in revolt. "This is precisely why I did not want—a husband! You're just like my father, the way you order me around. You don't hear a word I'm saying! For all the good it does me, I might as well be talking to the wall!"

"If I were just like your father, you wouldn't be sitting

for a week! Now stop fighting me and do as you're told. Your parents love you, and I won't have your relationship with them destroyed."

Her words calmed. "I know they love me. I'm not saying they don't."

"If you have things that you want us to take, pack them. I'll be back to get you in a little while."

Elizabeth glared in contempt as he strode from the room. Standing to her feet, she grabbed her crutches and hobbled her trembling frame toward *his* bedroom. With every fiber of her being she wanted to defy this overbearing man, but what good would it do? She was still trapped in this marriage she wanted no part of with a broken ankle and all that snow. In the end fear won out, she did as she was told.

He Loves Me!

Chapter Eight

Battles Within

AFTER PUTTING THE kitchen back in order, Kaleb let his father and mother know that he and Elizabeth were going to her parents'. Then he headed for the barn. He needed time to get a handle on his temper, and more than ever he needed to pray.

The drastic change in his wife's personality had him baffled. Kaleb could recall several instances where Elizabeth had challenged him and Jesse as a child, but never to such an extreme. Last night he made it clear that he had no hidden expectations. Didn't she believe him? As much as he wanted her to feel secure with him, he was at a loss.

The evening they shared talking and praying together had ended so well. He had been hopeful that a good night of rest would help her to see their marriage in a different light. In some ways she did seem to be coming around. At least that was true before he opened up this can of worms.

Personal experience had taught him that fear had a tendency to eradicate clear thought. Was it possible that this whole episode had little to do with them and much to do with her not wanting to face her father? After giving it some thought and spending time in prayer, he was convinced of it. He hated to pass the buck, as her father would say, but it did bring him a measure of relief to think that all of this was not just about their union. This knowledge would do nothing to dissolve his wife's anxieties, yet it would help Kaleb to better understand where her anger was stemming from. He would feel responsible if he sat back, said nothing, and allowed her relationship with her father to disintegrate. He refused to do that. Although he didn't like being so harsh with her, her emotions were a bit too frazzled to have settled this in quiet debate.

After pulling the sleigh in front of the house, Kaleb walked into the bedroom to find his wife leaning on her crutches, staring out the window.

She didn't hear him come in, so his abruptness startled her.

"Get your coat on and meet me at the door, Elizabeth."

Kaleb grabbed the bag off of the bed and left before she could offer a response. He had every intention of discussing this further, but not until they were well on their way.

She needed time to work through her trials. If she could settle this rift with her father, maybe then she would begin to see their union in a positive light.

It's difficult for her right now, Lord; I know she's hurting. Ease her despair and fill her with Your peace.

They were down the road a ways before Kaleb broke the

icy silence that hung between them. Her gaze remained on the distant fields.

"You're angry, Liz, and I can't say that I blame you. I feel very strongly that the struggles in our marriage should be a private matter. With that in mind, we should try to talk this through before we go into your parents' home. I have a few things to say, and I hope you'll listen. You only had a day with your family before we were wed. We both know it was not enough. I'm beginning to think we should have stayed with them from the start. We can't live with them, but there is no reason not to have an extended visit if you choose."

Kaleb waited for a time, hoping she would respond in some way. When it became obvious that she had no intention of giving him the time of day, he stopped the sleigh.

"Liz, please look at me." When she continued to ignore him, he reached out and drew her to him. "I'm sorry we quarreled, but snubbing me will not make me go away. I have to know what you're thinking—I have to know if you'll be all right when we get there."

His tone was kind, yet her aversion to his high-handedness inhibited her ability to think rationally. A curt, "I don't know!" was the best that she could offer.

"Is there anything I can do that would make this easier for you?"

"I was beginning to think you were nice—that we could find a way to make this marriage work ... I don't like you very much right now."

"From where I'm sitting, you're running from your fears. I'm not about to let you do that."

She stared, nonplussed. "I'm not a child, Kaleb, and you are not my father. I am capable of deciding what's right for me without any help from you."

"Liz, I know you'd like to erase what has taken place over the last twenty-some hours, but it won't happen. You are my wife. If you're doing something that will hurt you, I won't just stand by and let it happen. If you don't agree with me, I'll hear you out, but I *will* have the final say."

"Well, I don't agree, and I don't have to like it!" When she tried to free herself from his hold, he would not release her. In her angered state, she began to cry.

Since nothing had been resolved, Kaleb continued, "After spending the day with your family, if you decide you need to go home, we can discuss your reasons for wanting to leave. I'm not trying to be mean, Liz. You need to find a way to make this right. We both need your family to be a part of our lives." When her tension eased, Kaleb knew that his words were getting through. He relinquished his hold.

Elizabeth, realizing how horribly wrong she had been, wanted to be alone to sort through her whirling emotions—to hide her embarrassment. Unfortunately, that wasn't possible. With no escape, she buried her face in Kaleb's chest. She had no more regained her composure and was ready to talk when she felt his arms come about her, drawing her into an embrace. *Oh, Kaleb, please don't do this! I can deny myself anything but this!* Resisting him was not an option when he held her in the circle of his arms.

Elizabeth couldn't fathom why he would want to comfort her. She was so blinded by her own vulnerable state of mind that she couldn't begin to see how much he cared. She saw herself as nothing more than a thorn in his flesh—an imposition, at best. Kaleb's words said otherwise, but why would any man want a wife who was such a mess? In the silence that lingered, she began to pray.

Your Word tells me that if I delight in you, you'll give me the desires of my heart. If that's true, then why are you putting me through this? To what end? I have no desire to have a husband, even if his hugs are irresistible. Kaleb can't be part of Your plan—is he? If he is, Lord, then I don't know my own heart. Is it possible that I'm shunning him because I didn't agree to this union? Am I angry with Kaleb, my father, or is it You, Lord, for allowing this marriage in the first place? Forgive me if I am. Give me direction; I feel so lost. I need Your peace to fill my mind like it did the night of the terrible storm. Show me, Father, what to do with this man who for some reason unbeknownst to me wants me for his wife!

Her discussion with the Lord helped, but it was keeping her from talking to the one she had wronged. "Kaleb, I've been treating you like you're the enemy when all you've done is try to help me. I'm frustrated. I don't like being ordered around, but I have no business treating a brother in Christ—let alone my husband—with so little respect." She paused for only a second before peering up. "I really am sorry. Will you forgive me?" His gentle smile was healing oil pouring over her wounded soul.

He held her face in his hands and gazed into her soft blue eyes. "I already have, Liz. We were both angry and it solves so little. Will you forgive me as well?"

"Yes."

"Can we go now? I don't want you catching a chill."

"I suppose ...."

Kaleb reached in his pocket for his hanky and dried her tears before placing the damp cloth in her hand and moving the team forward. "Blow your nose, My Sweet, before it freezes."

Her husband was so intent on driving the team that he didn't notice her watching him. After a time, her gaze fell on the snow-covered terrain.

"I'll bet you're having regrets now, aren't you, Kaleb?"

"I'll never have regrets. It's tough right now. I'm in no hurry for things to be on an even keel. We haven't done this before, and we're bound to make mistakes along the way. We just have to keep at it. Sooner or later we'll get it right."

Although she couldn't say that she was any closer to accepting this change in her life, she did appreciate his level of patience and most of all his friendship. "Kaleb," she asked in earnest, "can you tell I've been crying?"

Her sudden change in character made him laugh. "Yes, you look dreadful!"

She slapped his coated arm. "Be serious."

"A little. We have a ways to go, Liz—you'll be fine."

Seconds passed. "You do know that you're something else, don't you?"

"What do you mean?" She had no idea what he was referring to.

"You were madder than a tormented bull a few minutes ago, and now your only concern is that someone might know you've been crying. How do you change your moods so fast?"

She grimaced. "I don't know! You do have a way of getting

under my skin like no one else can. Who knows, maybe someday I'll be glad we're married."

"I certainly hope so, but you haven't answered my question."

"It's simple. Granted, it may take me awhile to come to my senses, but I'm willing to admit when I'm wrong. I asked your forgiveness. To me, it's over." A wave of doubt passed through her. "You do forgive me, don't you, Kaleb?"

"Yes."

They were pulling into the farm, and her attention was drawn away from their conversation. Her uncertainties were written all over her face when she said in a rush, "Kaleb, take me with you to the barn."

He shook his head. "I'd better drop you off at the house. Your hair's damp, remember? It'll take *days* to dry!"

Her eyes glistened as she mustered a halfhearted smile. "You, Mr. White, had better be nice."

"I'm always nice." He bumped into her on purpose, adding, "I can't believe I forgot to tell you that."

She rolled her eyes at his candid remark but made no bones about contesting it. "If that were true, all of my troubles would be over. You know, Kaleb, I've had time to think about it. I've changed my mind."

"About what?"

"Drop me off at the house. And you, My Dear Husband, should head back home."

His brow rose on her flippant remark. "I don't think so."

"It's obvious you're in no condition to be out visiting. I'll never survive the night, let alone a few days, if you and Jesse gang up on me. I really think it's for the best."

Kaleb grinned at her playful words, but while he was thrilled to see her smiling again, he had to set her straight. "I'm sorry you feel that way. Our home is with each other now, Liz. You'll have to get used to me tagging along." Taunting brown eyes encountered timid blues. "You met your match when you said I do. If necessary, I can be just as ornery as my feisty bride. So keep that in mind the next time you decide to fly off the handle."

It was the worst thing he could have said. Her mouth dropped open in revolt. *How could he think this was all her fault?* "You're the one who started this whole thing!" she insisted. "If you weren't so busy ordering me around, none of this would have happened!"

Before she could anticipate his next move, he reached out and pulled her flush against him. "While I wouldn't recommend it, I'm beginning to think you're trying to start another fight. Am I right?"

"I wouldn't dream of it, Kaleb. Let me go!" Her attempt to free herself was futile. His closeness made her tremble, but he was toying with her, and she knew it.

"You just go ahead and fight all you want. I'll warn you ahead of time. You start any more trouble, and you'll pay the penalty for your crimes. Understood?"

Her eyes flew up. Not out of fear. She had been on the receiving end of Kaleb and Jesse's threats many times before. All of them ended with the same result.

"I'll let you off this once, with a warning. Next time, I'll show no mercy."

She turned away, trying to hide her smile. "You'd better

not, or I'll find a way to get you back."

"I doubt that! Shall I assume this means you'll be on your best behavior from now on?"

When she offered a cheesy grin, he would not be put aside. "You know better than to ask. I won't make a promise that I'm incapable of keeping. You married me with your eyes wide open—for better or worse, remember?"

"Keep in mind that goes both ways."

When Kaleb pulled the team up in front of the house, he jumped down to carry Elizabeth in. While he hated seeing her so tense, he had to believe that time spent with her family would change all that. Her strained look tore at his heart. When he could stand it no more, his wiggling fingers gave her a small sampling of his threatened penalty for future crimes.

"Kaleb, stop!" Though she would never admit it, being tickled did have a way of easing her weighted soul.

Kaleb knocked on the door, and the huge smile that lit her mother's face as she opened it warmed their hearts.

"Hey, Jesse," Jayne called to her eldest son, "come and see who's here!" Since he had just mentioned heading over to check in on the bride and groom, she knew he'd be glad to see them.

"Mom," Kaleb said, "we came for an extended visit. I hope you don't mind?"

"You're always welcome." Jayne hugged her son-in-law and Elizabeth as well.

Kaleb was right. Elizabeth thought, *I did need to feel my mother's touch and see her smile.* Her father could be a greater challenge, but the embrace she received from her brother eased her struggling mind. When Jesse released her, he took Kaleb's hand and shook it. Kaleb grinned, and said, "Good to see you."

"I hope you two are staying for a while."

"We'll see how long it takes to wear out our welcome, Jesse."

Jayne touched Kaleb's arm, and said, "Dad's in the barn if you want to get the team settled."

"Thanks!" He reached for the handle on the door, calling back to Jesse, "help your sister find a seat by the fire. Her hair's still damp."

Elizabeth had just gotten comfortable on the sofa, when Jesse reached for her hands to pull her back up. She tried to wave him off. "I'm fine, Jesse. Kaleb worries too much!"

"That may be, Sis, but you're not getting me in hot water with your husband right off." She laughed when he shivered in mock fear. "You're sitting by the fire, hear me?"

"All right, already!" Jesse was just as persistent as Kaleb. If she didn't give in, he'd never let it rest. She heard footsteps coming down the stairs, and looked up to find Suzanne and Louise running toward her, squealing in delight.

"Lizzy, Lizzy!" they echoed.

"How are you?" Louise asked, and then added, "We've been hoping you'd come. We miss you!"

"I was only gone for the night, silly."

"But we didn't have the chance to get caught up. How long can you stay? Is your foot better?" Louise paused, searching the room before she asked, "Where's Kaleb?"

Elizabeth smiled in the light of her exuberance, and tried to answer her questions. "Let's see ... I'm fine, but missing all of you. Kaleb thought we should come for a visit. I'm not sure how long we'll stay. My ankle is about the same. Kaleb's in the barn with Dad and should be back soon." Elizabeth heard laughter behind her and turned to find her mother standing by the entrance, enjoying their interaction.

Jayne harbored no doubts; Elizabeth adored her little sisters and never seemed to tire of their endless babble. "Girls, why don't you take a seat and visit with Lizzy. I need to put the roast in the oven and brew some tea."

Jesse, seeing Elizabeth had been crying, wanted to know why. "Lizzy, how are you really doing? Is my friend treating you right?" His question made her smile, but he wasn't sure why. "What's the grin about?"

"I would have expected you to ask if I was treating *him* right."

He scowled. "You'd better be!"

She shook her head. "We've managed to chase his family out of the room twice. Fortunately, they don't seem to mind. I wish I could tell you that everything is fine, but having Kaleb for a husband will take some getting used to."

"You seem to be handling this whole thing better than I would have."

"Looks can be deceiving." She giggled. "You didn't see us about an hour ago." Leaning over, she whispered in his ear, "He's bossier than you and Dad put together."

Jesse's brow furrowed. "That may be, but sooner or later you'll quit fighting him and maybe even find a way to love him."

Her mouth dropped open. "Jesse Somers! I can't believe my ears! What makes you think only women need to change?"

"Not all women do," he sent her a lighthearted wink, adding, "but you, My Dear Sister, have a serious tendency to be high-strung."

Elizabeth, feigning shock and dismay, said, "Me? Never! Jesse, you know how calm I am. What would make you say such a thing?"

He shook his head in complete denial of her embellishments. "If Kaleb finds a way to settle you down, I'll be amazed!"

"Thanks a bunch! It's good to know my brother thinks so highly of me."

"Lizzy, you know I love you ... you also know that I speak from years of experience."

"I do. I'm just giving you a hard time. Pray for us, Jesse ... pray a whole lot!"

"You know I will."

For a moment she lowered her eyes. "Promise you'll still come around and do things with Kaleb. We both need you in our lives, and besides, I'll go crazy if he hovers."

Jesse chuckled. "I'll see what I can do, but you need to do what you can to ease his mind. You told me you would try, Lizzy. I'm expecting you to honor your word."

The girls had been so quiet she forgot they were there until Louise asked, "Lizzy, don't you like being married to Kaleb?"

Apparently her conversation with Jesse worried them. "I'm finding it hard to believe that I'm anyone's wife. Kaleb's a good friend. I'm sure we'll find a way to be happy together eventually." Elizabeth looked at her brother, who was watching her with hawk eyes. "Besides, I made Jesse a promise, and I can't go back on my word, can I?" They seemed content with her answer, so she opted for a lighter subject.

"Enough about me. I need to hear what the two of you have

been up to."

Louise started prattling again, tickling Elizabeth right down to her toes. She looked at her brother, who had his hand over his mouth, suppressing his own laughter, and suddenly Elizabeth realized how much she missed all of them. Although she hated to admit it, even to herself, she was thankful that Kaleb had insisted they come.

"Have you started any new projects, Suzanne?"

"I did this morning, but it's a surprise for you and Kaleb for Christmas, so I'm not telling."

Elizabeth smiled at her sister's declaration. Louise and her both had a horrible time keeping secrets. "With everything that's happened, I haven't had time to make gifts, girls. I hope you'll forgive me. I promise to plan ahead and make you something special for your birthdays."

"Lizzy," Louise said and Suzanne agreed, "We're so happy you're alive—you're all the present we'll ever need."

Elizabeth gathered them in an embrace. Tears were standing in all of their eyes when George and Kaleb walked into the room.

"What's this? You've only been together twenty minutes and already my girls are crying!"

Kaleb didn't miss his wife's hesitation when she heard her father's voice, but as always her ability to overcome adversity astounded him.

"You know us, Dad. Always fussing about one thing or another."

Her father leaned down for a hug. "It's good to see you, Honey. As he stood, he gave an exaggerated sniff. "You smell good, Lizzy Girl. What'd you get in to?"

"I took a bath in lavender salts." She caught her husband's grin out of the corner of her eye. Ignoring it, she asked, "What are Jared and Joe up to, Dad?"

"They're in the barn working on a Christmas gift for your mom. They'll be in soon."

"Speaking of Christmas," Kaleb said, "Mom wanted us to come up with a list, so she knows who's making what."

"Lizzy, let your mother know what we're supposed to bring."

"I will, Dad."

Kaleb had a request. "I'm not sure about anyone else, but I'll be happy as long as you show up with the apple pie and fudge!"

Shocked by her husband's announcement, she tried not to overreact. Elizabeth held her breath, hoping her father wouldn't tell him that they were her creations. No such luck! She winced when he smiled in her direction—just before letting the cat out of the bag.

"Elizabeth, aren't you the one who makes the apple pie and fudge?"

Kaleb didn't miss her deepening shade, or the twinkle that danced in her eyes as she skillfully avoided his gaze.

"Yes, Dad, so you don't need to bring them." Feeling a sudden need to leave the room, she encouraged her sisters to join her. "Girls, why don't we head out to the kitchen and see if Mom needs us."

Kaleb helped Elizabeth to her feet, handed her the crutches, and whispered in her ear—deepening her shade even further. "I think it's wonderful to know my wife possesses so much talent in the kitchen."

She needed to shift his attention, and asked, "Kaleb, we didn't have dinner. Would you like a sandwich?"

"Just a little something to tide me over. I can smell the roast in the oven and I don't want to spoil my appetite."

"Are you coming into the kitchen, or should the girls bring it out here?"

Her father answered for him. "Jesse said he's hoping to beat Kaleb at a game of checkers."

Elizabeth nodded. "Dad, would you like something?"

"No, I'm fine, but I'm sure Jesse will be looking for something hot to drink."

As the evening moved along in good fellowship, Kaleb sensed a growing tension in his wife. He was about to question her when her mother called from the kitchen.

"Lizzy, can you come to Jesse's room for a minute? I finished something for the girls and I need your opinion."

"Oh, Mom!" Elizabeth exclaimed as she entered the bedroom and saw the new dresses. "The ivory trim is perfect with the burgundy fabric. I like the higher waistline. They'll love them."

"I hope so. With the way they're stretching up, I can hardly keep up with their wardrobe."

Elizabeth's gaze fell on her mother. "I wish I had time to make them something."

"Honey, listen to me. I don't want you worrying about Christmas gifts this year. You have enough on your plate trying to adjust to your marriage. No one will be expecting a thing."

"That's what the girls said."

Jayne patted her arm. "If you'd like to make a gift for Kaleb, I have an extra piece of medium brown shirting fabric. You're staying for a while, so I'd be glad to help you get it started."

"I would like to have a little something for him. You're sure you don't mind?"

Jayne noticed the way she chewed on her lower lip as if she had no need for it. "Honey, what's wrong?"

A warm flush kissed Elizabeth's cheeks. "I'm just wondering where you want us to sleep?"

"Lizzy, you have nothing to be embarrassed about. You and Kaleb are married. Tell me, where did you sleep last night?"

"I thought I would be in Sarah's room, but when I asked Kaleb about it, he made it clear that as his wife I would share his bed."

George had mentioned that he would expect this. With compassion for her daughter Jayne asked, "How are you really handling all of this?"

Elizabeth mulled over her question before saying, "I think every woman dreams of falling in love before marriage. In many ways I feel robbed of my dreams. I'm sure you'd feel the same if someone had dictated who you should marry."

"This marriage is the only way we could protect you."

"Everything happened so fast, I didn't know what to think. To be honest, I feel like all of you abandoned me when I most needed your understanding."

Jayne's heart went out to her. "I'm sorry we didn't have time to talk before the ceremony. You're our daughter. Our relationship has changed because of your marriage, but we would never want you to feel so alone. Lizzy, you were young when Kendal went through this same thing. Her mother and I were good friends. It was awful. Kaleb remembers, and he had no reservations about making you his wife."

"He explained all that last night. I understand why everyone's concerned, but it changes nothing for me. I want to finish school and be free to do things with my friends. Now that I'm married I won't be welcome at the youth socials or the barn dances. Everything that matters to me, including living with my family, was taken from me. Dad pushed me into this to save my reputation, and now I'm expected to pick up the pieces and just accept that Kaleb is my husband. If I had chosen to be with him I know I'd feel different—instead I feel trapped. Do you have any idea how frustrating it is to know that because these women couldn't control their tongues, life as I knew it is over?"

"This isn't going to be easy, Lizzy. Life rarely turns out the way we think it should. God's thoughts are not ours—you know that! I'm listening to what you're saying. I hear an awful lot about what Lizzy wants, but where does your Heavenly Father fit in to all of this? You've been asking God to show you what He wants for your life. Have you stopped to consider that maybe Kaleb is what He wants? Does He also know you wouldn't have agree to be Kaleb's wife any other way."

"I wouldn't have."

"I know that. Pray about it. Ask yourself if being Kaleb's wife is in fact part of God's plan for you. If it is, are you rejecting God's very best for you? Be careful you don't miss out on all He has for you because you're so busy dwelling on all you've lost."

She heard what her mother was saying and she would pray

about it, but it was all so overwhelming. "I'd like to believe you're right, Mom. I really would."

"Kaleb cares for you more than you know."

"I didn't ask him to care. I wanted him to annul the marriage and bring me home, but he wouldn't."

Jayne scowled. "Why would you do that?"

She couldn't believe her mother had to ask. "Mom, you know I don't want this marriage. Besides, I liked Kaleb so much better as a friend. As a husband he annoys me! I can't relax and be myself."

Jayne smiled at her daughter's absurd expression. "Your father and I were in love with each other when we married, but we both had adjustments to make. I had been living on my own for quite some time, and all of a sudden his opinion had to be considered. At first he irritated me as well. Over time I learned to accept his leadership, and now I wouldn't have it any other way. I depend on his strength to see me through the tough times. He depends upon my support, even when I don't agree with him. Becoming one isn't only physical, Lizzy—it's spiritual as well. It doesn't happen over night, it happens over time. I know I'm repeating myself, but I can't stress this enough. Be sure you don't miss out on the blessings God has for you by staying focused on what you've lost. Concentrate on what you're gaining. We all need to learn to be content in whatever situation we're in. Read through Acts and Philippians; think about Paul's life and all he went through. Our problems seem less significant when we look at someone else's trials."

"You know me, Mom. I need time to sort all this out. I'm glad we talked. You always find a way to encourage me. I really do appreciate your support. Promise you won't quit praying."

"I won't, Honey."

When her mother stood, Elizabeth thought she was going to leave without answering the question. "Where would you like us to sleep?" Elizabeth couldn't bear the thought of sharing her old bed with Kaleb—it was hardly big enough for her.

"I'll have Jesse take your old room, and the two of you take his."

"He won't mind?"

"Not at all."

She sighed with relief. "Mom, would you ask Kaleb to bring our bag in? It's been an exhausting day. I want to get settled."

"I'd be glad to. I'll see you in the morning, Honey." After a much-needed hug, Jayne left in search of her daughter's husband. She found him relaxed as a cat, leaning back in his chair, enjoying a game of checkers with Jesse. Kaleb had been an active part of all their lives since before Jesse was born, so becoming Elizabeth's husband was an easy fit. She could only hope that in time her daughter would agree. As much as she hated to interrupt their fun, Elizabeth did look worn out.

"Kaleb," Jayne said from the entrance to the sitting room. "Lizzy is in Jesse's room. She's wanting to get settled for the night and asked if you'd bring her the bag."

"Sure." Glancing at his friend he said, "Give me a minute. I'll let you know if we'll finish this now or tomorrow."

"Take your time."

When Kaleb walked into the room, Elizabeth was tugging on her boot, trying to get it off. He sat next to her on the bed, and offered to help.

"I'm used to prying it off with my other foot. It doesn't work with this bad ankle."

Kaleb could see that the boot was too small. Recalling her reaction to him buying fabric, he kept his observation to himself. He would simply buy her a new pair when they went to town. "Liz, we were planning to read. Your mother said you're tired. Would you like to choose another time?"

"You don't mind?"

"Not at all. Are you comfortable staying? You seemed anxious earlier."

Kaleb turned her away from him, moved her hair to the side and unbuttoned her dress. His touch was so gentle; she relaxed enough to answer him. "Our sleeping arrangements had me a little unsettled. I'm fine now—just need some sleep."

"I'll be in as soon as Jesse and I finish our game. Could I steal a hug?"

She turned to face him, realizing that he was not the only one in need. Surrendering to his warm embrace eased her heart in a way she could not comprehend.

As Elizabeth readied for bed, she thought about the difficulties in her first day of marriage. The battles that raged within were challenging her faith as nothing ever had before. If she had the chance to go back, there were things that she would change and some that she would not. She still felt trapped but like it or not, tomorrow she would face another day as Kaleb's wife. Could her happiness really depend upon her own willingness to yield? Her mother seemed to think so. When Elizabeth snuggled into the quilted warmth of her brother's bed, she wasn't convinced it was possible. But by the time she finished praying, she'd begun to wonder ....

He Loves Me!

Chapter Nine

Her Despicable Giant

HE COVER OF darkness still permeated her brother's room. It was early morning, but Elizabeth simply couldn't sleep another wink. She shed the warmth of Jesse's quilt, removed her gown, and slipped into her brown woolen skirt, white blouse, and the warm beige sweater her mother had knit for her sixteenth birthday. No one was stirring when she left the room, so she bundled up and headed out the door. Over a week had passed. She was anxious to see Lady.

Several days had gone by without a fresh snowfall, and the snow that remained seemed safe enough for her crutches, so she proceeded with caution toward the massive structure. The familiar barnyard smells assaulted her as she pushed on the big door, slid through the opening, and made her way in. Fond memories filled this building. Litters of kittens had been spoiled; various animals had come and gone. So many childhood adventures were played out with her siblings—her husband too for that matter. Lady, the object of her delight was standing in a stall about twenty feet away. Elizabeth stood silent, waiting to see if Lady would pick up her scent. As she fully anticipated, Lady whinnied out loud, hanging her head out as Elizabeth approached. The times they'd spent together over the years had formed a close bond. The thought of not having her close at hand saddened Elizabeth's heart.

Her desire to ride overwhelmed her, but there were too many men in that house who would have her hide for allowing that thought to enter her mind, never mind actually doing it.

"Hello there, girl. I've missed you too." Removing her glove, Elizabeth pulled some sugar cubes out of her coat pocket. Lady stuck out her soft, fuzzy muzzle and removed them from the palm of her hand. As Elizabeth reached up to drape her arms around Lady's neck, her husband's deep voice startled her from behind. She turned and saw him standing in the open door.

"I missed holding you this morning," he said.

"You were sleeping, so I came out to greet my friend." Until Kaleb reached her side she couldn't be sure, but Elizabeth had the distinct impression he was annoyed with her. The thought of his imminent reproach put her stomach in knots. She averted her eyes a moment too late. As he often did, Kaleb read her unspoken words.

"I know you wish I'd go away, but I have something to say." When she didn't respond, he insisted. "Elizabeth, turn around and look at me."

His gruff tone was the last thing she wanted to hear. "Kaleb, I came out here to be with my horse, not to be scolded." She cringed when his large hands slid around her waist and turned her to face him. As much as she wanted to free herself, fighting him would be futile. He was much too strong, and it would only serve to spark her temper when it became impossible to escape.

"Liz, if you want to be in the barn, I'm more than willing to come with you. You could have fallen."

"You were sleeping, Kaleb. I'm not a child; I am fully capable of making these decisions on my own." But he went on as if she hadn't spoken, and she fought against her urge to lash out.

"Until the splint is off and the crutches are no longer needed, you will have one of the men in your life come with you."

A warm flush covered her face—her body shuttered with frustration, but she had nothing to say to him. Unfortunately, he wanted an answer.

"Elizabeth, am I understood?"

Her narrowed gaze flew up at his face. She despised his choice of words! She balked every time her father used them and now they were spewing from her husband's lips. That they required a response only added to her frustration! Although the desire to let him have it with the sharp side of her tongue overwhelmed her, it would accomplish nothing. Besides, then she would have to apologize for not controlling her temper. He overreacted—even so it was out of concern for her safety. How could she fault him for that?

No doubt being married to her brother's friend was bothersome at best. Before they were wed, Kaleb, Jesse and she were always cutting up and carrying on as friends do. Now much of what transpired between them rubbed her the wrong way. *I know the way I respond to him isn't right, but how do I get past feeling so vulnerable where he's concerned? I just want to be his friend again so I can relax and be myself. No matter how much I want it to be so, I can't go back, Lord, can I?*

"Liz, have I lost you?" Kaleb soft words interrupted her thoughts.

"I'm fine ... I'll do as you ask. I just like being out here with Lady."

Her willingness to yield pleased him. As Kaleb tenderly tucked some wayward wisps behind her ear, her gaze met his.

She was coming to recognize this gesture as his wordless way of letting her know that all was well. In truth, she kind of liked it.

Lord, I'm so confused, how can he be so wonderful one minute and frustrating the next?

"You haven't been able to ride Lady for some time now."

She nodded, while working her fingers through Lady's long red mane. "We've only been married a day and I miss her already."

Kaleb watched her for a moment. "Why would you miss her, Liz? We can go riding all the time." The sadness in her eyes melted his heart. He needed to tell her of her father's news, but she spoke before he could get it out.

"Lady belongs to my family. She's not mine."

Kaleb, knowing how thrilled she would be to hear his news, couldn't withhold a smile.

"Are you laughing at me?" She was about to turn away when he pulled her firmly against him.

Without any more hesitation, he admitted, "No, My Sweet Wife, I'm not laughing at you. I did have something I was going to tell you—but since my presence is only annoying you and you don't like surprises, I'll leave you to visit with your hairy friend."

Kaleb was a terrible tease when he wanted to be and this was obviously one of those times. She watched as he nonchalantly released her and walked away.

"Kaleb, please don't tease me. Tell me what you know."

When he turned, her glittering blue eyes sparkled with excitement. How could he refuse her? "Lady is a wedding gift from your family."

"You're serious?"

"Yes. I'm not cruel, Liz, I wouldn't toy with you about such things. I know how much you love that silly horse. Look at the way she nuzzles up to you. She'd be lost without you."

For a moment their eyes met tenderly, but she was frightened by what she saw.

Kaleb, noticing her distress, made a suggestion. "Would you like me to get Lady out and lead you around for a while?"

Stunned, she questioned his sincerity. "You wouldn't mind?"

Kaleb smiled in the light of her pleasure and answered honestly, "I wouldn't have offered if I did. Can you stay on with just a blanket or should I get her saddle?" When she rolled her eyes at his ridiculous inquiry, he laughed out loud.

"I ride bareback all the time, and backwards in races with my brothers. I promise, I won't fall. I'll grab her blanket from the tack room while you take her out of the stall."

Elizabeth dashed off so fast Kaleb didn't have time to respond to her reckless admission, so he bellowed to her fleeting back. "Slow down before you fall—and Elizabeth, if I ever see you riding backwards on any horse, I'll tan your hide—do you hear me?"

Oh brother, she thought. *Have I lost a friend and gained another father? Will he ever see me as the woman I've become, instead of the little girl he and Jesse cared for?* Having no desire to allow his censoring eyes to read her contrary thoughts, she lingered in the tack room a moment longer. In her opinion, Kaleb had a tendency to be overly cautious, if not prudish at times. She believed with all her heart that everyone should avail themselves of a little all-out foolishness now and then. After all, didn't the Lord say that laughter was good for the soul, and a merry heart was like a medicine? Concessions would have to be made where Kaleb was concerned—after all, he was her husband. Even so, she was not about to throw in the towel and give up everything she enjoyed with her siblings, just because she was married.

As she hobbled out with the blanket, her mother's words from the night before went through her mind, forcing her to begin looking beyond the difficulties in her marriage and concentrate on the adventure at hand.

Kaleb lifted her up and carefully placed her on Lady's warm back. She felt like a child being led around by her papa on her first pony ride, but she didn't care. This pony ride was more fun than she'd had in days. Besides, the fresh air had a way of clearing her mind.

As they walked along and began to talk, Kaleb was encouraged to see signs of effort on his wife's part. Her father's wisdom in giving Lady as a wedding gift could turn out to be the healing bridge she desperately needed to move forward in their new life together.

"So tell me, Liz. Will I ever be allowed to ride Lady?"

"She was a gift to both of us. As long as I'm not riding, feel free."

He couldn't tell if she was serious or not. "Shall I take that as a 'no'?"

An ornery smirk lit her face and she responded to his question with one of her own. "Will I be allowed to ride Lightning, or am I still forbidden?" On numerous occasions she had begged him to let her, but he always had one excuse or another.

"He's not predictable like Lady, Liz. As long as you're careful I suppose it wouldn't hurt to let you try." The dense snow drew Kaleb's attention away from his wife and back to the trail.

She tried not to come across as being overly zealous, but she couldn't help it. Her mind raced with excitement. Lightning was such a tall, agile mount, she simply had to ask, "Can he fly, Kaleb—can he fly?"

"When I need him to. But you're going to behave yourself and ride at no more than a slow canter, are we agreed?" He knew she'd never make a promise she couldn't keep. Even so, he would not have her taking unnecessary risks. When she didn't respond, his head craned around to find her arms spread out above her upturned head, mimicking a bird in flight. This was so much like her. Although his weakness would cost him, it couldn't be helped—he exploded with laughter.

"I'm beginning to think I married you with blinders on. How could I forget how daring you are?"

"I have no idea!"

"Will you do me a favor?

"What's that?"

"Since we both know you're determined to test him for speed, will you promise only to race him when I'm with you?"

"As long as you won't hold me back."

He shook his head.

As she fully expected, his words that followed were parental to a fault.

"As long as you're reasonable, I won't."

She gleamed with enthusiasm. "I think you'll be surprised, Kaleb. Lady can run a close race. You're a tad bigger than me, so you might slow her down some."

"I know how fast Lady can go. Jesse and I ride in your wake quite often—remember? You didn't give me your word, Liz."

"I promise! Now I'll go crazy waiting for the snow to clear so I can try him out."

"Well, I want spring to get here so we can get into our own place."

The silence lengthened as they plodded along. Kaleb was chiding himself for not building last summer. His wife, on the other hand, was thanking God that he had not.

"Liz, let me know if you get too cold."

"I'm fine. If I forget to tell you, thank you for bringing me home."

"You're not upset with me?"

"I was furious at first; not anymore. I probably shouldn't admit this, but I'm glad you didn't listen to me. Mom and I had a chance to talk last night. She had no idea how alone I felt going through this. I've been thinking. It doesn't look like the snow will allow us to travel this weekend, do you mind if we stay until after church next Sunday? I'd like to have more time."

"Not at all."

"Kaleb, look ... can you see the buck and doe with their fawn in the field?" She leaned forward to point them out.

He did turn, but lost interest in the deer the moment Elizabeth came into view. Entranced by the woman before him, he noticed everything about her: the curve of her mouth, the faint trace of freckles across the bridge of her nose, the slender line of her jaw and the way it was framed in soft golden waves cascading over her shoulders and down past her waist. Jesse's little sister, now his wife, was opening windows in his heart that he never knew existed. He could have lost himself in such ponderings for hours if he hadn't been jolted back to the present by the one now consuming his thoughts.

"Kaleb, are you all right?"

He grinned at the strange expression on her face. "I'm fine—just doing a little dreaming, I suppose."

"I'd ask what about, but the way you're looking at me is scary enough—!"

❀ ❀ ❀

"Liz, let me help you," Kaleb offered, as he opened the door to Jesse's room and found his wife standing next to the bed struggling with the many buttons down the back of her calico dress. He waited, confused by her lack of response.

For a moment she only stared, contemplating his offer. Her warm winter coverings needed washing and the summer ones she had on covered so little. He was her husband. It shouldn't matter. But it did. Since the task was impossible balancing on one foot and she needed to move beyond her dreadful apprehensions, she ignored them and turned in acceptance.

Kaleb gathered her silky hair in his oversized hand, laid it across her shoulder, and sighed. Had her timid eyes not fallen back on him, he would not have known it was an audible response.

How could he not notice the change in her unmentionables? The sight of her pale peachy skin against the delicate lace trim of her camisole took his breath away. While the desire to run his hands along its softness consumed him, he reminded himself that his caress would not be welcome. To have and to hold—but not touch—became more of a challenge with each passing day. Since gaining her trust was everything, Kaleb clung to the hope that in time she would truly be his.

"Liz, I need to talk to you."

When she turned, his lips were only inches away. "Is something wrong?" Her spirit quickened. She withdrew.

His heart beat out of control. He wanted to kiss her in the worst way, but her vulnerable look set his mind to rights. "No. I'd just like to run something by you."

They sat on the bed, and Kaleb, needing to touch her, reached for her hands. "Jesse and I are heading out to check the fence lines. I won't be around this morning." Kaleb noticed her changing mood and asked, "Honey, what is it?"

In her reluctance to tell him, she lowered her head, but Kaleb gently lifted her chin, bringing her gaze back to his.

"Tell me."

"I'm overreacting," she admitted. "Jesse and I always worked the lines ... I miss our times together."

It was no mystery that Elizabeth and Jesse did almost everything together. So why had Kaleb never stopped to consider all that she had given up to become his wife? "I'd take you with us if I could .... You can't help with your ankle the way it is."

"Letting go of my past isn't easy. Maybe in time I can go with you?"

"I'd love that."

"I don't know why I'm so emotional. I'm fine, really. What did you need to talk to me about?"

"Mind if I ride Lady? The other horses are in use and the team we brought isn't saddle-broke."

"She was a wedding gift to both of us, Kaleb. Aren't you the one who keeps insisting that all we have belongs to each other?"

"Yes, but ..."

The soft touch of her fingers on his lips stopped the flow of words. "There can be no buts .... If you want me to feel comfortable having you see to my needs, then *everything* we have must be shared. Would you talk to me before riding Lightning?"

"No.

"You should feel the same way about Lady. She's just as much yours as Lightning."

"As long as you're sure."

"I am. Just keep in mind that she hasn't had a good workout since the storm."

He smiled as his warm hand caressed her face. "I'll be easy on my wife's prize mare. I promise."

She grimaced. "I can't wait until this splint comes off, so I can start riding again."

Kaleb scowled. "You're going to take things slow, Elizabeth. I won't have you doing more damage to your foot."

He had been so tender with her over the last few minutes that his sudden unyielding tone startled her. "Riding won't affect my ankle, if that's what you're worried about. Besides, with Lady, I don't need the stirrups, unless, of course, I'm trying to keep my brother's bluchers on."

Kaleb, needing to get a handle on his strained emotions, stood, and moved to the window.

The tension in his jaw reminded her of how appalled he had been to learn that the boy he rescued in the storm was, in fact, she.

"Your days of wearing men's things are behind you, Elizabeth. You're my wife. Since you'll be with me when you're out, I want you looking like the woman God created you to be."

His possessive tone rubbed her the wrong way. However, the intensity in his glare told her she would have to get used to it. As expected, when she attempted to stand, he came to her aid. Instead of responding with words, she tried something new, hoping to soothe his frazzled nerves.

When his wife pulled on his vest and sweetly kissed his cheek, a blissful tranquility settled over him, body and soul. Did she know how her simple gesture affected him? Wondering what had brought this on, he savored the moment, but he wasn't about to ask.

Her husband's silence made her smile. "Kaleb, you'd better get going, Jesse will be looking for you."

Without warning, he wrapped his arms around her, lifting her off the floor in a tight squeeze, but Elizabeth didn't last long.

"Enough of this closeness ... you're making me nervous."

He chuckled as he put her down, but he couldn't help longing for the day she would finally be at ease in his arms. He made sure that she was stable on her crutches before turning to leave. Stopping at the door, he said, "I'd feel better about going if I knew you were going to eat something." When she didn't respond, he added, "Liz, you can't afford to lose more weight. I can barely find you inside that dress as it is."

How could she resist rubbing it in? "It's all that weight I lost from your wonderful cooking."

"Ha! Ha! Ha! Aren't you a funny gal." He motioned with his hand, saying, "Get out there and eat, woman. Your mom did the cooking and the food's delicious."

Kaleb stayed long enough to see that she had a full plate of food and a steaming cup of tea. Although her sisters would have been more than willing to help her, he took pleasure in seeing to the task himself.

"Mom," Elizabeth asked, "do you have any plans for this morning?"

"Nothing too pressing. Did you have something in mind?

"Since the men are out of our way, could we work on their gifts? Kaleb and I will be heading back to his parents' place on Sunday."

Jayne tried not to think about how much Elizabeth would be missed and said, "Sounds good to me. If I don't get going on your dad's gift, I won't have anything for him either."

That settled things. Everyone listened as Jayne gave the orders and the girls gladly did their part. "Suzanne and Louise go ahead and get the gifts you're working on. I'll grab the fabrics we need. Lizzy, you wash up the breakfast mess and start another kettle for tea. If we sit out here, we should all be able to fit."

The fun ensued around the table for the rest of the morning hours. Her mother and sisters were in the process of making the noon meal when they heard voices outside. The girls scampered off to tuck their gifts away, and Jayne took Kaleb's. Elizabeth was sitting at the table with a cup of tea, sipping at it as if nothing were out of the ordinary when Kaleb meandered in the back door.

The way he rubbed at his hands and arms, she suspected he was chilled to the bone.

"Did you and Jesse have a good morning?"

"A productive one. Had several repairs to do." He came up behind her, leaned over, and snuggled his cold unshaven face into her warm neck.

Shivering, she pulled away. "Kaleb, you're freezing!"

"I am. So come here and let me hold you so I can warm up."

She shook her head no, but apparently that was not the response he was looking for. Her eyes grew wide when he scooped her into his arms, grabbed her crutches and headed for the sitting room.

Squirming, she demanded, "Kaleb White, put me down!"

"In a minute." He sat in the big fluffy chair that faced the warming flames.

He did put her down, but she was in his lap—the last place on earth she wanted to be. "Kaleb, this is not what I meant and you know it." She pushed at his chest when he drew her close, insisting, "Let me go!"

He leaned over and whispered in her ear. "If you can tell me that you had your ankle elevated for at least an hour, I will."

"That's not fair," she pouted, "you know I can't lie to you."

"I would hope not. Tell me, how long did you have it up?" Her profile exposed her deepening flush. There was no need to press her further. "Put your leg over the arm of the chair, you can visit with me until dinner is ready." She trembled in his arms, and, while it bothered him, he knew she'd never get used to his closeness if he didn't exercise an occasional form of gentle persuasion. Minutes tumbled awkwardly by.

"Kaleb, you're embarrassing me. My family will see you holding me."

He rolled his eyes. "Liz, you're my wife. I see your dad holding your mom all the time."

"That's different; they've been married for years, and besides, she likes him. I don't—" Her hand covered her mouth as if doing so would erase her horrible blunder.

He wasn't offended, just surprised that she would voice such thoughts. "Liz, you can quit blushing. I already know you don't like me very much now that I'm your husband."

"That's only true some of the time ... please let me go."

Her pleading eyes were hard to resist, but he so loved having her close. While he could live to regret it, he ignored her plea, and tried again to snuggle her close. She wanted no part of anything he had to offer. In fact, she sat stiff as a board.

When Jesse sauntered into the room and took a seat across from them, she stiffened even more. She seemed to be waiting for her brother to comment on her position. Jesse never did, so she eventually relaxed and leaned against Kaleb, who could only assume that her yielding was more out of discomfort than anything else. For a time, the three of them visited without a moment's tension until she heard her father talking as he came in the back door.

Panic-stricken, she begged Kaleb to release her. Again, he refused. She watched as Jesse sat back, taking all this in— seemingly as an innocent bystander. She knew better. *Why,* she berated herself, *did I allow anyone to bully me into marrying my brother's friend?* Jesse had to be an intricate part of this little conspiracy. They had just spent hours alone.

Kaleb leaned down and whispered in her ear, *"Your freedom for a kiss on the lips!"*

Her mouth dropped open. She couldn't believe the audacity of this overbuilt man. Didn't she just kiss him on the cheek? Wasn't that enough? Perhaps she shouldn't have. That innocent kiss put other ideas in his head—or was it that ornery brother of hers? Noting a look that passed between them, her eyes zeroed in on Jesse. The impish grin on his face said it all.

"I'll get you back, Jesse Somers. There is no question in my mind. You were the mastermind behind this plot!" The sound of heavy footsteps coming their way interrupted her barrage of threats. Anything was better than the mortification she would endure if her father were to see her in Kaleb's lap. Why, he might think she wanted to be there. Perish the thought!

She kissed her despicable giant! Like his hugs, it was actually quite nice. But she would never give him the satisfaction of knowing that! The second Kaleb released her, she left the room, piercing him with a fiery blue glare.

Elizabeth, having given much thought to Kaleb's earlier manipulation, had devised a plan to make her unsuspecting husband pay a small price for a few of the crimes he had committed against her. To pull this off, she had to stay awake until everyone else went to bed, or her family members would give her away. For Elizabeth, this was not an easy task. No doubt the risk of impending torture was high ... but only if her husband found out what she was up to. "Kaleb," she asked with no show of emotion, "how about a game of checkers before we call it a night?"

His thoughts of going to bed early forgotten, he agreed. They moved to the game table and set it up.

This particular round could have been won many times over, but she kept that piece of information to herself. "Kaleb, this is a close match, would you care to make this a little more interesting?"

He scowled. "You know I won't gamble, Liz, and you won't either."

Him and his orders, she thought. *Remember the plan, Elizabeth; don't let him ruffle your feathers.* "I was only thinking of a favor freely given to the winner. What harm could there be in that?"

His interest peaked. "What did you have in mind?"

She lowered her gaze and became very interested in her next move. It would never do to have him read her thoughts.

Kaleb's were much different than hers. *Another kiss would be nice. Several would be even better.*

"Shall we say ... the loser has to rub the winner's back for five minutes before we go to bed."

It wasn't a kiss, but he nodded. "Sounds good. I could use a good back rub after the morning I had."

Finding it difficult not to smile, Elizabeth dug her nails into her hand and managed to keep a straight face. The game played on. She stretched it out as long as she could without being obvious. Even so, she won with no effort.

Kaleb watched the little imp as she moved toward her brother's room, knowing his lovely yet devious wife had hornswoggled him. He smiled, remembering the smirk she tried to hide. Having played these games for many years, he would have to come up with some form of retribution. Luckily, he had something in mind.

When Kaleb meandered into the room, she was lying on her

stomach, waiting to receive her prize. If Elizabeth could have read his mind she would have been running out the door.

Kaleb blew out the candle. Her eyes didn't have time to adjust to the darkened room before she felt movement on the bed. She knew he was there, but he didn't lie next to her as she had expected.

"Kaleb!" she squealed as the hands that were supposed to be rubbing her back tickled her sides without mercy!

As the seconds turned into minutes, she begged him to stop. "Kaleb, please!" She was laughing so hard, she could barely breathe; tears were pouring from her eyes as his hands went from her sides to her neck and then again to her sides.

"Kaleb, I'm going to be sick!" The magic words! Before he released her, he leaned into her face, nose-to-nose, and his big brown eyes sparkled in the moonlight.

"I will pay my debt, but you and I both know that game was fixed. Don't mess with your husband, Woman!"

When he agreed to her terms, he hadn't stopped to consider how soft she would feel unbound in her blue flannel gown. In an attempt to relieve his whirling emotions, his hands slid toward her shoulders. His eyes betrayed him though, taking in every curve. *Heaven help me!* His thoughts exclaimed. *She's my wife, I have every right, but she's not ready. Slow down, Kaleb!* Just as he was about to flee the room, her timid voice cooed softly in his ear, rescuing his tortured mind.

"It was worth being tickled, Kaleb. This feels wonderful. I'll just have to be wiser next time and make sure you're not on to me."

"Next time, we'll take turns; no games will be necessary."

"Maybe someday I'll like being married to you, Kaleb White."

"Good, `cause you're stuck with me!" The sweet smile on her face as he kissed her cheek stayed with him long after she found her rest.

He Loves Me!

Chapter Ten

A Child in His Eyes

KNOWING THEY WOULD be going back to Kaleb's parents' home after church on Sunday, Elizabeth went out of her way to savor every passing moment.

George and Elizabeth spent as much time together as possible. Their mutual desire to salvage their tattered relationship allowed healing to begin from the first hug they shared. She now understood that her father had acted out of love.

True to his word, Doctor Taylor stopped by to check on Elizabeth. Pastor had been in his office the other day with some questions about the children he was adopting, and had mentioned marrying them. Doc wasn't surprised, just thankful they were willing to make a go of it. *If he only knew!*

Kaleb had insisted on being in the room with Elizabeth, and the first words out of Doc's mouth were directed at him.

"Kaleb, as far as I can tell, the swelling is down. If you

can assure me that your wife will take things slow, I'll take the splint off."

She scowled. Apparently she was old enough to be a wife, but not wise enough to take care of herself. "Why are you asking him? I'm the patient here."

"He knows what you're like, Liz. Give the man a break."

Doc turned to Elizabeth. "Lizzy, listen to me. The last thing I want to do is be the cause of marital discord. You're going to have to take things slow, or you'll do more harm than good."

"I'll do anything you say if you'll take this thing off." She cast her eyes on Kaleb.

His young wife was begging him to say yes. Recalling some of her earlier comments, he decided to make a point while the good doctor was here to answer his questions.

Kaleb's big brown eyes staring back at her revealed his intent. "What will happen if she doesn't do as you suggest?"

"The pain will increase and the splint will have to go back on."

"Be specific. What can she do?"

"Use the crutches if you need them for a few days, weeks, whatever it takes, Lizzy. Only do what your ankle will allow—without pain. Can I count on you?"

"Yes."

Doc glanced at Kaleb, awaiting his approval.

"Go ahead—I'll never hear the end of it if you don't. You'd better do what he's saying, Elizabeth, or I'll have him put it right back on."

Having the splint off felt wonderful! When Doc asked her to put a little weight on her leg, she was pleased. What used to be intense pain was now more like a dull ache. Oh, it was stiff, sure, and her skin was itchy, but this was a big step in the right direction.

※ ※ ※

"Jared," Elizabeth asked as she hobbled into the sitting room Saturday morning, "did Jesse and Kaleb happen to tell you when they'd be back?"

"Nope." He could see that she had something on her mind, so he asked, "Is there anything I can help you with?"

"Well ... my ankle's doing better and I need to get out of here for a while. Want to go riding?"

"I'd love to, but ..." His scrunched expression was not a good sign. "Dad said my paper had to be done before he gets home. He seems to think school's gonna be back in session on Monday."

"What's Joe doing?"

"Sorry, Sis, he's worse off than me. He has a book report to do, and he just started the novel this morning." Jared took her disappointment personally. "I'd be glad to saddle Lady. When you get back, just bring her up to the house and I'll put her away."

"You don't mind?"

"Not a bit."

"Thanks Jared. I'd see to it myself, but the giant I'm married to would have a cow!"

Jared chuckled as he slipped his coat on and tied his bluchers. "What's up with him anyway?"

"Apparently, he's having too many flashbacks from my childhood to see me as an adult." She shrugged, adding, "Who knows, maybe I'll always be a child in his eyes."

"I've seen the way he looks at you. Trust me, he likes what he

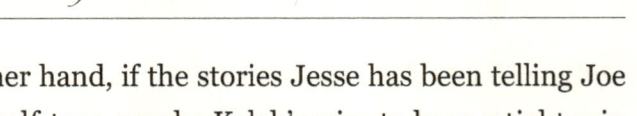

sees. On the other hand, if the stories Jesse has been telling Joe and I are even half-true, maybe Kaleb's wise to keep a tight rein on you. You make the rest of us look like angels, Sis!"

She smacked his arm. "I wasn't that bad. What's Jesse been telling you?"

They were on the way to the barn when Jared asked, "Did you really pull all Mom's carrots out of the garden, and then hide them around the farm so the rabbits would stay out of it?"

"Yes, but I had the best of intentions. Mom scared me. She said the next rabbit that ate out of her garden would be dinner. I figured I was doing her and the rabbits a favor. How could I have known we needed those carrots more than the rabbits did?"

Jared shook his head in disbelief, got Lady out of the stall, and went for her gear while Elizabeth brushed Lady down. She was glad Kaleb didn't need Lady today. Too much time had lapsed since she'd been able to ride and she needed some time alone. "Jared, if Kaleb gets back, let him know I'll be home in about an hour."

"That's fine, but I need to confirm one more tale before you take off."

"Which one is that?"

"The day Jacob Woods came out to fetch a hog."

She giggled in remembrance.

"Did you really hide in the back of the wagon, so you could go home with him?"

"Sure did. I saw his wife at church the previous Sunday. She told me she had bought gumdrops at the store for the next time I came for a visit. I was going to collect."

"I heard Dad wasn't too pleased when Jacob had to bring you

all the way home."

"That would be putting it lightly. I found out just how long his list of chores was for a little girl who chooses to be sneaky. I think it took me more than a week to work off that adventure."

Jared threw his head back and laughed out loud. "Jesse didn't tell me that part." After Jared helped her mount, he reached for her hand. "Do me a favor will ya, Sis?"

"What's that?" She didn't miss the ornery fleck in his eyes.

"Don't do anything impulsive while you're out today. I don't need Kaleb getting angry at me for helping you out."

She stole the hat off his head and threw it back at his face. "I'm not a child anymore, Jared. Remember that!"

Jared muttered as she moved out of sight, "Whatever you say, Sis—whatever you say."

In no hurry, Elizabeth rode the path along the Huron, taking the time to enjoy the scenery and the animals that came to the waters edge. Deer were always coming and going. Today, a rather timid red fox came as well. Although one didn't appear this morning, the coyotes intrigued her the most. They rarely came close, but they could often be seen off in the distance, watching. She wondered what God was thinking when he created them. Their oversized heads looked so displaced on their thin, agile bodies. She hated to end her peaceful outing, but when she came to the old Indian trail, she knew time had to be getting away from her. She wouldn't give her family or Kaleb cause for worry.

Jesse and Kaleb pulled the team into the barn when they returned from their outing. Kaleb noticed right off that Lady was missing. He tried not to panic as he moved toward the house and stuck his head in the back door.

"Hey, Mom, do you know where my wife is?"

"She said something about getting Jared or Joe to go riding with her."

"Lady's the only horse missing."

"Then she must have gone alone." His anxious expression did not go unnoticed. "She won't go far, Kaleb. Want me to check with the boys?"

"No need."

Jesse was finishing up with the team, when Kaleb came toward him. "Jesse, mind if I borrow Shadow? Liz went out alone."

"She'll probably be back before you get him saddled, but feel free." Jesse thought his friend was getting worked up over nothing, but he wasn't going to interfere.

Kaleb hadn't been looking for more than five minutes when he spotted Elizabeth down by the river. She heard his approach and glanced up.

"Hi, Kaleb. Did you just get back?" Had a large rabbit not distracted her from across the river, she would have noticed his reaction to her nonchalance.

As soon as it scampered off she looked back at her husband. He hadn't answered her question. A second glimpse gave her a clearer picture. *Here we go again!*

"Kaleb, I needed to get out of the house, and both boys had homework to do. Jared helped me get Lady ready." His look intimidated her. "They couldn't come," she explained.

"So you came alone?"

She averted her gaze, wondering why he was acting like this.

"We need to talk, Elizabeth. Would you like to go back to the barn and get out of the wind?"

"No. If you have something to say, say it here!"

Kaleb contemplated his words. "To start with, your ankle has not had sufficient time to heal."

"That's your opinion."

"And besides that, you shouldn't be out riding alone. "

"I can appreciate your concern, Kaleb. I assure you I am fine."

"Yea!" he exclaimed, "as long as the bears stay in their dens and the panthers and wolves stay away and the drifters you run into have your best interest at heart and ..."

"Enough, you're making a mountain out of a mole hill."

He had no desire to put a wedge between them, but he needed this issue resolved. "You're not understanding what I said to you the other day, or what I'm saying now. If you need to be out and about, I am more than willing to take you."

"You weren't here. Besides, I like being out on my own—you know that."

The steeled look in his eyes told her more than she wanted to know. She could not avoid him for long, but she refused to discuss this when her anger was flaring. Had she been thinking clearer, she would have taken off in the other direction. When she nudged Lady forward, his long arm reached out and snatched her from her mount. "Let me go!"

"No! We're not finished."

"Yes we are!" Her aversion to his highhanded obsession with keeping her safe was growing old. "I can understand your wanting me to be cautious while the snow is on the ground. But you'd better change your mind before spring, or you're going to have a major war on your hands."

The veins in his neck twitched. "Elizabeth," he began, barely

holding his temper in check, "a woman out alone is only asking for trouble. Your accident more than proved that."

"You're wrong. My accident could have happened to anyone— even you! My father understands my need to have time to myself. You knew what I was like before you married me. Did you think you could change me?"

Kaleb held the utmost respect for her father, but in this they did not agree. "Your father and I are not going to agree on everything. You're my wife. I expect you to abide by my wishes."

"Your wishes! What about mine?" *He's unbelievable!* "You're not trusting the Lord to take care of me, Kaleb." As she continued to stare, her thoughts rambled on. *You can't see the truth as I do. God alone brought me safely through that storm. He used you, Kaleb, but you were only a vessel.* When it became obvious that he was not ready to see that, she took a deep breath and tried to calm down.

"I'll pray about it. Until I tell you otherwise, please do as I ask."

"Let me go before I say something I'll regret."

"When you quit struggling and look at me, I'll take you back."

In her exasperated state, Elizabeth hadn't noticed that her horse was gone. "Where is Lady?"

"She'll be in the barn when we get back. Are you going to do as I asked?"

What she wanted to do was slither off Shadow and take off running. Her ankle wasn't strong enough to walk in the deep snow, and she wouldn't give Kaleb more fuel for the fire.

"Elizabeth, I need to know you're safe. I can't do that if you're alone. I'm sorry you don't agree. For now this is how it has to be."

Her lids slid shut. "Are you finished?" Her actions were childish, but what did she care? He insisted on treating her like a child, she might as well fit the bill.

"Yes ... take me back." When Kaleb relinquished his hold, she turned away. He was asking too much! She needed to calm down—she needed to pray, but how could she? She was so angry she could spit nails. To a degree she could see where Kaleb's fears were coming from. After all, he was the one who found her in that desperate state. She could see that a man alone in the same situation couldn't have done better. Kaleb could not. He was wrong for giving in to his fears, but in so many circumstances he had been there for her throughout her life. She would have to give God time to work on his heart.

Elizabeth couldn't stand to be at odds with anyone. She had to talk to him to try and ease the tension between them. As she peered over her shoulder, his gaze held on to hers. "I'm sorry, Kaleb. I don't agree with you, but my anger is wrong. Can you forgive me?"

"You know I will." She made no attempt to pull away when he drew her to him, ran his long fingers through her hair, and snuggled her close. "Ya know, Liz, coming to love you is not where the challenge will lie .... The hard part will be waiting for you to feel the same way about me. I appreciate your patience in this. In some ways you could be right. I still see you lying helpless in that mound of snow. I need to know you're safe until I can work things out in my mind."

"Just promise you'll pray about it, Kaleb. Will you?"

"I will."

"I *will* bring it up again, you know that, don't you?"

He chuckled. "I figured as much. Just so you don't get your heart set on me changing my mind ...."

Chapter Eleven

A Place to Start

*S*TREAMS OF LEMON light shimmered through the windows as Sunday came to greet the Somers' household with the promise of a beautiful day. The aroma of coffee brewing and fresh cinnamon muffins coming out of the oven filled the humble home as everyone scurried around, readying for church.

Kaleb was seated at the kitchen table with a cup of coffee, savoring his last bite of crisp bacon, when his mother-in-law whispered in his ear.

"You might want to check on Elizabeth. She was struggling when I came by her room."

He turned to face her. "I just left her. She was fine."

"She's not now."

Entering their room, Kaleb was shaken by the change that had come over his wife in such a short time. The color had drained from her face and she was sitting on the bed holding her stomach. Perhaps her pale gray suit added to her pasty appearance, but he couldn't help wondering if something else could be making her ill. "Honey, what's wrong?"

"I feel like I'm going to be sick, Kaleb. I need to stay home."

He hated to ask. "Is it your time?"

Her brow furrowed. "What?"

He took a deep breath. This was more difficult than he thought. "You know ... your female time?"

Appalled that he would ask, she turned away. "That's none of your business!"

He should correct her, but he was sweating bullets already. Since her questionable denial narrowed things down, he had a pretty good idea what was upsetting her. "Liz, you're going to be fine .... You're just uneasy about seeing everyone for the first time. We've talked about this. The people at church are our friends."

"What if our friends think the worst of us?"

Kaleb wrapped her in his arms. "We can't control what everyone thinks. You know that. The people who love the Lord and us haven't changed. You'll see that for yourself. I'll stay by your side."

"I can't go ..."

Kaleb wanted her to face this and put it behind her, or she'd be sick every week until she did. "Liz, you're not staying home. This is our first Sunday to attend church as husband and wife. I need you by my side. I'll go hitch up the team and we'll take our time getting there."

Elizabeth wondered if a cup of tea might help, so she picked up her crutches and headed for the kitchen. She joined her mother at the table, poured a steaming cup from her grandma's cherished teapot, added a little honey, and took a sip.

"Thanks for everything, Mom. I'm glad we've had this time together."

A gentle smile brightened Jayne's face. "I am too. Did you remember to pack the gift for Kaleb?"

"Yes, but I don't like him very much right now." Elizabeth shrugged. "I suppose I'll finish it."

"I'd ask what's wrong, but I shouldn't interfere. You and Kaleb need to work through your differences together."

Elizabeth took another sip of her tea. "He doesn't seem to need my help. He solves all of our disagreements the same way. I tell him I don't care to do something and he says I have to. I'm sick of his orders already and we've only been married two weeks."

"Lizzy, you can't put all the blame on Kaleb. In some ways, you're trying—I can see that—but you're keeping him at bay. You're Kaleb's wife, and hanging on to resentment won't change that. The way you respond to him can. It's really up to you. If you're asking me, it seems like an awful lonely existence for both of you if something doesn't change. Maybe instead of being so intolerant, you should begin to thank the Lord for His goodness. Kaleb cares about you more than you give him credit for."

Although her mother meant well, Elizabeth's irritation would not allow her to accept the criticism. She changed the subject. "Did you decide what you're bringing for Christmas dinner?"

Jayne knew what she was doing. She also knew that Elizabeth would have to make her own way. No matter how hard it was to see her hurting, she could not do this for her. "I'll make a sweet potato casserole, rolls, and the rest of the desserts."

Elizabeth had a certain hankering. "Are you open to requests?"

"From you? Yes. What did you have in mind? Pumpkin?"

They shared an intuitive smile. Elizabeth offered a definitive "Yes! You don't mind?"

"Not at all."

The thought of not being home Christmas morning was difficult for Elizabeth. She would miss her father's excitement that always overflowed on this special morning. The smiles his antics would bring to her mother's face only added to their celebration. Knowing her family would be coming to Kaleb's parents' house for dinner made it easier to bear.

Elizabeth could hear Kaleb calling from the front door, so she said her farewells. Although her stomach had settled to a degree, her mood remained dark and dreary. Because she had only heated words for Kaleb, she kept them to herself. Preparing her heart and mind for worship was impossible today.

Kaleb pulled the team into the churchyard, helped his silent wife out of the sleigh, and handed her the crutches. As much as he wanted to say something, offer a hug, anything that would ease her mind, he was at a loss. He had never seen her in such a somber mood.

Elizabeth scanned the room, hoping to see some of her friends from school. Disappointed, she slid into the pew after Kaleb. She did everything she could to ignore the inquisitive eyes that turned her way, but it wasn't working. Some of the girls who usually sat with Kaleb and Jesse were put out that Kaleb was sitting with her. Why she didn't notice that Kaleb had been holding her hand was beyond her. She remedied the problem, but the damage had already been done. If she were thinking clearer, she would have realized that her marriage was the real clincher.

His family joined them from the other side. Elizabeth nodded in greeting, but her mind was preoccupied with her churning stomach. Everything else became a blur. When her mouth began to water, she grabbed her crutches, flew towards the door, and went down the steps so fast she almost fell. Although she heard Kaleb calling, she couldn't stop. She made it to the outhouse just in time.

Minutes had passed before Kaleb asked, "Liz, are you all right?" She didn't respond at first, so he waited.

"That depends on what you call all right? You don't have to wait, Kaleb. I need to be sure my stomach's settled before I go back in."

He wasn't going anywhere—even if it took all day. "Maybe you should come out. The smell could be making you worse."

Elizabeth wanted to go home, but she couldn't bring herself to ask. A denial could be her undoing. Since she was not prepared to carry on a face-to-face conversation with her husband, she waited it out in the odorous confines of the outhouse.

When the nausea passed, she slowly opened the door and hobbled out. Kaleb did look concerned, but she was so tense she couldn't accept anything from him right now.

"Liz, would you like to try and catch the end of the sermon?"

On her hesitant nod, he followed her. Pastor had begun to give the closing announcements, so they slid into the back pew. Had she known what he was about to share, she never would have come back in.

"We would like to congratulate Mr. and Mrs. Kaleb White on their recent marriage."

Oh no! she thought, as every eyeball in the church turned their way. Her flaming face had to be purple. If only she could melt into the floor. As if Pastor hadn't said enough, he added, "Please be sure to stop by and wish them well. Mr. Somers has informed me that there will be a house-raising party in the spring. We'll look forward to participating in that."

Elizabeth's eyes slid shut. She needed to find a sense of peace in the midst of her overwhelming circumstances. How could she accept congratulations when she hadn't found a way to accept this union herself? She had no desire to be bombarded by well-meaning friends.

People did stop to talk, but they left her feeling more confused than ever. They really did seem happy for them—in fact, most were elated. How could she have been so wrong?

Kaleb and Jesse were talking when Elizabeth made her way to the sleigh. She didn't mind. In truth, she needed a few moments alone. Her thoughts were going in all directions. Would she ever find clarity?

Elizabeth wrapped the blanket around her legs, made herself comfortable, and sat in silent wonder. Her life was such a mess. Granted, much had been thrown her way, but how long could she go on feeling sorry for herself? How could she go about picking up the fragmented pieces of her life and find joy in them?

Although she had no desire to have a husband and everything else that went along with the package deal, that had to change. She couldn't live her whole life complaining like Jonah did in the face of God's blessings. Like it or not, she had a husband who seemed to care a great deal.

Kaleb had been so right insisting that she see her family. The healing that had taken place in her relationship with them was nothing short of miraculous. He'd insisted on her coming to church, and everything turned out just as he said it would. In a way, she resented him for being right so much of the time.

I was angry when he insisted on me coming today. It's over, and I saw with my own eyes—our friends really do care. I'm still fighting this marriage, Lord. I don't like feeling so vulnerable and out of control. I know I have to do my part and quit being so selfish or we'll never be happy, but how? How do I get beyond feeling so violated—so wronged? I forgave my father and I think I've forgiven Kaleb. Am I still angry with You for allowing this marriage in the first place? Forgive me, if I am. Help me to open my heart to this man, who has so graciously opened his heart and life to me. Thank you for this realization, Lord. Show me how to go about this. Give us a place to start.

"Liz!"

Startled by Kaleb's deep voice, she snapped out of her meditation. "I'm sorry. Did you say something?"

"I asked if you're feeling any better?"

Her brow furrowed.

She appeared out of sorts, so he tried again, "Your stomach, Liz. Did it settle?"

"Yes. Mom had some peppermint. That helped."

He could only assume her quiet reserve had something to do with her rough morning, so he didn't question her further.

Elizabeth gazed at the view before her, trying to enjoy the

ride, but her present circumstances kept pressing in on her. She had to find a way to work this out—to tell her husband of her changing heart.

"Kaleb?" Elizabeth asked, though again her mind trailed off.

"Did you want something?"

"Have you ever noticed how easily our parents get along in their marriages? They make everything look so easy. It's not easy, is it?"

"They've had years to work out their differences. My parents had a rough start, and I'm sure yours have had challenges as well."

His eyes traveled back and forth between her and the trail in front of them.

"You've never been married before, so you might not know how to answer my question—but you are my husband, and I don't think I could ask anyone else."

"All right."

"How do we get from where we are to where they are?"

He was both shocked and elated with her inquiry. *Could she be asking what I think she's asking?* The beat of his heart increased with every breath. He forced himself to focus on the question at hand. "You have to go back to the day we were married. This time something has to change."

Elizabeth's eyes never left him as he stopped the team on the side of the trail.

Offering up a silent prayer, Kaleb turned to her. He was all-too aware this conversation could make or break the chance of their marriage ever getting off the ground. "Will you humor me for a minute?"

"All right."

"Close your eyes, Liz."

She complied without hesitation.

"Now, picture us standing in front of Pastor. When you recite your vows this time, no one is forcing you. The words you speak have to come from your heart. You have to want me to be your husband—you have to be willing to open your heart and life to me. Not because your father said you had to, but because you're committed to us. You're willing to move toward becoming one with me. Until you arrive at the place where you begin to want me, as I so desperately want you, we're at an impasse. We can't attain what our parents have because they've accepted each other as life partners. They've chosen to love each other through the good and bad. I want you to want this marriage as much as I do, but only you can give me your heart."

Kaleb touched the soft skin of her face, and her lids opened— their eyes held each other in a hopeful embrace.

"Remember, Liz. This is a gift that only you can give. My wanting your love doesn't make it mine. You alone can open that door and begin to let me in."

Speech evaded her. She was stunned. This man was only five years older than she. How could he know this? He had answered her question with undeniable clarity.

For the first time since she uttered her vows, she understood that this marriage really was theirs to make or break. Her mom was right. If she wanted to find happiness with this man, she had to open her heart. This decision was hers to make. Sure, Kaleb had to want this as well, but he just said that he did. This endeavor could not be self-seeking or it would never pan out. Although she didn't have all the answers, somehow it didn't matter. She had to tell him. He had given her a place to start.

Both happiness and unfathomable relief flooded her soul at the same time. She wanted to jump for joy—shout from the rooftops!

He cares, Lord, did you hear him? His heart is open to me! Not because he feels obligated, because he really wants to give me—Elizabeth White—his heart. Thank you, Father God. Thank you!

With awe and wonder the sealed portal of her heart peeped open, offering her husband what he believed to be a glimmer of radiant hope.

Kaleb's protective words broke into her rapturous thoughts, and for the first time since she uttered her I do's, she was ready for him.

"Liz—Honey, are you all right?"

Her smile went from ear to ear. "I've never been better!" There was so much she needed to say. She wouldn't give him false hope—she couldn't say that she loved him. But he did deserve to know that she would give it her all. Elizabeth now understood, beyond a shadow of doubt, that if she didn't give their marriage a chance, she could be missing out on all that God intended. "Kaleb, thank you!"

His thudding heart raced out of control as her slender arms wrapped around him, attempting to squeeze the life out of him. But why was she thanking him? He needed to know. Did she want to be his wife in life as well as on paper? He returned her hug, hopeful that she would fill him in.

As if she hadn't confused him enough, she yanked on the front of his jacket, bringing him down to her level. She kissed him full on the mouth. Kaleb, feeling stunned and out of control, waited breathlessly, expecting that at any moment she would enlighten him.

When she finally spoke, he chuckled at the way her exuberance spilled forth. Words he had been waiting to hear poured over him, like cool water on a hot summer day. Remembering her forceful kiss and wanting another, his scrambled brain took a bit to catch up.

"Kaleb, we can do this, I know now that we can. You said that your heart is open to me and, starting now, mine is to you. I want you to be my husband. Not in every way just yet, but you've given me a place to begin—oh, Kaleb, how I want to begin! I hate being frustrated with you so much of the time. I'm ready to let go of my anger. I want to move forward."

She gazed in delight at the caring man smiling before her. The devotion emanating from his dark amber gaze did little to ease her thundering heart. When his long fingers weaved their way through the hair at the nap of her neck, there was no doubt in her mind that she was about to be kissed. Although she trembled in his arms, this simple act of submission brought so much more than she could have ever imagined.

Kaleb's lids slid shut, longing to savor this precious moment, feeling the tenderness of her sweet lips ensconced in his own. Moments passed before he released her, hoping that this kiss would be the first of many yet to come. Having no desire for the enchantment to end, he drew her into his fond embrace—held her, squeezed her, and gazed into her soft blue eyes.

"Now do you understand how much my heart is open to loving you, Liz?"

She flushed before him, feeling shy in his presence. "Yes, Kaleb, I do. We have much to sort out. Some things still terrify me, but I do want to move forward. I can promise you that."

"So do I. Maybe we should head home. It's awfully cold, and I wouldn't want you to be sick for the first holiday we share as husband and wife. We have the rest of our lives to figure all this out."

Her hand reached up to caress his face. "Always the protector, aren't you, Kaleb?"

"I can't help myself where you're concerned."

"By the way, I'm sorry I was so anxious about church today. Once again, you were right and I was wrong. Will you forgive me?" He smiled and squeezed her hands.

"Yes ... but I think it's only fair that you make amends."

"Kaleb White, I ..." Her impending threats were disarmed, and she melted in his arms when another sweet kiss came to her lips—as payment for her crimes. She found her voice about the time they pulled into the barn.

"Kaleb, promise me something?"

"What's that?"

"If you ever kiss me when I'm standing, promise you'll hang on tight." The dreamy look in her eyes made him smile.

"Why is that?"

"You drain every ounce of strength I possess. I'm afraid I'd fall."

He laughed out loud. "You do wonderful things to my heart, Liz. You know that ... don't you?"

"Well, mine isn't a closed book."

"I know. You've made me the happiest man on earth."

Reaching out, he tucked her stray locks behind her ears.

"Do you really mean that?"

"With all of my heart ...." He jumped to the ground and alighted her. "Look, Liz." Her gaze followed his long finger to a nearby stall. "Your brother brought a friend of yours over before church." Kaleb didn't miss the way Lady sensed Elizabeth's presence before she even approached. Lady's head bobbed up and down and she whinnied out loud, like she was carrying on a conversation with her best friend. Elizabeth egged it on with the way she spoiled her, but they really were quite a pair.

Elizabeth took the time to be sure Lady was all settled in while Kaleb put the team away. The moment he finished, he came up behind her and slid his arms around her waist.

"Are you ready to head in?"

"Sure. Lady doesn't seem to mind her new home, does she?"

"She seems to be handling the change better than someone else did her first night here."

Elizabeth leaned against him, giving him a bit of a shove. Her words were soft and teasing as they gazed into one another's eyes. "If she had to sleep next to a big grizzly like I did, I'm sure she'd be frightened as well."

He shook his head. "What is it about me that you find so frightful?"

"At first it was because I wanted nothing to do with being your wife. Now it's more about disappointing you."

"You could never disappoint me, Liz."

"I had so many preconceived ideas about what having a husband would be like. I'm finding out that many of them were wrong. I still have insecurities, Kaleb, but I'm getting there."

He tightened his hold. "I know you are. If I forget to tell you, thanks for giving us a chance."

She smiled in response as they headed towards the house. Her heart was so much lighter—so much fuller, practically bursting with renewed hope!

❀ ❀ ❀

From the moment Kaleb reached for her hand to pray, Elizabeth noticed the different effect his touch had on her. Up till now, she had only tolerated him. Her acceptance of their union had changed more than she anticipated. Kaleb must have sensed something, but not recognizing the look he sent her way, she made an attempt to shake off her new findings and join in with the conversation.

"Mom, was Sarah excited about going home with Suzanne and Louise?"

"Yes. I could hardly get her to set still in church."

Samuel scolded his wife, "I told you not to tell her until after service, but you wouldn't listen."

"How could I resist?"

In truth, Elizabeth wondered if they sent her away until they were sure their new daughter-in-law was a bit more agreeable. Since she had no intentions of revealing her thoughts, she contained the giggles that threatened to escape.

"Dad, did you see the latest addition in the barn?"

"Yes, I helped Jesse get Lady settled before church. She's a fine looking mare. The way your father talks, you'll enjoy having her here."

"There's no question about that."

Kaleb watched his wife throughout the meal. She pushed her food around on her plate, eating next to nothing. Something had dampened her appetite and he needed to know what.

When his mother stood to begin cleaning up, Kaleb told her to go ahead and visit with his father. He and Elizabeth would do the dishes.

Elizabeth made her way to the counter, leaned her crutches against the wall, and started washing, while Kaleb cleared the table. He was quiet, but she had things on her mind, so she didn't think much of it until he sidled up behind her.

"Kaleb, what are you doing? Your parents ..."

"My parents will think there's something wrong with me if I never put my arms around my wife. Besides, they're in the other room."

Her timid eyes met his. "What if I need you to let me go?"

"I will in a minute." He leaned to kiss her cheek. "Can you tell me what has you so tense you're not eating again?"

"I did eat, just not very much. I keep thinking about the things that are still unsettled."

"Would you like to talk now?"

Her eyes followed the sound of his parents' voices. "I'd rather no one else heard what we're saying, Kaleb. I'd never survive the humiliation if they did."

He gave her a squeeze and moved away. When he swatted her backside with the dishtowel, he winked and said, "Then we shall wait, my bashful wife, until we are alone."

The terrible scowl she sent his way was dispelled by the smile that followed.

"Your mom and I had a nice chat while we were fixing dinner. She told me about how your parents got their start. Makes ours look like a piece of cake, doesn't it?"

He nodded. "I still find it hard to believe that my father treated my mom with so little respect. I'm glad he woke up before he destroyed their chance for happiness."

"It helps to hear testimonials that stand the test of time."

"I'll agree with you there."

Kaleb had things to put in the cold cellar. When he returned Elizabeth asked, "Are you up to playing some checkers after were done with dishes?"

"That's fine, but first we're going to discuss these things that are bothering you." He stared at her for a long moment. "It would seem that my wife is trying to avoid the inevitable."

"How did you know?"

His heart went out to her. "Honey, don't fret over the little things. We'll work them out."

"To me, this is huge."

He, while waiting for her to finish the big roasting pan, hung his head on her shoulder, and nuzzled into the side of her neck. She shivered and pulled away.

"Kaleb, don't do that, I can't stand it!" She shivered again, just thinking about it.

"Is your neck ticklish, My Dear?"

Her back was to him, so he missed her smile. "I'm not telling." She could hear the wind picking up, and peeked out the window, expecting to see snow flakes.

"Ah, but I have ways of finding these things out." His tone was fiendish, in a taunting sort of way.

"You'd better be nice, Kaleb White, or you won't get your pie or fudge for Christmas."

He turned her to face him. "You wouldn't torture me like that, would you?"

She grinned at the huge man holding the towel. "Without a second thought!"

His brow furrowed. "Let's see, that means I have to be nice for six more days. Ummm—I can do it!"

She giggled.

"What are you going to do to stop me after that?"

She couldn't believe his boldness. "Put a halt to kisses, that's for sure!" She washed the last dish and set it on the counter before he grabbed her, threw her over his shoulder and headed toward their room. While she had every intention of demanding he put her down, she was laughing so hard she couldn't get the words out. He plopped down on the bed, secured her on his lap and attempted to set her straight.

"Why would you say such a thing?" He looked worried, but he asked, so she felt obliged to tell him.

"It's obvious—they've scrambled your brain, Kaleb. I can't have you running around acting like a lovesick schoolboy—I'll die of embarrassment! You're much too big to be acting that way. And besides, you're sure to make a regular habit of making me blush."

"That would be a shame! Your kisses do scramble my brain and mine make you weak in the knees. You can't do this to a man— not this one anyway! I kissed you and you kissed me back. That door will forever remain open—it can never be closed. Do you hear me?" He seemed serious enough. She had to be certain.

"You're serious, aren't you?"

"Absolutely!"

She offered her cheesy grin and he knew in that instant, he'd been duped.

"Finally!" she said, as her hands rose towards the heavens, "we agree on something!" Her teeth came over her lower lip. "I don't think I've seen you that intense since our first meeting in the cabin. It was really hard not to laugh, Kaleb!"

He grabbed her face in his hands, and scolded her again. "You, Young Lady, are a terrible tease. Why ... if you don't stop I'm going to be forced to ..."

His words were cut off by his wife's inflection. "Forced to do what, Kaleb, punish me again?" Her husband roared with laughter just before finding her lips and devouring them once again.

If only the fun could have gone on and on. Unfortunately, Kaleb, wanting these other issues resolved, relaxed his hold and leaned against the headboard. His nonchalance did little to ease her mind.

"Liz, since you're the one with reservations, I think you should lead this conversation."

Her brow furrowed. "But ... where do I start?"

"You said that some things frighten you. Can you tell me what they are?"

"Oh ... I don't know, Kaleb ..." As she contemplated his question her pulse thudded in her ears, impeding clear thought. "I don't think I can do this. I can't! I just can't ...."

"If you give me a clue, maybe I could help you along."

She hesitated, lowering her eyes. "Since the day we married I've felt like a dark cloud is hanging over me. It keeps me on edge and makes it difficult to relax and be myself around you."

His wife was now a deep shade of crimson, so it wasn't difficult to read her thoughts. "Are we talking about intimacy?"

She nodded.

He lifted her chin. Her eyes did not follow. "I haven't asked you for intimacy, so why does it have you feeling unsettled?"

"You don't give me much warning, Kaleb. I don't like not knowing when you might spring this on me. Kissing you is one thing. I'm not ready for more."

Since she was the one who kissed him first, he was perplexed by her admission. "Sweetheart, I know you're embarrassed, but I want you to look at me." He sat up and waited until her eyes met his. "Are you saying you want to know when?"

"If you could be patient and wait a while, yes. I'm not as naive as you think. I see the way you look at me. It scares me. I don't want you thinking I'm ready when I'm not."

Curious, he asked, "Did you have a timeframe in mind?"

"I'd like to wait until we're in our own home." He shook his head, furrowing his brow just enough to worry her.

"That's a long time away, Liz."

Seconds passed. "Can I tell you why I feel this way?"

"Of course."

"Most people fall in love and then get married, am I right?"

"Yes, but there are exceptions."

"I understand that. To me, it would be like planning our wedding. Our first night in our new house could be like our wedding night. To me, it would be something to look forward to—special. We would have this time to prepare our hearts and minds to be open to one another." She could see Kaleb was thinking.

The silence unnerved her.

"You've made a good point." He held her gaze. "The night of our wedding celebration will be our first night in our own house."

She nodded.

"That night I will make you my wife in every way. That means no matter how frightened you are there will be no holding back. Do you agree?"

The tears streaming down her face were a mixture of joy and relief. Placing her arms around her husband's neck, she hugged him like she had never hugged him before. When she released him, she looked straight into his big brown eyes, her own dancing with happiness. "Yes, Kaleb, I agree. Thank you for understanding."

Kaleb, though he delighted in her pleasure, had to make one thing clear. "That doesn't mean I won't want to be kissed—often! I'm talking real often!"

She smiled at the desperate look on his face.

"I mean it, Liz. This man has to have something to keep him going till spring."

She laughed through her tears and watched as he slid his hand in his pocket to retrieve his hanky.

"There is one thing that I need to add. At any time, should either of us change our minds about this waiting period, we need to be honest with one another. God's Word tells us that it's all right to abstain for a while, but only if we are both in agreement. I'll talk to you if my needs change and I'll expect you to do the same. Agreed?"

"Yes, Kaleb, I agree." Curious, she asked, "When would you like to have the celebration?"

"If you're asking me, tomorrow would suit me just fine!"

Her lips disappeared inside her mouth in an attempt to ward off laughter. "Be serious! We can't build in the winter."

"That's true, but I can fell the trees and get them ready. I'm sure if I tell Jesse that I'll help when his turn comes, he'll be glad to put in the extra hours. We can set the date together, all right?"

"Yes!" She felt like a weight had been lifted off her shoulders. She could breathe again. Her husband had the strangest look on his face, so she asked, "What does that expression mean, Kaleb?"

"I want you to kiss me." A look of panic came over her—he wasn't sure why.

"I will if you close your eyes."

"That's silly!"

"Maybe so, but kissing you on our bed makes me nervous and you're the silly man who married me, so that's my offer. Take it or leave it."

Willing to do whatever was necessary to alleviate her fears, his eyes slid shut. Kaleb could feel his wife's presence as she scooted beside him, could feel her slender hands as they touched his face and then, softly, the smell of lavender brushed his nostrils, just before her tender lips pressed against his. The kiss was brief, but what it did for his heart was oh-so-sweet!

He Loves Me!

Chapter Twelve

Fears Denied

NEEDING AN EXTRA blanket for the sleigh, Kaleb knocked the snow off his bluchers before making his way through the narrow passage that led to their room. Without thinking, he swung open the bedroom door and was taken unawares by the vision who stood before him.

A deep flush covered Elizabeth's delicate face, and he told himself if he was any kind of gentleman he would look away—but he could not. Her slender frame was ensconced in a pink lacy underthing of sorts, the likes of which he had never seen. But oh, was it nice. The color against her soft creamy skin, the way her long golden tendrils framed her sides, took his breath away. Entranced in the wonder of the moment, Kaleb met her gaze as her timid voice came softly to his ears.

"Kaleb, turn around."

He complied, though not before saying, "Honey, I like

that outfit."

"I can see that. Now turn around." As soon as he did, Elizabeth slipped her dress over her head and asked, "Did you need something?"

He snatched a blanket off the quilt stand, sent her a playful wink, and said, "All set!" before turning to leave.

Kaleb's heart soared as he made his way to the barn, thrilled with how far he and Elizabeth had come in such a short amount of time. Their conversation the day before had done them both good. Getting some things out in the open had lightened her heart, alleviating many of her fears. Setting goals had eased both their minds. This waiting period would be difficult for him—possibly pure torture—but he would survive. Her sweet kisses would have to hold him. His love for her could not be self-seeking. He must be patient above all else. Time had a way of working things out, and he would give her all the time she needed.

While the hazy sky held the promise of snow, Kaleb was reasonably certain it would hold off until they got back, so he pulled the team around and opened the side door to collect his blushing bride. She was ready and waiting with her coat on, wearing a smile to match his own. Before she could deny him the pleasure, he had whisked her into his arms.

"Kaleb, you know this isn't necessary."

He pressed a kiss to her lips. "I do, but it's become a habit I'm in no hurry to break."

"You're in a funny mood. What's going on?"

He climbed in beside her, tucked the quilts around their legs and they were heading towards town before he took the time to reply.

"I always feel a little different around the holidays. This year's ... special."

She nodded in agreement and settled back for the long ride. The brisk morning air brushing against her skin was invigorating. She, having missed so much in the last month being stuck inside, was determined to take full advantage of their time away. For the first time in days, she wasn't frustrated about something or angry with anyone. In truth, it was quite liberating.

Kaleb took pleasure in watching her face light up as the scenery unfolded before her vigilant eyes. As she scanned the open lands, wild rabbits leapt across the icy fields. The way they scampered about, running to and fro, indecisive as to which direction they should go, made her wonder ... "Kaleb, do you think those rabbits have a destination in mind?"

"I'm sure they stay close to their homes."

She giggled. A young fawn, determined to follow its mother, kept toppling. The poor little spindly legs kept slipping through the crusty snow as it struggled for balance.

"Don't you love the way the snow weighs everything down, especially the pines?"

"It's pretty all right."

The view was breathtaking, but she had to wonder if she would ever see the season in the same way she used to. "Being lost in that storm was frightening. I wouldn't wish that experience on anyone."

Kaleb could see that she was struggling, but gave her a moment. She would say more when she was ready.

"This winter wonderland was our beginning, Kaleb. If you didn't find me, I wouldn't be your wife. I'd be home with the Lord."

Kaleb reached for her gloved hand. "That would have been my greatest loss."

She couldn't imagine life without him. "Mine too ...."

"There isn't a day that goes by that I don't thank the Lord for his protection over you."

She smiled up at him. With heartwarming clarity, Elizabeth was catching glimpses of the depth of Kaleb's feelings for her. He didn't marry her because it was the right thing to do; he genuinely cared—and the knowledge of it was wonderfully reassuring.

When he wrapped his arm around her, pulled her to him, and pressed a kiss to her brow, she saw no reason to move away. They enjoyed the rest of the trip in silence.

Kaleb stopped the team in front of the livery and called out to the smithy, motioning for him to come to where he and Elizabeth stood, "Jeff, I'd like you to meet my wife, Elizabeth."

"Your wife! You never told me you were engaged." He reached to shake Kaleb's hand. "I suppose congratulations are in order."

Turning to Elizabeth, Jeff couldn't resist giving her a hard time. "Lizzy, why didn't you tell me you were spoken for?"

She hadn't been, but then some things were better left unsaid.

"You got yourself a good man. Kaleb and I go back a long way."

She nodded, finding it strange that he didn't know she had been around Kaleb her whole life. "How have you been, Jeff?"

Kaleb listened to their light conversation. "I can see you already know each other."

Elizabeth thought Kaleb looked confused, maybe even a little uncomfortable with Jeff's familiarity. "Kaleb, Jeff takes care of Lady whenever I come into town and need to stay for a while."

"Oh. Well, um, well—good to see you again, Jeff. We won't be long." As Kaleb helped her across the street, his mind was back at the livery.

"Kaleb, is something wrong?"

His brow furrowed. "I still find it hard to believe that your parents let you do so much alone."

"I'm a grown woman. Why wouldn't they?"

"I just don't think it's safe, that's all."

This conversation had disaster written all over it, so she attempted to end it before it got too far off the ground. "Could we discuss this some other time?"

"That's fine."

When Elizabeth was confident the topic had been laid to rest, she latched onto Kaleb's arm and gave it a squeeze. There was something in his tender smile that eased her mind.

"Are you ready?"

She nodded. "Ready as I'll ever be." A brisk gust of wind caught her skirt as Kaleb reached for the brass handle and followed her in. The country store was alive with shoppers like themselves, and the aisles were packed with extras for the Christmas season.

"Kaleb, did you have something in mind for our parents?"

"Nothing specific. I thought it would be nice to get them something for their houses."

"Sounds good, but what?"

He scanned the room, looking for ideas. "Looks like Grant got some new lanterns in. My parents could use one for the sitting room. What about yours?"

"If they had a new one, they could use the old one in their bedroom." That was easy enough.

"Liz, would you mind finding something for the girls, while I look for the guys?"

Her eyes searched the room for a glimpse of Mrs. Grant. "That's fine, but if you see any flying crutches, you'll know I've changed my mind."

"Elizabeth!"

She rolled her eyes playfully. "I'm toying with you."

He glared down at her. "You shouldn't tease about things like that."

"Tell me, Sir, what did you do for excitement before you married me?"

Without answering her question, he leaned to whisper in her ear, "Be good, Young Lady, or I'll torture you when I get you home."

"You're not so scary with that smile on your face." She shrugged. "I'll do my best to accommodate."

"Don't forget to pick up your bath salts ... and there had better be at least two other items you need in that basket."

She bowed on his command and spoke as an obedient servant. "As you wish."

Kaleb chuckled as his sober-faced wife left his side. She wasn't a bit happy when he told her she had to pick out some things that she needed, but he managed to persuade her.

Spending her husband's money would not come easy—knowing he would do the choosing if she did not, spurred her on. *A second pair of warm socks would be nice, and I really could use another set of winter underclothes.* She meandered toward the feminine aisles, browsing through the different styles and colors of undergarments. Elizabeth started when she heard her maiden name squealed out in that high-pitched tone that could only belong to—Amy!

"Elizabeth Somers, what a nice surprise!" They shared a hug before the words began to fly.

"My father was in town and heard that you had gotten lost the day of the storm. I had no way of knowing if you were found or not. What did you do to your foot, Lizzy?"

"I broke it trying to get home that day. I have so much to tell you, Amy. I wish I could come for a visit, but we're busy getting ready for the holidays."

"That's okay. We can catch up when school resumes after the New Year." Elizabeth's eyes welled up with tears and Amy's heart plummeted. She reached for her friend's hand. "Lizzy, what's wrong?"

"It's a long story, so I'll give you the shortened version. I won't be coming back to school. Kaleb White found me in the blizzard and we were stuck in an abandoned cabin for a week. Rumors were started, and my father insisted that we marry."

"Lizzy, that's terrible!"

"It was at first. I've decided Kaleb's not so bad after all."

"I suppose if you had to get married, at least you were lucky enough to get stuck with one of the two good-looking guys in town."

"If it gets too unbearable, we could always go back to our original plan and skip town!"

Surprised by her admission, Amy had to ask, "Would you do that?"

"The way I feel right now, I wouldn't. Believe you me, the thought crossed my mind more than a time or two."

"I know what you're like, Lizzy. Forgive me, but I feel sorry for Kaleb. How will he ever manage to turn someone like you into a submissive housewife?"

They hadn't heard Kaleb's approach, so when his deep voice broke into their conversation they both jumped and flushed with embarrassment. "I'm not convinced it will happen either, but I can see why my wife chose you for a friend.

Amy asked, "Why is that?"

"Not many women blush as deeply as my Liz." He shook his head, astounded by their appearance. "I'd say you're both a nice shade of cherry."

Elizabeth slapped his arm. "You'd better be nice, Kaleb. Amy here is the friend I planned to travel with and we could always proceed with our plan."

Her admission shocked Amy. Kaleb, on the other hand, didn't seem surprised at all. Horrified, Amy asked, "Lizzy, did you tell him about our plans?"

"Yes, I'm sorry, I did. Now if we disappear, we're sure to have this massive farmer hot on our trail." The three of them burst into laughter.

"I don't know, Lizzy. It could be kind of fun if he brought along that handsome side-kick."

"Amy Potter! You know full well Jesse is not your type."

Amy glanced up at her friend's husband and took a chance. "Well, Kaleb isn't exactly yours, and you married him."

Kaleb chortled out loud—he had to pursue this further. "Let me see if I can get this right. I'm too big, strong—and don't forget bossy!"

Amy had to grab the counter for support—she was hysterical. "Lizzy, I can't believe you told him all those things!"

"I had to! I was sure that if I did, he'd send me home. Something went terribly wrong. He still wants me. I haven't figured him out, but I suppose as husbands go, he's not all that bad." Kaleb snuck his arm around his wife and gave her a hug.

Amy was impressed with Kaleb's ability to make light with a complete stranger. To her, this said a great deal about Kaleb's character. Her friend needed someone who could laugh at some of her blunders. She even began to wonder if Elizabeth hadn't fallen into a wonderful thing.

"I'm glad to meet you, Kaleb. I've heard good things about the White family. Feel free to ride along when Lizzy comes for a visit. You'd be more than welcome. Now, my pa might talk your ear off, so don't say you haven't been warned."

"I'll do that. I need to check on the leather for Dad, Liz. Let me know when you have your things collected. And here," he said as he handed her two pairs of boots he'd been holding behind his back. "Try these on and see if they'll go over your bad ankle."

Her eyes flew up at him. "Kaleb, I don't need boots."

His brow rose. "Is that so?"

"Yes."

"Then you won't mind lifting your skirt and showing us what you have on under it!"

Her eyes widened as her gaze went back and forth between her husband and Amy. She couldn't possibly do that. "Kaleb, my other boot will fit soon enough."

"No it won't. The one on your good foot is too small. Just try these on and don't be stubborn."

They were an awful price. She didn't want to cause a scene, so she put them in her basket. She even agreed to try them on, albeit reluctantly.

When Kaleb moved away, Amy scolded her friend. "Don't fight a good thing, Lizzy. Let him dote on you. You know those boots have been hurting your toes for months."

She grinned. "I suppose you're right. I shouldn't be so stubborn."

"I'd best get moving. My father will worry if I'm gone too long. It's a big relief to know you're safe and happy. You are happy, aren't you?"

"I'm trying to be. We could use your prayers. You know better than anyone I didn't plan to be married this young."

"God's timing isn't always our own, Lizzy." They hugged again and promised to visit after the holidays.

A sense of relief washed over Elizabeth as she watched Amy move away. *Thanks, Lord. I needed that.*

🌼 🌼 🌼

Elizabeth sighed with relief as the horses turned into their farm. The way the cloud formations were darkening on the way home set her on edge. Another storm was on the way.

Kaleb drove the sleigh into the barn. After setting the brake, he was about to jump down, when Elizabeth's softly-spoken words drew him back to his seat. He turned to find her gazing bashfully in his direction. "Liz, did you say what I think you did?"

She nodded, and slid toward him on the seat.

His spirit leapt within. He was enthralled with her request, but remained silent, allowing her to make the first move.

Her slender hands tugged lightly on the front of his jacket.

Finding no resistance their lips met once, tenderly, then again with sweet passion.

When his heart calmed, Kaleb asked, "Don't take me wrong. I'm elated that you changed your mind, but you told me before we left that I'd already had my allotment for the month."

"I was teasing, Kaleb. Besides, I owed you a real kiss from the day we were married. I'm afraid to think of what I might have done if you would have insisted on kissing me that day."

He chuckled lightly, admitting, "You looked like you might slug me. I didn't think it would be a good way to start our marriage. Just so you know, for future reference, you don't ever have to ask. I'm your husband, Liz. You have an open invitation to kiss me anytime you want."

"I've been thinking about it since yesterday. It's not quite as scary now that I don't have to worry about—well, you know."

Her reference to intimacy brought a smile to his face.

"You confuse me. You'll fight me tooth and nail on certain issues, yet when it comes to something as simple as a kiss, you're timid and shy."

"I can't help it! Kissing my brother's friend is strange enough. Knowing you're my husband is still intimidating."

"Well, I'm glad to be married to your brother's sister, and I'm growing more fond of her with every passing day. I'm sorry it feels odd to you, but I love your kisses. There are so many things about you that confuse me, but if I understood you completely it would take the mystery out of getting to know the real you. What fun would that be?"

Kaleb jumped down from the sleigh and lowered Elizabeth to her newly booted feet. He handed her the crutches, and his eyes followed her as she headed towards Lady, who had been nodding excessively since she'd entered the barn.

Hearing the swishing of hay on the barn floor, Kaleb glanced over to find his wife attempting to walk on her own. "Elizabeth, don't push it."

When her eyes met his disapproving glower, she simply smiled. "I'm just testing it out."

Kaleb went back to what he was doing, while Elizabeth looked around the barn, realizing as she did how little she really knew about the inner workings of the Whites' farm. Her broken ankle had been keeping her from working alongside of Kaleb, so it pleased her to find that the new boots gave her the added support she needed to move about.

The workload on a farm was never-ending. Since Elizabeth had toiled alongside of Jesse for so many years, farming was second nature to her. No matter how difficult the chore, she never complained. When given the choice of helping in the house or being with her brother, she would always choose to work with Jesse—Kaleb too, when he was around.

She hadn't talked to Kaleb about what her place would be in his parents' household. Perhaps when the time came for them to have their own home, she would be ready to assume her role as wife and, someday, mother.

Elizabeth knew this barn inside and out from all the times the White and Somers children had spent playing together. Still, she knew so little about how Kaleb and his father like to do things. To her, it was a travesty that she didn't know all the names of the horses, never mind the cows, cats and other critters. She would have to get on the ball and learn some things before spring hit.

Then there would be no time for such frivolities.

Elizabeth's favorite time of year had always been haying season. The two families would work together for days bringing in load after load of hay. Their fathers would always reward everyone's efforts with a huge dune of hay inside the barn. They would climb up the ladder into the loft, swing out on the rope tie that hung from the rafters, and land in the soft pillow of hay, sliding the rest of the way down. About the time everyone was dripping wet with sweat, their fathers would call a halt to their games and demand that everyone march down to the river for a cool swim. The laughter and fun their families shared over this simple celebration of a job well done held wonderful memories. Some traditions just had to be carried down from generation to generation and this was one of them.

Elizabeth, hearing her husband's approach, was drawn from her recollections. She eased against him as his arms slid around her. "Kaleb, I've been thinking. It might be fun to breed Lady. What do you think?"

"Is that what you want?"

"Your father's right. She does belong to both of us. Would we be able to keep her foal or would you have to sell it?"

"I'd like to keep it, but you can decide after it comes."

As if Lady knew they were talking about her, she pressed her nose into Elizabeth's coat, expecting her to pet her. "Could I go with you when you take her to the Bemis ranch?"

Kaleb turned her in his arms. "Liz, you'd have to trust me on this. I'm afraid Mr. Bemis is from the old way of thinking. You wouldn't be welcome."

Suspecting this she asked, "Do you like his stallion?"

"Yes, he's ebony with a white star. I think they'd make a nice foal."

She smiled. "You do what you think is best."

A sense of pride swelled within him. For Elizabeth, this was a huge step in his direction.

"Kaleb, I should collect the eggs before we head in."

"Leave them till tomorrow. The snow is coming down pretty hard. I'll have enough trouble keeping you from falling."

He was acting a little strange as they moved toward the door. At first she didn't question him. When he grabbed her and threw her over his shoulder like a sack of feed, she assumed he was clowning around. It didn't take long to find out that he was not. From her rather odd position, she asked, "Kaleb, what are you doing? Put me down!"

He shushed her.

She had no way of knowing what had put him in such a state, but his silence began to annoy her. She waited for a while, but she was hanging upside down. Growing impatient, she tried again. "Kaleb ..."

She had barely spoken his name when he commanded, in a whisper, "Hush, Liz. I can't hear!"

Her thoughts were anything but calm. *Maybe you should tell me what you're trying to hear—you're scaring me, Kaleb!* Within seconds, he'd moved out the barn door, barred it, and ran towards the house. Once inside, he set her down and went for his gun. She had never seen him like this.

"Elizabeth," he began as he reentered the room, "no matter what happens or what you hear, don't leave this house." She was so dazed he couldn't be sure if she heard him. Lifting her chin until their eyes met, he tried again, "Are you listening to me?"

"Kaleb, you're scaring me. Tell me what's wrong?"

"You know we have problems with stray dogs that run wild." She nodded, so he continued. "I heard them while we were in the barn. It sounds like a good-sized pack. I can't let them get to the livestock."

"You can't go out there alone!"

"I have to. I'll be fine."

She was not at all convinced, but what choice did he have? No one was here to help him.

"Promise me, Liz."

"I promise. Be careful, Kaleb." Though tears pooled in her eyes, she refused to let them fall. Elizabeth closed the door behind him. She felt so useless, standing in the safety of the house when someone should be helping him.

She paced the floor, praying frantically for his safety. Why was it so easy to put her own life in God's hands during the storm, and not her husband's in this? He was alone facing a pack of wild dogs, but God was still God. Nothing was beyond Him.

Shots were being fired off and on. She couldn't see Kaleb from the kitchen, so she headed for the sitting room. As she peered out the big picture window, she whispered her thanks. His parents' sleigh had just pulled up to the front of the house. The snow must have brought them home earlier than they had planned. Or was it the Lord? Must have been.

She met them at the door, and Samuel, noticing her tense expression, asked, "Elizabeth, what's wrong?"

"The wild dogs ... they're back. Kaleb took the gun, Dad—I don't know where he is. Please help him."

Samuel pulled her into his arms and tried to reassure her, "There is no need to worry, Elizabeth. This happens off and on. Kaleb is used to dealing with them."

Ruth led her to the couch so Samuel could be on his way. Elizabeth rambled on for a while, but Ruth let her. The more she talked, the calmer she became.

"I'm sure the men are fine, Honey. Don't you think it's a good idea to hold them up in prayer?"

"Yes," she admitted as she shrugged apologetically. "I have been praying, but I'm not sure if I've made much sense."

Ruth reached for Elizabeth's hand and began, "Father God, we thank you for watching over our husbands. Give them the wisdom they need to deal with whatever they come against. We entrust Kaleb and Samuel to Your safekeeping. Help us to put our trust in You. We love You, Lord, Amen."

Ruth, thinking that Elizabeth could use a diversion, made a suggestion. "Why don't we start on supper? The men will be hungry when they come in."

As Elizabeth and Ruth walked towards the kitchen, Elizabeth felt the need to explain. "I'm sorry about the mess we left. Kaleb planned to wash the dishes while I was cooking. I'll get them out of the way before I help with supper."

"That's fine. Did you and Kaleb enjoy your trip to town?"

"We did. I saw Amy at the store. It was so good to talk to her. Did you and Dad have a nice visit with the Coxs?"

"Yes. Did Mary Lou tell you she's engaged to the Williams' son, George?"

"No. Did she say when they plan to tie the knot?"

"Sometime in the spring."

"I've always thought spring was a wonderful time for a wedding. The early flowers that are in bloom make a nice bouquet.

Ruth could hear disappointment in Elizabeth's tone and wondered if these were things she had wanted for her own wedding. She understood. Just like Elizabeth, she'd had no time to prepare for her own nuptials.

Elizabeth dried the last bowl and put it away. "Mom, I've got a hankering for something sweet. Would you mind if I make some dessert?"

Ruth smiled. "Kaleb won't complain about that. What'd you have in mind?"

"Since we're having pies for Christmas, how about oatmeal cookies with chocolate in them? I'm not sure why, but Kaleb bought enough chocolate to keep us going all winter."

Ruth smiled. "Sounds wonderful. I haven't had anything chocolate in a while." Ruth didn't miss the way her daughter-in-law peered out the window every chance she could. Her actions told Ruth much about Elizabeth's changing heart toward Kaleb. As a mother wanting her son to find love in his marriage, she was encouraged. "Lizzy, there's no telling how long Kaleb and Samuel will be ... would you like to go ahead and eat?"

"No, you go ahead if you want to. I don't think I could swallow a bite until they come through the door. I'd rather keep myself busy, so if you have any unfinished gifts I'm more than willing to help."

Ruth was elated with her offer. "There's hand work that needs to be done on Sarah's dress. Do you mind?"

"Not at all."

"Honey, does your mom struggle as much as I do trying to

stay caught up around the holidays?"

"Yes. She always says, too much to do, too little time."

"If you'd like to get your foot up, I'll gather everything and bring them to you." Only moments had passed when Ruth bustled back into the sitting room continuing their conversation as if they never parted.

"Lizzy, I like your new boots. Are they comfortable?"

"Yes. They give my ankle the extra support I need to walk. Kaleb didn't think you'd mind if I wear them in the house."

"Don't give it another thought."

Ruth handed Elizabeth the sweetest red dress. "Mom, this is adorable."

"I hope she'll like it. Here, let me show you where I left off. I have the hem and the cuffs all pinned up. They just need to be stitched. If you finish that, I have the buttons in my room."

Elizabeth had no trouble picking up where Ruth had left off, and they were enjoying the rare opportunity to visit without anyone else around.

"Samuel mentioned that he and Kaleb would be heading into town day after tomorrow ... wonder if the snow will keep them home."

Elizabeth glanced at the window. "Nothing would convince me to chance going out in another storm."

"I can understand why. Isn't it wonderful to sit back and see the way God protected you throughout the entire ordeal?"

"Now, yes. But this marriage definitely threw me for a whirl."

Ruth finished her next stitch and looked up at her daughter-in-law. "I'm beginning to notice little things that make me wonder if you've changed your mind. You seem happier. Are you, Lizzy?

Or is it my imagination?"

"I'm getting there. Kaleb's not alone anymore, if that's what you're asking. I want this marriage to work as much as he does."

"Samuel and I were introduced by our fathers but I didn't know my papa had offered my hand to him until the day we were married. At least you have the advantage of having known each other for so many years."

Elizabeth offered a halfhearted grin. "I'm not so sure it's an advantage."

Although Ruth wondered what she meant by that, she didn't want to pry. "If I can do anything other than pray, you let me know."

"I will." Elizabeth had finished one cuff and was starting on to the next, when she asked, "There is something I've been wondering about. Is Dad always with you when you go out?"

"That depends—why do you ask?"

"Just curious. Kaleb's paranoid about me going anywhere alone. He doesn't even want me going to my parents' without him. I thought maybe it has something to do with how Dad is with you. Guess not."

"Give him time. It wasn't easy for Kaleb finding you the way he did."

"I kind of thought that."

Elizabeth had a few more stitches to do on the last cuff when she looked over at her mother-in-law and smiled. The men were coming in the back door and they were laughing—a sure sign that all had gone well. The ladies set their work aside and joined them in the kitchen.

"You two don't appear to be any worse for the wear," Elizabeth said, and then asked, "Are they gone?"

Kaleb kissed her rosy cheeks before responding to her question with a desperate plea, "We're starving! The aroma in here is killing me, so can we talk and eat at the same time?"

The men washed up while Ruth and Elizabeth put the food on the table. The four of them joined hands, and Samuel offered a prayer of thanks.

As the food was being passed, Kaleb filled them in. "The pack was larger than I anticipated. Several of them won't be giving us any more trouble, but some got away."

"What?" Elizabeth didn't find this comforting in the least.

"Won't they come back?"

Kaleb nodded. "They could, so until we tell you otherwise, you and Mom should have one of us with you when you go out to the barn. Those dogs are wild, Liz. They won't think twice about coming after you."

Kaleb had no more swallowed his last bite when his narrowed gaze flipped back and forth between Elizabeth and his mother. "Did I smell something chocolate when we came in the back door—or was it wishful thinking?"

Elizabeth's eyes flew to her mother-in-law, who was grinning from ear to ear.

"All right you two, hand it over!" His wife taunted him.

"I don't know, Mom. Should we make him wait?" Kaleb pulled her against him so fast she chortled with glee.

"If you know what's good for you, you'll give it up."

She scowled at the desperate man who held her in a vice-like grip. "This is a fine way to thank your wife when she makes you a special treat."

Samuel shook his head. "You might as well bring it out, Lizzy, before he really gets ugly."

Elizabeth's eyebrow arched. "You mean he gets worse?" Her tone was incredulous.

"Only if chocolate is involved."

Kaleb sported a triumphant grin—confident he had won the prize. Elizabeth, on the other hand, was thrilled with her newfound knowledge. It could prove to be invaluable in the future. With pleasure, she retrieved the plate from the cupboard and placed it in the center of the table.

"Hey!" Kaleb said after biting off half a cookie, "these are really good!" He held it up for further inspection, then proceeded to devour the rest of it and several more.

The men cleared the table before going off to play cards, while the ladies worked together on the dishes and discussed their thoughts for the coming holiday.

Elizabeth was fighting sleep when they joined the men, but her determination to complete the handwork on Sarah's Christmas dress kept her from giving into her need for rest. After securing the last button, she said good night to everyone, and went off to bed.

"Kaleb," Elizabeth asked when he join her in the room, "is it extra cold tonight, or just me?"

"It's just you. Give me a minute. I'll warm you up."

The changes taking place in Elizabeth's heart where Kaleb was concerned pleased her. The security she was finding in his arms had taken their relationship to a different level. Her fears were dissipating, and the wall of defense she had built between them was crumbling. For a time she lay there, listening to the beat of his heart and thanking the Lord for His protection over him. "Kaleb?"

"Hmm?"

"I'm glad you weren't hurt out there today."

"Dad said you were pretty upset when he got home. I'm sorry I had to leave you like that ... couldn't be helped."

Peering up, she found his eyes on her. "I'm used to my dad and brothers helping each other when something like this happens. I didn't like you being out there alone. I could hear the dogs growling and shots being fired, but I had no way of knowing if you were all right. Mom and I prayed ... that helped."

"I appreciate your prayers."

Seconds passed. "Liz?"

"Hmm?"

"Would it scare you if I kissed you?"

She had to be honest. "Yes ..."

As much as he wanted to press her, he knew she felt more vulnerable in their bed.

"But I'd like you to anyway."

Kaleb sighed as he caressed her warm face, savoring the pleasure she found in his every touch.

The indescribable way his kisses made her feel were opening windows—windows that were releasing her fears and replacing them with something entirely new.

Elizabeth wondered if her in-laws had ulterior motives when they announced at breakfast that they would be going to stay a few nights with her family. In truth, it didn't matter. She looked forward to the time alone with her husband.

On the second night Kaleb helped her set up the big tub. After a nice relaxing bath, she dressed in her nightclothes before making her way to the sitting room. She threw another log on the already-burning embers and stoked up the flames. Shivering, she huddled close to the radiating warmth.

Kaleb joined her after his own bath, picked up her brush, retrieved the afghan and wrapped it around her. She couldn't help but smile as she took in his appearance. *I like him like this,* she thought. *That wavy blonde hair all askew, and his shirt missing. He's so at ease in my presence. Are we getting their, Lord?*

"Liz, if you sit in the chair, I'll brush your hair."

"You don't mind?"

"Not at all." Her lids slid shut as he worked the brush through her damp tangles. Every moment they spent together was drawing them closer, binding them in ways she could not define. Her decision to open her heart to this man had altered her every response.

Her thoughts went back to the novel they were reading, *The Last of the Mohicans.* She was dying to know what would happen next. If it were up to her, she wouldn't have put it down until she had finished it. Not Kaleb. The suspense didn't seem to bother him. In spite of their differences, they both had a deep appreciation for Cooper's ability to present a true picture of the good and evil that exists in every race.

Growing up in Detroit, she had heard so many stories about farms raided by renegade Indians. Entire families had been wiped out. Women had been taken captive, and men savagely killed.

But who bothered to write about how we took over their lands, and devoured their food? No wonder they fought back. They had a right to protect their way of life. She couldn't understand why people couldn't live in harmony as descendants of Adam—equals in God's eyes. Kaleb's words broke into her pondering.

"If I can read your thoughts, will it earn me a kiss?" Her heart surged as Kaleb set the hairbrush aside, drew her into his arms and brushed the tip of his nose against hers.

"One never knows."

"You're thinking about Cooper's book."

Her mouth dropped open. "How did you? ..."

Kaleb didn't wait for her to finish. He gave in to his desire and was astounded—delighted—overwhelmed by her response.

Where her longing came from she did not know, but she suddenly needed him, wanted him as much as he did her. She had to touch him, run her fingers through his hair. Heaven help her, she lost herself in his delicious kisses, returned every one, yearned for the next.

The enchantment ended as swiftly as it came, leaving husband and wife content in one another's arms.

Moments passed before his hazy thoughts had cleared enough to say, "Just think, Liz, when we're in our own place, we can have quiet nights like this all the time. Won't it be nice?"

"I suppose." Her feelings, so new and undefined, thrashed around inside her. She cared. She cared deeply. She could not deny that she found him desirable, his kisses wonderful, his hugs beyond description. But why did she not long for more?

With Kaleb, there was no containing his deepening desire. She saw it in his eyes every time he held her gaze. He wanted a real marriage in every way. She whispered a prayer. *Give me time, Lord. I don't want to be afraid of what lies ahead—I merely want to be ready.*

"Liz, you're awfully quiet. Are you all right?" The nodding of her head did not convince him that she was. "Honey, please don't think I'm trying to rush you. My feelings are growing all the time, but I'm more than content with the plan we've laid out."

Why did she have to be so transparent? "I'm realizing a little more each day how much I enjoy having you in my life. I like being your wife, but I don't want things to move too fast."

His reassuring smile eased her doubts. "Thank you for telling me ... can I ask you something?"

"Anything!"

Kaleb stooped down in front of her and reached for her hands. "If you and I were only courting and I was to ask you to be my wife, knowing how you feel right now, what would you say?"

An illuminating smile lit her face. "I'd say yes. But, I'd still make you wait until spring!"

"Hold that thought for just a minute."

She grimaced. "But ... where are you going?"

He flashed her a smile. "I'll be right back."

She could hear him fumbling around in their room and wondered what he was up to. The second he came back, he snatched her from the rocker and sat with her in his favorite chair.

"I planned to give you this on Christmas day, but knowing you would accept my proposal makes today special." Kaleb held out a little box that was tied with a pink satin bow. Before placing it in her hand, he asked, "Liz, will you wear these rings as an outward sign to the world that you're my wife?"

Through glassy eyes, she removed the ribbon. Lifting the lid, she found two rings; one, a golden wedding band, the other a ruby ring with diamonds on either side, in a delicate gold filigree setting. "Kaleb, they're beautiful!"

She hesitated a beat, maybe two. "Yes! I will wear your rings to declare to the world that I have chosen you, Kaleb White, to be my husband."

He liked her choice of words. As he slipped the rings on her finger, the tenderness they shared was only a glimpse of what the future could hold. Basking in the warmth they were finding in each other's arms, neither wanted this moment to end, but Elizabeth's protesting stomach broke into the silence with loud rumblings.

"You sound a little hungry, My Sweet."

"It's an hour past supper."

He chuckled, tweaked her nose, and asked, "Would you like some more of that delicious soup you made for dinner?"

"Yes. Give me a few minutes and I'll warm it up."

A log shifted in the fire. "Let your hair dry, Liz. I'm sure I can heat the soup up without doing too much damage to it."

Elizabeth couldn't help but smile as Kaleb moved away. Her lids slid shut as she thought about all that had just transpired. She drifted off and awoke to Kaleb calling, "Liz, supper's hot."

After a luxurious stretch, she replaced the afghan. "I'm coming." The wonderful aroma heightened her senses as she strolled into the kitchen to find her husband in his mother's apron dishing up the soup.

"That apron suits you."

He glanced over his shoulder and grinned, "As long as I don't get too creative, right?"

"You're a wise man." She tore off a bite of bread and popped it in her mouth.

"The water's hot. I'll let you make the tea while I get the butter out of the cold cellar."

When he reentered the kitchen, she asked, "Kaleb, when did you buy the rings?"

"The ruby belonged to Grandma White. She gave it to me last summer and told me in no uncertain terms that I'd best have a wife wearing it by the time she came back. I should have given it to you sooner, but I wasn't sure you'd wear it."

Since Kaleb wasn't courting anyone, she found this strange. "How often do you see her?"

"Once a year. I told her she was dreaming. Now I wonder if she knew something I didn't. I picked the band up this morning."

Elizabeth's thoughts trailed off. "I think I'll like this Grandma of yours, Kaleb. Everything I hear about her tells me we'd be close."

"I want you to meet her, but don't set your expectations too high. My grandfather was extremely abusive. She lived with his tyranny for so long, it has made her a bitter woman."

"Then we should be including her in our prayers."

He looked at his wife and reached for her hand. "I couldn't agree more. I'd love to see her set free."

"So would I." They did include her in their prayers before sharing their simple meal.

"Liz, what would you like to do this evening?"

"Oh, I don't know. Surprise me."

His wheels were turning.

"We should feed the animals, don't you think?"

"That goes without saying. I suppose I can do that while you clean up this huge mess."

She looked around the room and smiled. All of the bathing things were put away, and there were only a few dishes. "I think I can handle this without too much trouble. Did Mom and Dad take the cobbler I made with them?"

He grimaced. "Elizabeth, please tell me you know me better than that?"

She giggled. "You don't part with sweets easily, do you?"

"No, Ma'am! I hid it in the pantry for a snack later."

"Sounds good."

Elizabeth had time to do the dishes and mend one of Kaleb's shirts before he strutted into the sitting room in his stocking feet. He had his Bible in his hand, so more than likely they were going to read together. Whatever he had in mind, he was heading her way. He set her mending aside, reached for her hand, pulled her out of the rocker, and led her back to his chair.

With Elizabeth snuggled in his arms, Kaleb opened his worn Bible and explained his thoughts. "Normally couples meet with Pastor for counseling before their wedding day. I know we're having to handle things backwards, but if you're in agreement, I'd like us to start in Genesis and work our way through passages that pertain to husbands and wives."

"All right."

Kaleb read through the whole creation story, but verses twenty-one through twenty-four held her thoughts captive. It was one thing to read these passages when they didn't pertain to her. Now that they did, they gave her much to think about.

" *'For Adam there was not found a help meet for him. And*

the Lord God caused a deep sleep to fall upon Adam, and he slept: and he took one of his ribs, and closed up the flesh instead thereof; And the rib, which the Lord God had taken from man, made he a woman, and brought her unto the man. And Adam said, This is now bone of my bones, and flesh of my flesh: She shall be called Woman, because she was taken out of Man. Therefore shall a man leave his father and his mother, and shall cleave unto his wife: and they shall be called one flesh.' "

When Kaleb closed his Bible, he tried to lighten her pensive mood. "God must have taken my smallest rib when he made you."

She knew what he was doing and couldn't withhold a smile. "Does it bother you that I'm small, Kaleb?"

"No, but I'll feel better when you put some weight back on."

"I'm not worried. Mom said she was built like me until after she had children."

Kaleb smiled as a deep shade of crimson graced her face. "I know you won't agree, but I hope I never run out of ways to make this happen." His hand caressed her warm cheek.

Flustered, she said, "If I would just think before I speak, I'd quit embarrassing myself."

"Honey, promise you won't do that. If you're embarrassed, wait until we're in the dark, ask me to turn around, or write me a letter. Remember what we just read. God knew that it wasn't good for man to be alone. How can we help one another if the lines of communication are broken?" She was holding back. "Will you come to me when you can talk about whatever's bothering you?"

She nodded, so he left it alone. *Help her to know my heart, Father.*

"Liz, we've never talked about children. Have you ever

thought about having them someday?"

His big brown eyes held her captive. "I have on occasion."

"So you're not opposed?"

"No, Kaleb, I'm not. My only drawback is how you view me."

His brow furrowed. "What do you mean?"

"Think about it. As long as you know where I am, you're fine. It's when you don't that you overreact—as if I'm still a child needing your protection. When we do decide to have a family, I want our children to see me as a mother who can lead them. If you don't see me that way, you'll confuse them and they'll take their cues from you."

He would love to tell her how wrong she was, but he knew how much he struggled with this issue. "Liz, you have to admit, you do tend to be carefree and daring, willing to take chances I would never want you to take."

"We approach life in different ways, Kaleb. I accept that you are the way you are—I find comfort in it. I wouldn't want you to change on account of me. But you can't expect me to be like you either. We need to find a way to meet each other halfway. God made me who I am for a reason. I shouldn't have to suppress who I am because of your fears. I know you care—you show me that every day—but you don't see me as a woman with needs and desires of my own."

With a raised brow and a tilt of his head, he said, "In some ways I do."

She rolled her eyes. "Let me guess! When you kiss me?"

"How'd you know?"

"Just a hunch." She gave him a moment to sort this out.

"I know God sustained you in that storm, and led me to

you. As your husband, I feel accountable. I know I'm holding on too tight, but when I don't know where you are, I see you lying helpless in that mound of snow. Can you give me time to pray about this?"

"Of course."

Wanting to do something unselfish for his wife, Kaleb led her to their room and lit the lamp. When she sat on the bed, he bent down and removed her slippers. As he looked up, he could see that his actions were scaring her. That was the last thing he wanted. "Liz, I should have explained. I was thinking you were overdue for another back rub. Sound good?"

"Sounds wonderful."

The silent couple readied for bed and climbed in. When Kaleb asked her to roll over, she didn't have to be asked twice. How could she not be at ease with his tenderness? Kaleb was pleased when after a time she sat up and announced that it was his turn.

Lying on his stomach, he found himself relaxed as a cat, under her gentle yet effective touch.

A strange noise in the dusky room set Elizabeth's nerves on edge. When she realized that it was only Kaleb snoring, she giggled softly. Unlike her husband, she was wide-awake and somewhat hungry. So she picked up the lamp and went to the kitchen.

The peach cobbler she made earlier was calling her name. At first she felt guilty even thinking about eating sweets without Kaleb, but she reassured herself that it wasn't as if he didn't know it was there. Elizabeth poured the rest of the warm tea into a cup, grabbed the peach delight from the pantry, dished up a piece and sat at the table, savoring every bite. She salvaged her guilty conscious by saving her snoring husband the final piece.

Since she had never been alone in this room at night, she found the unfamiliar sounds in the dimly-lit kitchen a tad unsettling. On second thought, it was more than a tad. The wind was howling like a pack of wolves on the prowl, and when she glanced towards the window she could have sworn she saw something move. On shaky limbs, she stood and moved that way. After scolding herself for giving into her fears, curiosity pushed her forward. A quick peek revealed the winter winds whipping the tree limbs to and fro. The massive maples and oaks were bending and swaying to the rhythmic movements of the variable billowing breeze. She knew herself well—if she allowed her overactive mind to wander, she wouldn't sleep a wink. Had she gone through with her original plan and moved out on her own, she'd be dealing with severe weather like this—alone. She shuttered at the thought, and made her way to her husband's side.

Elizabeth covered Kaleb with the quilt, blew out the lamp, and for a moment, sat down beside him. Since he had fallen asleep before their evening prayers, she prayed alone.

"I come before you Holy Father, with a grateful heart. Thank you for bringing this man into my life, and for giving us this time to draw closer. My father was right, Lord; Kaleb is a good man. I have to believe that if we continue to open our hearts to each other, the possibilities are endless. Thank you that all things work together for good and for guiding our lives."

At this moment, Elizabeth could envision why her husband liked to watch her when she slept. Knowing he was unaware gave her the opportunity to really look at him. His deep-set lids were concealing those big brown eyes that could expose her every thought. She remembered running her fingers through his wavy blonde hair during that wonderful kiss. Without actually touching him, she ran her finger just above his brow, his nose, then his jaw. When it came to his lips she couldn't resist. With feather-like moves she touched their thick velvety softness, yearning to kiss them, while not desiring to wake him. When she lay down beside him, she felt his comforting limbs draw her in. How did he know she was there? Apparently he sensed her presence. Elizabeth still had her vulnerable moments, but Kaleb's gentle ways showed her repeatedly that her fears were unwarranted, and must be denied.

He Loves Me!

Chapter Thirteen

The Woods

ELIZABETH, HEARING HER brother ride in on Shadow, finished buttoning her coat, picked up the package of food from the table, and moved out the back door to greet him. "Good morning, Jesse ...."

Her ear-to-ear grin made him smile. "I can see you're thoroughly depressed about something. Does this mean you're going?"

After he dismounted, she hugged him tight. "If you knew what I had to go through to convince that friend of yours to let me go, you'd be more understanding."

"So, where is Kaleb, anyway?"

"In the barn saddling the horses. He wanted to bring the sleigh, but I helped him change his mind." Jesse laughed at the devious look she sent his way.

"I won't ask how you managed that. I am surprised he's

letting you ride that far with your ankle the way it is."

"My ankle is fine. I merely told him that if ..." Her words were cut off when Kaleb snuck up behind her, kissed her cheek and finished her sentence for her.

"... I didn't let her ride alone, she would be riding with her brother."

Jesse's brow arched into his hairline. "Oh, you did, did you? Now what makes you think I want to ride all the way to the Woods' with an imp hanging on my back?"

"If you're bent on picking on me, I'll head over to Mom and Dad's, and you two can go alone."

Kaleb leaned over and spoke for her ears alone. "You'll do no such thing. Go ahead and get the horses, they're saddled in the barn. I need to run back in the house and tell Dad something ...."

Elizabeth gladly did his bidding. After securing the cookies and muffins on the back of Lady's saddle, she led the horses out by Jesse, who was now back on Shadow. Had Kaleb not drawn Jesse's attention away from her, Jesse would have noticed that she handed him Lady's reins instead of Lightning's.

She didn't know what Kaleb would say, but she wanted to ride Lightning in the worst way, so she attempted to mount. Why she had never realized the vast difference in Lightning and Lady's height was beyond her. It took great effort to reach the stirrup, and while it didn't help that Lightning pranced about, she wasn't about to let that stop her.

"Elizabeth!" Kaleb bellowed, as he ran towards her. Lightning was moving away of his own accord and she brought him easily to a halt. Her soft plea reached her husband's ears as he arrived at her side. "Please Kaleb, just for a little while? I'll stay close—I promise."

He should have made her stay home for even trying to mount Lightning with her sore ankle. But how could he deny her when he knew how much she longed to ride his horse?

Jesse was in the background, taking in the entire exchange. Kaleb's weakness with his sister warmed his heart, yet Jesse knew what Kaleb was like. He would not take chances where Elizabeth was concerned. If Kaleb gave in, Jesse would be surprised.

Elizabeth regretted having pressed him in front of her brother. "Kaleb, you know Lightning. If you don't think I should, if you really don't, I'll wait."

Her acquiescence pleased him. "See how he does. No one else has ever been able to ride him, so stay close." He placed his hands over hers and gave them a squeeze. "Do you need me to adjust the stirrups?"

"No, I don't use them." She waited until their eyes met before adding, "Thanks!"

"Just don't make me regret it."

"I won't." Her gentle smile was followed by her husband's placating wink.

The snow would keep her from testing him for speed, but the long ride would give her the chance to get to know Lightning better.

About an hour into the trip, Kaleb forced himself to stop watching his wife so closely. She handled his horse with ease. He never should have doubted her ability.

Kaleb and Jesse talked on and on about farming and the upcoming changes they were hoping to make—a subject that held minimal interest for Elizabeth. Before long she was bored with their conversation and quit fighting Lightning's desire to take the lead.

The couple they were going to see had been members of their church since it began. Jacob and Anna were in their mid-to-late seventies and a constant example to those who had the pleasure of knowing them. Never having had grandparents close by, Elizabeth was pleased when they introduced themselves as Grandpa and Grandma. She loved their sweet spirits, their silky white hair, and the feel of their soft skin, but more than anything about them, the love and devotion they held for each other, after all these years.

Elizabeth found the difference in Lightning and Lady's dispositions astounding. She enjoyed the opportunity to ride him but found he wasn't trustworthy like Lady. She had to be constantly on her guard, and eventually grew weary of his antics. By the time they reached Jacob and Anna's home, she was more than ready for their journey to end.

Kaleb smiled at his yawning wife, reached for her waist, and helped her dismount. Holding her close, he asked, "Didn't get enough sleep last night?"

"I was up for a while after you fell asleep."

He nodded. "You haven't ridden this far in a while. Are you going to wobble if I let you go?"

She hated to admit it, even to him. More than likely she would crumple to the ground if he unhanded her. "Can you keep your arm around me till I'm sure."

"Absolutely."

"Kaleb, did Jesse get the package?"

"Already in the house."

Jacob and Anna were thrilled that Elizabeth had come along.

After hugs were shared all around, Anna informed her guests that dinner was ready.

Elizabeth poured the tea and coffee, added the muffins and cookies she brought to the array of foods already on the table, and took a seat between Anna and Kaleb.

Jacob led them in prayer. While the men discussed the work Jacob needed help with in the barn, the women talked about their latest endeavors.

Elizabeth did some investigating of her own and found several things that could use her attention. "Grandma, would you like me to help with the dishes, or should I try to get rid of those cobwebs that are too high for you to reach?"

Anna glanced up at the ceiling and giggled. It had been a long time since she'd been able to see to them. "I don't know, Honey. Don't you think you should just relax and visit for a spell?"

Elizabeth knew what she was thinking. "No, Grandma. My ankle's doing better, and besides, I came to help. We don't want those spiders getting too settled in their new home, now do we?"

"I suppose not. The broom's in the corner, Lizzy, and the hand towels and string are on the shelf."

Grandma started the dishes as soon as Elizabeth removed the spider webs over her worktable. The ceiling was low in their bedroom, so that was easy enough, but the sitting room held its challenges. The rafters were high. Apparently, the small home had been built so that another floor could be added at a later date.

"Grandma," Elizabeth asked as she moved back into the kitchen. "You don't happen to have a ladder, do you? I can't reach the webs in the parlor."

She turned to Elizabeth. "There's one hanging on the back of the house. You'll have to be extra careful though. It's old and I'm not so sure it's any more stable than I am."

"I will."

She was making her way around the room when Kaleb strolled in and startled her. "Elizabeth! What are you doing?"

His words, though softly spoken, annoyed her nonetheless. She scowled. "What does it look like I'm doing?"

"I'm not talking about the webs. You shouldn't be on that rickety ladder. Get down from there before you fall."

"You know, Kaleb, I really do wonder how I've managed to stay alive these sixteen years without you guiding my every step. Honestly! I think I can handle this! Go back to whatever it was you were doing and pretend you didn't see me!" She turned away from his insistent glare and continued to work, hoping he would leave. She should have known better.

"Kaleb! she shrieked when she heard his approach. "Go away! ... Quit!" She tried to shoo him off, but knew it was a lost cause when he wrapped his arms around her legs, and she fell across his shoulder. She laughed so hard she could barely speak.

Kaleb could hear Anna snickering and turned to find her leaning against the doorjamb. "Grandma, if it's all right with you, I need to borrow your bedroom for a minute."

"You go right ahead, Kaleb—long as you don't hurt my girl."

"Grandma!" Elizabeth pleaded, "You're supposed to be on my side."

"I'm sorry, Honey. I learned a long time ago not to get in the middle of marital squabbles."

"I won't hurt her, Grandma. I'll just tickle the sass out of her ... what do you think?"

"I suppose you know what's best." Anna went back to her dishes, laughing with Elizabeth, who was squealing in delight.

As Anna listened to her grandchildren's antics, her heart fluttered with joy as memories of her younger years with Jacob came to the fore. He had a tendency to be protective like Kaleb, but he too was playful at heart. She was pleased to see that God had given Kaleb someone like Elizabeth, who would lighten his heart.

"Kaleb," Elizabeth said, as he opened the door. "I really am fine to finish this alone."

"You'll be careful?"

The roll of her eyes brought that glare from him, which told her she had better answer him—and quick. "I will!"

"That's better." He kissed her cheek and turned to go back through the kitchen. "Grandma, I came in for the extra hammer. Know where it is?"

"You passed it on the way in. On the shelf next to the door."

"Thanks," he said, yelling back before he moved out the door, "Let me know if she gives you any trouble!"

"Kaleb, Kaleb, Kaleb," Anna murmured as she ambled into the sitting room. "What are we going to do with that husband of yours, Lizzy?"

Elizabeth smiled from her place on the ladder. "I don't know. My sides hurt. I'm not sure if it's from laughing so hard, or his tickles."

"He seems so happy, Honey. Are you happy, too?"

"For the most part. We have fun together, but we need time to work out the details. We didn't exactly have time to plan for this marriage."

"I'm glad you're together. He needed a wife, and I can't think of anyone who's better qualified for the job."

"Thanks Grandma. It means a great deal coming from you."

"Tell me, Lizzy. Are you anxious for spring, so you can get into your own place?"

"To be honest, I'm not. You might say I'm not trusting the Lord to work them out, but I have insecurities about our relationship."

"I can understand. My Jacob tends to be overbearing like Kaleb."

Anna's insightfulness surprised Elizabeth. "How long did it take him to begin to trust you?"

"It didn't happen over night. I talked to my mother about it, but she insisted that too much attention was better than the alternative. I agree with her now, although back then I wasn't so sure. Give him time, Honey. For three years Kaleb has longed for a wife. Now that he has you, he needs to see that your life is in God's hands, not his."

"I'm sure you're right."

"We don't always understand the overall picture, but God wants us to be content in whatever situation life puts us in. Learn what He's trying to teach you through these difficult times and you'll be a better person for having gone through them. Praise Him for the good you can find in every experience, and never forget what Pastor is always telling us—life is a journey, preparing us for eternity."

"Everyone has been telling me the same thing. Do you think it might have something to do with the fact that the people whose opinions I trust most are studying the book of Philippians with Pastor?"

Anna beamed in the light of her comment. "I do!"

"I'll put the ladder back so we can get to these other chores."

Anna hated to see the children working so hard every time they came, but the dust was building up on the curtains and she would love to get them washed and hung back up. While Elizabeth went to haul more water from the creek, Anna set the pots to boil.

"Lizzy," Jesse scolded as he came toward her and took the full buckets from her drooping arms. "You could have asked us to do this!"

"I did fine until I was halfway up the path. That incline got to me."

"Will this be enough, or do you need more?"

"Two more should do it."

Elizabeth took the curtains down, carried them outside to shake the worst of the dust off, and had them soaking in the sudsy water before her brother came back inside.

"How are the repairs coming along, Jesse?"

"We've got another hour of work before we'll have to head back. Can you be ready?"

Anna answered for her. "I'll be sure she is, and since you'll be missing supper I'll make some ham and cheese sandwiches for the road."

"Sounds good to me," Jesse said as he moved back out the door.

"Grandma, could you do me a favor while I finish the curtains?"

"You name it, Honey."

"Lightning was acting up when I tried to mount him, and the seam on the back of my coat gave way. It needs mending. Would you mind?"

"Not at all." Anna took Elizabeth's coat from the hook, got settled in the rocker, and had her needle threaded before she took a better look at the area that needed mending. The threadbare fabric held no warmth, and the tear was beyond repair. She could patch it, but she had another solution that would be even better.

Without a word, Anna went to the storage closet on the far side of her bedroom. If memory served her correctly, she had something that might fit her slim granddaughter.

"Elizabeth," Anna said as she came back into the parlor. "Do me a favor and try this on."

Inquisitive, Elizabeth peeked in the box. "What is it?"

"I'll tell you if you'll promise not to make a fuss and accept it as a gift from the Lord."

"Grandma, you shouldn't be giving me things."

"Now, Lizzy," she teased, "do I need to call that husband of yours in and tell him you're giving me a hard time?"

"Grandma!"

"Well, do I?"

"No." Elizabeth conceded, tickled by her persistence.

"Then try it on. Jacob had it made for me last Christmas and it's too small. He'd love to know you could make use of it."

"Are you sure?"

Anna pulled the beautiful brown wool coat out of the box and Elizabeth sighed as she fingered the material. "Oh, Grandma. It's so nice and warm."

"I know. Jacob has wonderful taste in fabrics and we both know Carolyn's a talented seamstress. I'm always complaining about being cold, so she added extra warmth. Well ... don't make me wait. Try it on."

Elizabeth did as she bade her. It thrilled Anna to see how nicely it fit. "Lizzy, if you'd like to get a closer look, I have a full-length mirror inside the left door to my armoire." Anna couldn't resist following her, elated with the pleasure she saw in Elizabeth's eyes as she caught her reflection in the mirror.

Wrapping her arms around herself, she turned to Anna. "I can't thank you enough! The coat I've been wearing belonged to my grandma on my mother's side. She wore it for several years before she went home to be with the Lord. I'm afraid it's seen better days."

"I noticed. I know it's dear to you, so perhaps you could cut it up and start a braided rug for your new home."

"That's a wonderful idea."

"Good."

Elizabeth gave Anna a great big thank you hug before removing the coat and going back to iron the curtains. When they were hung on the windows, she took all the rugs outside, laid them over the porch banister and gave them a good beating. While they aired out, she swept the floors then thoroughly cleaned them before putting the rugs back in place. Although Anna protested the entire time she worked, by the time the men were ready to leave she was pleased with all their accomplishments.

Kaleb and Jesse went on and on about Elizabeth's new coat, but the joy she saw in Jacob's eyes when she slipped it on brought tears to her eyes.

"How did we manage to get such fine grandchildren, Anna?"

"They are a blessing."

"They are at that."

Goodbye hugs were shared, and hopes of seeing each other

on Sunday were spoken of, but they all knew the heavily-clouded sky could alter the best-laid plans.

Elizabeth noticed the added warmth her new coat gave her the second she flounced down the porch steps and walked out into the brisk afternoon air. She whispered as her gaze rose to the heavens, "Thank you, Lord!"

A yawn caught her unawares as Kaleb boosted her up on Lady. He hemmed and hawed about her ability to stay awake, but she insisted she would be fine.

About an hour into the trip, the men were hungry, so she passed them each a sandwich, and nibbled on one herself. Had she known the effect a full stomach would have on her weary body, she never would have touched it. Not fifteen minutes later, her head began to sway. As she slumped over Lady's neck, she felt Kaleb's arms come about her and he settled her in front of him. She thought to tell him that she would be fine, but the words did not come. Perhaps it was the warmth of his body, or her new coat, but she slept in contented bliss the rest of the way home.

"I think your sister wore herself out."

"No question about that."

"Anna was pleased that she had come along."

Jesse nodded. "Kaleb, you'll never guess who I ran into while I was in town yesterday."

"Who?"

"Okemos, the Ottawa chief. He was here with some of his warriors trading at Browns."

"I can't remember the last time I saw Okemos. Must be getting up there in years ... I'll have to remember to stop by Browns and pick up some Indian sugar before it's gone."

"Makes your mouth water thinking about a tall stack of hotcakes smothered in it, don't it?"

"Enough! You're making me hungry."

Jesse chuckled. "The path that leads to the river is just around the bend. If it's all right with you, I'll take Lady home and bring her back Christmas day."

"Thanks, Jesse. Liz will be so busy getting ready for the festivities she won't have time to miss her. Tell everyone we said 'hi'."

"Will do. Be sure and let my sister know how peaceful the trip home was."

"Forget you—she'll be clobbering me!"

Jesse yelled back as he moved down the hill towards the Huron, "Better you than me!"

Kaleb smothered his wife with kisses as they rode into the yard, trying to wake her, but she didn't stir until he laid her on their bed.

"Kaleb," she insisted, "I'll be fine, put me back on ..." The opening of her eyes revealed her shadowed surroundings, leaving her all the more confused. "When did we get home?"

"Just now."

"I slept the entire way?"

He smiled, nodding. "I need to get Lightning settled. Why don't you slip into your gown and warm up the bed. I'll be back in a few minutes."

"What about Lady?"

"Jesse took her home. He'll bring her back Christmas day."

"Do you want some tea, Kaleb?"

"I'm fine." He leaned to steal another kiss. "Get ready for

bed. You'll need your rest for tomorrow."

"You're probably right."

When Kaleb returned Elizabeth had the lantern lit for him, but she was curled around her pillow, sound asleep in her pale yellow gown.

Chapter Fourteen

The Eve of Their Savior's Birth

THE BRIGHT MORNING sun filtering through the curtains drew Elizabeth from her slumber. As she slipped into her tattered brown frock she smiled, remembering what day it was. She loved every aspect of Christmas, and the preparations were a big part of what made their celebration special. Since the baking was a top priority, eggs would need to be gathered.

Elizabeth fastened her new coat, stepped out into the biting air, and shivered as the bone-chilling winds hindered her steps. She prayed that the storms would hold off until after tomorrow. Although she loved seeing the snow fall on the eve of her Savior's birth, she would be devastated if anything were to keep her family away. Tiger, their big tomcat, weaved around her legs, crying for attention. How could she deny him? He purred in contented bliss as she stooped down to pet him before continuing on her way.

Elizabeth was almost to the barn when she heard Kaleb bellow her name. For the life of her, she couldn't imagine what was wrong. The coffee wasn't on, but surely that wouldn't upset him. By the time she realized that this could be about the dogs, he was standing beside her.

"What did I tell you?" he asked as he reached for her hand and led her out of the wind, then stood before her, waiting for an answer.

Why did he insist on doing this? Couldn't he see that he was treating her like a child again? While she had every intention of setting him straight, and would have, when she looked up, she lost her nerve. The tension in his jaw silenced her.

"I told you not to come out here alone."

"I know you did. Days have passed. I thought ..."

Kaleb could see that his actions were scaring her, so he took a deep breath and forced himself to calm down. He captured her face in his hands, and kissed her firmly. "Check with me next time, okay? My father and I saw those dogs again just the other day. They would rip you apart without a second thought."

She had no way of knowing if he was angry with himself for overreacting, or with her for not thinking. Before she could ask, he turned away and went about his chores. Apparently, he needed time alone.

Disheartened, Elizabeth walked toward Lightening, her thoughts a mull of confusion. *Just when I begin to feel safe and secure with him, Lord, I do something that irritates him. Will I ever understand the way he thinks? I'm so used to my father's ways, I fail to remember that their opinions often differ. I want this marriage to work, but every time my heart feels wide open, something happens and I'm floundering again. Help me to be worthy of my husband's trust.*

Elizabeth knew Kaleb was in the barn. Until his arms came about her, she had no idea he was so close. She trembled in his gentle hold but forced herself to turn and look at him.

"Liz, I should have talked to you instead of snorting like a bull. Can you forgive me?" His hands rubbed at her arms while his eyes pleaded for understanding.

"I'm not sure if I'll ever get this right, Kaleb."

His eyelids slid shut; he was kicking himself. The last few days had been wonderful and now he made her feel inferior—as if his lack of faith could somehow be her fault. "You're doing fine. This is my problem, not yours."

She released the breath she'd been holding. She could see it in his eyes. He did understand—and his understanding meant the world to her. In a daring attempt to ease his anguish, she chanced a halfhearted grin. "You were really mad, weren't you, Kaleb?"

"My mind does crazy things when I think you could be hurt." A sparkle lit her tearful gaze. He was learning that his wife's playfulness seemed to be her way of moving past her insecurities, so he could hardly anticipate her next words.

Elizabeth wiped the last of her tears away with her gloved hand. Her baiting words totally altered their moods. "So, Papa, tell me—how long do I have to wait before I can come to the barn alone?" She earned an evil glare that she returned with much flair.

"That's it. Turn around."

Fully aware of his intentions, she giggled and bit her lip. "I don't think so!"

His thoughts raced. How can she be dispirited one minute

and tantalizing the next? She looked so adorable he wanted to squeeze her. Instead, he opted to give her a portion of what her playful heart seemed to be begging for. But when he waited a bit too long to put his plan into action, she slithered out of his grasp and ran towards the stack of hay. Had they been out in the open, his long strides would have brought her into his grasp within seconds. In the barn she had him at a disadvantage. Her agility amazed him. She hiked up her dress and scampered up the mound so fast he was taken aback. Since she had nowhere to go, he took his sweet time.

As Kaleb glanced up, his heart dropped in his chest. Elizabeth stood on the ledge they would swing off of during haying season. Before he could catch his breath, she grabbed the rope that dangled from the rafters and swung up into the loft.

His first inclination was to scold her for giving him such a fright, but that would never do. She'd really be calling him *Papa* after that. He loved her whimsical spirit. And while he wouldn't mind taming her a bit, he would never set out to dampen the lighthearted woman he was coming to love. He smiled as her moving portrait played over in his mind, flying through the air with the ease of a bird in flight, golden hair and skirts flaring out behind her, then that graceful landing on one foot. She mystified him. He had no doubt that if he tried the same move, his oversized frame would drop to the barn floor with an excruciating thud.

What now? He opted to climb back down the mound and head for the stairs, changing his mind in the process. Elizabeth's heart must be racing, and he could only imagine how swollen her ankle would be after this escapade. He'd check into that later. Before he could do anything, though, he would have to catch her.

He decided the best course of action would be to let her stew in her own brew, allowing her to make the next move. He went about his work, keeping an eye on her without her knowledge—or so he thought.

She taunted him from the loft, pacing back and forth, but he ignored her. Her blood ran wild; she was ready for action. The smile that crossed her husband's face as she plunked down on the hard floor and tried to catch her breath did not go unnoticed. He was not oblivious to her movements, so she stayed on her guard.

They were both playing like children, and she loved it. There were, however, advantages and disadvantages to knowing each other so well. While Kaleb knew she would not give up without giving it her all, Elizabeth was well aware he would not easily let her off the hook she was hanging herself from. As much as she enjoyed toying with him, the adult in her was thinking of all the baking that was not getting done. If she came down, she would be forced to pay the piper. Her taunting had gone too far. Kaleb would never let this fall by the wayside. If she could only get to the chicken coop and gather the eggs, he might let her pass, just to keep them from breaking. She could say she needed them for his fudge and pie. That would be enough to grant her safe passage, but it would also be a boldface lie—not an option.

On silent feet, she moved towards the back of the loft where the hay was stacked at its highest. She shuddered with renewed excitement, lifted her skirts and took a flying leap off the edge, landing in the middle of a slightly lower storage shelf—exactly where she was headed. Her bad foot slipped between the boards. No harm had been done, so she pulled it out and began her descent. About a third of the way down, a big chunk of hay dislodged, sending her tumbling—right into her husband's waiting arms. She was trying to figure out where he had come from, when her frantic blue gaze met his deep brown glare. What would he do? She'd given up without a fight—well, sort of. Maybe he'd find it in his heart to be merciful.

Kaleb sat on the lower shelf, trifling with the woman in his arms. "What, My Dear Wife, do you suggest I do with you?"

Her insides were all in a twirl, her eyes wide with a mixture of apprehension and delight, her words soft and oh-so-humble. "You could just let me go," she teased.

He tried not to laugh. "Are you done being sassy?"

Though she nodded her head in affirmation, Elizabeth saw the flicker in his eye. He would not release her without some form of retribution; she knew that, so she attempted a bribe. "If you'll be kind, I'll make you more oatmeal cookies with chocolate in them."

Kaleb burst into laughter. He couldn't believe she would try to use chocolate to lure him. He thought, *my wife is wise for her sixteen years*. Those tasty little morsels she created were just the temptation required. He gave in without so much as a second thought.

"All right, but you'd better be on your best behavior the rest of the day." When she tried to get up, he forestalled her a moment longer. "At the very least, you owe me a kiss."

She gladly gave him a quick peck on the cheek and grinned like a possum.

"A real kiss or the deal is off!" Elizabeth rolled her eyes, before pulling herself up in his lap. Her slender hands slid behind the nape of his neck, drawing him in. Her penitent lips earned her more than absolution—Kaleb, seeking one in the same, offered his own form of penance—leaving husband and wife breathless and entirely serene.

"Kaleb, you didn't answer my question. How long before I can come out to the barn alone? I'd rather not have my husband seething like a dragon!"

"I wasn't that bad—was I?"

"Yes!"

He tweaked her nose with the tip of his finger. "Check with me in about a week."

She grimaced then turned to walk away, her irritation clear. Kaleb's deep thunderous tone turned her head.

"Elizabeth!"

"You're serious?"

"If it takes the rest of the winter, you will wait for one of the men in your life to come with you. Are we agreed?"

"Do I have a choice?"

"No, you don't."

Elizabeth moved away, exclaiming under her breath yet loud enough for him to hear, "High-handed husband, he's worse than my father and brother—put together!" She was not surprised when a playful swat connected with her bum. Her head whipped around, flashing a frolicking grin that made him laugh out loud.

"So tell me, Liz. Why did you come to the barn in the first place?"

"To play with my husband. I thought you knew?"

"Aren't you the funny gal?"

"To see the piglets and collect the eggs."

"Well, go ahead and finish while I do my chores."

❦ ❦ ❦

The spirit of Christmas began to fill their house, from the first tray of cookies that came out of the oven. Samuel and Ruth came home just after lunch to join Kaleb and Elizabeth in their preparations. The hours they had already spent cooking produced many trays of various delights. By early evening, the billowing winds had brought in their own form of holiday cheer.

"Mom," Elizabeth asked as she peered out the kitchen window, captivated by the falling snow, "can you get along without me for a few minutes?"

"Sure. Take your time."

Elizabeth went in search of her husband and found him in the sitting room next to the fire. Her attempt to drag him away from his book failed—at least at first. What he wanted her to do was join him in his chair, but Elizabeth would not be put off. Leaning, she whispered in his ear.

With raised brow and an impish smirk, Kaleb winked at his father, whose eyes followed their every move.

Samuel relished the opportunity to witness their playfulness. Because he had acquired his wife's hand through lies and deception, he had missed out on the delight young couples share with each other. He was thankful Kaleb and Elizabeth would not have to go through some of the same struggles he and Ruth had experienced. While his son and daughter-in-law may not have married for love, he knew in his heart that if they pressed on love would come, if it hadn't already.

After pulling on their coats and boots, Elizabeth shoved her reluctant husband out the door, off the porch, and into the yard.

"Kaleb, look at this. Isn't it beautiful? I love it when it snows on Christmas Eve!" She lifted her hands toward the heavens. "To me, it's a gift straight from the Lord."

Kaleb gazed in elation as his whimsical beauty danced in circles in the glittering white flakes. The snow trickling from a darkened sky did present a peacefulness that only Christ's love could bring. This year Kaleb's added blessing came in the form of a beautiful lady now twirling before him. With awe and wonder, he joined her in a simple dance of shared happiness and utter joy. They really did have so much to celebrate, so much to be thankful for on the eve of their Savior's birth. Sweeping his bride into his arms, Kaleb and Elizabeth danced on to a rhythm and beat of their own making, a tune that they hoped would play on throughout the years to come.

Arm in arm, Samuel and Ruth stood in the picture window, partaking of the scene in the yard. With tears of jubilation streaming from their eyes, they marveled at the way God had blessed them. The celebration of Christ's birth held so much meaning for them. Knowing Him had drastically altered their lives and, somehow, seeing their son so blissful made them all the more aware. The rewards of raising this young man in the ways of the Lord were in full view before them. Kaleb wasn't perfect—he would make mistakes—but the way he put Elizabeth's needs above his own melted their hearts. When Kaleb slowed to caress the abundance of all that God had given him, Samuel and Ruth turned to embrace and delight in their own love. A union whose foundation began on sinking sand, now stood firmly on solid ground—all because of what their Savior had done.

Daisytales

He Loves Me!

Chapter Fifteen

Christmas

*E*LIZABETH AWOKE TO kisses tenderly given on Christmas morn and deep amber eyes sparkling with happiness—or was it contentment?

"Merry Christmas, Liz."

"Merry Christmas."

Kaleb found her sleepy state very entertaining. That she was powerless to do anything about it only added to his joy. Her gaze fixed on his as he ran his fingers along the soft skin of her face. How could he not chuckle when an exaggerated stretch and irrepressible yawn caught her unaware?

She gave into a sudden urge to goad him. "You're up kind of early, aren't you, Mister?"

"I've been up for a while. You must have worn yourself out with all the baking you and Mom did yesterday. We finished breakfast an hour ago."

Elizabeth sat up with a start, feeling guilty for having

overslept. "Kaleb, why didn't you wake me? Your mother ... she must think I'm horrible."

"You're fine. Mom's the one who insisted I let you sleep. Besides, I helped her."

She grinned, probing him further. "Did she chase you with the wooden spoon when you nuzzled her neck too many times?"

"No, I love my mother, but I don't enjoy baiting her like I do a certain feisty beauty who sleeps so peacefully in my arms. You'd be impressed. I was quite helpful."

She wasn't buying it. "What did you do, make the coffee, tea, and set the table?"

"How did you know?"

"Oh, just a wild guess .... Kaleb, you should leave so I can get dressed." He just sat there in a dreamy stare; obviously, he had no intentions of going anywhere. "Why are you being so silly?"

"I have something I'd like you to wear today."

"You gave me my gifts. I'll always treasure them." She held up her hand to show him.

"I'm glad you like them, but they are your wedding rings, not your Christmas gift."

"They're more than I need, Kaleb White." His long finger came to her lips, silencing her protests before reaching for a rather large package he had behind him on the floor.

"Kaleb, what have you done?"

The astonishment in her eyes made him smile. His wife couldn't comprehend his need to give, even though she gave of herself without expectations every day. He wondered if she still saw herself as an imposition. If she could only recognize how much he delighted in having her in his life, his joy would be complete.

"Kaleb, shouldn't we wait to exchange gifts?"

"No. Not this time."

Filled with timidity, her eyes met his. "Will it embarrass me? Is that why you're giving it to me in private?"

His brow arched. "I hope not. Now quit with the inquisition and open it." She did as she was told, though not without letting him know how she felt about such overabundance. "You shouldn't spoil me so ...."

"I couldn't resist. To be honest, this gift is as much for me as it is for you. I can't wait to see you in it!"

Elizabeth, beaming in the light of his exuberance, lifted the lid. She was awed by the beautiful, deep plum dress she pulled out of the box. The bodice was fitted with tiny tucks and a slight scoop to the neckline. The sleeves were long, puffing at the shoulder, tapering at the cuffs, and the full skirt hung straight to the floor. Under the dress she found a new chemise, and a complete set of ivory unmentionables trimmed in the same ivory lace that adorned the gown. As if all this were not enough, she uncovered another warm pair of socks, ivory wool with knitting needles, and a pattern written out for a matching shawl. The gift was everything she could have ever dreamed of, but the thought of wearing something so nice brought on those confounded tears.

Kaleb drew her into his arms. "Honey, this was meant to make you smile, not cry."

"You did make me smile on the inside. It's just ... well, you know ... I'm overwhelmed." After sharing a tender kiss, he reached for his hanky and proceeded to dry her cheeks.

"Where did you find something so beautiful?" Without

waiting for an answer, she informed him, "It's too nice to wear, Kaleb. I might spoil it cooking."

"Nonsense! I was hoping you'd like it. I hired Carolyn to make it for you. She was thrilled to have the distraction while she waited for Ron and Phyllis to bring the children."

"Did she say how long the Bodtke's would be staying? I'd love to see them."

"I'm not sure? I didn't like you not having a special dress the day we were married. Not for my own sake, but for yours. Besides, this deep shade of orchid will accent your lovely features, and show off that golden hair."

"Kaleb ... stop," she ordered as she tried to turn away.

He captured her chin, bringing her gaze back to his. "If I don't tell you I like the way you look, how will you know?"

"I can't help it. The same words coming from my father feel so different."

He couldn't withhold a smile. "I'll take that as a good sign. Come on," he said as he threw back the covers, "let's get you out of that nightgown and into this dress."

His boldness staggered her. "Kaleb, what's gotten in to you?"

"I'll turn around while you put it on." When she only stared, he added, "I promise to be good. I'd like to be the first to see you in this."

"I'm not sure that's possible," she said, as her eyes fell on the long string of ivory beads down the back of her new gown. "I suppose I'll need help with all these buttons."

She looked at the splendid dress as it fell into place, and knew without seeing her reflection that she loved it. "Kaleb, you can look now."

His mouth gaped in surprise. With all of her other clothes faded and worn, this was a nice change. "Liz, you're exquisite!"

"Thank you. My husband has wonderful taste, don't you think?"

"He does at that." His wife was speaking of her attire; he, on the other hand, was thinking of the woman herself. "Turn around. I'd better get started on those buttons, or we'll be here all morning." Kaleb had just begun when she heard him murmur, "The new unmentionables look nice too."

Elizabeth spun around with every intention of setting him straight, but the innocent brown eyes that met her glare made her smile instead. "What am I going to do with you, Kaleb White?"

He shrugged. "Anything your heart desires."

Her twinkling eyes held his a moment longer. As Elizabeth turned in wonderment, allowing Kaleb to finish what he had started, the realization struck her: *something is changing here, Lord. I like how I'm feeling about this husband you've given me.*

The dress was a perfect fit and Kaleb's triumphant grin revealed his pleasure. She suspected he had something to say when he fingered her long braid.

"Liz, I'd like you to leave your hair down today."

She swirled in his arms. "But, it'll be in my way when I'm cooking ...." The persuasive power in his pleading eyes was impossible to ignore. "Does it mean that much to you?"

"What do you think?"

Gently she caressed the rough skin of his face. Needing more, her arms slid around his neck. Her intentions were more than clear and Kaleb was more than willing to comply.

Thoughtful, she moved to the mirror. Unraveling her braid,

she brushed through her rippled hair, her eyes never leaving the good-looking man who glanced back and smiled at her reflection, just before he walked out the door.

Elizabeth, knowing the hour had to be getting late, tidied the room. She felt like a princess going to a ball, all decked out in her finery. Temporal things had never held much of a draw for her, but she had to admit, it was nice to feel pretty on this special day. Kaleb liked the way she looked in this dress, and his opinion had begun to matter more than anyone's.

Ruth was working on the preparations for the holiday meal when Elizabeth bustled into the kitchen.

"Merry Christmas, Lizzy. Don't you look nice." Elizabeth twirled before her.

"As you can see, your son has been full of surprises already this morning." They shared a hug and Elizabeth said, "You look lovely yourself. Merry Christmas, Mom."

"Kaleb mentioned that he gave you the rings the other night. Did you like them?"

Elizabeth held out her hand to show them off. "I do, but," she said, sticking out her lower lip, "now everyone will know I'm an old married woman." Her façade made Ruth smile.

"They already know, Honey."

"I'm sure you're right. If someone had told me in advance that I'd be a wife at sixteen, I would have left home without a second thought."

"Then I'm glad you didn't know. You're a gem, Lizzy. My son is blessed to have you."

"I felt the same way about him." Elizabeth could hear Kaleb's bluchers on the wooden floor and turned as he came into the room. Looking quite distinguished in his new jeans, a crisp white shirt, black vest and necktie, he strutted towards her.

"You are a married woman," he said, "and it's best the other men in this community know you're mine."

She shook her head. "You were eavesdropping, Kaleb. Shame on you."

"No shame. Only pleasure."

"You're incorrigible!"

"Mmm, hmm! Best they know you're mine." Kaleb's eyes ran up and down her attire, as if drinking in the view. His words slowed .... "Especially when they see you in this dress. I don't know, Liz. You'll have to give me some time to think this through."

"Quit."

"I may have to insist that you only wear this around family."

Her husband's frankness made her giggle as she turned to pour a cup of tea. Within seconds, Kaleb's arms came about her waist, and he whispered in her ear. "You're blushing, My Dear."

Leaning against his chest, she murmured her plea. "Please settle down, Kaleb—or I'll never survive this day."

His mother was otherwise occupied when he glanced her way. "Mom, would you please inform my charming wife that I am always over-zealous on Christmas Day."

"I'm sorry, Lizzy. It's hopeless to try and change him. He's an overgrown child on Christmas and his birthday. I can only imagine what he'll be like when you give birth to your first child. We won't be able to live with him!"

Since this was not a subject his wife would want to discuss with his mother, Kaleb made an attempt to steer the conversation in another direction. "Mom, would you like me to peel potatoes?"

Ruth smiled. "If you don't mind it would be a big help. Your father brought them up from the cold cellar. While you are in the pantry, grab the big pot from the shelf."

Elizabeth savored every bite of a fresh cinnamon muffin and poured herself a second cup of tea before joining Kaleb in his efforts. The three of them worked and laughed together, reminiscing about Christmases gone by, but the morning was getting away from them. Other things had to be done before their guests arrived.

Kaleb had chores to do in the barn. His parents were putting the extra chairs that were scattered around the house into the sitting room. Elizabeth formed the yeast rolls. While they were rising, she started the vegetables and then popped the rolls into the oven. She had just pulled them out and put the apple cider over to simmer when Kaleb came in the back door announcing her family's arrival. Her heart soared. Their day of celebration could commence.

The house had chilled by the time all the food and gifts were brought in, so after greeting her family Elizabeth grabbed her shawl off the hook and went to the sitting room to warm up by the fire. Everyone else had the same idea and the chairs filled fast. When Jesse walked in and there was no place to sit, Kaleb's remedy for the discrepancy left her feeling more than a little unsettled. Without time to protest, she found herself in his lap. She didn't mind being in this position when they were alone, but her parents were now seated across from her. The scowl she sent Kaleb's way did not have the effect she had hoped for; he squeezed her even tighter, and her dander rose. If she took him to task the heat rising up her neck would deepen. Instead, she swallowed her pride and tried to make the best of her uncomfortable position.

When all of them were gathered, Samuel handed Kaleb his Bible and said, "Since this is Kaleb and Elizabeth's first Christmas together, I'd like him to read the account from Luke chapter two.

Elizabeth, feeling more at ease, snuggled against her husband as he began to read.

"And it came to pass in those days, that there went out a decree from Cesar Augustus, that all the world should be taxed. (And this taxing was first made when Cyrenius was governor of Syria.) And all went to be taxed, everyone into his own city. And Joseph also went up from Galilee, out of the city of Nazareth, into Judaea, unto the city of David, which is called Bethlehem; (because he was of the house and lineage of David:) To be taxed with Mary his espoused wife, being great with child. And so it was, that, while they were there, the days were accomplished that she should be delivered. And she brought forth her first born son, and wrapped him in swaddling clothes, and laid him in a manger; because there was no room for them in the inn. And there were in the same country shepherds abiding in the field, keeping watch over their flocks by night. And lo, the angel of the Lord came upon them, and the glory of the Lord shone round about them, Fear not: for, behold I bring you good tidings of great joy, which shall be to all people. For unto you is born this day in the city of David a Savior, which is Christ the Lord. And this shall be a sign unto you; ye shall find a babe wrapped in swaddling clothes, lying in a manger. And suddenly there was with the angel a multitude of the heavenly host praising God, and saying, Glory to God in the highest, and on earth peace, good will toward men. And it came to pass, as the angels were

gone away from them into heaven, the shepherds said one to another, Let us now go even unto Bethlehem, and see this thing which is come to pass which the Lord hath made known unto us. And they came with haste and found Mary, and Joseph, and the babe lying in a manger. And when they had seen it, they made known abroad the saying which was told them concerning the Christ child. And all they that heard it wondered at those things which were told them by the shepherds. But Mary kept all these things and pondered them in her heart. And the shepherds returned, glorifying and praising God for all the things that they had heard and seen, as it was told unto them. And when eight days were accomplished for the circumcising of the child, his name was called JESUS, which was so named of the angel before he was conceived in the womb."

In keeping with tradition, everyone joined hands in a prayer of thanksgiving, before exchanging gifts.

The women went off to the kitchen to put the finishing touches on the meal, and Kaleb and Jesse were elected to slice the ham.

Elizabeth couldn't resist giving them a hard time as she set the table. "The way the two of you are going at that meat, you won't have any room left when it comes time for dinner, never mind dessert."

Kaleb said, "You should know better, Liz. Do you really think I'd risk missing out on that fudge and apple pie?"

"I suppose not," she admitted, reaching for a knife to slice the nut bread.

The pan of potatoes was so big the three women had to take turns mashing them. By the time the rest of the meal was on the table, the women's shared effort had paid off—the potatoes were nice and smooth. Jayne finished the sweet ham gravy before their families gathered around to say grace.

Elizabeth glanced around the room and sighed with pleasure. It really was good to have everyone together again. Their parents filled their plates and went to the sitting room while everyone else squeezed in around the table. The group had no more begun to sample their meal when Joseph had a question he was itching to ask.

"Lizzy, Jesse shared a story with us the other day and it seems to be missing a certain detail that's been troubling Jared and me."

His playful smirk told Elizabeth she was about to be harassed in some way, but she let him go ahead.

"Just how far did you have to chase that chicken after you lopped off its head?"

Jesse got the evil eye for divulging private information.

Confused, Suzanne piped in, "What are you talking about, Joe? Lizzy won't butcher a chicken!" The boys erupted in laughter.

After jabbing Kaleb in the ribs for joining in their elation, Elizabeth sent her words of warning to her teasing brothers.

Kaleb couldn't tell if she was upset or not when he unwittingly added, "Honey, the expression on your face was hysterical when you thought I'd make you kill that chicken—it took me forever to quit laughing."

Elizabeth stood suddenly. "You don't know me at all, if you thought for a second you could *make me* do something so grotesque!"

Kaleb looked to Jesse for help.

With a sympathetic tilt of the head, Jesse said, "You blew it now!"

Kaleb reached for Elizabeth's arm, trying to make amends, but she wanted nothing to do with any of them. Picking up her plate, she sat down on the bench between her little sisters. Elizabeth berated herself for letting them get to her. They usually didn't. Since she did not care to give it another thought, she turned to her sisters and asked, "So tell me girls, did you have fun together this week?"

Louise said, "We did, Lizzy. You'll have to come and see. The boys made us hope chests for our rooms. They're beautiful!"

Elizabeth smiled in the light of their enthusiasm. "I saw them before I left. Now we can begin to fill them. I want you girls to be better prepared when it's *your* turn to get married." She touched Sarah's hand. "I'll have Kaleb build you one soon."

"Thanks, Lizzy. I'd like that."

Suzanne said, "Dad made us a new sled. He let us bring it so we could try it out. Maybe ..." Suzanne paused, needing to be sure she had their attention, "since the men are doing dishes, we could go alone. Lizzy, wouldn't you like to go with us?"

Their excitement was hard to ignore. She would love to go. However, Kaleb might not be so agreeable. She hated having to check with him about everything, but if she didn't he might embarrass her in front of her family and that would be worse.

"Let me see what Kaleb says. Did you girls bring play clothes? I wouldn't want you to ruin your new dresses."

"Yes!" the three of them shouted in unison.

A quick look at her younger brother made Elizabeth think of something she had left at home. "I wish I had Jared's jeans. It's so much easier to go sledding in pants than a dress."

"Actually..." Louise said, as a mischievous twinkle brightened her eyes. "I mentioned that to Jared before we left, and he gave me an old pair you can keep."

"You didn't!" Elizabeth's teeth went over her lower lip.

Louise's golden head bobbed up and down as she whispered, "I did. And ... we confiscated an old pair of Joseph's for Sarah. What do you think Kaleb will say when he sees them on you again?"

I suppose I'll find out, she thought. "Well, girls, I'll talk to Kaleb, but if you hear any loud noises in the room, you'll know it's not going well." While her lighthearted inflections made them giggle, Elizabeth did not join in. She had a pretty strong inclination as to how Kaleb would respond. If history repeated itself—which it often did—she might not handle it well.

"Kaleb," she whispered in his ear, "could I talk to you alone for a minute?" Knowing they weren't on solid ground because of the conversation added to her unease. When the door clicked shut, she took a moment to clear her thoughts before turning to face him.

"Kaleb, the girls brought the new sled they got for Christmas. They want me to take them sledding ...." Kaleb was shaking his head no. Her calm demeanor vanished. She kept her voice at a respectful tone, but made no bones about giving him a piece of her mind.

"Kaleb, it's been almost a week since those dogs were here. This is absurd! Even our fathers can see that there's safety in numbers. I'm an adult and I'm sick to death of you treating me like a child. You're going to have to get a handle on your fears and start trusting the Lord."

His lack of expression did not help.

As angry tears began to fall, she added, "You're making me feel like a prisoner in my own home!"

Seconds crept by before he pompously asked, "Are you finished?"

"Yes."

"This is one of those times where you have to decide. You're either going to trust my advice, or you're not. Jesse and I will be more than happy to go with you when we're done with the dishes. It's obvious you don't agree, but I don't think the potential danger is worth the risk of going without us. If you can't live with my decision, then make your own." On that note he turned and walked out the door without a backward glance.

Once again, she might as well have been talking to the wall. As much as she would love to defy him, Kaleb knew she could not. Her acquiescence did nothing to curb her mounting frustration, and his unwarranted fears were the cause. She hated the way this made her feel inside. How could she tell the girls that they would have to wait for the men to take them, without revealing her own frustration? They could read her like a book. In her husband's opinion, she wasn't capable of protecting herself, let alone anyone else.

Determined to find a peaceful resolve, she threw herself across the bed and cried out to the only one who could soothe her despondent heart. *Why can't he see what he's doing, Lord? How much longer is he going to keep this up? Father, forgive my impudent heart! It's not Your fault Kaleb is the way he is. Open the eyes of his heart, Lord. Help him to put his trust in You.*

The girls lingered at the table, waiting for Elizabeth to come out. After questioning Kaleb, he told them they were welcome to check on her. When they found her sleeping, they knew something must have gone wrong. Kaleb was all too quiet and the only time Elizabeth slept during the day was if she was crying, discouraged, or ill—and they were quite certain it was not the last.

He Loves Me!

Chapter Sixteen

Mutual Trust

ELIZABETH AWOKE TO the wonderful sound of her mother's laughing. Slipping her feet into her house shoes, she pulled her disheveled hair into a loose braid and headed out the door. She found her mother and mother-in-law in the sitting room, chatting over a pot of tea and a plate of holiday cookies. They didn't notice her, so she moved back towards the kitchen for a cup before joining them again.

"Is this a private party, ladies?"

"Of course not," Ruth said. "Lizzy, come. Sit and talk with us."

"Lizzy," Jayne asked, "are you not feeling well? The girls said you were sleeping. The men ended up taking them sledding."

"I'm sure the girls will do fine without me."

Jayne noted the strain in her daughter's tone, but didn't question her in front Ruth.

"Lizzy, Ruth tells me Kaleb hasn't been able to beat you

at checkers."

"That's true." After taking a sip of tea, she smiled, and added, "He wants me to divulge my strategy. You know I can't do that; besides, I kind of like having the upper hand in some area of our relationship."

"My father used to say that if I wanted a young man to stick around, I should never beat him at anything. I took his advice and George was quite surprised when he realized I had been holding out on him. Checkers is the one game that no one has ever beaten him at."

"Dad taught me much about the game, but he's been careful not to show me how to beat him. Kaleb and Jesse are a different story. They're not even competition."

"You should play with Samuel some time, Lizzy."

She nodded, picked up a cookie, and took a bite.

The women heard voices in the pantry and assumed everyone would be coming in looking for desert.

Elizabeth stood and said, "I'll put the drinks on the stove. You two just sit and visit." Experience had taught her that the best way to work through her frustrations was to spend time alone with the Lord. Once night fell, she would have to resolve this with Kaleb. She had every intention of having her emotions well under control before then. Her father and father-in-law were warming themselves by the stove when she entered the kitchen.

"Lizzy, we missed you out there. The girls were disappointed you didn't join us."

She smiled at her father and skirted his comment. "I've been visiting with my mothers. They're in the sitting room chatting."

"In that case, I'll join them." Samuel said as he snatched a butter cookie off the tray, leaving George to talk to his daughter.

Elizabeth put the pots on the stove, and her father slipped his arms around her for a hug. She adored her father—loved being in his arms—but her emotions at the moment were too unstable.

"How's My Girl?"

Her father could read her thoughts better than Kaleb, so she kept stirring the chocolate into the warming milk, avoiding his eyes. "I'm fine, Dad. Did you have a good morning?"

"We did, but we missed having you there. You seem to be fitting in around here. Are you happy, Honey?" His voice was hopeful.

Why did he have to ask this of all things? "I'm trying to be." Desperate to discuss something less emotional, she changed the subject. "Did Kaleb tell you we're having Lady bred when she comes into season?"

"That will give you something to look forward to."

"That's a long ways away."

"Yes, it is. Is there a chance I'll be having a grandchild to spoil before next Christmas?"

Elizabeth, stunned by his inquiry, said, "Dad, you shouldn't ask such things."

George turned her in his arms. She sounded all too close to tears and he needed to see for himself that she was fine. "Oh, Honey, what has you so tied up in knots?"

Her eyes filled with tears under her father's tender gaze. "Dad, I don't want Kaleb to come in and find me crying. It's Christmas. I wouldn't want to upset him."

"Bundle up, Lizzy. We're going for a walk."

As she fastened the buttons on her new coat and pulled

her scarf over her head, she questioned her ability to open up to her father about this. He had a way of making sense out of her most trivial problem, but she was no longer a little girl with little girl issues to solve. How could he help when she didn't understand herself?

Outside they strolled along in silence for a while, enjoying the peacefulness of the day. The snow that fell the previous night was just enough to give their world a fresh glow.

"We couldn't have asked for a more beautiful Christmas, could we, Dad?"

"It has been nice."

As he often did, he reached for her hand, and she savored the comfort she found in his touch.

George led her in the opposite direction of the sledding hill, hoping they could talk without interruptions.

"Dad, before we begin I need you to understand that although I was opposed to this marriage at first, that's no longer true."

"Then what has you so upset?"

Where could she begin? "Last Sunday, Kaleb and I had a rough start to our day. I was a mess. I couldn't get beyond feeling so wronged. Forgiving you and Kaleb was no longer the issue. Understanding why God allowed any of this to happen in the first place was. The way I saw it, other people were dictating who I should love. I felt trapped. Then I got to thinking: who would I be hurting if I continued to sulk? The people who started the rumors could care less if I have a good or bad marriage. The evil they set out to do was accomplished. If I continued, I would only be hurting Kaleb and myself."

"You have to find a way to forgive them as well, Lizzy."

"I know. Christ's command for us to love all men isn't always easy to accomplish. I keep reminding myself that no one will ever see Jesus in me if I allow what brought us together to destroy me. My life would be for nothing. I'm beginning to see now that God is able to take what others meant for harm and turn it into something wonderful. Kaleb made it clear that he's offering me his heart, but mine is a gift that only I can give. He went even further to say that his wanting my heart didn't make it his; I had to give it freely. Most of my frustrations were of my own making. I knew that. We couldn't continue as we were. I was making both of us miserable. I needed to accept him as a gift from the Lord— part of God's plan for my life. I suppose I was so blinded by all that I had lost, I failed to see all this marriage could bring to my life. I was finally ready to try."

"*Was*? I hope that doesn't mean you're giving up?"

"No, Dad. Kaleb is my husband and walking away is not an option for me. You and I both understand the permanency of this covenant. That's why I was so opposed to it at first. I wish I could say that everything is fine .... I'm sure every couple has problems to iron out."

"We're all in process, Honey."

"At this point in my life, I couldn't agree more with you. It's easy to have faith and go on when everything's moving along just fine. It's these bumps in the road that throw me."

George smiled. "It's good to know some of what I've tried to teach you got through. Can you tell me what's bothering you *now*?"

She grimaced. "I'm not sure it will do any good."

George, muddled by her confession, looked at his daughter,

searching for clarity. Tears spilling down her cheeks told him much. It didn't matter who was in the wrong—his child was hurting. At the very least, he had to try and ease her pain. He slipped his arm around her. "Honey, what is it? I can't help you if you don't tell me."

"I really need to have someone to talk to, but I don't want you thinking badly of Kaleb. He's been placed in an awkward situation and I would never set out to hurt him. He's been wonderful in so many ways."

"Elizabeth, your union with Kaleb made him my son. I love you both. My desire is to see the two of you happy. If my counsel can help you move towards building a strong marriage, then let me help. I'm not saying I have all the answers. You'll have to pray about our discussion and allow God to lead you. You're young. It's all right to admit you need guidance. Kaleb's your partner in life. It's my hope that someday you'll be able to go to each other for advice. Until that happens, you can always come to me."

"I appreciate that, Dad. Promise you'll be honest and tell me if I'm wrong?"

"That goes without saying ...."

"I used to think you and Jesse went overboard when it came to your protective ways. Boy, was I wrong! Trust me when I say that Kaleb has you both beat by a long shot." George found it difficult not to smile. For Elizabeth, this was no laughing matter.

"Kaleb started by informing me that riding alone is a thing of the past. Now I'm to have him with me to go anywhere except the outhouse. He doesn't even want me going to the barn alone."

George tried not to overreact. "Does he have a reason for thinking this is necessary?"

"At first I thought it might be because of my ankle. That had little to do with it. He said that even though you didn't have a problem with me riding alone, I'm his wife now. He doesn't think it's safe for a woman to be off on her own. My accident only strengthened his resolve."

"He's right, Lizzy. We're bound to see things differently."

"I told him I would honor his wishes—for now." She paused for a few seconds, before adding out of desperation, "Dad, the wild dogs were here almost a week ago. I could understand him not wanting me to go to the barn alone for a while. But a week—please! His fears are getting worse. I know they're stemming from my accident, but it's no excuse. I feel like a small child having to ask my daddy's permission to go out. I'm not handling it well."

"Did something happen since we arrived? You seemed fine when we got here."

"Yes. The girls wanted me to take them sledding. My first mistake was not telling them right off that we'd have to wait for Kaleb and Jesse."

"Kaleb didn't want you to go? There were four of you?"

"No. He said that I had to make a choice. I was either going to accept his advice or I wasn't." She started to cry again. "You know me, Dad. I don't know how much longer I can live like this! I told him he's not trusting the Lord. All he says is that he'll pray about it." For a while, her father withdrew. He seemed to be thinking, so she waited. Minutes had passed without a verbal response and although she would love to have his opinion, she needed to ease his mind.

"I'm sorry, Dad. I shouldn't have put you in the middle of this. I'll try to be patient and allow God the time He needs to change Kaleb's heart."

"Come over here, Lizzy." He led her to a large stump from an old fallen tree. They sat together.

"I'm going to ask you a few personal questions, because I'm trying to understand where Kaleb's coming from."

"All right."

"You do realize that men and women don't think alike?"

She nodded in passing, though her thoughts were resolute. *Boy, do I ever!*

"If you're uncomfortable with what I'm about to ask, I'll understand. But I think it might help you to discuss it."

"All right."

"Do you and Kaleb share an intimate relationship?"

Elizabeth faltered. She recovered quickly when she saw no reason not to tell him. "We've agreed to wait for more than kisses until we're in our own place." The concern that filled her father's face held no comfort.

"Kaleb is only human, Honey. He sleeps beside you every night. He may have agreed to wait, but his needs must be changing. Anyone with eyes can see that the man's in love with you." Since George had been the one to ask Kaleb for patience in this area, he owed it to him to go on.

"Lizzy, something wonderful happens between a husband and wife when they become one physically. If you see this step as something to fear—let me assure you, nothing could be further from the truth. I won't tell you that the problems in your marriage are going to disappear if you open this door, but it should be opened. The fulfillment of the blood covenant will strengthen your union."

"I'm not sure fear is the issue, Dad. At first, it consumed me. Now, it's more about being ready. I didn't have time to get used to the idea of becoming Kaleb's wife before we were wed. Maybe I'm wrong. The way I see it, becoming one in the physical sense is more about trust. I only have one chance to do this right. You say that he loves me, and yet he doesn't trust me. How can I feel secure in his love? How do I give myself to a man I care about, but don't love?"

"Will withholding yourself from him change your marital status, or his needs?"

"No ..."

"Until you're willing to give to each other freely, you're bound to butt heads more often. Your commitment to this union is weak, halfhearted. If you want your marriage to be strong it cannot be self-seeking. It will never last. Love expects nothing in return. It's a risk, but it's one that's so worth taking."

"So, you think waiting is wrong?"

He nodded. "I do. God's Word says that you shouldn't withhold yourselves from each other unless you've made that decision together, and then only for a time."

"At first he wasn't sure he wanted to wait that long. After we talked about it, he said he would. We want our first time to be special."

"Honey, whenever it happens it will be special. All I can say is, pray about it. Allow God to lead you in spite of your reservations. Ask yourself if Kaleb only agreed to wait because he knows that's what you want. It isn't as if he felt secure in your love when you married. If you remember, you made it very clear that you wanted nothing to do with him. Only *you* can show him that you're willing to move toward a loving relationship with him."

"But he doesn't trust me. How can I trust him?"

"Marriage isn't about you. It's about both of you. Someone has to take the first step, and from where I sit, Kaleb is making concessions he shouldn't have to make."

Her gaze stretched over the distant field. "So many times I want nothing more than to flee this place and never come back. Other times I'm happy and I want to make him happy. Will I ever get to the place where I find level ground?"

"Keep working at it. Give him all of you, and God will take care of the rest. Kaleb is the one who found you in that desperate situation. I'm not trying to make excuses for him, but it's bound to take him a while to realize you're safest in the Lord's hands. Just keep in mind, this is Kaleb's sin, not yours. We need to hold him up in prayer, but the battle he's waging is between him and the Lord."

"In the meantime, as his wife I have to find a way to live with his unreasonable demands."

George reached out to caress Elizabeth's face. "He's so focused on keeping his bride safe, he can't see that he's smothering you."

George smiled. He really did understand Kaleb's overzealous heart. In reality, they were not as different as Elizabeth thought. Kaleb hadn't lived with her persistence as long as he had—Kaleb hadn't seen the need for compromise. His daughter would not last long if her husband didn't lighten up, but at this point George would not intervene. He would, however, continue to pray that God would lead his new son, strengthen his faith, and that soon his daughter would not only recognize, but experience, the love that can exist between a man and his wife.

Elizabeth appreciated her father's advice, and she would pray about it. She couldn't see herself taking this step, but talking to him did make her burden feel lighter.

By the time Elizabeth and George got back to the house, the cover of darkness had begun to fall. They slipped in the pantry door and found the desserts spread out on the table, half-eaten.

"Dad, I'm making some tea. Would you like some?"

"Sounds great."

"Go ahead and take your pie to the sitting room. I'll bring the tea when it's ready. He was moving away when she added, Dad ... thanks for lending your ear."

"Stay in the Word, Honey. Seek the Lord's advice. Unfortunately there are no pat answers."

"I will."

Elizabeth's needs were pressing in, so she stuck her coat and boots back on and ran toward the outhouse.

Kaleb stood when his father-in law came into the room, expecting his wife to be with him. Offering his chair to George, he went to look for her. He was angry with himself for putting a damper on their first Christmas together. He didn't find her in the kitchen or their room. When he noticed her coat and boots missing, he grabbed his own and ran out the door. His emotions tossed and turned as he ran toward the barn, bellowing her name.

Elizabeth could hear Kaleb calling, but she was indisposed at the moment.

Lady was in her stall. That relieved his mind to a degree. Did he miss seeing her in the house? He'd asked about her whereabouts earlier, but no one seemed to know if she went for a walk with her father or not. As Kaleb approached the back entrance, the outhouse door squeaked open, drawing his attention. He sighed with relief when his wife came into view, ran toward her, and lifted her off the ground in a bone-crushing embrace.

"Kaleb," she squeaked, gasping for air, "I can't breath."

Her words brought him back to his senses. He set her down. "Liz, I couldn't find you. I thought you were gone!"

She stared into his dark, frantic eyes. "I may want to be at times, but I wouldn't do it."

His emotions still tumbled within as he scooped her up into his arms and sat on the back step. He had to touch her, kiss her, calm his restless heart.

She surrendered to her husband's unusual appeal, understanding that nothing had changed except her state of mind. At the moment, that was all that mattered.

"Kaleb," she said, as she ran her fingers through his honey-blonde hair, "I started the kettle. We should head back in before it goes dry."

He nodded, stood, and held the door for her. "Liz, I had some of your apple pie. It was delicious."

"I'm glad you enjoyed it. I have my heart set on something else." Elizabeth's mouth watered in anticipation. "My mother made pumpkin."

His brow furrowed. "So, I take it apple is not your favorite?"

"No, Kaleb, it's not." She giggled. His downcast look was too much!

"How will I ever get you to make it if you don't crave it as much as I do?"

"Oh, I'm sure you'll think of something. You're resourceful when you need to be—downright manipulative, if you ask me."

"Persuasive, Dear."

"Call it whatever you want. It accomplishes the same thing." She could feel her irritation rising. Determined to set her own feelings aside and find peace instead of contention with this man, a thought ran through her mind. *I've always considered Kaleb to be a peacemaker. Maybe the tables are turning and it's my turn to take on that role. When two stubborn people are joined for life, both of them can't be right all of the time. Maybe I can just agree to disagree and leave it at that, even if I know in my heart that I'm right.*

"Kaleb, would you like something to drink with your pie?"

"Sure—coffee, please. My mug's sitting on the counter, right next to the pot. How big of a piece are you looking for, Liz?"

"Huge!"

Kaleb chuckled as he added a second slice to the one he'd put on her plate. He carried the tray into the sitting room, where they joined the rest of their family.

Tradition called for the evening to end with the singing of Christmas carols, and by the time George announced the last song, everyone, except Elizabeth, was pretty well spent. Her family packed up the sleigh, and they said their good-byes. Louise handed Elizabeth the pair of jeans she'd confiscated from Jared and stole a hug. Kaleb and Jesse were in a deep discussion about something, so Elizabeth slipped into their room and tucked them away. She may never summon the courage to put them on, but at least she knew they were handy if she wanted them. Lost in thought, she started when Kaleb poked his head in the room.

"Liz, throw on some old clothes. I'm taking you sledding." He was gone before she had a chance to respond.

In a sudden wave of boldness—or maybe a touch of defiance; she didn't know, or care—she removed her dress, added a second pair of long underdrawers and pulled her brother's jeans on over top. They were looser than she remembered, so she tied a piece of hair ribbon around her waist to hold them up. As if the jeans weren't pushing things far enough, she added the old flannel shirt she wore when she went to town as Eli. All she needed to top it off was her brother's old Scottish cap, but she'd left that at home. Her short riding coat put the finishing touch on the ensemble. She was ready to face the cold. Now all she had to do was walk out the door. She glanced back at her reflection in the mirror, wondering, *what will my husband say?* She quivered in anticipation.

"Liz, what's holding you up? Come on."

She sighed with relief when Kaleb didn't come in. He was calling from the sitting room. The moment of reckoning had come. It was now or never. She took the coward's way out and snuck through the breezeway to the pantry, yelling out before she moved through the door: "Kaleb, I'll wait for you outside!"

Husband and wife were well on their way to the barn before he captured a glimpse of her attire. Elizabeth continued walking, but Kaleb's steps slowed, and then came to a halt when he realized his eyes were not playing tricks on him.

"Elizabeth, where did you get those?"

"What?"

He smiled at her oh-so-innocent response. "You know exactly what I'm talking about. Now turn around and answer me."

She stopped and turned. Her chin was out and ready for war. "They were Jared's and now they're mine. You said to put on old clothes. I merely did as I was told. I wear them when I mend fences with Jesse or when I'm doing other odd jobs around the farm. I also use them for sledding. They're actually quite comfy."

He had never seen her in them before the cabin incident, so he knew she didn't wear them all that often. "Well, don't get too comfortable. If you don't want me to burn them, you'll ask my permission the next time you take a notion to put them on."

His words, though written in granite, did nothing to alter her response. Childish or not, she couldn't resist! She backed out of his reach, stuck out her tongue, and tried to run. The shock that registered on Kaleb's face made her explode with laughter. He tackled her before she took ten steps. As he pulled her into his lap, his scolding started her laughter all over again.

"Don't you ever, do you ... hear ...?"

"Then don't be such an old stick in the mud or I'll burn all my dresses and wear jeans all the time."

"No you won't!"

Her head tilted. Her brow rose in obvious delight. "The way I see it, all I need is my Scottish cap to hold all this hair and I could pass for your cousin Eli."

"We both know I don't have any cousins. And, if I wanted a wife who looks like a boy, I wouldn't have married you."

"What are you saying, Kaleb?"

"You're far too delicate and lovely to ever pass for a boy."

His tone sent trickling shivers through her frame. Her father's counsel—the unmistakable desire in her husband's eyes—thoughts she had hoped to suppress—now swirled fantastically. *Kaleb, please don't love me—not until I can love you back!* Leery of his unspoken words, she leapt to her feet and ran for the sled.

Kaleb came to her side, reached for her gloved hand, and

they were off to the hill. Although he would love to know what had just happened, he didn't press her.

The peaceful stroll in the moonlight brought to the surface emotions she would rather ignore. And the strange feeling in the pit of her stomach didn't help.

Kaleb sat on the back of the sled; his long jean-clad legs stretched the distance to the steering bar with much room to spare. Reluctant, Elizabeth sat between them, grabbed his bent knees, and they were off. The brisk flight down the hill was exhilarating. The joy they shared—acting like a couple of children—was exactly what their unsettled hearts needed—nothing pressuring them, just all out fun. As they crested the top of the hill for the eighth time, Kaleb announced that this would be their last ride before heading in. Unlike his wife, he was spent.

"Let's do this one up right, Liz. Lean back and we'll really soar!" He was right. Within seconds they were sitting at the bottom of the hill.

"Thanks for bringing me, Kaleb. I enjoyed myself."

"That makes two of us."

"Good!" Elizabeth kissed his cheek. When she moved to get up, he pulled her into his lap.

Removing his glove, his long finger's outlined her face. "Before we go, I need to apologize to you. The way I responded to you earlier was wrong. It upset me that you would even ask when you *knew* how I felt." For a time, their gaze held.

"I wish I understood what goes on in your head, Kaleb, but I don't. You knew what I was like when you married me. Did you hope to change me that much?"

"No, but until we find a compromise we can both live with,

I would appreciate you honoring my wishes, even if you think I'm wrong."

Staring off into the distance, she murmured her reply, "I thought I was doing that."

He reached for her chin and gently brought her eyes back to his. "You're fighting me."

"I'm frustrated, Kaleb, and I don't like the wedge it puts between us."

"I'm so afraid you'll get hurt again. Can you let me take small steps towards working this through?"

"I suppose." What choice did she have?

"I appreciate your patience."

"I wish I could say that I'm being patient. I'm no longer a child, Kaleb. I have wants and desires just like you. I'm not saying that I don't have areas that need improvement, but if you can't begin to have a little faith in me, how will we ever have a relationship based on mutual trust?"

"I'm trying, Liz."

"Then show me you are by taking the first step."

In the shadows of the moonlit night, Elizabeth watched as her husband's gaze lowered and his expressions went from fearful to contemplative. When his emotions finally reached resolution, she could no longer restrain her desire to kiss him. Maybe it was seeing effort on his part that prompted her yearning. She didn't know, but his response was amazing. And suddenly her supple heart was willing to accept whatever his tortured mind could avow.

"I'm sure it's safe enough for you to go to the barn alone. Will you let someone know, or leave me a note on the counter if you're going further?"

"Sure." It wasn't much of a concession. For Kaleb it was a beginning. Elizabeth wondered if her father had said something, but the thought had no more crossed her mind when she realized it didn't matter. She was thankful for whatever had mellowed his heart.

Chapter Seventeen

His Golden Beauty

THE FOREBODING WINTER storm proceeded to cover their world in a pristine white blanket. By noon, a foot of snow had fallen, with no relief in sight. Not only were their plans for the New Year's Vigil at church canceled, but Kaleb informed Elizabeth at dinner that they wouldn't even chance going to see her family. Disheartened, though understanding this news, she busied herself with mending and such.

After the noon meal, Elizabeth set her own project aside and finally got around to teaching Sarah how to crochet a blanket for her doll. Several hours had passed before she had Sarah working well on her own.

Kaleb had been outside with Samuel moving snow for the better part of the afternoon, but he didn't come in when his father did. Thinking that some fresh air would do her some good, Elizabeth bundled up and went to join him in the barn. He didn't hear her come in and started when she walked up behind him. "Kaleb, you've been out here a long time. Is something wrong?"

He shrugged. "No. Just thinking."

She pressed him further. "I don't think you're being honest with me."

Her boldness surprised him. "Well, I don't think you're ready to hear what's on my mind."

The rapid beat of her heart did nothing to weaken her resolve. Since her talk with her father, she had become more aware of Kaleb's changing needs. As much as she'd like to keep denying what she could clearly see, it was time to discuss this openly. "I'm not as fragile, or naïve, as you seem to think. Your eyes speak volumes. Besides, even if I am uncomfortable with what you have to say, I need to hear it."

Her fervor was more than apparent, when he reached for her hand and led her to the bench in front of Lady's stall so they could sit together. His eyes held on to hers.

"You're my wife, Liz. I love what you've brought to my life, but I can't help feeling as though you're only partially committed to this marriage. In all fairness, I should have talked to you before now. I'm struggling with the agreement we made. This waiting period is more difficult than I ever could have imagined."

Her lids slid shut. Hearing his confession was harder to take than she thought. "So you're saying you've changed your mind?"

He tucked her stray hairs behind her ears. "I would never want you to do something you're not ready for."

"But you are, aren't you?"

"Yes. I realized it the night we went sledding."

Elizabeth said nothing at first. In truth, his admission came as no surprise. But would she be able to ... go through with it? "My father and I had a long discussion on Christmas Day. He asked if we shared an intimate relationship."

This surprised Kaleb. "What did you say?"

"Since he was the one who asked you to give me time, I saw no reason not to tell him."

Kaleb nodded.

"Dad said that if you wanted intimacy, and you're holding back on my account, I'm in the wrong. Why didn't you tell me before this?"

"You weren't ready. For a while I suppose my pride was involved. I wanted this to be a mutual longing, but ..." He held her face in his rough hands and gazed into her caring eyes. "I'm in love with you, Liz ... I yearn for the day that you'll allow me to show you how much."

Moments passed as she comtemplated her response. "I care for you, Kaleb. You've become so much more than a friend, but I won't say that I love you until I'm sure."

He pulled her into his arms. "Oh, Liz, don't let this get you down. I know you care or you wouldn't put up with me. My love comes without conditions."

Her eyes glassed over. "If that's true, where do we go from here?"

He understood her uncertainties—he had some of his own. "That's up to you—you know where my heart is. I won't press you. When you're ready to come to me, let me know. I'll be waiting with open arms."

Her heart wanted to say yes. She had to be sure she could follow through. After sharing a tender kiss, the quiet couple walked back to the house.

❦ ❦ ❦

How the day had come so quickly to a close, she did not know. New Year's Eve had always been a time for staying up late and celebrating in her family home. Things were far different in the White household. Kaleb and Elizabeth were the only ones awake at half-past eight. Perhaps it was for the best.

Her husband's preoccupation with a book he'd been reading gave her the time she needed to come to a decision that would change her relationship with Kaleb—forever. She tried to be rational as she mulled this over, but her anxious mind was all in a dither. When she stopped thinking and began to pray, she was able to give her fears to the Lord. Denying the inner prompting of her heart was no longer an option.

Arriving at this conclusion was one thing. Now she was faced with an even greater perplexity than before: how could she summon the courage to enlighten him?

Recalling Kaleb's passionate reaction to her pink summer camisole gave her an idea. She smiled at her own ingenuity and headed off to their room. Because she had made it clear that he would not see her in this outfit again until they were in their own home, she was certain he would take the hint.

A quick glance at her reflection told her all was in order, except her hair. She pulled it from the chignon, brushed through her long tresses, and left it hanging loose. Kaleb loved her hair down. Since she normally braided it for bed, she smiled, thinking this would be another insinuation. Looking at her image in the mirror, she thought, *as long as I don't have to tell him, I should be able to maintain my resolve.* Securing her robe, she stuck her feet into her slippers and murmured a prayer as she walked out the door.

As she rounded the corner and found her husband's gaze fixed on her, Elizabeth willed her thundering heart to calm. Slouched in the chair, his deep amber eyes held an invasive glare that seemed to examine every inch of her mind. *Does he know?* she asked herself, and then answered. *No, Elizabeth, how could he? You haven't said a thing.*

"Liz," he implored, in a soft, yet masterful tone, "come here."

He knows! Her legs felt like willow branches, void of strength—surely they would bend and sway if she dared take a step. All the courage she had summoned abated, like dew in the morning sun.

Sensing her trance-like state and progressive panic, Kaleb stood, captured her slender hand, and led his timid wife to their room. The door clicked shut. Her eyes never left him as he turned the lamp down low. Removing his bluchers, he loosened his shirt, sat on the edge of the bed and drew her into his lap. She trembled at his gentle touch that was only meant to soothe. With slow deliberate moves, his long fingers slid down the soft skin of her cheek. He looked at her with undeniable devotion. His words, though barely detectable, surprised her nonetheless. "Are you coming to me willingly, Liz?"

"Yes," she said, though she could not be sure it was an audible response until she saw the elation in the depth of his gaze.

He was thrilled with her decision, but her trembling heightened and that concerned him. "Sweetheart, are you frightened?"

She managed a single nod and admitted, "Petrified!"

Drawing her closer into his arms, moments passed in silence before Kaleb sought to expose his own floundering emotions. "Liz, this is new for both of us. I'm unsure as well. Maybe if we keep in mind that God created us to delight in one another ...."

His admission was too absurd, though a glance in his direction revealed otherwise. "You are?" She never would have thought Kaleb could be anything but confident. "Would you mind if we take things slow?"

"Sounds wonderful." Yielding to one another, his passionate kisses brushed softly against her lips. He paused, simply had to know. "Honey, can I ask you something?"

"Absolutely."

"What do you have on under your robe? Because I know it's not a gown." The intimation he saw in her glittering blue eyes told him all he needed to know.

Abandoning her own reluctance, she could not deny him. "You could help me out of my robe and see for yourself." Where her sudden display of courage came from, she did not know, nor the boldness that followed. No longer was she afraid of this wonderful, caring man. Rising to her feet, she watched as his clumsy impatient fingers worked at the many buttons. His face lit up as her robe slowly opened revealing the delicate lace of her pink summer camisole.

Kaleb beheld her loveliness. Knowing he had her permission to claim what was rightfully his, he drew her to him. "Do you have any idea how lovely I find you, Liz?"

Her fingers skimmed the rough skin of his jaw, as the

windows of their hearts held on to each other. "I think you're pretty amazing yourself."

"I love you, Elizabeth Brenae White ...."

Capturing his golden beauty in a warm embrace, his oh-so-desirable kisses were a wonderful place to start. As their uncertainties dissolved into undeniable pleasure, the evening of celebration held discoveries beyond imagination. Husband and wife both gave and received and found contentment and belonging in each other's arms.

He Loves Me!

Chapter Eighteen

The New Papa

ELIZABETH HAD BEGUN to wonder if the heavy winter storms that held them captive would ever let up. What she wouldn't give for a day's reprieve, a nice long visit with Amy, anything that would break up the monotony of her ordered life. On the rare occasion that the weather would break, Kaleb would take her to see her family, but those times were few and far between.

Kaleb and Jesse were spending every spare moment preparing lumber for the new home. Whenever possible, Elizabeth would work with them removing limbs and smaller branches. So many wonderful memories were brought to remembrance as the three of them worked to accomplish their goals. Unfortunately, some things would never change. On the days when the men were cutting down trees, she was a child again in their eyes and sent back to the house or the barn. As much as she resented their

superior air, two against one was never fair—especially when the two against her were Kaleb and Jesse. Her wounded pride was involved, but she pressed on, refusing to give those wounds time to fester.

Out of desperation, Elizabeth picked up the novel she had begun to write during her last semester at school. She loved the way it drew her in and allowed her an escape. There was nothing like creating a story that entailed a fine mix of truth and fiction. She giggled, cried, and smiled as her life experiences filled the blank pages. At times she wrote things just to see them in print and then erased them. Silly? Yes. Healing? Immensely! Her frustrations were interwoven in the prologue, but it worked well for what she needed to accomplish. As much as she enjoyed the diversion, reality had a way of sweeping in the moment she tucked it away. Elizabeth's anxious spirit and unpredictable stomach were dragging her down. She was convinced that her mood swings had everything to do with feeling like a caged bird.

On the second Saturday in February, her mom stopped by, wanting her company on a ride into Ann Arbor for supplies. Kaleb's response would not be favorable, of course, but on this day Elizabeth was determined to press him. She found him alone in the barn working on furniture.

Listening halfheartedly to Kaleb's excuses to delay or reschedule the trip, Elizabeth came to one firm decision. She was going! Her father said that a good marriage required give and take on both sides. If that was so, it was time for him to start giving and her taking. Only thing was, she hated conflict. Since she would prefer to be in agreement with her husband, she attempted a calm visage. "Kaleb, the sky is clear and my mother could help me pick out the fabrics you've been wanting me to buy for spring clothes." He seemed to be considering her request, so she waited.

He took a deep breath and slowly exhaled. "You would come home before dark?"

"Yes. Mom needs to be back before supper."

"I don't like this—but I suppose it wouldn't kill me to compromise. Go on ... get ready. Let me know when you're heading out."

She nodded and turned to leave before a huge smile erupted on her face. Containing her elation was not an easy task. She wanted to shout, jump for joy! Instead, she hustled toward her room, added the necessary pieces of clothing, and wasted no time in frivolous endeavors. She needed to get back to the barn before a certain tall blonde giant had too much time to think. Elizabeth heard her mother's voice in the kitchen and stopped to say, "I'm ready, Mom. I'll be back in just a minute. I need to tell Kaleb we're leaving."

She slid inside the crack in the big barn door and found her husband planing the top of their new armoire. "Kaleb, Mom and I are heading out." She cringed when he set his tool aside, reached for her hand, and pulled her into the tack room, away from her brother who had just arrived and was otherwise occupied.

"You and your mother stay together, Elizabeth. Do you hear me?"

"Yes, Dear."

"Do you have enough layers on under that dress? Do I need to check?" When he lifted her skirt to do just that, she squealed.

"Kaleb, stop! What if my brother comes in?" As usual, he

ignored her protests and went on.

"You put on extra socks, didn't you?"

"Kaleb, I'm not a child. Now kiss me and quit being such a worry-wart. My mother is waiting."

Since their marriage, this would be the first time Elizabeth went anywhere without him, and his reservations were many. "I'd feel much better if you'd stop by and see Doc while you're in town. You're looking pale and you should mention your lack of appetite."

She loved the way he kept touching her. "I'm fine, Kaleb. I don't need a doctor to tell me that my overprotective husband worries too much!"

When he reached around and swatted her backside, a roll of her eyes brought on more of his threats. "You'd better be good or I'll torture you later."

Her chin went in the air. "Since you only have threats to issue, you don't need a farewell kiss, I'll be off. See you later, Kaleb White." With a flick of her hand, she turned to leave and found herself scooped into his arms for a wonderful send-off.

"Mom," Elizabeth asked when they were almost to town, "after we pick up the things we need at the store, would you mind if we stop by the parsonage to say hello? I thought it would be fun to take some candy to Mikayla and Theodore."

"That's fine. I'm sure the children would love it."

After dropping the team off at the livery, they headed for the general store.

Elizabeth walked to the counter and greeted the proprietor as if nothing were out of the ordinary. "Hello, Mrs. Grant. How are you?"

"I'm fine, Lizzy." She recalled how withdrawn the young bride had been on her last visit. Elizabeth's lack of apprehension at the moment astounded her. "I haven't seen you around these parts since before Christmas. I hope you haven't been ill."

Her brow rose. "I thought you knew. Kaleb and I were married."

"Oh that's right, he confirmed that the last time you were here. I'm a little confused. You told me time and again that you and Kaleb were only friends. Did something change? I'm curious as to why you agreed to marry him." Without giving Elizabeth a chance to respond, she added, "Do you live with your family, Lizzy, or his?"

My, my, my! You ask so many questions for such a fine upstanding lady. "As you know, it's customary for a bride to live with her husband after they're wed. I live with his family, not mine. You don't see me because, unlike my father, Kaleb rarely lets me out of his sight." She hoped this would be the end of her interrogation. It was not.

"I'm sure your family misses having you around."

"I miss them too, but when false tales were spread about us, my parents and Kaleb didn't feel as though we had an option. You know what it's like. Folks forget that the Bible speaks about those who bare false witness against their neighbors. I'll continue to pray for whoever those people are, that God will convict their hearts and show them a better way. In spite of their intent, though, I'm happy to convey that I've been a fortunate victim. I have no regrets. Kaleb White is a wonderful husband." Elizabeth stopped and brushed a piece of lint off her coat. "So you see, Mrs. Grant, God can use *anyone* to accomplish His purpose in our lives. What others intended for evil turned out to be a huge blessing for Kaleb and myself."

The proprietor stood dumbfounded by Elizabeth's proclamation, and Jayne was flabbergasted as well.

"I'm glad you and Kaleb are happy. Is there anything I can help you with today?"

Apparently Mrs. Grant was ready to change the topic, and Elizabeth, having said more than she intended, agreed. However, her heart did a flip when she looked up and saw Mr. Grant. She could only assume from his shocked expression that he had taken in the entire exchange.

"Mom and I both have lists. If you don't mind, we'll leave them with you while we head over to pick out our yard goods."

"Take your time, ladies."

Elizabeth led her mother toward the fabrics, and the second they were out of earshot, she asked, "Mom, are you all right?"

"Yes, but you said all that without an ounce of animosity. You're really okay with your marriage, aren't you?"

Elizabeth smiled and kissed her mother's cheek. "Yes. God knew my stubborn heart and blessed me in spite of it. Even if Kaleb had asked until he was blue in the face, I wouldn't have agreed to court him, never mind marry him. I convinced myself that I wanted to travel, see some things before settling down. Looking back, I can see that Amy's influence played a big part in that. Funny how things work out, isn't it?

It could have been disastrous is what Jayne thought.

"Now mind you, we have our differences of opinion, but if Kaleb would quit smothering me, I'd go so far as to say I've found my match."

Jayne pulled Elizabeth into her arms. "Honey, I'm so happy I could just burst!"

"I suppose I should have told you long before this. I really didn't think about it. Promise me you won't quit praying for us. We need it." Her mother's smile warmed Elizabeth's heart.

"We'll never quit praying, Honey."

"Good! Tell me something, Mom. After we pick out the yard goods, would you mind staying to have them cut? Kaleb wanted me to stop by and ask Doc a question or two. I shouldn't be long."

Concern filled Jayne's eyes. "You're not sick, are you, Lizzy?"

She shook her head. "Kaleb thinks I'm losing too much weight. I think he worries too much. Since we're here, it can't hurt to talk to Doc. Just don't tell you-know-who where I'm going."

Jayne grimaced. "I wouldn't dream of it. Would you like me to pick up the candy and meet you at the parsonage?"

"Sounds great." Her mother's input made her selections easy. It took a while to gather everything she would need to complete her projects, but she now had the notions and fabrics to make two lightweight dresses and a skirt and blouse for herself, along with three shirts for Kaleb.

"Mom, Mrs. Grant's busy with Rena Wilson. Just tell her I said goodbye. I'll see you at the Williams'."

There was no doubt in Elizabeth's mind that Kaleb would not be happy if he knew she was going off alone. But what choice did she have? If she had to take her mother along, she wouldn't be going at all. Some things were private. Besides, depending on what Doc said, she might not tell Kaleb about their visit at all. Setting her concern aside, she made her way down the boardwalk, stepped out into the street, and glanced up the way. Jack and Tom

Bemis were outside the saloon. In no mood to put up with their shenanigans and hoping to slide by unnoticed, she avoided the worst of the slush and moved to the opposite side of the street.

Elizabeth couldn't begin to comprehend how two kind-hearted people could have raised such rotten kids. Their mother, God rest her soul, had passed away about five years ago from a weak heart. No wonder. That was about the time the boys began building up their reputation as the town bullies. Elizabeth would have thought they'd be settling down by now, but that wasn't the case. *Surely only a divine intervention from God would turn them around.* Her judgmental thoughts had no more run through her mind when she realized what she was doing and berated herself for it. *Who are you to talk, Elizabeth? Look at what it took for you to listen. We're all sinners in need of a Savior. You should be praying for them, instead of judging them!* Elizabeth started when Jack's comment took her by surprise.

"Well, well, well. Would you look at who we have here, Tom? If it isn't the charming Elizabeth Somers."

A wave of panic passed through her. She could probably out-run him in his drunken state, but that would draw attention from other townsfolk, so she stood her ground.

Leaving Elizabeth no time to react, Jack darted towards her, grabbed her upper arm, and said, "Where have you been hiding yourself, Elizabeth? Haven't seen you around in a while."

Jack ran his thick, grubby finger down her cheek, giving her the whim-whams as he said, "You and I could be having all kinds of fun if you'd just give us a little time to get to know each other better." His perverse chuckle made her cringe. And his awful smell brought bile to her throat.

"I'm sure your father and Jesse could let you out of their sights long enough for you to come for a visit of sorts!"

"Now that wouldn't be such a good idea, Jack. Besides, what do you suppose my husband would say?" Her words did not have the effect she was hoping for. Jack jerked her arm so hard she wondered if she would find bruises where his fingers were wrapped around it.

"Don't you go telling me a story now, Girl. A fine lady like yourself should know better than to be lying to a nice gentleman who's sweet on you."

Nice, my eye! His breath reeked of booze and his body stank. Since when did the words *nice* and *harassment* go hand in hand? Perhaps she should have been frightened. In truth, she found them pathetic. Jesse's warnings were going off in her head, but she didn't think they would do anything in broad daylight. Clinging to the hope that they were only giving her a hard time, she decided to mention her gentle giant again.

"It's no story, Jack. If you don't unhand me and back off, I'll have to let my husband, Kaleb White, in on this rather suggestive conversation you insist on having." It was as if she'd admitted to having the plague. He let her go and backed off so fast that she had to suppress a laugh. Kaleb's overwhelming size often had a strange effect on folks. Fortunately, no one had witnessed the encounter. If it got back to Kaleb that these not-so-gentle men had accosted her, he would not be happy with them or her.

She hurried down the street, reached for the brass handle on Doc's door, and moved inside. He wasn't in the office, so she wandered down the hallway that connected to his living quarters, calling out. "Hey Doc, you here?" She found him coming out of the kitchen with his sweet wife Martha wrapped in his arm. Seeing their open display of affection warmed Elizabeth.

"This is a nice surprise," Doc said, "What brings you in to see us today, Lizzy?"

"Mom and I had a little shopping to do, so I thought I'd stop by to say hello."

"And?"

Her eyes flew up. He knew her too well. "Kaleb wanted me to run a few concerns by you."

He nodded. "Let's head down to the office so we can talk."

"Good to see you, Mrs. Taylor."

"Same here, Honey. Come again when you can stay for a while. And, Lizzy, bring that handsome man you're married to next time!"

"I will, thanks."

As expected, Doc got right to the point. "So tell me, Lizzy, other than the weight loss, what's going on?"

She groaned. "Is it that noticeable?"

"Yes."

"Truth is, my stomach hasn't been on level ground of late. I can't eat very much if I want it to stay down. It's the strangest thing—some days I'm horrible and other days I'm fine."

"You haven't talked to your mother or mother-in-law about this?"

She scowled. "Of course not! Kaleb doesn't even know I've been sick." The way he stared unnerved her. She tried to explain: "You know what he's like, Doc. If he thinks I'm ill he'll insist I stay in bed. I just can't do that. You'll keep this visit between the two of us, right?"

He shook his head. "Lizzy, your husband has a right to know what's going on with you."

"That may be, but you have to let me decide what to tell him—and when."

He couldn't believe she was acting this way. "You made it sound like he knew you were coming to see me."

"He asked me to. I told him he worries too much." Feeling a twinge of guilt, she added, "I am fine ... some of the time at least."

"Lizzy, girl, you confuse me. Come up on the table and let me examine you."

After a few um-hm's and ah-ha's, he seemed to come up with a diagnosis, but he was in no hurry to fill her in. He went to his desk and began writing on a sheet of paper. When he finished, he looked up and said, "I'll give you two weeks to tell Kaleb, or I'll do it for you."

Since he'd always been like this with her, she should have expected no less. "Honestly, Doc, you don't know what it's like living with Kaleb. I know he loves me, but he barely lets me out of his sight. It was like pulling teeth to convince him to let me come to town with my mom today. I don't want him to know if there is something wrong with me."

Doc's response was matter-of-fact. "Your husband has the right to know he's going to be a father, Elizabeth."

She was stunned, speechless! She'd expected him to tell her to take a pill and all would be well. "A baby? You think I'm ..."

"Yes Lizzy, you're pregnant. I've written out some instructions that should help you to keep food down. If you get any worse, I want to know about it right away. Your husband is right: you can't afford to lose any more weight. Even if you feel ill, I want you to eat small meals often. Have Kaleb bring you back in March unless something comes up before then."

"You're sure about this?"

He started to laugh. "Lizzy, I've been bringing babies into the world for thirty years. I know an expectant woman when I see one." His expression went from humorous to imploring as he glared above his spectacles. "Remember what I said, Lizzy Girl! You have two weeks before I tell him myself."

"I will." She paused for a moment. "You can tell Mrs. Taylor— no one else, please."

"She'd like that, but I wouldn't dream of telling anyone else. This is your news to share."

"Thanks, Doc. See you tomorrow at church."

"Send the new papa my congratulations!"

"When I tell him, I will. I have two weeks, remember!" They shared a heartwarming smile as she walked out of the office. Elizabeth took a seat on the bench outside the door and attempted to clear her thoughts. If she didn't snap out of her dazed state, her mother's questions would never end, and she'd be forced to tell her.

She didn't know what to think. When she placed her hands on her flat stomach, reality began to set in. A wave of excitement ran through her, along with questions—unanswered ones. No sense worrying when the man who could put an end to her quandary was just inside.

"Doctor Taylor. Are you still back here?"

"Yes, Lizzy. Did you forget something?"

"I'm unsettled about a few things. How many months before this baby will come?"

"From what I can tell, the beginning to middle of October."

"So there is no way folks will get the wrong impression, because it takes nine months, right?"

"Honey, when did you and Kaleb consummate the marriage?"

Her cheeks flushed.

"Lizzy, I'm your Doctor. If you tell me, I might be able to ease your mind."

"Oh … I suppose that makes sense. New Year's Eve."

"Then you have nothing to worry about. It does take nine months for a baby to be full term. Even the folks who started those rumors can count. Relax and enjoy the blessing that's growing inside of you."

Elizabeth sighed with relief, offering a hug that he accepted with gratitude. "Thanks, Doc. I feel much better. And just so you know, as long as Kaleb's home when I arrive, I'm going to tell him about the baby."

"Now that's what I like to hear. I don't care if you need to see me every day until your concerns are exhausted. Just eat, and let God take care of the details."

"I will. Thanks again." She reached for the handle and sent him a mischievous smile. "I really am leaving this time—promise!"

Doc was pleased to see a smile on her face, and he thanked the Lord for small favors. Moving to the window, he watched with joy in his heart as Elizabeth moved on down the street with a confident skip in her steps.

❀ ❀ ❀

"Hello, Carolyn. How are you and your little ones doing?"

Carolyn smiled as she ushered Elizabeth in, took her coat, and answered her question.

"We're doing fine. Your mother and I are having tea and visiting with the children in the parlor. Come, join us."

Elizabeth reached for her hand. "Before we head in, I wanted to thank you for the time you put in on my gift. Kaleb loves the dress on me. It was such an unexpected surprise."

"I wish you could have seen him, Lizzy. He has excellent taste, wouldn't you say?"

"Carolyn," she said, somewhat befuddled. "I assumed you were the one to pick everything out."

She shook her head. "I went with Kaleb, but he did all the choosing—even the trims."

Elizabeth could not wipe the smile from her face. This news astounded her. Growing up, she couldn't remember a single time where her father showed an interest in anything but the finished product.

"You look amazed, Honey."

"I suppose I am. Kaleb's full of surprises, but this goes above and beyond."

As they rounded the corner and entered the parlor, a sweet young boy stepped up to greet her. "Who do we have here?" Elizabeth asked, as she reached to shake his hand. He was a handsome little guy with features much like her Kaleb's. In the boy's reluctance to speak, Elizabeth introduced herself. "I'm Lizzy to most of my friends and family. Am I correct in assuming you're Theodore?"

He seemed to hang on her every word. "My family and friends call me Teddy."

"Very nice to meet you, Teddy."

His eyes, so gentle, left Elizabeth long enough to smile up at Carolyn with affection before he turned back and said, "My new mother tells me that your Kaleb is very tall like I am."

Elizabeth thought she would burst into tears when she realized how swiftly the boy and Carolyn had bonded. "Yes, he is. In fact, I've always thought of him as somewhat of a giant."

Theodore chuckled.

"Kaleb's looking forward to meeting you."

When Elizabeth saw Carolyn's daughter leave her own mother and hide behind her brother's leg, her heart about went to pieces. There stood this petite two-year-old dolly, with a head full of raven hair that hung down her back in massive ringlets. She had a baby soft fullness to her cheeks and amber-colored eyes that danced on her little round face.

To seem less threatening, Elizabeth sat down on the rug and carried on a conversation with this shy little wonder. "Hello, Sweetheart. You must be Mikayla. I'm Lizzy."

Her head bobbed up and down in the cutest way. "Yep, I'ms Kayla Sue Wi-mms."

"Williams," her brother corrected.

She was so serious. The women in the room had all they could do to hold their laughter. "Yep, Wi-mms, T-dy says!"

"I think you say it just perfectly for a young lady." Elizabeth turned to Mikayla's brother and asked, "Teddy, did you know that Mrs. Somers is my mother?

"Yes. She said you have brothers and sisters. I'm going to meet them tomorrow at church."

"Teddy," Carolyn asked, "do you remember what you were

going to ask Lizzy?"

"Oh yes! My father said that we're coming to your house tomorrow. Would you take me for a ride on Lady? I've never ridden a horse. Mother says she's nice."

Elizabeth smiled in the light of his hopeful inquiry. "Teddy, it would give me great pleasure to share my Lady with you, and Mikayla too if she'd like to ride." Theodore beamed as he moved to Elizabeth's side and joined her on the floor. Within seconds, Mikayla abandoned her reluctance and, to everyone's astonishment, plopped her tiny self down in Elizabeth's lap.

They visited for a while before Elizabeth and Jayne needed to be on their way. The children were delighted with their gift of sweets and waved at the window as the women walked away.

"Hey, sleepy head! Dinner's ready. Are you going to join us, or sleep right through the night?"

After a long stretch, Elizabeth opened her eyes to find her husband smiling down at her. "What time is it?"

Kaleb, thinking his wife looked awfully tired for someone who had just taken a two-hour nap, didn't hear her question. "I tried to kiss you, Liz. Your breath's horrible. Is your throat sore? Are you ill?"

She offered her pat answer. "You worry too much." His arms were straddling her on either side, so she couldn't get up.

"Did you see Doc like I asked you to?"

"I did. Martha too. They're both doing well. Martha wants us to stop by for a visit. She's so sweet, Kaleb. We really should plan to see them more often. Mom and I had a wonderful visit with Pastor's children. I can't wait for you to meet them. They're so cute. Did your parent's tell you they're coming for dinner tomorrow, after church?"

"No."

"Teddy's never ridden a horse, so I told him I'd take him for a ride on Lady."

"That's fine—but you haven't answered my question."

"I did, to a degree. Besides, your family's waiting for us to eat. The food will get cold."

He chortled out loud. "That may be, but you are not off the hook. You will tell me what he said later, agreed?"

She should have *agreed* and left well enough alone. His persistence, as it often did, had a way of bringing out the worst in her. "Are you trying to make up for lost time, Kaleb?"

"No ... we both know you're a master at avoiding the inevitable. Now, are we agreed or should I tell my parent's we'll eat when we're finished?"

She rolled her eyes and groaned. "Do you have any idea how insufferable it is being married to someone like you?"

"God knew what he was doing putting us together, Liz. Are we agreed?"

If he asked that question one more time, she was going to scream. "You're like a hound dog going after his prey."

"Elizabeth! You're trying my patience."

"Then we're a matched set. I'll tell you when I'm ready, and not a moment sooner."

His long finger running down the side of her face soothed her frazzled nerves. She even managed a halfhearted smile when he tucked her hair behind her ears. "I'm sorry I upset you. I think we both know this is getting us nowhere ...."

She held his gaze. "I shouldn't be so stubborn. I really do want to tell you, but I'm hungry and I have no desire to rush this conversation."

He nodded. "In that case, I'll ask my parent's to do the dishes and we'll talk in the loft after supper. Is that all right with you?"

"Yes. I need you to do me a favor though."

"What's that?"

Her brow furrowed. "Don't say anything if I can't eat much dinner. My stomach's touchy. I would rather the others didn't know. I'll explain later."

"Would you like me to bring you a tray, so you can stay in bed?"

"No!"

"Settle down. It was only a suggestion."

"I'm sorry. I don't know why I'm so edgy. Go ahead, Kaleb. I'll be right out."

He kissed her forehead, and glanced back before making his way to the kitchen. Trying to get his wife to stay in bed was like trying to tame a rattler: either one would strike without warning.

❀ ❀ ❀

"Doc said that I'm having a normal reaction to what's going on inside my body. But before we go into all that, you have to promise that you're not going to overreact.

"I'll promise you nothing until I know what he said."

"Then I won't tell you!" She folded her arms, her

declaration unwavering.

"Yes, you will, or I'll ask him tomorrow at church."

She grinned in triumph, and declared with confidence, "It will do you no good! He promised me two weeks of silence."

She loved the way his deep-set eyes almost bounced out of his head. Finally, she had him over a barrel! He would have to agree to her terms; he had no other choice.

"Ya know, Elizabeth ..." he said, his tone patronizing, "I could tickle you here in the loft for hours ...."

Well, crackin' ice! What am I going to do now? Doc's words ran through her mind, answering her question for her. *"He has a right to know he's going to be a father."*

"Will you at least try to discuss your concerns instead of spouting your orders?" Her pleading eyes were begging him for some sort of concession.

"I'll try."

She shook her head. "You're not making this easy, Kaleb."

Clueless as to what she was trying to tell him, he grew more impatient as the seconds ticked on. Unfortunately, she went off on another tangent.

"You and Jesse are making furniture for our new house and I would like you to add one more piece to your list."

"That's fine, but what does furniture have to do with what Doc said?"

She raised her hand to forestall him. "Humor me for a minute."

He sighed. "Go ahead."

"I think it should be about," she held out her hand's to show him, "this long and this wide."

"Elizabeth! You're stalling!"

Appalled by his lack of forbearance, she returned her own barrage of intolerance. "I certainly hope you're more patient with our child than you are with your wife!"

"What has that got to do with this discussion?" He was not listening and she enjoyed his irritation more than she should have.

"We're going to need a cradle, Kaleb. So you see, furniture has everything to do with what Doc told me."

His mouth dropped open. "A baby? Are you sure?" He was bewildered, so completely flustered.

"I thought you'd be happy ...." His reaction confused her.

"I'm thrilled. It's just ... well, you know. How did this happen so fast? I thought these things took time."

"Kaleb White, I won't even justify that comment with a response!"

Her irate tone made him laugh as he pulled her close for a kiss. "Liz, this is wonderful news. What else did he say?"

"He's concerned about my weight loss too. He wrote out some suggestions to help me keep food down."

"Did he say when the baby would come?"

"About the middle of October."

Since she'd been hiding her sickness for a while, it was time for some gut-level honesty. "How long have you been sick and not telling me, Elizabeth?"

This one small detail had slipped her mind.

Kaleb insisted, "Honey, look at me, I want the truth. This isn't just about you any more. We have a baby growing inside of you that needs nourishment."

She cast her reluctant gaze on him. "Several weeks."

"How many times a day?"

"Some days once, some twice—usually more."

Kaleb grew pensive, trying to take it all in. They would need to discuss this further, but that could wait. For now, he only wanted to share in her joy. "When do you want to tell everyone?"

"Would you mind if we wait a while?"

"That's fine, but you might have to remind me to wipe this grin off my face."

Elizabeth understood. She had the same problem with her mom and Carolyn. "When we do, I'd like it if we could tell both of our families together?"

"I couldn't agree more." Kaleb snuggled Elizabeth close. The enormity of God's blessing had begun to sink in, and in truth, it overwhelmed him.

"Kaleb, there's one more thing I should tell you." She stared at him, trying to decide if he was going to make a mountain out of a molehill. "I didn't do well on the long ride to Ann Arbor and back. I'd love to go to church tomorrow, but I'm not so sure it's a good idea. Not until some of this sickness passes."

"That's fine. Your health and the baby's have to come first."

"If you'd like to go, don't stay home on my account."

"I wouldn't hear of it. Now let's get you in the house. You haven't been well. You need to rest."

Frantic, her eyes flipped up. "Kaleb White, this is precisely what I was just talking about. I'm having a baby. I'm not sick."

He shrugged, giving no indication that he understood.

She took a firmer stance. "I'm not going back to bed—I just slept for two hours."

"All right," he conceded, with more aplomb than he felt.

"Will you promise to rest when you need to?"

"Yes." She needed to move beyond this tense moment and said, "Doc wanted me to offer his congratulations to the *New Papa.*"

Kaleb was suddenly all smiles...

"I'll get on Lady first, Teddy, okay? Then Kaleb will put you on in front of me." Teddy's little hands clenched in anticipation when they were both on Lady. Pastor and Carolyn stood at the picture window with their reluctant daughter. Mikayla liked watching her brother, but she wanted no part of being anywhere near that large animal.

"What do you think?" Elizabeth asked Theodore as they came around the back side of the barn. "Shall we go a little faster?"

His wavy blonde head spun around. "Could we?"

"Of course." The minute she moved past the front of the house, she nudged Lady into a trot, which made Teddy giggle and then into a slow canter. As much as Elizabeth wanted to keep going, the bouncing was unsettling her irritable stomach. When spots began to float before her eyes, fear overwhelmed her—not only for herself and the baby, but for Theodore as well. She didn't want his first experience riding to end in a fall.

"Kaleb!" she called out in desperation as she rounded the corner.

Alarm slammed through him as his feet propelled forward. The color had drained from his wife's face. Elizabeth had barely latched onto Kaleb's neck when she crumpled into his arms. He had her cradled against him by the time Jesse reached his side.

Jesse demanded to know, "What's wrong with my sister?"

Kaleb grinned at his frantic friend and whispered in his ear. "She'll be fine, Jesse. You're going to be an uncle, that's all. The jostling must have been too much for her."

Jesse's eyes grew wide. This news relieved him to a degree, but the way his sister's unconscious frame appeared in her husband's arms made him shudder. "Go," he insisted, "get her in the house. Teddy and I will go for a ride. We'll be back in a little while."

George and Samuel were at the door helping as Kaleb carried his wife to their room. Jayne grabbed a wet cloth, and when Elizabeth opened her eyes Kaleb was sitting next to her. Their friends and family were gathered around her bed.

Feeling uneasy being on display, Elizabeth glanced back at her husband. "Kaleb, what happened?"

"You passed out." He tucked her hair behind her ear, leaned close and asked, Would you like to relieve their minds, or shall I?"

She smiled. "You do the honors."

"I know all of you are worried, but there's no need. Elizabeth went to see Doc Taylor yesterday. He said our first child will arrive sometime in October."

Jayne and Ruth looked at each other and squealed in delight, "A grandbaby!" The joy on all of their faces was a sight to behold. After hugs were shared, Kaleb shooed everyone out. His wife needed rest and he had every intention of seeing that she got it.

He Loves Me!

Chapter Nineteen

Abducted

*T*HE COLD CHILLS of February gave way to a milder March than they had seen in years. Kaleb's determination to get them into their own home was unrelenting. The stacks of lumber were piling high. It wouldn't be long before he and Jesse could begin laying the foundation.

Kaleb and Elizabeth were trying to decide where to build. Having narrowed their choices down to two areas, they brought it up over supper one night and Samuel had a definite opinion on the matter. He wanted his son's growing family to have the privacy they would need to lead their own separate lives. He encouraged them to build on the opposite side of a long row of massive pines. Elizabeth was enthralled with the setting the moment she laid eyes on it, and Kaleb readily agreed. They wouldn't be able to see each other's homes from this location, but they would have equal access to the barn.

The first week in April, Kaleb and Elizabeth, along with his parents and sister, were invited to have dinner with friends from church. Elizabeth had been hopeful Kaleb would give in this one time and agree to go. It was not to be. Her fear of him overreacting to her illness had been realized. His resolution to keep her from traveling until the sickness passed was unwavering. Although she understood his concerns to a degree, he didn't stop to consider how much an outing would lift both of their spirits. She so longed to fellowship with other believers. Their social life, other than occasional trips to her parents' house, was non-existent. His mother and sister were always around—but her husband, the one person she needed more than anyone, became more distant with each passing day.

Sitting at the table with a cup of tea, Elizabeth looked up as her mother-in-law bustled into the kitchen to say her farewells. Elizabeth had gained a deep appreciation for the way Ruth always treated her with kindness and understanding. "You have to promise to have a wonderful time so you can tell me all about your visit when you return."

Elizabeth was fighting tears and Ruth did all she could to keep from joining her. Concerned for Elizabeth's state of mind, Ruth wanted to confront her son about getting her out more, but Samuel didn't feel it was their place to interfere. She couldn't help wondering if part of Elizabeth's sickness was directly related to the way Kaleb had withdrawn his affection over the last few months. If only he could see what she saw. Since her hands were otherwise tied, she continued to pray for both of them. "I'll do my best, Honey. Promise you'll take it easy. Do something you enjoy."

Elizabeth swallowed her sip of tea. "I thought I'd start a gown for the baby."

"That should be fun. Do you know if Jesse is coming by to

work on the house?"

"I'm not sure. Kaleb's in the barn—you could ask him on your way out."

She shook her head. "That won't be necessary. Your mom wanted to borrow a set of my knitting needles. Would you be a dear and send them with your brother if he shows up? I set them on the end table in the sitting room."

"Sure. By the way, Mom, you look wonderful in your new dress. The deep rose is definitely your color." Elizabeth thought her mother-in-law looked like a porcelain doll. The paleness of her softened skin held so few signs of aging, and the contrasting color against her deep brown hair presented a delicate picture of beauty and elegance. They shared a hug and Elizabeth watched with a heavy heart as Ruth walked out the door.

The Whites would be sharing dinner with Sheriff Henry Kane, his wife Donna, and their two children, Catherine and William. Having come to America from Ireland as a young man, Henry's accent remained strong. Elizabeth loved the expressive way his words rolled off his tongue. He had such a kind way about him that she found it difficult to envision him dealing with thieves and scoundrels. Knowing she could be visiting with these people if her husband wasn't so unreasonable did nothing to relieve her despondent heart.

Elizabeth had been struggling for weeks now, striving for a contentment that would not come. Some of the problems in her relationship with Kaleb were of her own doing, she admitted that. So much had gone wrong. Her marriage had become a lonely place. It started the week she told Kaleb of their coming child. The passionate caring man she was falling in love with had withdrawn a little more each day. At first, she wondered if he was afraid to touch her for fear of making her condition worse. In truth, she didn't know. Although deep down she had to believe he still cared, there was no evidence to lead her to that conclusion. He expected her to be content living within the walls of his parent's home until she was well. What if she was sick for the whole nine months? She didn't understand. No matter what she wanted to do or where she wanted to go, he would refuse her request, and take off like a coward to work on the new house—the house she was supposed to share with a man who had become nothing more than an acquaintance—her brother's friend.

She so longed to have him take her in his arms and gaze into her eyes with that feverish glow—that look that told her he couldn't possibly live without her. Even his wonderful kisses had diminished to an occasional peck—the kind he would give his mother.

Where was the laughter and joy they once shared? How could she get it back? Knowing that God alone could heal their union, she spent much of her time talking with her Heavenly Father. Try as she did, she couldn't make sense of it all.

Father, I come before you again with a heavy heart. I'm at such a loss. Doc tried to get through to Kaleb, told him we can't live in fear of what may or may not happen, that we should live each day to the fullest, but his words had no effect, at least it seems that way. I was so hopeful. He's worse than I could have ever imagined. Forgive me, Father, for my grumbling heart. Calm my ailing stomach. Soothe my weary soul. Help me to look to You, the source of true joy and contentment. Your Word tells me that a merry heart is good like a medicine, but a broken spirit dries the bones. I so want to be happy again. I have to believe this is only a season and joy comes in the morning. Thank you for bringing Kaleb into my life and thank you for our precious baby. Renew the joy we once found in each other. Show us both where we're wrong. I place my marriage in Your hands and look forward to the blessings that lie ahead. Thank you that I don't have to see a light at the end of the tunnel to know You're standing there with open arms.

Elizabeth rose from her place at the table and moved toward her room. She needed her sweater. For the first time in weeks, her heart was lighter. She had to see Kaleb right now and do whatever it took to turn things around. It didn't matter what had induced this downhill spiral—she wanted it to end, and now. The gloominess that had been hovering, robbing her of her joy—it had to go! If happiness were indeed hers for the taking, she would claim what was rightfully hers.

Hearing the latch on the back door, her heart soared. A smile erupted on her face. Kaleb had come to seek her out. As she neared the kitchen, she could have sworn she heard unfamiliar voices. After listening for several seconds, she assured herself it had to be Jesse with Kaleb. Who else could it be? Her ears were playing tricks on her.

But when Elizabeth reached the entrance, fear assailed her. Two of the scruffiest-looking men she had ever seen were staring at her as if she had been the one to invade *their* home. Evil prevailed in their dark sinister eyes, telling her all she needed to know. Their intentions were anything but honorable. Frantic, her mind spun out of control. Coming to her senses, she was about to bolt, but the bigger of the two realized her intent and lunged toward her, snagging her arm.

"Now where do you think you're going in such powerful big hurry, little Missy?"

Alarm spiraled through her as his filthy hands slid around her waist, pulling her flush against him. His ominous glare gave her the once-over before he flashed his loathsome friend a ragged-toothed grin. "We're taking this one with us, Butch. It's been a long time since I've had such a tasty little tart in my arms. Besides, we'll bring in more revenue from her than anything else we'll find in this quaint little abode."

Elizabeth shuddered in horror, repulsed by his insidious plan. When she thought she had heard all that she could stand, the ruffian holding her spewed his chaw and spoke again.

"Gus will take her off our hands when we've had our fill—and offer a hefty fee as well."

His friend—partner—whatever he was, nodded and laughed with disdain. The scoundrel that held her captive ran his hands up and down her back, as if she were his for the taking. When he grabbed her derriere with his oversized paw, common sense eluded her. She punched him hard in the nose. Unfortunately, he didn't just stare back like Kaleb had; he backhanded her with such force, she was thrown to the floor. Clutching her burning face, her eyes filled with tears. His thunderous words shook her to the core.

"Let's get one thing straight you little vixen! You raise a hand to me again and I'll beat you within an inch of your life! Do I make myself clear?"

She managed a nod. The foreboding malice in his venomous eyes told her he would squash her like a bug without a second thought. She refused to do anything that would bring harm to her baby. For now she would be still, bide her time and look for a chance to break free.

The big man grabbed the supply bag from the hook and slung it at her, along with his spewed orders. "Fill it with food. We got a long ride ahead, and you're too skinny for my liking. She's a looker, Butch, but she'll be much more pleasing to the new men in her life if we plump her up a bit."

She trembled, nearly out of control. But, sensing she needed to comply, she rose to her feet and did as she was told. Praying, she glanced out the window from time to time for signs of Kaleb, or even her brother. She saw nothing.

Butch called the big brute Hank, so now she knew both of their names. They were checking out the place for hidden treasures. Unfortunately, their watchful eyes never left her.

Since it looked like she would be going with them, she chanced a question. "Would it be all right if I pack a few things to take along?" She addressed Butch, the smaller of the two men. As scoundrels go, she found him the least frightening. Her opinion, however, was based solely on the fact that he hadn't hurt her yet.

"What do you think, Hank? She'll need extra clothes to take the chill off. If we let her get sick, she'll be no more use to us than a horse with a broke leg."

"Be quick about it," Hank snarled. "We need to be on our way. Grab the thickest blanket you got. The nights are cold. This ain't no pleasure trip. We sleep under the stars."

On shaky limbs, Elizabeth went to her room, and pulled on two more pair of long underwear. Butch watched her every move, but right now keeping her baby warm was her only concern. She

brought along two extra pairs of socks, buttoned her cardigan, and added one of Kaleb's flannel shirts to the ensemble. Although it swallowed her up, shielding herself and her baby from the cold was all that mattered. By the time she pulled her coat over top, she was ready to face an arctic storm.

Butch belly-laughed. "If you think for a minute that all those layers are going to keep you safe, you're mistaken, Little Lady." His tone softened. "If it puts your mind at ease, you go right ahead. Shove an extra dress in that bag, case it rains."

"Butch, keep an eye on her while I saddle a horse." Hank glanced at Elizabeth and queried. "You got a favorite mount in that barn?"

Surprised that he would ask, she thought about it for several seconds. *Lightning would be best for speed. On the other hand, if she couldn't escape, she needed stability.* "The chestnut mare in the first stall on the left, her bridle is right outside her door. Her saddle is the second one hanging inside the tack room to your right."

He nodded and moved out the door.

Since Kaleb hadn't come to her rescue, she could only assume that someone had prevented him from doing so. *Father, help him. Give us the strength we need to get through this seemingly impossible situation.* She was petrified, but she refused to allow her fears to get the best of her. If she did, she'd put herself and her baby in more danger than they were already in. *Father, remind me every step of the way to look to You.*

Hank strutted into the house. Without a word, he gripped Elizabeth's arm and practically dragged her into the yard. "I have a few ground rules that need settin'. We can do this the easy way or the hard way—makes no difference to me. You ride this mount without taking off or you'll spend the rest of the trip in so much pain, you'll wish you hadn't. We meet up with any strangers, you'd best act like we're the best friends you ever had, or you'll die with 'um. Understood?"

"Yes ..." She could feel her resolve wavering as she mounted Lady and they moved away from home.

Hank had been watching her. "We'll be on the trail for a week, so quit frettin', and enjoy the ride."

Enjoy the ride, she mused. *Is he kidding? Does he think for a second that I could enjoy any of this? My husband is injured, if not dead. My life, and that of my unborn child, has been threatened repeatedly, and I'm supposed to enjoy the ride! Father, already my faith wanes. Help me to put my trust in You. If you get me out of this one, I'll never grumble again about Kaleb's overbearing ways. He may barely acknowledge my existence, but compared to these men he's an angel of mercy.*

Elizabeth's heart ached as she thought of Kaleb. The sudden need to know if she would have a husband to go home to preyed heavily on her mind. "Can I ask you a question?"

"Sure."

"There was a man in the barn ... did you hurt him?"

Hank had the audacity to grin. "You must be asking about that big brother of yours."

She nodded. No need for them to know Kaleb was her husband. Luckily, she'd left her rings in Kaleb's top drawer. For some reason, she felt safer letting them think she was an unblemished maiden.

"Don't ya worry your pretty little head about him. He'll be

fine once that bump on his head heals. We tied him up good, just in case he wakes up and takes a notion to come after his baby sister. We have plans for you, Honey, and we're not about to let anyone get in the way."

As they rode deeper into unfamiliar territory, she made every attempt to pay attention to landmarks. Her sense of direction left a bit to be desired. If the sheriff wasn't able to track them down, she could be on her own trying to find her way home.

Her father would tell her that if she didn't pay attention to what was around her, she would end up in Timbuktu. She had no idea if this was a real place, but the word itself had a way of lifting her spirits.

Hank made mention that their destination would be a seven-day ride. That would mean they were going further than Detroit. She was guessing Mt. Clemens or Pontiac.

"Kaleb, what happened?" Jesse asked, his frantic mind racing as he crouched down to untie the rope that bound his friend. "Who did this to you?" In Kaleb's muddled silence he reached for the back of his head, grimacing in obvious pain. Jesse's heart thudded with dread. There was blood dripping freely from Kaleb's long fingers when he pulled his hand away. Kaleb had been hit with such force that his head was split open, leaving a deep gash and huge lump in his skull. "I'll need to go for Doc, Kaleb. You're a mess."

Jesse helped him to his feet, steadied his faltering frame, and headed toward the house. After lowering him to the edge of his bed, he ran for a glass of water. "Drink this, Kaleb. I know you don't feel much like talking, but I need to weasel a few things out of you before I leave."

Kaleb downed the cool liquid. "Jesse, where's Liz?"

"Was she here?"

Kaleb was struggling to maintain consciousness when Jesse pressed him. "Yes, my parents went to Sheriff Kane's for dinner. Liz and I stayed home. Please Jesse, tell me you'll find my wife. I don't deserve her, but I can't go on without her!"

Jesse didn't miss the desperation in his good friend's eyes before he fell back into darkness. After bandaging Kaleb's head, Jesse settled him in the bed, ran out the door, mounted Shadow, and tore off towards home.

Jared and Joseph came out of the barn as Jesse galloped into the yard. "Don't ask questions, boys. Hitch up the team and bring it around. Saddle both your horses and Dad's too. We'll be right out, I'll explain on the way.

Jesse plowed through the door, bellowing for his family who was already gathered in the sitting room. "I just found Kaleb in the barn. He was hit over the head and I have reason to believe whoever did this to him took Lizzy hostage. Kaleb's in his bed, Mom; he passed out after begging me to find Lizzy. I need you and the girls to go over there in case he wakes up. He might try to do something crazy. I'll have Jared and Joe go for Doc. They can stop by the sheriff's home on their way back. His wife will let them know what our plans are."

Jesse turned to his father, trying to keep from imagining the worst. "Dad, something horrible's happened here. We need to get moving. Kane will know what to do." He turned to leave, but then he remembered. "Mom, the house has been ransacked. Take some supplies. There's no telling how long you'll be there."

"Girls," George said, as his eyes narrowed in on them. "You go with your mother. Under no circumstances do any of you leave the house, hear me? That goes for you too, Jayne."

Jayne nodded.

"Lock the doors and stay put." George wanted to kiss his wife, but she was all-too close to tears. She would break down if he tried. Instead, he offered words of encouragement. "Pray, Jayne. God's in control, we need to trust Him. I'm sure Ruth and the boys will be back before long. Listen for them. Jesse, we'd better saddle a horse for Samuel just in case we begin our search from Kane's place."

Elizabeth wondered how much further she could go without falling from her mount. Her extreme hunger and unquenchable thirst plagued her as exhaustion settled in. Desperate to stay awake, she recounted the events that had transpired that morning. In a moment of boldness as Hank had pulled her out the door, she lunged for Kaleb's wide-brim hat that hung from the hook in the pantry. Hank's hand came up to strike her again, but he let it slide when he saw what she was grabbing. After a day in the intense sun, it had been worth the effort. Thoughts of what the night could hold horrified her. Knowing who was really in control brought a sense of peace to her troubled mind.

The shadowy grays darkening the evening sky made Elizabeth wonder if a storm could be approaching. It was obvious that Hank and Butch were staying clear of any form of civilization. Still, she found it strange that even the wild animals were sparse in this desolate place. Spring had scarcely begun to work its wonder. The scenery along the way was drab and dreary—a true depiction of the way she felt inside.

So many times she had tried to get Kaleb to let her ride Lady again. Now she would do almost anything to be safe in the confines of his parents' home. *Please God, keep him safe in the shelter of Your arms.*

Elizabeth hated to ask her captors for anything. She had been riding all day without a drop of water or a crumb of food. She needed nourishment of some sort or she would faint from hunger. "Hank, I'm sorry to bother you. Is there a chance we'll be stopping soon? I could use some water, maybe a little food. My legs are numb."

He chuckled, in an irritating sort of way, but it wasn't long before he took Lady's reins and led her down an embankment towards a line of trees. He stopped when they reached a small stream and jumped off his horse. Elizabeth held her breath as he came to her side. She didn't know what to think. What would he do? Her insides calmed as he helped her down and even held her up until the feeling came back into her limbs. Although her legs were as wobbly as a newborn filly, she made her way to the water.

Butch came alongside of her, handed her a tin mug, and asked, "You all right?"

She wondered where the sudden concern for her welfare came from, but decided they were just protecting their investment. This "Gus" person, whoever he was, probably didn't accept damaged goods.

She started when a bird flew up as she bent over the gurgling stream. She emptied one cup then another. Quenching her insatiable thirst had been her only thought. How could she have known the cool water would react the way it did in her empty stomach? In a moment of desperation, Elizabeth ran for the trees. Hank and Butch came after her—halting the second she began to heave.

"Ya got no sense!" Hank snarled, smacking the back of her head. "That water's too cold to be drinking so fast."

"I'm not used to depriving myself, so lighten up."

His brow rose on her bold inflection. Surprisingly he let it pass. "I have an extra canteen. And I suppose if we're gonna fatten ya up we'd best start feedin' ya more. Now, get yourself another mug—to sip on. Then get over there and fix our supper." He pointed to where Butch had started a fire.

Curious, Elizabeth asked, "Are we staying here?"

Butch answered, "Yes, but we'll be gettin' an early start, so don't get yourself all worked up thinking your family might find ya. We got too much ridin' on this venture."

Elizabeth stared in disbelief. She should have been angered by their blatant disregard for human life. *To them, I'm nothing more than an animal to be used and sold to the highest bidder ....*

Her thoughts were rudely interrupted by Hank's threat. "Are ya gonna do as you're told and make us supper, or do I need to smack ya round for a while?"

Elizabeth, needing to clear the cobwebs clouding the good sense she was born with, filled her cup with water and hustled over to the bag of food. While it wouldn't be much, she would do her best to prepare a meal that would fill them up and hopefully make them sleep.

When dusk fell into darkness, their bedding was placed on the ground next to the fire. From the looks of things, she would be in the middle. This did not bode well, but the choice was not hers to make? Hank tied a rope around her hands, binding them together, and another around her ankles. He then tied one of the loose ends around his waist and Butch did the same with the other. From all appearances, she would be safe from their advances tonight as long as neither one of them rolled in their sleep. If they did, it could be a long night of being stretched from stem to stern.

Elizabeth had begun to lose hope of anyone finding them. Every day held the same drudgery—endless hours of riding, without enough to eat. Then, to make matters worse, she was never allowed to get enough sleep. All this had taken its toll on her pregnant body.

Hank and Butch were determined to cover their trail. Sometimes they'd be heading North, and then they would veer off towards the East or West and ride the shallow creeks as often as possible. Lady, never having liked the water, seemed to be especially skittish on this particular day. In Elizabeth's weakened state, she found it difficult to keep fighting her horse. Every chance Lady got, she would leap up onto the bank in search of dryer ground.

The warm temperatures had forced her to shed her layers of extra clothing. This left her more vulnerable, but she had no choice. The heat and her foul stomach were not a good

combination. Hank and Butch were edgy from lack of sleep. Elizabeth had been extremely ill during the last few nights. Since they were tied together, she had no choice but to waken them.

When Lady leapt onto the bank for the fifth time, something snapped in Hank. He latched onto Elizabeth's arm, and took his frustrations out on her—beating her with his crop. She cowered in excruciating pain and begged him to stop, praying that he would before it was too late. Nothing! She peered up at Butch, desperate for some form of mercy. To her horror, a morbid grin covered his face, as if she was finally getting what she deserved. Blood seeped into her calico. She didn't know which was worse, the excruciating bite of the whip or the unyielding despair filling her body and soul. Beyond tears, she could no longer breathe. She fought to maintain consciousness, but darkness prevailed ....

Kaleb awoke with a start.

"Take it easy," Doc said as he rushed toward his bed.

"You've got a bad head injury, Kaleb. I don't need you doing more damage."

"How long have I been out?" His head was booming, but he needed answers.

"About four and a half days. We weren't sure you'd make it for a while there. Let me get Jayne and Ruth; they wanted to know the minute you were awake."

"Doc, wait a minute. Have they found Liz?"

His heart went out to him. "Kaleb, you have to concentrate on getting well."

"If it was Martha, you'd want to know. I have a terrible feeling. Something is desperately wrong. That's what woke me up!"

The tears forming in Kaleb's eyes were Doc's undoing.

"Seven men are out looking for her. We haven't heard anything, so you know as much as we do."

"I have to go after her. I didn't take your advice and now I've lost her. All this is my fault, Doc, don't you see? She has been so sick. I allowed my fear of losing her to destroy what we had. We've both been miserable. I have to make it up to her."

"I understand, Kaleb, really I do. The best thing you can do for Elizabeth and your baby is to get well. Forget any crazy notions you have about going after her. You're no good to her dead and that's what you'll be if you move from this bed. You say you should have taken my advice, then start now. Pray for your wife and child as never before. Place her in the Lord's hands and leave her there. Don't let your fears consume you. Give yourself the chance to heal and let your brother-in-law, father, and father-in-law find her."

After a moment, Kaleb stiffly nodded. Reluctant he agreed.

"Ladies," Doc announced moments later, "we have our first answer to prayer. Kaleb's awake, sitting up and hungry."

Kaleb was understandably overwrought, but he calmed after they all joined hands and prayed together for Elizabeth and the baby. He promised that he would stay put until Doc felt his life was out of danger.

"Ruth," Doc said, "I'm heading home for the night. I'll be back tomorrow. If he wakes up and can't sleep, mix this with a cup of water and have him drink it. I don't care if you have to hog-tie him, don't let him leave that bed."

He Loves Me!

Chapter Twenty

Earthly Angels

ELIZABETH AWOKE, PLAGUED by the horrific pain ripping through her back. With caution, she opened her eyes, knowing the men who did this to her could be close by. Slivers of vibrant beams shot through the small cracked window, exposing her meager surroundings. She was face down on a bed in a cabin, not unlike the one she and Kaleb had stayed in during the blizzard. The only sounds she heard were birds singing their morning songs and the last of the burning embers crackling in the fireplace.

Could she be alone?

After several tries, she pushed herself up to a sitting position. The movement drew fresh blood from her wounds, but at the moment that was the least of her worries.

As Elizabeth stood to her feet, her head began to sway. She had to take it slowly. With vigilance, she moved toward the makeshift kitchen. She found a bucket of water and took a few sips to moisten her dry mouth. The food bag from home sat on the table. Reaching for the last dry crust of bread, she nibbled on it. Her extra clothes were in a heap on top of Lady's saddle. *Lady's saddle is here!* Her wary heart leapt with renewed hope. Did they abandon her? *Oh, please God, let it be so.* Leery of getting her hopes up too high, she opened the dilapidated door, drinking in the warm breeze as it tussled her matted hair. Every step exuded pain. But she forced herself to go on. When she found Lady hobbled next to a small stream eating grass, her tempered heart beat a little faster.

At first she thought she should saddle Lady and get out of there as quick as she could. After praying about it, she decided to take some time to clean her wounds. If they got infected, she might pass out and then where would she be? Besides, she had no way of knowing how many days she'd been unconscious. Both she and the baby would need nourishment.

The day was warmer than usual, so she gathered her extra clothes and made her way to the creek. In an attempt to keep her wounds from opening up and bleeding excessively, she lay down in the shallow water and soaked her back until the fabric of her dress came away from her skin. Although the process was excruciating, by the time she finished, she actually felt better. Maybe not well enough to dance a jig, but nonetheless determined to begin her long journey home. *Home*, the word alone warmed her heart.

After eating a small meal, she saddled Lady, and thought by the sun's position in the clear blue sky that it had to be getting close to noon.

"Thank you, Lord!" Elizabeth shouted in exaltation as she mounted Lady and her gaze rose toward the heavens. "You made this glorious day, in all its splendor, and what a beautiful day it is! The pain in my back is unbearable. I'm tired from all my efforts. Still, my heart is as light as the air knowing You set me free! Father, I thank you! Thank you! Thank you! For whatever caused those men to release me, thank you! Protect and guide me along the way."

The long afternoon ride proved to be uneventful. She had no way of knowing if she was heading towards Detroit or Ann Arbor. Twice she had taken the time to stop, stretch her legs, fill her canteen, and eat a little something. She didn't know how long it would take her to get home, so she used the food sparingly. The warmer day had brought the wild rabbits and squirrels out in abundance. She had to be watchful because the skunks were on the prowl as well. She could only imagine how her stomach would respond to such a smell.

Dusk slithered in like a thief to steal away the light of day, and fear reared its ugly head. She didn't like being by herself in a house at night—never mind outside. As Elizabeth contemplated a night alone in the wilds of Michigan, her thoughts rose heavenward. *Father, I know you understand my weaknesses. I need an extra measure of Your peace right now ....*

In her reluctance to stop, she kept moving until she spotted what appeared to be a campfire up ahead. While the uncertainty of who it could be left her feeling anxious, she reassured herself that this could be anyone. Securing Lady, she made her way through a copse of trees toward their camp. For a time, she watched from a distance. A man around Kaleb's age, with dark hair and a full beard, was sitting next to the fire. He had something cooking over the open flame. As the aroma wafted past her nose, her stomach growled unmercifully. Disappointment washed over her when no one else moved about. After all that she had been through, she wouldn't even consider putting herself and her baby in a vulnerable position with a lone man. As she turned to walk away, she heard a child giggle. At the moment, it was the most wonderful sound she had ever heard. Sure enough, a mother and daughter came out from behind their wagon. She couldn't be sure, but it looked like the woman was expecting again.

With hopeful anticipation, Elizabeth moved with care into their camp. Since her approach had been silent, she startled the young family when her timid voice broke into their playful laughter.

"I'm sorry to bother you ...." Alarm slammed through her as she stared down the barrel of his long gun. *Oh, God! What have I done?*

The gentleman spoke as the woman scooped up her small child and moved behind him.

"I wouldn't recommend coming any closer, Ma'am. I will shoot to protect my family." He had no way of knowing if she was alone or not.

The strain of the last week came in like a flood. Falling to her knees, the dam broke loose. No matter how hard Elizabeth tried, she couldn't speak through her gasping, shuddering tears.

"Jake, please, let me go to her." Her heart was breaking for the frail woman. "Look at her, she's just a young thing. Surely she's no threat to us."

Seconds ticked by before they made their way to the

hysterical woman's side. Although it took Vicki a while to calm her down, she would give her all the time she needed after the way Jake frightened her.

"I'm sorry," Elizabeth managed. "Lady—my horse, she's over there." A trembling finger pointed to where she was tied.

Vicki, in her need to comfort her, tried to wrap her arm around her.

Elizabeth cowered.

"Oh, Honey, I won't hurt you." Vicki thought she had frightened her again.

"My back—those men—they beat me."

Jake and Vicki shared a sympathetic glance and wondered what kind of nightmare this young woman had been through.

"Jake will see to your horse, but first you go ahead and tell us what's happened. Maybe the good Lord put you in our path so we can help."

Her mention of the Lord was like music to Elizabeth's ears. Jake motioned for her to take a seat on the fallen log by the fire.

"My husband and I live in Ypsilanti with my in-laws and his little sister. They had no more left to visit with friends when two men came in the back door. They hit my husband over the head and made me go with them. Night before last, I was sick more than normal. None of us got much sleep. I'm expecting our first baby, and my stomach is a mess at times. My horse was acting up. One of the men decided to take it out on me. Needless to say, he beat me until I passed out. I woke up this morning in a cabin— alone. After cleaning my wounds, I started for home. I think I'm heading in the right direction. Not really sure. If all else fails, I'll follow the Rouge and land myself in Detroit. My husband's

grandma lives there."

"Our farm is in Detroit too, on the west side."

"Grandma is on the west side, but I'm not sure where."

The lady had a strange look on her face; in fact, her husband housed the same enlightened glint. The woman asked, "Her name doesn't happen to be Naomi White, does it?"

Now Elizabeth was the one perplexed. "Yes, do you know her?"

They were both grinning from ear to ear. "We do. Our names are Jacob and Victoria Smith. Our families have known each other for years. Our land's connected to the White farm. We know your in-laws, your husband Kaleb, and his little sister Sarah."

For a moment, Elizabeth was too overwhelmed to speak.

Jubilant tears hindered her. "I'll tell you what! When God sends me angels, he doesn't fool around. My name is Lizzy— Elizabeth White."

"It's about time Kaleb took a wife!" Jacob smiled, recalling a conversation they'd had on the subject last summer. "If we didn't have to be back to milk our cows, we'd love to take you back. Lizzy, I know you're itching to get home, but I'd feel better if you'd ride along with us until your husband can come for you. If I know Kaleb as well as I think I do, he'd agree. We could take you to Grandma's. If you write Kaleb a note letting him know where you'll be, I can have it posted the day we arrive.

"That would be wonderful." Her relief knew no bounds. She wanted to shout for joy, but she managed to contain her exuberance. Vicki had a small child in her arms and Elizabeth had no intentions of frightening her. In truth, Elizabeth had hopes of them becoming friends right off. "How old is your little one, Jacob? She's so adorable."

"Sorry, I suppose I should make the introductions. This is our daughter Rebecca Karin; she's sixteen months. We call her Becky. And our baby is due the end of April. You mentioned that you and Kaleb are expecting. Do you know when?"

"Not until October."

"Most folks call me Jake, and my wife goes by Vicki."

"Kaleb calls me Liz, but I'm Lizzy to family and friends." After a stretch of silence, Elizabeth glanced up at Jake. "I should go for Lady. It's getting dark ... I don't want her to think I forgot her."

Jake stood and said, "What you need is some tea and nourishment for that baby. Just point me in the right direction, I'll find this Lady of yours."

While Jake was gone, Elizabeth asked Vicki to take a quick peek at her back. Her wounds were oozing and she didn't have another dress.

Vicki's breath caught in her throat when she first laid eyes on Elizabeth's inflamed flesh. Sickened by what she saw, she kept her thoughts to herself. After applying a salve to a clean piece of cloth, she laid it across Elizabeth's back. "This should help until we can get Doctor Bert to take a look." She had her all fixed up and covered before Jake meandered into camp with Lady.

"I'll tell you what, Lizzy, you ever get a colt out of this mare, I'd be interested."

She smiled. "Kaleb plans to breed her the next time she goes into season, but you'll have a fight on your hands the first turn around. We'd like to raise her first offspring."

"Well, if she has twins, make sure you give me first option."

Elizabeth nodded and stood to take Lady's reins.

"Ah, ah, ah!" Jake admonished as he glanced at his wife. "Can you believe she's starting already, Vicki?"

Giggles randomly escaped as Elizabeth listened to Jake scold her in the same manor Kaleb had so many times before.

His eyes narrowed as he turned back to Elizabeth. "Am I going to have problems with you keeping your place, Young Lady? I'm the man in charge around here, and as long as you're with us, you'll do as I say. Understood? Just ask Vicki what a brute I can be with pregnant women who give me any lip. Now, sit back down there and sip at that tea!"

Biting her lip to keep from laughing, Elizabeth chanced a peek at Vicki, who had lost all composure when Elizabeth saluted Jake in mock respect. Laughter erupted in the open setting. As Jake and Vicki began preparations for their evening meal, the three of them knew they would be friends for life.

Jake's heart went out to Kaleb. He couldn't imagine the turmoil he must be in, having his wife stolen right out from under him. If only Kaleb could be here to witness the relief in his wife's eyes. *Soon enough*, he thought, *we can share a nice long visit together and I'll tell him all about it. There's no doubt in my mind, the woman we're bringing with us is my good friend's rarest treasure.*"

Chapter Twenty-one

Grandma

AN OVERWHELMING PEACE flooded Elizabeth's heart as Vicki drove the team around the bend and stopped in front of Grandma White's home. Her mind was a flurry of awe and wonder while she drank in the scene before her. The river had to be close; she could hear the sound of rippling water. A deep covered porch wrapped around the whitewashed, two-story farmhouse, possibly leading to a back entrance. Wooden rocking chairs sat next to the door facing each other, as if welcoming those who might care to take a seat and visit for a spell. The massive budding trees were sure to offer an abundance of shade against a scorching summer sun. And the gentle breeze put everything in motion. Elizabeth found it all so inviting.

"Vicki, I've wanted to meet her for so long ... but suddenly, I'm nervous. Do you think she'll mind my being here without an invitation?"

"Lizzy, look at me."

She complied without hesitation.

"We loved you from the moment we met. Just be yourself and allow Grandma to see the beautiful, kindhearted woman her Kaleb married. She'll adore you."

Elizabeth hugged her friend. "Thanks, Vicki. I couldn't love you and Jake more if I'd known you all my life."

With hopeful anticipation, she leapt down from the wagon. The two women climbed the three steps to the porch together. Sucking in a deep breath for courage, Elizabeth knocked on the big door; her eyes falling on Vicki when she heard Naomi yelling from within.

"Hold your horses ... I'm coming! Don't ya know it takes a old lady time to get her old bones a-moving?"

Elizabeth grimaced. "Do you think I've upset her?"

Vicki chuckled. "Nooo ... that's just the way she is. Has a tendency to be gruff, and somewhat hard of hearing." Her brow rose. "Now, if you're asking my opinion, I've come to the conclusion that her hearing disorder would be better termed 'selective'."

Elizabeth burst into giggles. "Well, blow me down, Vicki! Don't get me going before she comes to the door. She'll think I'm laughing at her." The door creaked open, silencing both women. And the craggiest female voice Elizabeth had ever heard presented itself.

"What can I do for you, Miss?" Naomi didn't pause long enough for Elizabeth to respond before announcing. "You're at the wrong house. There's another place up the way. The Smith's farm, that's the one you want!"

"Mrs. White," was all Elizabeth got out, before the door slammed in her face.

Vicki laughed at Elizabeth's dumbfounded expression. "Trade places, and let me try." After knocking again—rather hard—the door flew open.

"I told you ..."

"Grandma," Vicki said, interrupting Naomi's tirade, "are you going to talk to us, or do you intend to make a rather large, pregnant lady stand out here and knock all day?"

Naomi smiled. She had a deep appreciation for Vicki, who had as much cheek if not more than she. Somewhat bewildered, Naomi glanced at Elizabeth, and back to Vicki a few times before asking, "Who's this you got with you, Vicki? I'm afraid I was a bit rude to your friend here. Haven't seen her around these parts."

"No, you haven't, Grandma, but she's written to you before."

"You don't say ...." For the life of her, Naomi couldn't place her.

"Grandma, I'd like you to meet your newest granddaughter, Elizabeth."

"Nah ..! You wouldn't be pulling an old lady's leg now, would you?"

Vicki couldn't suppress a smile. "No, Grandma, I'm not."

Her brow furrowed. "You mean to tell me this little squat of a woman is married to my Kaleb?"

"Yes, Grandma, she is."

"Why, he'd swallow her up in one bite!" Naomi shook her head, scrutinizing the young woman. "I'll have to have a long talk with that boy—he's gone and robbed himself a cradle, that's for sure!"

Thankfully, Naomi looked back at Vicki, giving Elizabeth a moment's reprieve. Boy, did she need a reprieve! If she didn't say something soon, she'd burst into laughter, and she didn't want to do that. In reality, there was a time that she'd agreed with the woman. Not any more. Knowing how desperate she was for a cup of tea, a comfortable chair and little to no movement for several days, she joined in the conversation. "Grandma, I'm Lizzy. We've had a long trip and I'm sure the Smiths would like to get home."

"Oh, sure. You go ahead, Vicki. We'll be fine. Thanks for bringing her. Truth is, I could use the company. Been lonely around here of late."

Elizabeth turned to Jake, her words soft. She had no desire to wake the little angel sleeping in his arms. "Are you sure you don't mind caring for Lady until I get the barn in order?"

"Not at all. Take the time you need to heal, Lizzy. I think your husband would agree that you shouldn't be pushing yourself."

"I will. As long as you're sure?"

His eyes filled with amusement. "I am."

"Thanks again for everything."

"You're welcome."

"Grandma," Elizabeth asked after the Smith's had pulled away and she and Grandma turned back toward the house, "I'd love to be able to relax and get acquainted, but I don't know when the doctor is coming by. I feel so grubby. I need to get rid of some of this trail dust. Would you mind horribly if I took a bath?"

"Not at all, Honey. I'm used to being on my own, so you help yourself to anything you need. Make yourself to home."

"Thanks, I will."

"I have a tub hanging on the wall in the kitchen and you'll find the river out the back door and down the hill. The big pot is on the counter for heating the water." She leaned over and whispered in Elizabeth's ear, as if speaking the words out loud would be unacceptable. "I have some of those feminine salts. You know, the ones that smell like flowers."

Elizabeth slid her arms around Naomi and hugged her tight. "That sounds wonderful."

A little flustered, Naomi reached for the tub and said, "You go ahead and get your bath ... then I'll help you wash that golden mop."

"Thanks, Grandma. I hate to be a bother, but I have one more favor to ask. Do you have something I could put on until I wash my dress?"

Naomi wondered why she didn't have a bag with her, but didn't ask. "I have several I'd be glad to alter for you. Truth is, I've put on some weight over the last few years. Don't you worry, Honey. I'll get you all fixed up."

As Elizabeth followed her into her room, she couldn't help noticing how tall she stood for a woman in her advanced years. She wore her white hair in a bun at the base of her neck and it glowed like fine silk. Time had etched her skin; yet there was an attractiveness about her that the hands of time could not wash away.

Grandma lifted the lid on a carved wooden trunk, pulled several things out and laid them on her beautifully-quilted bed. "I'll need to take them in and shorten the length, but they'll be good enough for scrub dresses."

Elizabeth's eyes filled with pleasure as she fingered the fabrics. "Grandma, these are far too nice for scrub dresses. We can hem them, yes, but Kaleb and I are going to have a baby. The extra room around will be wonderful in the months to come."

Naomi's eyes widened. In fact, she was so shaken by her announcement she had to sit down. "You're carrying my great-grandchild?" Her voice crackled as if she was about to cry; but no tears came. Instead they shared their first heartwarming smile.

Elizabeth blinked. Naomi's countenance had changed in an instant.

"Do you mean to tell me that grandson of mine has no more concern for his pregnant wife than to let her go roaming the countryside alone?"

Elizabeth's brow rose on the sudden realization. "Grandma, no, you don't understand. A week ago I was abducted—taken from our home."

Naomi's features softened; her tone did not. "What?"

Elizabeth nodded and told her what had happened. "On my way home, I came across Jake and Vicki. They brought me here until Kaleb can come to get me."

"Oh my! Honey, that's terrible! Are you sure you're all right?"

"I will be. I'll feel better when I know how Kaleb has fared. Jake's mailing the letter I wrote to let Kaleb know where I am. He's also sending the town doctor out to check my wounds."

Naomi's brow arched. "I wondered why you needed a Doctor. Didn't think it was my place to ask."

Elizabeth frowned. "I have no need for secrets, Grandma."

Naomi looked relieved. "I'll help you fill the tub. If you don't mind having an old lady in the room, I'll fix us some tea and we can have a chat while you have a good soak."

"I don't mind a bit."

Naomi racked her brain for something that might sound appetizing to her weary guest. "I have a chicken coop out back.

How does some chicken fricassee sound?"

Elizabeth's pulse quickened at the mere mention of those dastardly birds. Unwilling to go through what she had with Kaleb, she told Naomi the truth. "I can't butcher one, but I'd be more than happy to cook one."

Naomi laughed out loud. Her new granddaughter looked as if she would faint dead away at the mere thought of having to accomplish such a task. "Don't you go worrying yourself. I'm not a bit squeamish about doing such things. I hate peeling potatoes, so if you're willing to take care of that, we'll make a fine team."

Elizabeth smiled. "I'd be glad to."

Naomi's first impression may have led her to believe that Elizabeth led a pampered life. However, she changed her mind when she took one look at the raw inflamed flesh on her back. "Oh Lizzy," her words caught in her throat; "you must be in horrible pain."

"I try not to think about it." Elizabeth's eyes fell on the open window as Naomi unbuttoned her dress.

"Lizzy, with all you've been through, I understand your fears, but no one comes around here."

She craned her neck around. "How did you know what I was thinking?"

Naomi winked. "Your expressions speak loud and clear."

Elizabeth giggled as she removed the rest of her clothes, stepped into the little tub, and sank slowly into the lilac bubbles. She cringed as the warm water flooded her wounds. It took a while, but after the initial shock wore off it actually felt good.

"It's funny you would say that, Grandma. If I don't want Kaleb to know my thoughts, I have to close my eyes or turn away."

Naomi spooned tealeaves into the pot, and filled it with boiling water. "Now what could a sweet little thing like you have to hide from Kaleb?"

She cleared her throat. "Trust me, Grandma, I'm not always the most agreeable wife. Kaleb and I have been a part of each other's lives since I was born. My natural tendency is to lip off, instead of bowing to his every wish."

"Well ... I love that grandson of mine, but he does tend to be a mite too big for his britches at times."

Elizabeth snickered. She loved the way Grandma spoke her mind.

"Ruth sent me a letter a while back. Said something about Kaleb finding you in a storm. I'd love to hear your version of the story. That is, if you feel up to telling it."

Elizabeth's face scrunched. "You might not like me very much if I tell you."

"I like ya just fine. No story will change that."

Elizabeth nodded. "The night after Kaleb brought me home, his family came over for dinner. As I was saying, our families have been close for years. I considered Kaleb a good friend until he went along with my father's outrageous plan to salvage my reputation."

Naomi smiled at the indignation she heard in her voice.

"Pastor showed up that evening to talk to my father about the rumors that were circulating. Now mind you, I had no intentions of being married for years, but Kaleb was willing, so my father gave me no choice. We were married that night. At first, my anger got the best of me. I had plans to be on my own for a while, before finding a very small, agreeable man to settle down with."

Naomi found this hysterical. "Did you tell Kaleb?"

"Yes, I wanted him to have the marriage annulled, so I spilled my guts. I was sure that if he knew the thoughts that ran through my head, he'd take me home as quick as he could get me there."

"But he didn't."

"No. He didn't give a lick. He found everything I had to say enlightening ... I found him annoying and high-handed. Deep in my heart I knew that eventually we could be good for each other, but I couldn't tell him that. I felt betrayed. When I finally let go of my anger, everything changed for the better until I got pregnant. I've been sick and Kaleb—well, let's just say he hasn't handled it well."

Not understanding, Naomi frowned. "I'd think the baby would bring you closer."

"I thought so too. Maybe this experience will help him to see that if I'm meant to be with him, I will be."

"Has he been good to you otherwise?"

"Before, yes."

"Before you told him about the baby?"

"Yes. God is my strength, Grandma. I promised to take the good with the bad, and I have every intention of helping him through, but it hasn't been easy. Kaleb is patient with me when I struggle—so how can I do anything less for him?"

"All you've been through wouldn't have set well with me, but then I don't have to answer to that God of yours. I decided a long time ago not to put my faith in a God who would allow a man to treat me the way Samuel did."

Elizabeth's brow furrowed as she contemplated her next words. "Grandma, we can't blame God for man's sin. Your Samuel chose to treat you the way he did. God had nothing to do with it."

"Well, I'm not convinced."

"The Bible says that there will come a day when we all have to answer to God. We have to acknowledge our sin and understand our need for a Savior. If we don't, we're responsible for our sins before God—no matter if we believe He exists or not."

Naomi was quick to put in. "I can't imagine why you believe that hogwash after all you've been through."

"God has given me the strength and peace of mind to get through this. I'm not perfect by any means. My heart is just as stubborn as the next person's. I've gone through times of fear and doubt, but because of the hope I have for eternity, those fears and doubts never last. If I die today, I know where I'll be. So you see, I don't have to fear what man can do to me. Having that man beat me like he did was horrible. Knowing God used my wounds to free our unborn child and myself makes me want to rejoice. Grandma, they had every intention of selling me to a man who owns a string of whorehouses. I'd take a beating any day over such a life. The peace that dwells in my heart reminded me that God was carrying me through."

Naomi was hanging on her every word.

Elizabeth didn't wish to press her. "I don't mean to change the subject if you'd like to talk more, but would you mind helping me wash my back?"

Naomi shuttered at the thought. "I'll just pour the clean water over it when you're ready to get out and call it good. Let's see what Doctor Williams says before we do anything else."

"All right ..." Elizabeth took the washcloth Naomi offered and scrubbed at her grimy skin.

"After we wash your hair, I'll braid it off to the side, Lizzy. You just sip on your tea while I look through my armoire for some clean undergarments."

Elizabeth's cheeks warmed. "I didn't think about needing those."

Naomi handed Elizabeth her mug, and for a moment their eyes held. "I can't tell you how glad I am to have you here, Lizzy. I hate what brought us together, but I have a wonderful feeling we're going to be good for each other."

"I told Kaleb months ago that I'd like us to be friends."

"I could use a friend. I've been doing some soul searching of my own lately. Maybe there *is* something to the things you've said—you've certainly given me some food for thought."

❀ ❀ ❀

Saturday afternoon Jake, Vicki and Rebecca stopped by to see how Elizabeth was coming along. Her wounds were on the mend, so they asked if Elizabeth and Naomi would like to go to church and have Sunday dinner at their place. While Elizabeth was thrilled with the invitation, she wasn't sure if Naomi would join them until the last minute.

"Grandma," Elizabeth called from the front door, after waving to her friends. "The Smiths are here. Are you coming?" Elizabeth's heart flooded with joy as Naomi came out of her room donning a cream bonnet, a delicately crocheted shawl and a soft green dress all trimmed in ivory lace. "Grandma, you look lovely." She reached to take Naomi's hand and gave it a squeeze. "I can't tell you how happy I am that you're joining us."

Naomi shook her head. "Land sakes, Girl, I've gotten used to having you around. What would I do with myself all day if I didn't come along? Besides, I'm not about to let you out of my sight. If something were to happen to you now I'd have that grandson of mine breathing down my neck."

Elizabeth laughed at Naomi's excuses as they made their way to the wagon. Inwardly, she was bursting with delight.

"Good morning, Jake, Vicki, and Miss Becky." Naomi tickled under Becky's chin. "How are the Smiths this fine, sunny morning?"

"We're good," Jake said with a smile. "I'm glad you could join us, Grandma."

"I haven't seen my granddaughter this excited since she arrived. I suppose this lonesome Granny would do just about anything for such a sweet granddaughter. I'll tell you what, I haven't had this much fun in years."

Elizabeth, hearing Naomi's heartfelt comment, did all she could to hold back tears. In truth, they had been a healing balm to each other's wounded souls. They spent hours taking about different things that life had sent their way. A bond of friendship was forming that neither Elizabeth nor Naomi had ever shared with anyone. Elizabeth found it uncanny to have so much in common with a woman sixty-two years her senior. The tears and laughter they shared over silly things that didn't matter, and the many things that did, were all part of the healing process. They both would agree that this was no chance meeting.

Elizabeth had been looking through Grandma's shelf of books and found a Bible buried under several old novels. At first, she read alone. After several conversations with Naomi about

God and the Bible, Elizabeth asked if she would be interested in finding out for herself what God's Word had to say. To her amazement, both morning and evening they were now studying the book of John together. Grandma was like a sponge. It didn't matter how much they read, she needed more. She was searching for answers that had been left unsolved in her life for too long.

God was using Elizabeth in a way that even she didn't fully comprehend. As much as she wanted Grandma to have a personal relationship with Jesus Christ, she didn't press her. Naomi would have to make this decision on her own. Elizabeth spent much time in prayer for her dear friend and simply answered her questions to the best of her ability as they arose.

When they pulled into the churchyard, Jake interrupted Elizabeth's thoughts. "Ladies, we seem to be knee-deep in mud today. I'll let you off close to the door."

Grandma and Elizabeth moved up the steps and into the sanctuary arm-in-arm. Vicki and Becky followed close behind. The Church in Detroit was huge compared to their meeting place in Ann Arbor. Elizabeth was awed. Many folks stopped to greet them and even Naomi seemed to feel at home as they sat down and the service began. The congregation rose to lift their voices in a familiar hymn. The pastor, a man in his mid-to-late forties, stood before the congregation and offered a prayer. From the moment he opened his mouth to preach, there was no doubt in Elizabeth's mind: this man knew God in a very real and personal way.

"I'd like you to turn in your Bibles with me to John chapter three. Nicodemus knew that Jesus was a teacher sent from God, so when Jesus said that except a man be born again, he cannot see the kingdom of God, this ruler of the Jews wanted to know how a man could be born when he is old. Jesus responded by saying that unless a man is born of water *and* of the spirit, he cannot enter into the kingdom of God.

"Read along with me, if you will, from verse sixteen.

'*For God so loved the world that he gave his only begotten Son, that whosoever believeth in him should not perish, but have everlasting life. For God sent not his Son into the world to condemn the world; but that the world through him might be saved. He that believeth on him is not condemned: but he that believeth not is condemned already, because he hath not believed in the name of the only begotten Son of God.*'

"Hold your finger in this passage and let's turn to the book of Romans. First, look at chapter three and verse twenty-three. '*For all have sinned and come short of the glory of God.*'

"Chapter six, verse twenty-three goes on to tell us that God made a way for our sin debt to be paid through the gift of His Son, Jesus. '*For the wages of sin is death; but the gift of God is eternal life through Jesus Christ our Lord.*'

"Can you say with the utmost confidence that if you were to die today, you would be in heaven? If you haven't come to that place, then you need to settle up with God right now. Don't wait. Before you take another step in this life, acknowledge your need for a loving Savior. Jesus died and rose again so that you might be redeemed from the curse of sin. Ask his forgiveness and invite him into your heart. Be born again. If you do this, Galatians chapter three, verse twenty-six reassures us, "*by faith in Jesus Christ, we are the children of God.*'"

The service was coming to a close when Elizabeth glanced over and found Naomi weeping. Naomi had been asking questions all week and, apparently, the pastor's words confirmed Naomi's need. Elizabeth reached for her hand, and when the pastor stood, encouraging those who wanted to have a personal relationship with Jesus Christ to come forward, Elizabeth was not surprised by Naomi's response. She looked to Elizabeth; her tear-filled eyes held a longing that only Christ could fill. Elizabeth pressed her hanky into Naomi's hand before Naomi stood and made her way up the aisle.

Naomi now understood the peace that filled her son. God had changed him from the inside out and he was doing the same for her. Her husband had been a horrible man, but Elizabeth and Samuel were right. She couldn't blame God for her husband's sin. For the first time in years, Naomi White was free of the bitterness and anger that had bound her for much of her life.

After sharing hugs, Elizabeth and Naomi walked toward the wagon, both assured of the fact that life for Naomi would be different from now on.

The delicious meal of roast pork was shared with much joy and laughter. Jake, sensing his guest's exhaustion, offered to take them home soon afterward. There would be other times for sweet fellowship; now was a time for quiet communion.

"Jake," Elizabeth asked as they moved toward the wagon. "How long should I wait before I send another letter to Kaleb? It's been almost six days."

Jake smiled with compassion. "I know you're anxious to see him, but the mail delivery isn't predictable, Lizzy. Give him another week. If he doesn't arrive, I'll see what I can do about sending someone to deliver a letter personally."

"I suppose you're right. My mind has a tendency to run away

when I should trust the Lord. It's just that I miss him terribly."

"I'm sure you do. I can't imagine being away from Vicki a day, let alone two weeks."

Chapter Twenty-two

Joy for the Journey

KALEB'S WOUNDS HAD begun to heal and the swelling was coming down, but Doc didn't want him moving around any more than necessary. Pastor and Doc were spending as much time with Kaleb as possible, encouraging him to keep his eyes off his fears and on the Lord. One of the thoughts Pastor had shared made so much sense. It kept running through Kaleb's mind as he lay back down on his bed that night. *"When you allow fear to take control of your situation, your desire for relief will weaken your courage. Don't seek instant gratification; endure the cultivation of your character. Accept what God is trying to teach you in this. He is able to do what you, as a mere human, cannot."* Pastor had told him to read Psalms forty-three whenever he grew discouraged. That happened often, so Kaleb had it memorized.

Lying around for thirteen days had given Kaleb time to reevaluate his marriage. If he and Elizabeth were ever going to share a union built on mutual trust, he would have to change his ways. He had failed her miserably, but he couldn't keep beating himself up. Should God, in his infinite wisdom, allow him the chance to make amends, he would do his best to make things right.

Doc had been by on Saturday, and Kaleb promised not to leave until Doc had checked him one last time. While Kaleb's mind was pretty well set on leaving, out of respect for the man, he agreed.

Jesse arrived as promised bright and early Monday morning. Kaleb and his parents were at the table waiting for Doc to arrive, so he joined them for a cup of coffee and cinnamon-raisin biscuits dripping with sweet butter.

Samuel asked, "How's your family holding up, Jesse?"

"Not bad, considering the circumstances. Dad and I have been over this whole thing time and again. Since no one in Mt. Clemens will admit to having seen Lizzy, it's possible they left her somewhere before they made their way into town.

Samuel said, "That would explain the disappearance of the third set of tracks. You could stop at the homesteads around that area. You never know what might turn up. I spoke with Henry yesterday after church. The men we brought back aren't talking. Without Lizzy for an eyewitness, Henry's afraid the visiting judge will release them when he comes through."

Kaleb heard Doc ride in and went to the door.

"You're on your feet, Kaleb. I'd like to think it's a good sign, but knowing your determination I'm not sure you'd tell me if you were ready to collapse."

"Of course I would. I'd still want to go search for Liz, but we can't have lies between friends."

"Tell me then. How are you really doing?"

"I'm unstable at times. We'll take it slow. I need to do this, Doc. If my wife is in some kind of danger, she'll be counting on Jesse and me to find her."

"I'm sure you're right. Sit down here and let me check your eyes." Doc reached in his bag, pulled a letter out, and handed it to Samuel. "Seth stopped me as I left the livery. Said this came to Ann Arbor by mistake."

Samuel glanced at the address. "Here, son, it's for you from Grandma. Stick it in your pocket, you'll need something to break up the monotony."

Kaleb did as his Father suggested, and allowed Doc to finish his examination.

Doc rubbed at his jaw. Letting Kaleb go went against his better judgment, but there were extenuating circumstances to consider. "Jesse, make sure he doesn't push himself too hard. If he has any problems get him back here as soon as possible."

"Count on it."

Kaleb and Jesse were down the road apiece before Jesse thought about the letter. "So tell me, Kaleb, how is your grandma these days?"

"Don't know. Liz and Grandma have been writing for a while, but the letters must be private. She hasn't offered to let me read any of them."

"Then open that thing and see what she has to say."

A grin stretched across Kaleb's face. "What's it to you? You hardly know her."

"I pray for her all the time. Open the letter!"

Reaching in his pocket, Kaleb pulled out the envelope and glanced at the handwriting. His heart flipped over as he ripped it open, slid off his horse and leaned against the trunk of a nearby tree. "Thank God!" he said. Looking up at his friend, Kaleb informed him with much enthusiasm, "Jesse, it's from Liz!"

"Well, read it! Is she all right?"

Kaleb's eyes scanned the page. "She's at my grandma's!"

Jesse, after tying their mounts to a nearby tree, listened as Kaleb read out loud. Neither of them attempted to stem the flow of tears.

My Dearest Kaleb,

Words cannot begin to express the yearning in my soul to be held within the shelter of your arms. So much has transpired since we were last together, I hardly know where to begin.

Today, I believe, is the sixth or seventh day since I was taken. I'll start by telling you that I am now free of those horrible men. I questioned them about you and, although they admitted to hitting you over the head, they also led me to believe that you would be all right. You have been constantly in my prayers. It's my hope that this letter finds you well. Kaleb, promise me you'll take care of yourself. I couldn't bear to lose you after all we've been through. I know all of you have been praying, because, once again, God has not only been my refuge, he has sustained me in spite of evil intent.

I passed out while being severely beaten by one of my captors, and when I awoke I was alone in a cabin (not unlike the one you and I stayed in during the storm). I know this news will concern you, Kaleb, so you should know right off that although I'm in rough shape, I'm fairly sure our baby is unharmed. With much effort, I sat up. I found the bag of food from home, a fresh bucket of water, and Lady hobbled by a nearby stream. Tell me that's not God at work in the hearts of evil men!

The day of travel went well. I was growing wary, thinking about having to sleep alone, when I saw the smoke from a campfire. You know me, Kaleb, I'm a big fat chicken. I probably wouldn't have slept a wink. It would seem that God understood my insecurities and met me on my level.

After all that I had been through, I wasn't taking any chances. I watched from a distance before approaching the camp. I found the most amazing young family. Last time, my angel came in the form of an abominable snow-covered man who went on to become my cherished husband. This time God sent me three angels, and these wonderful people have taken me under their wings as you did that night of the storm.

Jacob has informed me that he knows you quite well, and seems to think you would want me to stay with them instead of trying to make it home on my own. The Smiths had been visiting family in Mt. Clemens and were on their way back to their farm. Although Jacob would like to bring me home, the young man seeing to their cows will be gone and they'll need milking and fed tomorrow night. I will heed his recommendation, so this is now the plan. They will drop me off to stay with your grandma until you are able to make arrangements to come and get me. Vicki wants her doctor to take a look at my back and I'll also ask him to check on the baby. Jake is going into town to post this letter. He will send the Doctor out so that I don't have to go into town. Jake and Vicki tell me your families have been friends for years. They're looking forward to visiting with you when you come, so try to plan on staying for a short while. I owe them so much. Their full names, if you don't know already, are Jacob and Victoria Smith, and they have a small daughter, Rebecca who's a constant delight.

There is so much more that I could say, but we'll talk when we're together again. I can only pray that the time will pass quickly, as I miss you terribly already. Give my love to all.

I can hear the Smiths waking up, so I will end this now. If you are not well enough to travel, please hold off, Kaleb, or send someone else in your stead.

Until we meet again,

I am forever and always your devoted wife,

Elizabeth Brenae White

Kaleb, breathing a huge sigh of relief, wrapped his arms around his friend. "Oh, Jesse, she's alive! I hate what she's been through, but God has sustained her. She's coming back to us!" Wiping his tears with the back of his hand, he looked at his friend. The smiles that erupted on their faces was a true depiction of the elation filling them, body and soul.

"Well, Kaleb," Jesse asked with a twinkle in his eyes, "what do you say? Shall we go get the little imp and bring her home?"

"Oh, yes! Most definitely! We'll run back by the house and leave the letter with my parents. They can take it to your folks. We need to be on our way."

The Whites were standing on the porch saying goodbye to Doc when the men rode back into the yard. Samuel, wondering if they'd forgotten something, noticed the smiles on both of their faces and asked, "What's gotten into you two?"

"Dad, read this letter to Doc and Mom."

Samuel glanced down at the signature. "It's from Lizzy?"

"Yes! She's at Grandma's."

As Kaleb and Jesse rode eastward, towards Detroit, their hearts were bursting with joy—joy for the journey ....

Daisytales

He Loves Me!

Chapter Twenty-three

The Reunion

"GRANDMA," ELIZABETH CALLED from the kitchen, "your bath is ready. You should come and get in before the water's too cold." When she didn't respond, Elizabeth wondered if she had fallen asleep. She found her motionless in her rocker, snuggled beneath a heavy quilt. Gently nudging her shoulder, she asked, "Grandma, are you all right?"

With effort, Naomi's eyes peeped open. As much as she wanted to relieve Elizabeth's concerns, she really wasn't feeling well. "I'll be fine, Honey. I'm a little under the weather today, that's all. Maybe I should skip my bath and lay down for a while."

Elizabeth wrapped her arm around Naomi, helped her to her room, and tucked her in. She stayed with her until Naomi drifted off again.

Puffs of steam ascended from the small tub, and the aroma of bath salts filled the air as Elizabeth meandered into the kitchen. The thought of wasting all those glorious lilac bubbles was inconceivable, so she leapt up the stairs, grabbed her unmentionables, and made her way to the small tub. Dinner plans would not have to be altered. Naomi already had the chicken simmering on the back of the stove. Things would have to be added, but Elizabeth could see to that after she washed her hair and indulged in a leisurely bath.

As much as she hated to drag herself out of the tub, the mantel clock chimed twelve times, reminding her that dinner would not make itself. She dried off. Slipping into her under things, she left her golden hair hanging unbrushed behind her, allowing it to dry while she added seasonings and the necessary vegetables to the pot.

Elizabeth heard Naomi calling nonchalantly from the entrance to her room. She didn't expect her to be awake so soon.

"Lizzy, come and see who's here."

Elizabeth looked down at her attire and murmured her frantic appeal. "I'm not decent, Grandma!"

"Somehow, I don't think he'll care."

Elizabeth's blood ran wild—her heart beat at a murderous pace. *Could it be Kaleb?* her thoughts questioned. *Will he be cold and uncaring, or will he receive me with open arms?* She peeked around the corner just to be certain it was him. Sure enough, that blonde hair and those shadowy whiskers gave him away. Throwing caution to the wind, she ran towards him, leapt into his open arms, and wrapped her skinny legs around him. Without thought for those watching or even his response, she kissed him over and over again—at first out of desperation, then relief, and finally out of hope for restoration. Entranced by his presence, she pulled back and gazed into the depths of his amber eyes. He did care; he cared deeply. That much was clear. The smile that erupted on his face not only eased her anxious mind, it lifted her weighted soul. For a fleeting moment, they were one again. Her heart, so soft and supple, was putty in his hands.

"Should I take this to mean you're glad to see me?"

She flushed, somewhat embarrassed by her boldness. "How can you even ask that, Kaleb?" Her hands carressed his face, "Did they hurt you? Are you all right?"

"I am now. These last weeks without you have been torture."

She could see the truth in his eyes as she tenderly ran her hand along his beard-stubbled face. "I'm so glad you're here."

Their passionate reunion ended as quickly as it had come when it dawned on Kaleb how little she was wearing. His tone, though mild, was scolding. "Elizabeth, where are your clothes?"

She tried to get down, but he wouldn't release her. "I just took a bath. We weren't expecting company until later. Besides, it's only you and Jesse, so what's the big deal?"

"You're too old to be running around in your unmentionables in front of your brother."

Rolling her eyes, she shook her head and tried to push away from him. "If you intend to be such an old stick in the mud, Kaleb White, you can just walk out that door and come back when you're in a better mood!"

Naomi burst into laughter, and Jesse laughed as well, finding it so difficult to catch his breath that he had to take a seat in a nearby chair.

"You tell him, Lizzy Girl," Naomi cheered, and then added, "Don't put up with none of his guff!" Naomi had to admit, never in all of her years had she ever seen a woman so exuberant about seeing her man. Then to have Elizabeth do an about-face and be ready to send him away, it was too much.

Kaleb, aware that his actions were absurd, was determined to see her clothed. Ignoring his ecstatic grandma and friend, his piercing gaze fell on Elizabeth. "Which room are you staying in?" He made his way up the stairs, with his wife merely dangling in his arms.

"Kaleb, put me down! You're being ridiculous—and besides, I didn't hug my brother yet."

Nose to nose he informed her. "You can do that after you're dressed."

She sighed in disgruntlement. "I thought maybe, just maybe, this time apart would do you some good. You haven't changed a bit. You're just as bossy as ever."

"Bossy? Maybe I'll always be that way. But let me assure you, God has shown me my faults—and they are many."

As much as she would like this to be true ...

"Liz, there's so much I need to tell you." He walked into her room, kicked the door shut with the heel of his blucher, and plopped down on the bed with his wife in his arms. Running his fingers along her perfumed hair, his eyes scanned every inch of her frame, as if needing to see for himself that she was really all there.

"Perhaps it's selfish, but I had to be alone with you. Oh, Liz, I've missed you so ... I just want to look at you, to touch you without anyone watching."

"Why didn't you say so?"

A moment of silence hung between them before Kaleb

admitted, "I haven't been a good husband to you in a long time. I allowed my fears to cloud my judgment. I really don't know how you stood it. Please tell me I haven't lost you." His deep eyes were silently imploring.

She stared at him for what seemed like an eternity. The days of being afraid of upsetting him, disappointing him, had to be over. Their lack of communication put them into this mess in the first place. "Kaleb, you were so attentive and then there was nothing. I didn't understand—I still don't understand. I adore this baby that's growing inside of me, but you and I have needs that haven't been fulfilled in a long time. In truth," she said, her golden lashes sweeping down from the weight of her words, "I feel as though you stopped loving me."

Kaleb lifted her chin. Her lids opened and their eyes converged. "Nothing could be further from the truth, Liz. You've been so sick. I was so afraid of losing you. Forgive me, I lost sight of the important things."

"I'm your wife. Because you hold such a special place in my heart, your actions cut deeply; those wounds are still hanging wide open. My heart wants to trust you, but I don't want empty promises. I'm in a fragile place with all that has happened. Please Kaleb, don't build my hopes up and then trample them down again. I'm not sure I could take it."

The dark cloud hovering over their marriage had lightened to a hazy gray. While nothing had been resolved, his wife's desire for healing gave him hope. Leaning down, he pressed a kiss to her brow, before claiming her lips in a tender wave of passion.

Elizabeth fought against her insecurities, determined to move past them. She had to let Kaleb know how much he meant to her. "Memories of you holding me are what brought me through my worst times. If I closed my eyes, I could see you—I could feel the warmth of your touch. When I was sure that I could not go on, God used the love we once shared to give me hope. I had to believe you were all right, that I would see you again—and that somehow, if we were both willing to relinquish our fears, God would heal our marriage."

Her words touched him as nothing ever had before. "I'm more than willing to do whatever it takes to make things right."

For a time, they just held each other.

"I have to ask you something, Liz. The afternoon of the fourth day—is that when the man beat you?"

"Yes—how did you know?"

"I was unconscious and woke up with a start that afternoon. I knew something horrible had happened to you. I couldn't be with you physically, but I was there in spirit. After our mothers and Doc joined hands with me and prayed, a peace came over me."

"God answered your prayers. I thought I was dying, Kaleb. But as you can see, I'm fine now."

"I'm so glad. Don't give up on us, Liz. We'll get there—we'll just take things slowly. If I fall back into old patterns, remind me. I'll listen this time, I promise."

"Don't you know by now that I could never give up? We're in this together—remember? For better or worse." Needing to put some space between them, she stood to get dressed.

Kaleb reached for her hand. "Sweetheart, I want you to show me your back."

She hesitated, knowing how this would affect him. "Kaleb, I know it's bad, but Doctor Bert says it's healing nicely."

Nothing could have prepared him for the sight before him. He gasped, unable to squelch the tears that flooded his eyes. Deep gouging wounds marred her bruised skin. They were healing, but what these monsters had put her through was unthinkable. He turned her to face him. "Liz, this is horrendous. Something else has been plaguing me. I need to know ... did they ... hurt you in another way?"

"If you mean did they rape me, no, Kaleb. They talked about it all the time. Hank was furious because Lady didn't like walking in the water. They were trying to cover their tracks. In my weakened state I couldn't control her. It was like something inside him snapped. His rage was taken out on me. Kaleb, in my heart I know these wounds are what set me free. They planned to sell me to a man who runs a string of whorehouses. I would take that beating ten times over before I'd give myself to men in that way. Don't look at these wounds with anger in your heart. That will only destroy you. See them as I do—the price of freedom for your wife and our child."

His heart wrenched within him. Even knowing she was right did nothing to soothe his tortured soul. He reached for her and offered the only thing he could—physical comfort.

Kaleb only had himself to blame. If he hadn't been acting like such a fool, they would have been at the Kane's for dinner that night. His family would have come home to a robbery. Anything would have been better than this.

Sensing her husband's despairing mood, she tried to cheer him. "Kaleb, I have something wonderful to tell you." Her slender hands caressed his unshaven face.

He made a conscious effort to join in her elation.

"What's that?"

"I feel the baby move all the time now."

His eyes sparkled with renewed joy as his hand covered her stomach. "Is it strong enough for me to feel?"

"The movements are light, but I'm sure it won't be long before you can." She grinned, taunting him. "Maybe in a month or so, if you're very attentive." In a wave of excitement, she leapt to her feet and turned sideways "Look Kaleb, I'm getting a belly!"

He chuckled. How could he have known that it was the worst thing he could have done?

Crushed, she walked away.

"Honey, come here, I'm sorry. It's just that ..."

Her saddened tone interrupted his appeal. "If you knew my body the way a husband should, you'd see the changes without my having to tell you."

Elizabeth's words were like salt to an open wound. He had been so entangled in his ridiculous obsession that he'd missed almost two months—months that should have been spent enjoying his wife and the miracle taking place inside her body. He couldn't recoup what he had lost, but he could change the way he responded to her in the future.

Kaleb's long finger stroked his unshaven chin as his eyes followed her every move. She buttoned her camisole, went to the chest at the foot of her bed, and lifted the lid. For a moment she was lost inside. Before long, she stepped into a full shift and pulled a deep burgundy dress over her head. She struggled with the lengthy row of buttons trailing up her spine.

"Liz, please let me help you." As his clumsy fingers went to work, he racked his brain for something, anything he could say that might get them back on solid ground. When nothing came, he settled for a compliment. "This looks nice on you. Is it new?"

"Grandma did re-makes for me on a skirt and three dresses that didn't fit her anymore. She wants me to use them for everyday. I'm not sure when she found the time, but the other day she surprised me with two new gowns that will extend as I get bigger."

Her reluctance to look at him was breaking his heart. When he could stand it no longer, he reached for her hand and gently pulled her back into his lap.

"Sweetheart, please look at me." It took her a moment, but she finally obeyed. "I know better than anyone how much I've missed, and how much damage I've done to the joy we once shared. You're right; I don't know your body as I should. As much as I hope to see that change, I'm going to make mistakes. I'm trying."

"Grandma and I have had a wonderful time together. I've been unhappy for such a long time. I can't go back to that dark place again, Kaleb, not even for you. Our baby needs his mother to be joyful."

"I couldn't agree with you more. Her father wants her mother to be happy too."

She didn't miss his change in their child's gender. He always did that. She yearned for the friendship they had shared—the teasing, his wonderful kisses and, most of all, the laughter—exuberant, joyful, laughter. "I hope you mean that."

"I do!"

His Elizabeth, always willing to forgive, wrapped her arms around his neck, practically squeezing the life out of him. "Liz, will you please kiss me?" When she came towards his lips and then quickly pulled away, teasing him like she used to, her words were a sweet presence in Kaleb's ears.

"I don't know ... maybe you've already had your allotment!"

His eyes narrowed. "Ya know, Young Lady, I'm beginning to think it's going to take me months to get you back in line! Am I right?"

Elizabeth, not having heard a playful remark come out of Kaleb in far too long, felt a surge of hope transfuse her. *Maybe he really has changed, Lord.* Surrendering to his ardent kisses seemed so right—a soothing ointment to her ailing heart.

"Kaleb, Grandma has something wonderful to tell you, and I need a hug from my brother. Can we talk more later?"

After sharing a tender smile, he relinquished his hold and laughed at the way she flounced down the stairs as if she had lived there all her life.

"Lizzy," Naomi asked, as she entered the kitchen, "turn around and let me see."

Elizabeth twirled before her in obvious delight. Jesse's drawn-out whistle only added to her joy.

"Doesn't she look nice, Kaleb?"

"She looks wonderful!" Kaleb leaned down for a hug. "It's good to see you, Grandma. I can't thank you enough for all you've done for my wife."

"Lizzy's given me far more than temporal things, Kaleb. With her help, I've found a new way of life."

Kaleb, staggered by her admission, inquired further. "Are you going to share?" He didn't miss the radiant smile that passed between the two women.

"I've been throwing a barrage of questions at my newest granddaughter, practically since she arrived. Last Sunday we went to church with Jake and Vicki. The pastor confirmed much of what Lizzy and I had been studying. I asked Jesus to come into my heart, and he forgave me of my sins, but he also lifted the heavy load I've been carrying most of my life. I'm finally free! In many ways I feel as though my life has just begun."

Kaleb and Jesse glanced at each other through glassy eyes. This was definitely an answer to prayer, and a monumental moment in both their lives.

"Grandma, this is wonderful!"

"I hate what brought Lizzy here, but God knew I needed her."

Elizabeth reminded her, "We needed each other."

Jesse offered his congratulations, stood up, and drew Elizabeth carefully into his arms. "I've accepted the fact that I now play second fiddle to my best friend, but I still need a hug from my sister."

"That goes both ways, Jesse. I'm glad you were able to come."

"I had to see for myself that you were all right." Jesse pulled back and gazed into her eyes before playfully adding, "I couldn't be happier that you're safe, but I have a request."

"What's that?"

"Now that this is over, could you please call a halt to all this drama? Your family needs a breather!"

Her mouth dropped open. "Jesse Somers, you know full well that none of this has been my fault. I would love nothing more than to have my life settle into a calm routine." She started to laugh. "But I'm not sure what that would be like."

Naomi asked, "So tell me boys, do you need to get the horses settled in the barn or are you planning to steal my girl away without a proper visit?"

Kaleb couldn't withhold a smile; his grandma was such a character. "No, we'll stay for a visit as long as you'll feed us! I'm starving. What about you, Jesse?"

"Famished! You see, someone I know was anxious to see his wife. We've been riding since before sun-up. We never did stop for breakfast, and I haven't had a cup of coffee all day."

Elizabeth grinned, "Now, that would certainly explain a few things!"

Kaleb reached out, pulled her into his lap, and tickled her. "What's that remark suppose to mean?"

Her words were intermixed with giggles. "Kaleb, quit it! Everyone else understands what I'm talking about. Figure it out yourself."

"I'd like to say that Grandma's been a bad influence on you, but you and I know better."

"Look who's talking."

Kaleb glanced at his grandma. "Would you please set my wife straight."

"Sorry, Kaleb, you're on you're own. Don't you go asking me to play favorites, 'cause I won't do it. Now, if you press me, I'd have to say your wife knows you better than you know yourself."

Kaleb, seeing he was outnumbered, gave up.

"Kaleb," Elizabeth said, "I've been cleaning the barn over the last few days. Mind you, it doesn't look great, but it's much better than it was. Jake took care of Lady for me until this morning. I let her stretch her legs for a while and brought her here."

Kaleb couldn't believe she'd even think about cleaning the

barn in her condition. *And riding alone—she knows how ...* thankfully, he realized what he was doing before he opened his mouth. *Surely,* he thought, *Liz knows her own limitations. Slow me down, Lord; show me how to trust.*

Elizabeth noticed Kaleb's altered mood as the men went out the back door, but she chose not to question him. She understood that some habits were not easy to change. Just like her, Kaleb would have things to work on.

"Grandma, are you feeling better?"

"A little. Honey, don't you think we should make something to go along with the meal? If we don't, we'll never fill these boys up."

Elizabeth agreed, so after pulling the chicken out of the broth, she set it aside to cool and mixed up a batch of corn muffins. "Grandma , did you have something in mind for supper?"

"There's a ham in the cold cellar, or," she said, winking, "you could sneak out and try your hand at fishing again."

Elizabeth giggled, imagining Kaleb's reaction to her last expedition. "We'll see how the afternoon goes."

Naomi nodded. "Here, you can add these vegetables to the pot."

As Elizabeth took them from her, she asked, "Where did you say the rice is?"

"In the blue tin on the shelf."

Elizabeth had the chicken picked and in the pot, the table set, and still Kaleb and Jesse were nowhere to be seen. Naomi offered to keep an eye on the muffins while Elizabeth slipped into her old boots and scooted out the back door to check on the men. As she moved toward the barn, she noticed Jake's wagon. They were shaking hands and getting reacquainted as she approached.

"Hello, Jake." Elizabeth said as she came near.

"Looks like Kaleb got your letter!"

"Mmm-hmm."

Jake smiled at the exchange of glances between husband and wife. "When did you get in, Kaleb?"

"About an hour ago. I appreciate all you've done for my wife, Jake."

He nodded. "She was in a bad way when we found her, but it's Vicki and I who've been blessed by our time together. Our Becky adores her."

Kaleb grinned. "I'll bet she's getting big. I hear congratulations are in order. Liz tells me you're expecting again."

"Thanks. Same to you." Jake turned to Elizabeth and asked, "What's up with that horse of yours? She wasn't that peppy when I rode her the other day."

Elizabeth's eyes twinkled. "I can't help it if she likes me best, Jake. I thought she'd burst before I let her cut loose."

"I saw that."

"Too much time in the stall, I guess."

"Thanks for staying close," Jake said.

Elizabeth caught her husband's eye and said, "I didn't really have a choice."

Jake thought Kaleb looked flustered about something. *But then, why wouldn't he be? He's been separated from his wife for a long time.* "We should get this feed and hay in the barn," Jake said. "Vicki will be expecting me for dinner before long. The way that sky is changing, we could have some rain before the day's spent."

"I'm heading back in to finish putting the meal on the table. I'll see you soon, Jake. Tell Vicki and Becky I said hello."

"Be happy to."

"Mmm! Mmm! Mmm! Something smells wonderful!" Kaleb announced as he came in the back door, sliding his arms around his wife and kissing the back of her neck. As expected, she squealed and pulled away.

Jesse, who had just walked into the room, witnessed the exchange. "All right you two, none of that!"

Kaleb was about to tell him to get used to it, but Jesse spoke before he had the chance.

"Lizzy, have you decided which room upstairs is mine? After I fill my empty stomach, I'll have to catch up on some sleep or I'll never make it through the evening."

"First things first, Jesse. If I know your sister, we'll both be taking baths before we're allowed anywhere near the clean sheets."

"You got that right!" Elizabeth declared as she set the last bowl of soup on the table. Jesse poured her tea and Kaleb filled their mugs with coffee.

The three of them joined hands, and Kaleb prayed for Grandma and the meal before them. "Did Jesse mention that Jake invited all of us for dinner tomorrow?"

She looked at Jesse, who was so engrossed in devouring his meal he didn't look up. "No. Are we supposed to bring something?" Taking a sip of her tea, she didn't notice Kaleb's smirk.

"Apple pie."

Smiling, her eyes met his. "And I suppose you had nothing to do with that request?"

"I had everything to do with it! I told him straight up that my wife makes the best apple pie I've ever tasted and we'd be happy to bring one for dessert." He couldn't resist adding, "Now, if you happen to make two, Jesse and I will be glad to help you dispose of the extra one after our evening meal."

She laughed out loud. "I hope Grandma has extra apples in the cold cellar."

"She has plenty. I helped her put them in storage last fall."

She shook her head, knowing she could never deny him.

Jesse finished his meal, sat back and sighed. "That was delicious."

"There's more in the pot if you're still hungry."

"No thanks. I'm all set, Sis. Hey Kaleb, did you remember to tell your wife about those men?"

"What men?" Elizabeth asked.

Jesse filled her in. "The day before you were taken, Henry had chased a couple of trouble-makers out of town. When we came across them in Mt. Clemens, we brought them back with us. Kane's holding them until you get back to identify them. Do you have any idea how far they took you?"

"We didn't go into any towns, and I'm sure it was the fourth day when Hank beat me, but I can't tell you much more."

Jesse wanted her to describe them, and her reluctance puzzled him.

The affirmation in her brother's eyes when she described them right down to the clothes on their backs brought back a flood of memories she'd just as soon forget.

Kaleb, sensing her despairing mood, reached for her hand. His touch brought on a sudden rush of tears. "Honey, I would think you'd be glad to know these men were behind bars. What has you so upset?"

"They should have to pay for what they've done. You don't understand, neither of you do. I need to put this all behind me. A trial? If there's a trial the whole town will know everything. I've done nothing to deserve this. But if the thought of telling my husband leaves me feeling mortified, how can I tell a judge, in front of the entire town?" A well of emotions swirled inside her as she fled the room.

Muddled, Kaleb stood to follow her. "Pray for us, Jesse. They didn't rape her, but they tortured her mind in ways neither of us will ever comprehend."

Kaleb moved up the stairs, opened the door, and found his wife face down, sobbing into her pillow. Her slender frame was lost in a puff of burgundy fabric, with golden hair strewn all around. Searching his heart for anything that might soothe her, he moved toward the bed, kicked off his bluchers, and prayed as he lay down beside her. *Father, I'm sure I don't know the half of what took place while we were apart, but You do. Heal her. Shelter my wife through this storm. Show me how to be the husband and friend she needs.*

Kaleb gently massaged her scalp and temples, hopeful his touch would somehow ease her disquieted mind. For a time she didn't acknowledge his presence; but when her sobbing eased, she moved to lay her head on his chest. Kaleb produced his ever-present hanky to dry her face, which brought a halfhearted smile to her lips. Thinking that a bit of levity would do her some good, he asked, "Tell me what I did to bring on that smile, and I'll do it again."

She accepted his offering, and blew her nose. "The only

reason you carry this is for your blubbering wife."

He grinned. "I knew my mother had a reason for insisting I have one in my pocket at all times. When I married you, the mystery was solved." Her mock-scowl, though fierce, was not very convincing. "You don't have to tell me anything, but I know they must have said or done some awful things to upset you this much. If you do decide to talk about it, I'm more than willing to listen."

"They said and did such crude and vulgar things—things I'd like to forget. I don't know if I can tell you, Kaleb. How can I risk losing what we have left?"

He tucked her hair behind her ears. "Liz, what kind of a monster would that make me if I blamed you for their sin?"

"I'm scared. I want to trust you, but look at where we've been over the last few months. We're not exactly on solid ground."

"I can't change the mistakes I've made. I won't press you if you don't want to talk about it, but keep this in mind: if we don't do something, these men will go free, and then this could happen to someone else. Don't you think we should do our part to keep that from happening?"

"Knowing what I should do is one thing; following through is where the difficulties lie."

Kaleb understood this better than anyone.

"The thought of having to see them again makes my skin crawl. You weren't there. The things they said and did, the way they looked at me—I can't—I just can't!"

"Honey, think about it. If we don't put this to rest, our fears will continue to rob us of our faith. Look at what I've been doing to you. I know this now better than anyone. I was so afraid of adding to your illness, so obsessed with keeping you safe. Everything blew up in my face. You were taken from the very walls I was sure you were safest within. On top of that, I squelched the love we began to share. We can't go back there. I don't want to and I don't believe for a minute you do either. I want our child to be born to two parents who love and respect each other. Please tell me you're not too weary—not when we've come so far. Our faith is bigger than anything these men set out to do. Our God can move mountains. Remember?" Kaleb was struggling until Elizabeth peeked up and smiled.

"Have you ever considered the fact you might be in the wrong line of work?"

His mouth dropped open. "Now what is that supposed to mean?"

"You present a very convincing sermon. I'll do what I have to. I know you're right, but you might have to remind me from time to time why I'm doing it. God really is changing your heart, and I'm glad. Maybe there's hope for us yet, Kaleb!"

"Hope. Trust me, Liz, there is always hope!"

He Loves Me!

Chapter Twenty-four

Forgiven

*A*FTER A WARM bath, Kaleb pulled on a clean pair of jeans, and went in search of his wife, who seemed to vanish right after they finished talking. He opened the front door and was about to step outside when Naomi spoke from where she sat by the fire.

"If all else fails, look down by the river, Kaleb."

He turned to face her. His brow rose. "Why would she be down there?"

"Oh, any number of reasons."

Kaleb smiled as he walked out the door. Apparently his grandma knew more than she was willing to say.

The brilliant afternoon sun spread a shimmery glow across the fields as Kaleb leapt off the porch and rounded the corner of the house. A chipmunk scampered up a nearby tree, the birds chirped, and wild violet leaves were poking up through the last vestige of dormant grass. For a fleeting moment Kaleb wished they were in full bloom. He'd love to gather a small bouquet for

Elizabeth to enjoy. All in due time, he reminded himself. Spring had arrived, evidenced all around. As he moved further down the embankment, he was irrepressibly drawn to the rhythmic sounds wafting up from the river's edge. Elizabeth was well hidden by the budding foliage, so he had no idea what she was doing. Never having heard his wife solo before, he stayed out of sight, drinking in the sweet melodious sounds as she raised her soft alto voice in worship to her Heavenly Father. The tune was unfamiliar, but the words were taken from the twenty-third Psalm. Her singing stopped, as exuberant words filled the air.

"Oh boy ... here we go ... oh my!"

Unable to curtail his curiosity further, Kaleb swung around the huge maple. There stood his wife, in a pair of overalls he had seen on his grandmother many times before. She was standing in the cold water. He shivered at the thought. In her hands were the poles he had used with his father on numerous occasions, and the way they were vibrating, a fish had to be attached to each hook. Kaleb watched in silence, utterly amazed. She backed out of the river, plopped down on the bank, carefully laid the poles beside her, and held them in place with her bare feet. She then reached for a rag, took the first line, and brought the wiggling fish as close as she dared. He could barely believe his eyes. Laughter threatened to erupt. Next, she wrapped the rag around the first fish, never allowing it to touch her hand. This did not surprise him. After carefully removing the hook, she let the fish fall from the rag into the bucket. She did the same with the other line.

He could hardly wait. Now she would be faced with the part of fishing she hated more than anything. In fact, the only way she would attempt to fish is if he or Jesse would agree to thread them on. Again, Kaleb was shocked. Pulling a worm out of a smaller bucket with the same piece of fabric, she laid it on the ground. Without touching it, she ran the hook through it. It was sort of on, sort of off, but that didn't seem to matter to her. His hand came over his mouth to suppress laughter when he saw her shuddered in obvious disgust. Before long, she had both poles back in the water and the process began again. Elizabeth, lost in her endeavors, started when Kaleb approached.

"So much for the woman of my dreams smelling like flowers!"

His comment made her smile.

"Tell me, Liz, how's a man supposed to snuggle up to his wife when she smells like a stinky old fish?"

"That's the price you'll have to pay for a good meal this evening. If it bothers you, when Jesse's done, you can help me haul water for another bath."

"Be glad to. But what did I tell you about wearing men's clothes without asking me first?"

He didn't sound angry, but she peered up, just to be sure. "You'll have to take that up with Grandma. I told her you wouldn't like it. She made it clear that when I'm at her place, I must adhere to *her* rules. If I want to fish, I must wear these silly things. Of course," Elizabeth continued, tilting her head and rolling her eyes, before she flashed him a baiting smile, "this is the only rule she's told me about." False innocence exuded when she added, "Do you think it could have something to do with the fact that I told her you don't want me to wearing jeans without asking?"

Kaleb burst out laughing. "Knowing Grandma, it has everything to do with it. I'm not letting you off the hook that easy. You'll pay for your crimes, Young Lady, do you hear me?"

With a twinkle in her glittering blue eyes, she whispered, "I can hardly wait."

She looked so adorable in her makeshift clothes, he could hardly keep his eyes off her as he asked what he thought would be a safe question. "So, how many did you catch?"

"Ten." His expression was doubtful, so she motioned for him to take a look.

"You haven't been out here long enough to catch ten."

"Oh, ye of little faith," she said, without a smidgen of condescension.

"Ouch! I suppose I deserve that one. I should know better than to doubt your straight-forwardness."

"I was talking about the fish, Kaleb."

"I know you were. I'm harder on myself than you could ever be. If I listened to you in the first place, our relationship wouldn't be in such dire need of repair."

She set his comment aside. "Kaleb, do you remember that Sunday I decided it was time to quit thinking only of myself and give us a chance?"

"Yes."

"I couldn't believe it took me so long to see you as a blessing from the Lord."

"Some blessing *I* turned out to be!"

When he lowered his head, she reached for his chin and brought his eyes back to hers. "Kaleb, I forgive you."

"I don't deserve you, Liz. I've been such a disappointment."

Elizabeth reiterated something he had said to her during their stay in the cabin. "You could never be a disappointment. You're always lifting someone's spirits—but like me, you get a little side-tracked here and there. We all do." When he didn't readily respond, she added, "You're holding yourself to a standard that's impossible to attain." For a time she only stared, wondering why he was making this so hard. "You confuse me. You never think twice about forgiving me when I'm wrong. Why can't you accept my forgiveness and move on?"

"I'm trying to."

"Maybe that's the problem. Quit trying. Just let it go! The blood of Jesus covers our sins. You can't change what's happened, but I'm more than willing to begin again. Leave it at the cross where it belongs. I need my husband back."

Her gaze held nothing but adoration. She was right; they did need to walk in forgiveness. As his long fingers claimed her chin, their yearning lips collided in total surrender. Selfless love—an amazing thing!

A silence hung between them as Elizabeth went back to her fishing. Not an awkward silence, but a peaceful acceptance. Things would have to be discussed. For now Kaleb merely wanted to get reacquainted with his wife and enjoy their time together.

"So tell me, Liz: who did you have in mind to clean these smelly things?"

"You or Jesse." He shook his head, mouthing the word no, so she added, "If you or Jesse won't do them, I'll give them to Jake. He's more than willing to do them for Vicki."

"You know, you're still too sassy for your own good."

"I am, and you're too bossy."

"What am I going to do with you?"

She grinned. "I'm not sure if you remember, but the night we married, you asked me that same question. Then, nothing suited me just fine. Now ... well, let's just say that I've changed my mind."

"I'm glad, Liz—so very glad. And just so you know, I had every intention of cleaning the fish, I was merely curious."

"About what?"

"I wanted to know if your fishing experience had gone full circle, or if it ended with the catch. I have my answer, and I don't mind a bit." Kaleb stood. "I'll grab my knife and get to work. At the rate you're pulling them in, we'll have enough to stuff ourselves in half an hour." He had barely walked away when his wife was squealing again. He looked back to find two more anxious victims hanging from the end of her lines.

Kaleb hauled her bath water so it could be heating while he cleaned the fish. The long day of travel was catching up with him, and he had every intention of snagging his own lilac-scented beauty for a cozy afternoon nap.

❀ ❀ ❀

Elizabeth rounded the corner of the kitchen to find her husband and brother sitting at the table with a cup of coffee in their hands. The minute Kaleb saw her, his face lit with pleasure.

Jesse's head swung around so he could take a gander himself.

Kaleb asked, "Honey, where did you get that dress?"

Elizabeth spun around, proudly displaying the golden gown. "I was hoping you'd like this. Grandma made it. I think it's my favorite."

"You look wonderful in it!"

"I couldn't agree more," Jesse affirmed.

"I thank you both."

After checking on Naomi and finding her sleeping, Elizabeth swung her shawl around her shoulders and the three of them were off to the Smith's home. Kaleb claimed Elizabeth's hand with his free one and proudly carried the basket with her addition to the noon meal in the other.

As they approached the farm, they could see Jake in the yard playing with his daughter. The blonde-haired moppet had a rag doll draped across her elbow. Spotting Elizabeth, Becky dropped the doll and ran toward her with both arms in the air, informing her father, "Zizzy, Papa! Zizzy's here!", as if he hadn't noticed.

Elizabeth lifted the exuberant child and accepted her open display of affection with a welcoming smile.

Kaleb and Jesse found the small girl delightful, but she wouldn't give them the time of day. Her "Zizzy" was here, and that was all that mattered.

"As you can see," Jake said to Kaleb, "Papa loses his importance when Zizzy's around."

"I noticed. She's adorable. You're a blessed man."

"I'm well aware of that. Just wait, your day's coming—and it'll arrive before you know it." Jake looked at Elizabeth and smiled; his daughter was snuggled contentedly in her arms. "Lizzy, dinner's not quite ready. Why don't we head out to the barn and show the men our newest additions."

"I'd love to see them again, but shouldn't I head in and help Vicki?"

"We won't stay long. They're changing so fast, I'd like you to see them again."

She didn't need to be asked twice. Elizabeth led the way,

asking, "Becky, would you like to see Matilda and the puppies?"

"Til-dy." As fully expected, the minute Jake opened the stall, Becky wriggled out of Elizabeth's hold and toddled towards the massive dog. Having witnessed this marvel before, Elizabeth was not about to miss Kaleb and Jesse's reaction. They both seemed to be holding their breath as Becky tackled Matilda's head. However, they burst into laughter when the dog's long tongue ran up her pudgy cheek. Becky didn't mind a bit. She merely plopped herself down on Matilda and began petting the puppies who had settled around her. After a time, she peered up at her captive audience, pointed to the litter, and informed them with much enthusiasm "Bup-pys!"

Unable to resist, Elizabeth joined Becky on the fresh bed of straw. After allowing Matilda to smell her, she reached for the biggest of the fawn-colored puppies. The slits on his eyes were barely open, but Elizabeth was sure he'd be quite the bruiser once full-grown. She wondered what Kaleb thought, and peeked up to find his eyes following her every move. He joined her in the straw, reached for the puppy in her hands, and held it up for inspection. He smiled at the thought of his wife having a companion like this. He could almost picture the puppy full grown, following her everywhere, and Elizabeth enjoying every moment. While he didn't acknowledge a thing, Kaleb knew what she was thinking.

"Why is this one so much bigger than the others, Jake? Is he the only male?"

"Yes. When he's full grown, he could have an extra hundred pounds or more on top of what his mother weighs. The female mastiffs are more popular because they don't eat as much, but the males can be very intimidating." Jake could see that Kaleb was seriously considering his offer to give them one as a wedding gift.

Elizabeth stayed for a while before heading in to help Vicki.

Kaleb handed the puppy up to Jesse, and asked, "What do you think about this one, Jesse?"

His brow furrowed. "Why are you asking me?"

"The way I see it, you'll have to face the beast as much as anyone. Lizzy wants a puppy when we get into our own place. As far as I can tell, this one'll be the biggest guard dog I'd ever come across."

Jesse started to laugh. The words Kaleb had chosen were all too familiar.

"All right, Jess, what's so funny?" Jake stood aside, taking in the whole exchange.

"You do know my sister often refers to you as her guard dog?"

"She's mentioned it." Slightly annoyed, he asked, "What did she say to you?"

"Kaleb, think about it. You don't want her leaving the house unless you're with her."

"That's not true. She went into town with your mom."

Jesse caught Jake's reaction out of the corner of his eye, and Jake's hand came up to suppress laughter. "Once! You've been married for months. If getting Lizzy a big dog to have at her side when you're not around will help you to relax and give her back her freedom, then I'm all for it."

"Knowing what I should do and actually doing it aren't always the same thing," Kaleb said, looking up at Jake. "Am I the only man out there with this problem?"

"No. I think most men are overprotective by nature. Finding Lizzy the way you did in that storm, and then this latest tragedy,

I can see where your fears are coming from. But that doesn't change what you need to do. Think about what your actions are saying to your wife. You're telling her you don't trust her. Wasn't it God who led you to her in the storm? Wasn't He the one who set her free and sent her home on the very day that we were traveling through the area? If she's meant to be here, Kaleb, God is able to sustain her, not you."

"I know you're right."

Jesse snuggled the little fur ball in his hands. "I don't doubt my sister will adore this puppy. Just be sure you're getting it for the right reasons."

Kaleb nodded. "She doesn't like being alone in the house, so I think a dog will help both of us to get on with our lives." Turning back to Jake, Kaleb asked, "Will the male be as gentle as a female with our baby?"

"He'll be fine as long as he's raised with kindness."

Jesse started to chuckle. "Look at that horse of hers. Lady's spoiled rotten, and I'm sure this puppy will be no different."

Kaleb and Jake nodded in agreement. "I'd like this to be a surprise, so don't say anything. All right, Jesse?"

"That's fine."

"Jake, before we head in, Grandma wanted me to run a few things by you. She said your brother is looking for a farm out this way and asked about hers. If he's still interested, I'm sure we can come to terms."

"He is. In fact, when I saw him in town the other day, he brought it up again."

"Has he mentioned how soon he'd like to get things settled?"

"Tomorrow would suit him. He'd like to get a crop planted

this season, but he wouldn't want to push Naomi out until she's ready."

Kaleb's brow rose. "That wouldn't be a problem. She has her heart set on going home with us. Could you bring him by tomorrow?"

"Sure."

"I've been trying to decide how I should go about getting the women home. Taking wagons through the mud on the Sauk Trail could be challenging if the spring rains don't hold off. But, I can't expect Grandma to ride that far. She hasn't been on a horse in years."

Jake had a suggestion. "I'm sure Nathan wouldn't mind if you stored Naomi's things in one of the rooms. You could come back after planting season when things dry up and get the puppy at the same time. If you borrow my smaller buggy for Grandma and Lizzy, and only take the things she needs for now, you should be able to get through without too much effort. The women would also have a roof over their heads if the rains did come."

"That would be great. Lightening will pull and I can ride Lady home."

"Then it's settled. I have the buggy in the other shed. After dinner, we'll take it over to Grandma's so you have time to get it ready."

"Thanks, Jake."

Jesse interrupted their conversation. "Guys, I think we're being summoned."

Scooping Becky off the ground, Jake led the way into the house.

Kaleb, having met with Nathan Smith, signed the necessary papers and filed them at the land office in Detroit. Elizabeth would have enjoyed going along, but there was so much that had to be done if they were going to be ready to leave as planned.

At Kaleb's insistence, Grandma was to wander no further than her rocking chair while the rest of them did the packing. Naomi tried to tell him otherwise, but he informed her that if she didn't take the time to rest and get her health back, he would be forced to leave her behind. He never would have followed through on the threat, but he wasn't about to tell *her* that.

Naomi's limited movement did nothing to deter her from issuing orders she expected to be followed to the letter.

Elizabeth took pleasure in Naomi's ability to get Kaleb and Jesse to do things her way. She knew the men were only humoring her, because she caught them on several occasions laughing uncontrollably over Naomi's zany way of directing them. When Elizabeth questioned him, Kaleb's comment blessed her to no end. He told her that most of his laughter was pure, indisputable delight. His grandma had always been so crude and bitter, it did his heart a world of good to see her enjoying life for a change.

Elizabeth spent most of her time preparing mounds of baked goods. Although they were anxious to arrive in Ypsilanti, Kaleb and Jesse had no delusions of this being a quick trip. With that in mind, she filled tin after tin with more food than they could eat in a week, maybe two. By the end of the third day, all seemed to be in readiness.

Their vigilant efforts had not allowed Kaleb and Elizabeth

time to delve into some of the issues that had been squeezing the life out of their marriage. While this concerned her, in some areas they had begun to move forward.

Happiness was a powerful tonic. They were laughing again, teasing each other as friends. The tenderness was back in her husband's eyes, and it seemed to be growing in intensity. His arms were willing to receive her and his wonderful kisses were like cool water after a day in the hot summer sun—refreshing and exhilarating. She had to believe it was only a matter of time before their relationship improved, for healing had begun in both of their hearts.

Elizabeth held no illusion of things being easier when they arrived home. The planting season would soon be upon them. They would have to put in long hours to make up for lost time. As much as they wanted to be in their new place before the baby arrived, she couldn't see it happening. She reminded herself repeatedly that God would work out the details. She had to keep her eyes on Him, and do her part in this union.

She had so much to be thankful for. Again, she was in the arms of her husband, and Grandma, who was coming to live with them in Ypsilanti, had found the peace that passes all understanding. How could Elizabeth be anything less than overjoyed?

Daisytales

He Loves Me!

Chapter Twenty-five

Departure

THE DAY OF departure dawned with the assurance of a beautiful spring day. As Elizabeth stood at the picture window looking out over the farm, her heart leapt with excitement. The sun's luminous rays flickered in the sky, as if summoning her to come and bask in its warmth. The songbirds filled the air with their harmonious sounds. Giggles bubbled up as a pair of squirrels, enjoying a merry chase, suddenly halted and stood at attention. Her husband, coming out of the barn, was obviously the cause of their deflection. With a sense of urgency and elation, Elizabeth bustled towards the kitchen to help Naomi finish putting breakfast on the table.

After a filling meal, the women tidied the kitchen for the new owner, while the men went to the barn to saddle their horses. Naomi and Elizabeth shared a smile as Elizabeth placed the tin of cookies they had made for Nathan in the center of the table. After saying their silent goodbyes, they joined the men outside.

Elizabeth sat down next to Naomi on the padded buggy seat and took up the reins to guide Lightning. Her enthusiasm about leaving was now intermixed with apprehension. The way Lightning pranced over her misguided attempts to control him was more than a little unsettling. Elizabeth had driven a team and wagon before, but never a buggy of this sort. She had no idea what she was doing wrong. Why she hadn't thought to have Kaleb teach her how to drive before this, she didn't know. It was too late for regrets now.

Kaleb's repeated attempts to guide her from Lady's saddle were not working. In truth, he made Lightning more fidgety with every word he spoke. His spirited friend was so used to following Kaleb's commands that Elizabeth's orders had no effect.

Naomi, understanding the problem, told Kaleb in no uncertain terms to, "Shush! Go away! Leave us alone!"

Kaleb laughed at her stern demeanor and moved out in front of the buggy. If Lightning became unreceptive to their bidding, Kaleb needed to be close enough to bring him to a halt. While he didn't mind indulging his grandma, he wasn't about to chance injury to two of his favorite women, along with his unborn child. Fortunately, the difference in Lightning was astounding. He settled down and Elizabeth learned quickly under her grandma's patient tutelage. Other than an occasional fallen tree that needed to be removed from their path, the day moved along without a hitch.

Often, Elizabeth would find her husband watching her from a distance. She noticed everything about him: the way his wide-brimmed hat sat tilted at just the right angle atop his wavy blonde head, his weathered skin, the crease of his lips when he smiled. How dare he look so irresistible out there riding alongside her brother? Did he know the way her heart leapt at the mere sight of him? She couldn't help but wonder, *is my heart changing or have I loved him all along? Is it possible that I was merely too blind to see it before?*

Could she dare to hope that the changes in Kaleb were here to stay—or was it only a façade that would dissipate when they were once again at home, in their room together?

I can't live in fear of his rejection again, can I, Lord? He says that his heart has changed. I have to trust him. How can I do anything else? He's woven around all that I hold dear.

As the sun began its descent and the evening shadows began to fall, they made camp in a clearing. The women prepared the evening meal while Kaleb and Jesse started a fire and saw to the needs of the horses.

"Grandma," Elizabeth asked, while stirring the pan of beans, "if you grab the green tin from the buggy, we can have the leftover biscuits from breakfast with our meal."

"That's fine, but I've got a hankering for those shortbread cookies. Can you remember what tin they're in?

Elizabeth giggled, recalling how many Naomi had eaten as they came out of the oven yesterday. "The one with the blue lid."

By the time they sat down to eat, the sky had turned to a sullen gray. Darkness was settling in, covering them in a thick black blanket. If the moon was out, it couldn't be seen through the leaves on the hovering trees. The only lights in the quaint setting were the flickering flames from the campfire.

The men were suspecting rain, so they insisted on the women

sleeping under the buggy. Elizabeth found this request terribly disheartening. She so wanted to sleep with her husband, but how could she chance hurting Naomi's feelings?

An hour later, Elizabeth's concern for her grandma's feelings had dissipated. Naomi snored, relentlessly. Wide awake, Elizabeth came to a firm decision; she would rather be rained on all night than listen to another second of Naomi's thunderous roars. Unfortunately, the small campfire had burned out, making it impossible to see where she was going. Feeling her way to the extra blankets in the buggy, she stumbled around in the dark, trying to relocate. Elizabeth hadn't gotten far when she tripped over something in her way and startled one of the men. She wasn't hurt, but what happened next made her blood run cold.

A gun cocked, and her husband's threat sent rippling chills up her spine. "Don't take another step, or you won't live to regret it!"

Her eyes about shot out of her head as she swallowed past the lump in her throat. That is, until it dawned on her. Surely he couldn't see anymore than she. It was pitch black! Timidly, she chanced his name. "Kaleb?"

"Elizabeth," he scolded in a whisper, "What are you doing up? I could have shot you!"

Apparently, there were unspoken rules about walking around in the dark. "Kaleb, don't be angry. Grandma snores loud enough to wake the dead. I can't sleep with her!"

His soft chuckle broke the stillness.

She heard the shuffle of feet as he moved toward her, but she had no idea how close he was until he bumped into her. Not so much as a hello or how are you—just a soft possessive growl as his arms shot out to claim her. "You're coming with me! I can't have you running around in the dark and being shot at!"

She started to laugh. Thinking better of it, she covered her mouth, lest she wake her brother. At the rate things were going, *he* might threaten to shoot them both.

Within seconds she found herself ensconced in Kaleb's oversized frame. He wanted to sleep; she wanted to talk. Unfortunately, she waited too long to speak up.

Now Kaleb was snoring—unmercifully! *How,* she thought, *do I manage to get myself into these predicaments?* Eventually, his irritating clamor settled into a familiar sound that she actually found soothing. In due course, she drifted off.

❦ ❦ ❦

"Land sakes! Would you look at that, Jesse? I've been looking all over for my granddaughter, and where do I find her? Safe and sound in her husband's arms, legs, oh ... you know what I mean. Snug as a bug in a rug."

Elizabeth peered up through half-opened eyes, smiling at the elderly woman hovering over her. Her hands were perched on her ample hips, and her grin went from ear to ear. "Sorry if I worried you, Grandma, but your level of snoring beats Kaleb's by a long shot. Besides, he's kind of nice to snuggle with, if you know what I mean."

"I do, Honey. I'm just giving you a hard time. I forgot about my snoring problem. Come to think of it, Samuel used to complain about it too."

"Give me a minute, Gram. I'll help you put the meal on."

After sharing a leisurely breakfast, the caravan was back on the trail before the morning sun could collect the dew from the ascending blades of grass.

Elizabeth was pleasantly surprised when Kaleb handed her Lady's reins before climbing in the buggy next to his grandma. Mounting Lady, Elizabeth rode alongside Jesse in the coolness of the dawn. It seemed they would never run out of things to talk about. She missed her brother in more ways than she'd realized.

"Jesse, maybe it's none of my business, but I'm curious about something. Are you still looking for a wife, or has someone already sparked your interest?"

"No one yet, but I do have a plan. I'd like it if you and Kaleb will pray with me about it."

"You know we will. What are you thinking?"

"If I don't find a wife within the next year or so, I'll just have to go elsewhere looking for one."

"How long would you be gone?" The tears pooling in her eyes did not go unnoticed.

"Don't get yourself all upset, Elizabeth. I won't be gone more than a year, two at the most. I haven't said anything before this, but I've been working towards getting my teaching certificate. I have every intention of coming back to run the farm with Dad, but you know how much I'd love teaching. I have to be sure I won't have any regrets. Besides, the time away could serve a dual purpose. It is possible that I'll find that special someone to share my life with. I should think you, of all people, would understand."

"I do, but I don't have to like it."

He grinned. " I'll be looking for a nice brunette, with red highlights in her hair. And, if she happens to be tall, with long spindly legs, I'd consider it an extra bonus. What do you think?"

"Jesse, you're silly. You can't get that specific or you might miss the woman God has planned for you. Besides, my baby needs an auntie, so you're going to have to be more serious about this."

He couldn't resist giving his brassy sister a hard time. "I may not know much about my future bride, but I know one thing for sure: she'll be a tad more agreeable than you!"

She wasted no time in countering his baiting remark. "No woman in her right mind would even think about marrying a bossy fella like you, unless"—she paused before saucily adding, "she has ten times more sass than me!"

Jesse was teasing with her when he rode off toward the buggy, ranting and raving as he did. "That's it, I've had just about enough of this!" He looked up at Kaleb and continued, "I'm done riding next to that—that woman you're married to! You may have to put up with all that lip, but I don't! She's your problem now. You take Shadow and ride with her. Grandma and I will have a nice quiet talk."

Kaleb chuckled as he rode toward his wife, who was now lying on Lady's neck, trying to gain a semblance of control over her latest outburst. He could only imagine the conversation that brought this on. Whatever it was, he was glad for it. Kaleb loved to see her let down and carry on as if she hadn't a care in the world. *Laughter,* he thought, *truly is good for the soul!*

Daisytales

He Loves Me!

Chapter Twenty-six

Home at Last

"GRANDMA, CAN YOU believe we're finally here?"

"I can't wait to see the look on my son's face when I share my news."

"Me neither. I wouldn't miss this for anything in the world."

The band of weary travelers had stopped to greet the Somers and asked if they would join them at the White's homestead. They were more than happy to oblige.

"Grandma, look! Your son is standing in the yard. His mouth is hanging open, catching flies. I do believe we've managed to surprise him." Elizabeth stole an exuberant hug, brought Lightning to a halt, and watched as Samuel helped his mother down from the buggy.

"I don't know how they managed to get you here, but we couldn't be happier!" Samuel said, as he enjoyed the first hug his mother had offered in a very long time. When Naomi took it one step further and kissed his cheek, his heart faltered. In all of his years growing up, he couldn't remember a time when she'd been so affectionate. Not once. Gazing into her hazel eyes, he asked, "Something has changed you, Mom. Tell me, what is it?"

Naomi turned to Elizabeth. They shared a smile that beat all smiles.

Elizabeth took the time to gather everyone's attention, and said, "Grandma has something she would like to share with all of you."

Elizabeth turned back to her cherished friend and listened as Naomi shared God's intervention in her life and then added. "With Kaleb's help, I've sold the farm and plan to stay around for as many days as the Good Lord allows me to remain on this Earth. I'm warning you ahead of time, though: this new believer has many questions. So be ready to open your Bibles and be willing to teach an old lady all about living this new life in Christ."

Samuel pulled both his daughter-in-law and mother back into his arms. He knew without asking that God had chosen to use Elizabeth in a miraculous way. "I'm sorry for all you had to go through at the hands of those men, Lizzy, but I can't thank you enough for your part in all of this."

"Your mother has been an amazing lifeline for me, too, Dad. We have so many wonderful things to tell, but maybe we could go in to the house and talk over a cup of tea. We didn't stop for dinner and we're famished."

"Kaleb," Samuel said, "come on over here by your wife for a minute."

He complied, noticing that the group at large was acting strange.

"George, what do you think? Should we let Kaleb and Lizzy come in for tea, or should we just send them home?"

Dumbfounded by his question, Kaleb and Elizabeth looked at each other and then back to their fathers, who were both baiting them with smiles. Come to think of it, everyone else had the same look. When no one spoke up, Kaleb finally asked, "What's going on here, Dad?"

"Should we make them go for a walk?" Samuel repeated.

Everyone yelled, "Yes!"

Something was up, Kaleb and Elizabeth both knew it, but nothing became clear until they passed the line of trees that blocked the view of their new house, completely constructed and ready for habitation.

After the initial shock, Kaleb beamed at his wife, who asked, "How ... when ... who ... who did this?"

George, thinking this conversation could use a little help, spoke up, "Doc supplied the rest of the lumber and told folks all over Ypsilanti and Ann Arbor your story. Pastor and Doc put out an open invitation and people came to help build your home. Your family members put in some long hours to give it some finishing touches. We like to think of it as the house that love built!"

Reaching for his wife's hand, Kaleb tried to thank all of them, but the words would not come. He and his wife were so overwhelmed by the gift.

"We can't begin to tell you how much this means to both of us. Liz and I have had more than our share of struggles. Maybe this is God's way of helping us to begin anew." Turning to Naomi, he added, "God's timing really is everything, isn't it, Gram? We have our own place, just in time to give you our old bedroom."

Elizabeth was so excited she could hardly stand it. "Is someone going to lead the tour?"

Samuel motioned for George to go ahead.

They were just about to walk through the front door when George leaned over and whispered in Kaleb's ear. "If you're going to start this off right, shouldn't you carry her over the threshold?"

"Thanks for the reminder!" Kaleb said.

Without warning, Elizabeth found herself swept into her husband's strong arms, with no clue as to why. "Kaleb, quit being silly. Put me down."

"There's nothing silly about a man carrying his wife across the threshold of their new home. I'm not sure when the tradition started or what it means, but who am I to mess with a good thing?"

Kaleb and Elizabeth were mesmerized as they came through the door. The front room had been fully dressed with a dark floral couch on the far wall, while two matching chairs sat next to the hearth. End tables were on both sides of the sofa, and a long table sat in front of the picture window, complete with a lard-oil lamp and doily.

Elizabeth had to ask, "Where did all this furniture come from? It's beautiful!"

George answered. "A wedding gift of sorts, from the Grants."

Elizabeth and Kaleb were both shocked.

"Why?" was all Kaleb could think to ask.

"Somehow, Mr. Grant got wind of his wife's part in starting the rumors. He took the price of the furniture out of her savings. The other additions were her own doing—it seems she's been having a change of heart."

Elizabeth's eyes met her husband's. "It's never too late to

start again, is it, Kaleb?"

With no thought of those watching, Kaleb drew her to him and kissed her tenderly—as a groom would have kissed his new bride.

With clapping and joyful laughter, their families expressed their approval.

The moment Elizabeth's feet hit the wood floor, her exuberance, as it often did, spilled forth. A small staircase sat off to the left, leading to the loft, which, they were informed, would be finished at a later date.

George couldn't resist adding, "The loft is just as big as the main floor, so feel free to fill it with as many grandchildren as possible!"

Elizabeth's sparkling eyes flew up at her father. "Daddy, you have grandchildren on the brain! Let's take this one step at a time, can we?"

He nodded, and the crowd moved on.

They found a new cook-stove in the kitchen, a work board with cupboards below, and the table and chairs that Kaleb and Jesse had made. On the floor were rugs that Suzanne, Louise and Sarah had crocheted in dark blue. Their mothers had made the curtains and doilies that were scattered throughout. A new coffee pot and teakettle sat on the back of the stove, and the cupboards and pantry were fully loaded. As Elizabeth scanned the ample room that she would spend the better part of her life in, something came into view that didn't belong there. Her eyes riveted on the sight before her. Tears trickled down her cheeks. Her mother's cherished teapot sat pretty as a picture on the kitchen counter.

"Mom, you love that pot. I can't keep it."

"Oh, yes you can! I never told you, because I wasn't sure it would survive our large family, but it was a wedding gift from my mother and she made me promise to pass it down to my first daughter when she married. So you see, I have no choice but to give it to you."

"Thanks, Mom. I'll love having it." George led them through the pantry and into what they thought would be a breezeway, like Kaleb's parents' home. This room was larger—a small bathing chamber of sorts. Their commode sat in the right corner. A small stove for heating water had been tucked in the corner, and Jesse was standing proudly next to a bathing tub built for two. An impish smile curved his mouth as he explained, "This is my wedding gift to the two of you. I hope you'll enjoy it. I only wish you could have seen the look on Mrs. Grant's face when I insisted she order it for you."

Elizabeth's mouth dropped open. "You told her it was for us?" She was mortified.

"Yes, Lizzy, settle down. Even Mrs. Grant takes a bath now and then."

But this is different. Oh my! Finding no hope for her runaway thoughts, she let it drop. No sense warming her cheeks further.

As they moved through the small room, they ended up in their bedroom. The bed was made up with new sheets, blankets, and beautifully-quilted pillow shams. The embroidered square in the center of the sham was a small bouquet of mauve roses, with daisies and baby's breath arranged in a blue, quilted vase. The effect was lovely. She could only imagine the hours that had gone into making them. Kaleb and Elizabeth were told that their quilt was still a work-in-progress and would arrive as soon as it was

418

completed. The bed from Kaleb's room sat on the wall to the left, with end tables on either side. Their new armoire was in the right corner while the dresser sat off to the right, just out of reach of the door. The curtains hanging from the windows were made from the main quilt fabric. As they walked out of the bedroom through the door, they found themselves back in the sitting room.

George turned around and asked, "Well, guys, what do you think?"

Kaleb pulled Elizabeth into the crook of his arm, before turning to their family and saying, "We could never thank you enough for making this happen. Once we get settled, we'll have all of you over for supper."

Elizabeth piped in, "I promise to do the cooking. We can't have our first guests going home ill because I let Kaleb do it."

"You'd better watch it, Liz! I could tickle you for hours out here and no one would come to your rescue!"

Grandma came to her defense. "Honey, if he picks on you, you tell me and I'll fix his little wagon!" Naomi then turned to Kaleb, whose eyes brimmed with glee. "You better be good to my girl, Young Man, you hear me?"

"I won't promise not to tickle her, but I'll try to be nice once in a while."

Elizabeth laughed at their playful bantering and the worried looks on her sisters' faces added to her joy. Although she appreciated everyone's concern, at this point in her life she wouldn't want to be anywhere else.

Samuel invited everyone to come and enjoy a bowl of hot soup. While the women finished the meal, the men emptied the buggy, bedded down the weary horses, and set up Kaleb and

Elizabeth's old room for Naomi. Since Kaleb would be going back to pick up her furniture shortly, they didn't go to extremes, just enough to make her comfortable.

"Elizabeth! Where are you?" Kaleb called.

His first mistake was in using her full name. She was either in some kind of trouble, or he wanted something. No doubt it was the latter. She had heard him thudding around in the new bathing chamber and knew what he was up to. Elizabeth had no intentions of evading him for long, but she couldn't just give in. The fun was in the chase—especially when her husband didn't know she was running from him. Again, his cajoling words rang out.

"Elizabeth, where are you?" His booted feet made the full circle. Growing concerned, he tried again.

What he didn't know was that Elizabeth was in her stocking feet following him, just out of view. This went on for a while, until she gave herself away with that confounded giggle which always escaped at the most inopportune moment.

Kaleb spun and tore off after his squealing wife. Upon capture, her pleading eyes held his. "Kaleb, can't we wait until tonight to take a bath? "

His brow lowered. "We can wait until tonight to take a *second bath.*"

"Maybe I don't want to," she pouted. She was having too much fun to let it drop.

He turned her away from him, pointing towards the bathing chamber. "Too bad!" he growled."

She spun to face him, declaring, "You sure are bossy, Mister!" The fun ended when his wiggling fingers came after her ....

"Kaleb," Elizabeth whispered as they lay in their bed that night. "Don't move too fast, but if you put your hand on my stomach, you might be able to feel the baby move."

The motions against his skin were light. Like butterfly kisses. "Is that our baby?"

"Yes. Isn't it amazing?"

"Astounding!"

"I used to think motherhood began after the baby arrived, but now I know it isn't true. I love knowing he's growing inside of me. As much as I want to see him, I'm in no hurry. I'm glad I have this time to enjoy the changes taking place inside of me."

"You keep saying 'he'. I don't want you getting your heart set on this being a boy. What if God's plan for us is to raise six gabby little girls? I wouldn't mind at all, Liz. You know that, don't you?"

"I won't be disappointed if this is a girl, but I have a strong feeling it's a boy. Kaleb, have you thought about what you'd like to name the baby?"

"Yes, I have. If it's a girl, I'd like to reverse your name and call her Brenae Elizabeth."

"Hmm. I like it. What about a boy?"

"A first name hasn't come to mind yet, but I'd like his middle name to be Samuel. What's your father's middle name?"

"Cameron. That's what his father's first name was, and it's Jesse's middle name too."

"Don't you think it'd be appropriate to name the baby after

your dad, since he was the one who insisted we marry? After all, if it wasn't for his counsel, we wouldn't be expecting."

"So, Cameron Samuel White?"

"Yes. What do you think?"

"I like it."

"Are you sorry we didn't wait, Liz?"

"No. How could I regret having this baby? Just promise you'll never shut me out like you did before." She sounded so vulnerable.

"I won't."

She paused for several seconds. "We need to lighten up and enjoy each other, okay?"

"Absolutely. So tell me, Liz, how did you like the tub?"

"I loved it, but then, I knew I would from the moment I saw it."

Puzzled, he asked, "Then why did you give me such a hard time about taking a bath?"

"Kaleb, how many years have you known me?"

"Sixteen."

"And you have to ask?"

Understanding dawned. "You little imp! You were toying with me?"

She offered a mischievous grin. He countered with a taste of what her playful heart was looking for ....

Content in each other's arms, Kaleb and Elizabeth's thoughts were much the same:

It may have taken us a while to get here, but we're home at last!

Chapter Twenty-seven

Communication

ELIZABETH BREATHED A huge sigh of relief as they walked out of the sheriff's office. When her abductors heard about Elizabeth's return, they made full confessions in front of Henry. So after signing papers for the visiting judge, her part in this misadventure was over. For the first time in weeks, she felt like she and Kaleb could finally get on with their lives.

They stopped by Doc's to thank him for his generous donations, and also his encouragement while Kaleb went through his time of recovery. From there, they went to thank the Grants for their extravagant additions as well. Kaleb had a few purchases he needed to make before heading home, and although Elizabeth wanted to take a seat and wait for him, he insisted on her staying with him.

Understanding his wife's aversion to this particular item,

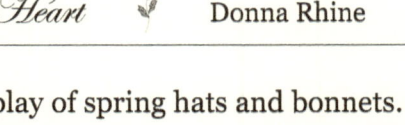

Kaleb led her to a large display of spring hats and bonnets. Most women would have been delighted to have their husbands buy them such a gift, but not Elizabeth. The moment she realized his intent, she turned away, but not fast enough. Those long arms reached out and brought her back to his side.

"Liz, listen to me ...." He spoke for her ears alone. "I want you to pick out a hat that you can live with or I will do it for you."

"I don't need one, Kaleb; they make me sweat. I hate the way they feel on my head."

"We've discussed this. You know as well as I do you're just being stubborn. I won't have the bright sun burning your skin. Am I understood?"

Her scowl was fierce. She hated being ordered around, especially by her husband, and then to top it off, he had the gall to use those three words that always ruffled her feathers. Even if she could overlook his first two blunders, she could not let him waste his money. More than anything she hated bonnets. Gritting her teeth, she issued her quiet response. "I have one already. I don't want another. I won't even wear the one I have."

"Pick one, Elizabeth!" he said out loud.

The scattered shoppers were now staring ... at her. Although her humiliation was a real factor to consider, her indignation impaired the good sense she'd been born with. She turned to the opposition, if only to seek refuge for her cherry complexion, and said in a fierce murmur, "Kaleb, if you like those silly hats so much, buy one and wear it yourself!" She foolishly clung to the hope that he wouldn't cause a bigger scene. When she tried to move away, her dress must have caught on something; she couldn't move. Looking back, Kaleb's large hand was wrapped in the fabric. Her flaming eyes flew up to meet his piercing glower. She knew at that moment that if one of them didn't concede, it would be all-out war. She wouldn't go that far—not in the store, and certainly not in front of all those glaring her way. Elizabeth reached for the woven bonnet with the loosest weave and shoved it at his chest. The moment he released her, she bustled out the door.

She watched from her place on the bench as Kaleb came out and scanned the boardwalk, searching for her. Since her anger was still at the fore, she remained silent, refusing to give her location away. Her actions were childish, she knew that, and she knew she would have to make amends, but not in her present state. Instead, she pierced his fleeting back with her uncompromising glare.

The Smiths' buggy came out of the livery, headed her way, and stopped in front of the store. Apparently he knew exactly where she was; maybe he'd known the whole time. He jumped down to offer her a hand up, which she promptly refused. She had no desire to touch him, let alone accept his help, and cringed when his oversized hands gave her a boost in spite of her refusal. The wall of silence continued the entire way home.

Elizabeth was sure that at some point Kaleb would say something. He did not, which infuriated her even further. About two hours into the trip, she asked herself, *How can he be so irresistible one minute and, so irritating the next? I know I'm wrong, Lord, but I'm so exasperated I can't think straight!*

Her eyes closed, she tried to sleep, but it didn't work. She couldn't let this go. She hated being at odds with anyone, especially her husband. Suddenly, a wave of panic assailed her. How could she have forgotten this one huge detail? She now lived

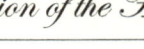

alone with this man.

I know what I'll do, she schemed, guilt washing over her as she thought it through. *When we get home, I'll need to use the outhouse. From there, I'll stop by his parents and visit for a while, and then—surely by then—he'll be busy with something else. Who knows? Maybe I'll have calmed down enough to make amends.*

Fortunately, he dropped her off in front of the house and went to the barn to put the buggy away. So far, so good! She moved towards the necessary room, took care of her needs and then slipped into his parents' home. Naomi and Ruth were sitting at the table, enjoying a cup of tea, and asked her to join them.

"I'd love a cup. Thank you!"

"How did things go in town, Lizzy?" her mother-in-law asked.

"You mean with the sheriff?"

Ruth nodded, somewhat befuddled by her clarifying statement.

"I couldn't have asked for it to go better. They made full confessions when they heard I was in town, so there's no need for a trial .... Grandma, are you all settled in?"

"I am," Elizabeth was acting strange, so Naomi had a few inquiries of her own to make. "What I want to know is how you and Kaleb are getting along, all alone in that new house?"

They were doing terrible right now, but that had nothing to do with how they were in the house, so Elizabeth kept that information to herself. Instead, she responded to Naomi's question as asked. "It'll take some getting used to. We had a nice evening together and left after breakfast this morning. Kaleb and I had lunch at Bloody Corners with Sheriff Kane. " Naomi's scowl gave Elizabeth a case of the giggles. She needed to explain.

"Mr. Allen built a block-house across the street from the Court House. It's a hotel of sorts for new settlers. They serve hot meals. Someone had the bright idea to paint it red, so the townsfolk dubbed it Bloody Corners. The special was roast beef with mashed potatoes and corn. It was actually quite good."

Naomi nodded. "I'm glad you enjoyed it."

"Mom? Did you happen to come across my needles when you were moving things around? I kept them under the paper that lines the drawers."

"Go ahead and check, Lizzy. I didn't think to look there."

Kaleb came in the back door just after Elizabeth left the room. Ruth watched her son as he leaned over to kiss her and then his grandma. Ruth sensed something was amiss, but didn't ask.

In the calmest tone he could muster, Kaleb asked, "Have either of you ladies seen my wife? She seems to have disappeared."

Ruth pointed towards Naomi's room. "She's looking for her needles."

Just as Elizabeth found her needles, someone grabbed her hand from behind. Her wide blue eyes flew up, to meet her husband's steeled glare. Without explanation, he led her along, said good-bye to the women at the table, and they were out the back door before she could utter her first word.

"Kaleb, why would you be so rude?"

"We have unsettled business to tend to. You shouldn't have left the house."

She sighed in disgruntlement. "I'm not about to ask permission to use the outhouse, or to visit your family."

Stopping in his tracks, he glared at her. "We both know you're avoiding me."

"And why wouldn't I? It does no good to talk to you when you're like this. I'd much rather share a cup of tea with some of the women in my life than be bullied by you."

He'd love to remind her that she was running from her problems, but knowing he was quite good at this himself, he opted for silence.

His grasp tightened as they began to walk again. Her strides were no match for his, and although she didn't think he would let her fall, he was so angry he did not seem to notice. She couldn't blame him; she hadn't been very congenial herself.

Moving in the back door, she sat down on the bench and took her time removing her boots. Kaleb did the same. After hanging his coat and her shawl from a hook, her slender hand was once again captured by his. He led her into the sitting room, and plopped down in the new fluffy chair. Patting his legs, he bade her to sit.

"Come on, Liz. Let's get this over with."

The last place on earth she wanted to be was anywhere near him, never mind in his lap. Perhaps he only wanted to settle their dispute. So did she, but not like this. If she fell into his trap, he would not release her until her anger had passed. In her impertinent mood, that could take hours. Thinking she could simply make excuses and move on, she soon discovered she was sadly mistaken.

"I need to fix dinner," she said.

Kaleb, unwilling to wait for her acquiescence, pulled her into his lap. "What we need to do first, *before dinner,* is get a few things settled."

Crossing her arms, she looked at the floor.

"Liz, we have to find a way to work things through. I was wrong to spring this on you the way I did, but you can't say I didn't warn you."

"You were supposed to forget ..."

"Honey, how could I forget something so important? The sun's getting hotter everyday. You told me you want to get the garden planted, and I knew you would need a bonnet before church on Sunday, so I pressed you. I'm sorry you're angry. In truth, I think you're being silly."

"I'm not surprised. Our opinions often differ."

"Is there at least an outside chance you would wear it, merely to humor your husband."

While she wanted to say yes, she couldn't help feeling as if they were slipping back into their old pattern. "Kaleb," she started, then paused. Summoning her courage, she went on. "I understand your concern. I do. Still, I can't help wondering if there will ever be a time where *my* opinion counts. Should I resign myself to the fact that you must have your way in *everything*?"

She dealt him a low blow—she wasn't a little girl anymore, but a woman capable of making her own judgments. His father had warned him against trying to control her; still, he had a tendency to overlook the advice of those who had been down the same road. If he really wanted a partner in life, he would have to find a way to ease up on Liz. If he didn't, his wife would be nothing more than a puppet on a string. He didn't want that.

"What you think *is* important to me, but you need to listen to me once in a while. It's important that you protect your skin."

He wouldn't give in on this issue; she knew that. Would they ever find a happy medium? She put him to the test.

"I don't believe you'll ever concede in anything, Kaleb."

In contemplative thought, his eyes fell on the open hearth. "Try me on another issue, Liz. Any issue."

"I think it's a waste of time, but here goes: I'd like to ride Lady over and visit with my mom and sisters tomorrow—alone."

He shook his head in amazement. *Should a seen that one coming.*

She gave him a moment before her hands went up to emphasize her declaration. "I knew it!"

"Now, just a minute. Give me time to think."

"There's nothing to think about, Kaleb. Yes or no?"

He knew he'd better say something, and fast. He was losing ground with every second that passed. "How long will you be gone?"

"Does it matter?"

"I'd feel better if I knew when to look for you."

"No more than four hours." His eyes about bounced out of his head. In fact, he looked so pitiful, she wondered if she might be pushing him too hard.

"Could you possibly have mercy on me, for this first time, and come home in two?"

She laughed out loud, literally couldn't believe her ears. In a state of disbelief, she clarified, "You're saying you wouldn't mind?"

"Yes, but ...

Here we go again! She thought, rolling her eyes. *He's changing his mind already!*

"If it rains, will you choose another day?"

"Gladly!"

"Just two more things, then I promise to quit being a worry-wart and trust your judgment."

"What now?"

"Will you promise to wear your new bonnet to keep the sun out of your eyes?"

"And?"

"*And,* if you feel dizzy or sick at all, will you have Jesse or Dad bring you home?"

"Agreed."

While he was in this kind of a mood, Elizabeth thought she might as well see how far he had come.

"Is this a one-time offer, or can I visit them whenever I want to?

"I'll be working and unavailable at times," Kaleb said, "so why don't we do this: leave each other a note on the counter when our plans change during the day. Oh, and one more thing: when you get bigger with the baby, you might need to consider taking the wagon instead of Lady."

"That's fine. You're getting there, Kaleb."

"Just make sure you remember where you belong."

"How could I forget that? I'm sorry I got so angry. Will you forgive me?"

His words came slow, as his fingers traced the thin line of her jaw. "I wasn't so even-tempered myself. I think we could come to some sort of a mutual settlement."

He obviously had something specific in mind. Holding her ever-so-gently in his arms, his deep amber eyes sparkled. As he lowered his head, her thoughts were crystal clear. *In this, Kaleb White, you can have your way, any old time!*

Kaleb picked up the hatbox he had next to him on the floor,

and set it in her lap. "I hope you won't be upset, but I didn't like the bonnet you picked out. I'm thinking this will better suit your needs. If you don't like it, I'll take you back and exchange it for another."

As she lifted the lid, her mouth dropped open—her words exclaimed her delight. "I don't remember seeing this one, Kaleb. I love it!" This particular hat had been woven like the one she had picked out, yet it wasn't a bonnet at all. The large circular brim stuck out on a slant, so the majority of it would not even touch her head. A small dome topped it off and the pretty lace ribbon circling around it came down on the sides. If the wind was blowing, she could tie it under her chin.

Elizabeth kissed him fiercely before going to try it on. When she came out, her hair was down, and she beamed as she spun to show him. "Do you like it as much as I do, Kaleb?"

He began to laugh, a deep, hearty laugh, as he stood to take her in his arms. "If you will wear it, then, yes, I like it. But you, Elizabeth White—I love you with all of my heart ...."

Chapter Twenty-eight

Brutus

ELIZABETH SMILED AS she awoke once again to warm hands sprawled across her protruding belly. Kaleb had grown quite content with this new method of waking her. As if their unborn baby had come to expect it, they shared this playtime in the morning. Elizabeth found them to be quite a pair already.

"Is it time to go, Kaleb?"

"Yes, I need you to come and bar the door. I made sandwiches for breakfast, so if you want to, go back to sleep. Jesse said your sisters wouldn't be expecting you until around noon."

"I think I will. I'm really tired for some reason."

"Don't push yourself, Liz. If you need to, send my dad to pick up the girls." She reached out, running her fingers through his mass of wavy hair and pulled him to her. Moments passed before he admitted that he really needed to be on his way. Jesse was waiting.

This time of separation would be difficult for both of them.

They had grown closer than either one of them could have hoped over the last few months. The crops had been in for a while, and his grandma needed her things about her.

Elizabeth's tears flowed freely as she stood in her husband's arms at the open door. He tucked her soft locks behind her ears, offering his tender parting words.

"When the baby wakes you up in the morning, be sure and remind him that Daddy loves him and his mama very much. Liz, don't cry. I'll be back before you have time to miss me."

"We miss you already!" She giggled through her tears when he pressed his hanky into her hand.

Drying her cheeks, she placed the bar on the door and moved to the big picture window. She watched as her husband opened the barn doors and slipped inside.

Why is it, Lord, that I can't tell him the way I really feel. You've brought us so far. Why are the words he freely bestows upon me, so difficult for me to say?

As the buggy pulled away, she frantically waved to her husband while saying the words he could not hear. She could only hope he knew. "I love you, Kaleb White—I love you with all of my heart!"

❀ ❀ ❀

"Hi, Mom, how are you this morning?"

Jayne smiled and opened her arms as her oldest daughter came into the kitchen.

The concern in Jayne's eyes warmed Elizabeth through and through. The two of them had always shared a close bond, but of late they were becoming friends on a different level. Somehow coming to love this child she was carrying had given Elizabeth a new insight into her mother's unconditional love.

"Honey, look at you! Your eyes are swollen from crying. I suppose that young woman who married her brother's friend, insisting that she didn't like him very much, is gone forever. Isn't it wonderful when we finally fall head over heals in love with our men?"

She stared at her mother. "How did you know?"

"That radiant glow could mean nothing else."

"I never dreamed it would happen so fast, or hit me so hard. I hated letting him go today. Maybe when he comes back, I'll finally be able to tell him how I feel."

Elizabeth's admission saddened her mother. "Why haven't you told him already, Lizzy? He needs to hear those words as much as you do." She paused only seconds. "How long have you known?"

"If I tell you, you have to promise not to say anything."

"You know I won't."

"In my own way, I think I've always loved him. Not in the way I do now. He's been like a brother to me, so for a while I wasn't sure I could ever love him as a wife should love her husband. I was infatuated with him as a child, yet I could also make myself believe that I despised him at times. He did have a way of getting under my skin. But it hasn't been like that since the day he bought me this hat."

Her mother smiled. "How could a hat change the way you feel?"

"I was furious when he insisted that I get one of those

annoying bonnets, but I knew how much he cared when I opened the box at home. He understood my frustration, so he didn't buy the one I threw at him; he chose this one because it blocks the sun without binding me. In his own way, Kaleb was compromising with me the best that he could. It's silly, I know … that simple act of compassion allowed me to see how much he has changed. He's not the same man to me anymore. He's my best friend. We're not fighting like we used to; we're walking together in unity. I'm no longer the little girl who always needed his care. He finally sees me as his wife—his partner in life."

Jayne's tears made it difficult to respond. "Sometimes it takes our stubborn hearts time to see the blessings God has for us."

"Our God is good all the time, isn't he, Mom? When Dad told me I had to marry Kaleb, I thought my life was over, that I'd never be happy again. I was so wrong. We've had struggles to go through. New problems arise, but I don't feel vulnerable when we face them because we're facing them together. I really do love him."

"Tell him soon, Honey. He deserves to know."

"I will."

"I think, for both of our sakes, we should call the girls and get off this serious note. My new grandbaby doesn't need his momma crying the whole time his daddy's gone."

"I agree. So, tell me, are they excited?"

Jayne rolled her eyes and shook her head recalling the previous night. "I thought your father was going to have to paddle them to get them to quit giggling and go to sleep. I just hope they don't keep you up with all their nonsense."

"I don't care if they do. The four of us will be on a vacation of sorts for the next week. Other than the sewing projects, I have nothing else lined up. I'm fortunate they offered to help. If I don't get moving, my poor little baby will come into this world naked and have to stay that way."

Jayne laughed at her daughter's over-exaggeration and insisted she follow her upstairs. "His grandmas have been busy, so he'll have a few things to get him started. I picked up a few more pieces of fabric I couldn't resist for blankets. I think your sisters would do fine working on them. If you're smart, you'll put them to work making diapers."

"That's a good idea. Let's talk after we get up there. I'd like to try and surprise them." On silent feet, Elizabeth climbed the stairs, reached for the doorknob, and swung the door open. "Did the fun begin without me?"

"Lizzy!" Louise squealed, her enthusiasm bubbling over. "Are you ready for us to come? Can we go now? Oh, Lizzy, we're so excited! Thank you for inviting us! Is Sarah coming too?"

Jayne, standing in the hallway just out of sight, tried to suppress her laughter. When she could stand it no more, she moved further down the hall into her own room.

After answering their questions, Elizabeth told the girls to take their things to the wagon. Her mother had suddenly disappeared, and Elizabeth knew why. Bustling in to her parents' room, Elizabeth found her mom sitting on the edge of the bed wiping tears from her eyes. "All right, you, what is so funny?"

"I'm sorry, Honey. They miss you so much; it's like they have to make up for lost time in the first few minutes you're together."

"I've noticed that, but I really don't mind. They're so cute."

"Yes, they are." Jayne placed a stack of gowns in Elizabeth's hands along with a nice warm quilt for the baby.

"Mom, these are adorable, thank you."

"You're very welcome. Here," Jayne took the clothing, set it aside, and handed her the other yard goods she had purchased. "Lizzy, should I send some extra thread along?"

"Do you happen to have an extra spool of white? I wasn't thinking about all the diapers when I bought thread."

Jayne reached in her sewing box that sat on the floor next to her bed and handed Elizabeth an extra spool.

"Mom, if you decide you're going to town, feel free to come by and pick us up. I have a few things I could use, but I promised Kaleb I wouldn't wander too far alone while he's gone. He doesn't seem to think the girls would be much help if I went into labor."

"He's right. Besides, you're getting too big to handle a team for that long."

"To tell you the truth, I don't have the energy to go much farther than your place."

"Lizzy, we'd better get downstairs before the girls come looking for us."

❀ ❀ ❀

With Elizabeth, Suzanne, Louise and Sarah's shared efforts, the baby would now be fully clothed and diapered whenever he decided to make his appearance. They had enough fabrics for extra blankets, several bibs, and a large bag to use for toting things.

Elizabeth expected Kaleb and Jesse any day now. She tried not to think about how much she missed them, but by late afternoon on Monday, her anxious mind was getting the best of her. Out of desperation she asked the girls to join her for a leisurely stroll.

The crisp chill in the damp air held the promise of coming rain, and the dark clouds confirmed her suspicions. She prayed for the men as she walked with the girls. Foul weather could do serious damage to Naomi's treasured belongings, and the Sauk Trail would be nothing less than a muddy mess, making it almost impassable. *Thank you, Father, that You're in control. Keep the men safe and help me not to fret so!*

"Girls, we'd better head home. I have a feeling were in for a real gully-washer."

The rains came down in buckets as the four women headed for cover. They ran up the back steps and through the door laughing and shrieking all the way. But the moment was shattered and their eyes flew up when a stern male voice broke into their chatter.

"Well, well, well! What have we here?"

"Kaleb!" Elizabeth squealed as she moved into his outstretched arms. Lowering his head, he accepted the many kisses she offered. "The baby and I have missed you terribly."

Kaleb loved the way she kept touching him as if she were afraid he might vanish if she let go. *We've come so far, Lord!* Although Elizabeth had never said the words, Kaleb knew without a doubt that his wife loved him, that they were truly becoming one.

"Liz, I need you and the girls to go into the sitting room and take a seat. I have something for you."

Elizabeth, anxious to see what it was, willingly played along. She could hear Jesse and Kaleb scrambling around in the bedroom. When they came out they were hiding something. Her mouth dropped open when Kaleb moved around her brother and placed in her lap the biggest puppy she had ever seen.

"Oh Kaleb, he's so adorable! This is Matilda's puppy, isn't it?" She lifted the soft fuzzy fella up to her nose, which he promptly licked. "Hello, Brutus. I've missed you, boy."

Kaleb was shocked. He didn't think she had allowed herself to become attached

"Look how you've grown," Elizabeth said to the dog. Turning to her husband, she asked, "Is he ours, Kaleb? Can we keep him?"

Kaleb started to laugh. "Do you think Jesse and I traveled all those miles with that wiggly thing just to bring him for a *visit*?"

She laughed and said, "I was thinking about him yesterday, wondering who would have the pleasure of watching him grow."

"Well, now you know. Jake and Vicki gave him to us as a wedding gift. I wanted to surprise you. Tell me, Liz, when did you name him?"

She glanced up and smiled. "The first time I held him. I didn't tell anyone. I just whispered in his ear: Brutus. I never dreamed he would be mine. Thank you, Kaleb, he's magnificent."

That's quite the description for a dog! he thought. "Just be sure he doesn't give me cause to be jealous!"

His insinuation made her giggle out loud. The thought of having such a large, playful pup living in their home was beyond her comprehension. Kaleb had an aversion to cats, but this oversized beast was acceptable. Although she found this unfathomable, she actually preferred the dog! Her sister's adoring looks told her how much they wanted to get their hands on him. Understanding, she placed him on the floor in front of them, turned to her husband, and said, "Kaleb, if you don't care for the name Brutus, we could always call him something else."

He thought about it for only a second. "I kind of like your choice. Besides, he's *your* dog, I think you should call him whatever suits you."

"Then Brutus it is."

Kaleb, immensely satisfied with Elizabeth's response to the gift, joined her on the sofa to watch their sisters' antics with their newest addition.

❀ ❀ ❀

"Kaleb, are you sure he'll be all right out there?"

He smiled. "He's fine. He's a dog, not a child."

"But he's all alone."

"Elizabeth, we need our rest. Close your eyes and go to sleep."

She tried but it wasn't working. All she could think about was that poor little puppy missing his mother. She waited until Kaleb had fallen asleep, slipping her feet into her slippers she tiptoed toward the door. She had one small problem. The bedroom door was shut and the new hinges squeaked unmercifully. She turned the handle, holding her breath as she pulled it open. Just as she was about to slither her lumpy self past the door, Kaleb's oversized hand reached out to grab the back of her gown. She about jumped out of her skin.

"Where do you think you're going?" he growled.

Taking a breath to calm the beat of her heart, she scolded, "Kaleb, you shouldn't frighten a pregnant woman like that!"

"If you were snuggled next to me where you belong, it

wouldn't have happened."

"I can't sleep. I have to see for myself that he's all right."

Her soft voice was so forlorn, he couldn't deny her, so instead he joined her. On silent feet they made their way to the kitchen, where they had blocked-in the puppy. Elizabeth's worries were swiftly put to rest. Sprawled out comfortably on the kitchen floor, the fuzzy fur ball was fast asleep.

Kaleb slipped his arms around his wife's ever-expanding waistline, leaned over and whispered, "Do you mind that I brought him home?"

She turned to face him. Her warm hands slid tenderly around his neck, drawing him closer. Her delectable kiss said it all. Lifting the source of his delight into his arms, he covered the distance, revealing his unspoken thoughts as they entered their room. "I think it's only fair to inform you, Mrs. White. I've developed a terrible craving for more of what you offered.

"You think so, do you?"

"Yes, Ma'am. I'm afraid I do."

"Are you sure you haven't overindulged already?"

"No, My Sweet, Liz, I could never get enough!"

Chapter Twenty-nine

Interwoven as One

THE PRESENCE OF autumn's splendid array of vibrant shades marked a vast turning point in Elizabeth's life. The time of her delivery was drawing neigh, as surely as winter's somber presence was moving in to steal away the last vestiges of summer. The birthing experience held no fear for her. She was learning not to question the plans that God had laid out for her. He had sustained her life thus far, and He was more than able to see her through this miraculous event.

The impatient, first-time grandpas gave up on the new papa finding time to make a cradle for the coming child and took matters into their own hands. If truth could be told, she believed they preferred it this way. The project gave them something to do other than ask her when she was going to quit hogging the baby. To Elizabeth's delight, they included a small dresser as an unexpected surprise. All of his or her little clothes were clean and tucked away. Now all they needed was a baby to fill them, as he or she would undoubtedly fill all of their hearts upon his arrival.

Since most of Grandma White's plans for the snowy season seemed to revolve around the hours she would spend loving on their coming child, she insisted that her rocking chair and matching ottoman from the farmhouse be added to their sitting room. Whenever Elizabeth would sit and rock, her arms would wrap about her baby, and his movement would bring on tears of happiness. She so wanted to meet this little person.

An expected knock resounding on the door saved her from the direction her emotional ponderings were taking her.

"Are you ready, Lizzy?"

"Yes. Let me put Brutus in the kitchen, and I'll grab my shawl. I won't be more than a minute or two."

"Come on, boy. You be good, and don't make any messes for me while I'm gone, hear me?" Brutus had grown by leaps and bounds in the last four months. He'd surpassed her weight a while back, but he was still as gentle as a kitten. She had only one problem with this gigantic puppy: he didn't have a clue as to how big he was. On occasion, he would catch her off-guard, and jump up to put his paws on her shoulders. Her ability to withstand his weight in her present condition was not always possible, and she would crumple to the wooden floor. Kaleb and Elizabeth were learning that although at first his actions were cute, his size had become a real and present danger to Elizabeth and the baby. Kaleb nearly had a stroke when Brutus all but knocked her over one day. From then on, he found it necessary to scold him for such measures. The dog was like an overgrown two-year old. He would pout miserably over any form of reprimand. It took every ounce of restraint she could muster not to baby him. Unfortunately, a certain blonde giant would watch over her to make sure she didn't give in to Brutus' antics.

Kaleb got himself in big trouble one day when he informed Elizabeth that training the dog was like dealing with her as a little girl. "Too bad," he had the gall to add, "I can't just tickle Brutus and get him to mind—like Jesse and I could you."

After being scowled at for almost an hour, he sidled up behind her at the kitchen counter and finally made amends. She wasn't sure; however, if his apology wasn't somewhat selfishly given. She had mentioned at breakfast that oatmeal cookies with chocolate in them were supposed to be part of the dinner menu, and a simple statement, letting him think they might be excluded, had brought forth a rapid change of heart. What he didn't know was that the dough was already made. She merely held off baking them until things were ironed out. *Men,* she thought, with an endearing smile. *Unless the aroma fills the air they can be so easily fooled.*

Whenever Naomi would come by to visit and help Elizabeth with her various chores, she was always full of questions. They spent much of their time searching the scriptures together for answers. They were both gleaning new insights. Time spent with Naomi was always a pleasure. Her never-ending comments about their oversized dog kept Elizabeth laughing, as they accomplished the tasks they set out to do.

Doc mentioned at church that he'd like to see Elizabeth on Monday. Since Kaleb had sows to deliver to a neighbor on the other side of town, her mother-in-law offered to take her.

Elizabeth was pleased to have a break from her normal

routine. For the last few weeks, she'd been cleaning everything in sight and, since there was nothing else to be done, the trip would help to pass the time.

"Mom," Elizabeth said, as she stepped down from the wagon in front of the livery. "I'll head over to Doc's. If you're not going to be long at Rena's, I'll meet you at the store."

"That's fine, Honey. Take your time. I'm in no hurry to get home."

Ruth watched as her daughter-in-law made her way down the street. Although Elizabeth never complained, Ruth had been keeping an eye on her over the last few days. She was convinced that Elizabeth's time was close. Her belly had gotten so big, Ruth wondered how much more her slender frame could hold. *Father, I know your timing is best. Guide her through these last days and may her delivery be swift and easy.* When she saw Elizabeth enter the office, Ruth turned towards Rena's home carrying her heavy-laden basket of food.

Doc had two patients waiting for him by the time Elizabeth came out of the back room. She felt a twinge of guilt for having kept him so long, but Martha, hearing her voice, had joined them for a short visit. It was good to hear that their prayers for Martha's sister were answered. She was recovering from a bad bout with pneumonia.

Elizabeth walked over to the store, lumbered up the steps, and sat on the bench outside the General Store. Mrs. Grant must have seen her coming because she was out the door in a flash with a tall glass of cool water.

"Lizzy, are you all right? You don't look so well. Should I get Doc?"

Elizabeth couldn't help but smile. "Thanks for your concern, but I'll be fine. I just came from there. I'm tired, that's all."

"Your time is close, isn't it?"

"He seems to think I have a couple more weeks. Who knows? I've been feeling odd the last few days, but he said that's to be expected."

"Maybe you should come inside and get out of the sun. This Indian summer might be playing havoc with your strained body."

"It feels good, doesn't it? I've always thought of it as God's gift before a long, cold winter."

"Maybe so ..."

"Mrs. Grant. Did you know I pray for you every evening when I sit in my lovely furniture?"

"I knew someone had to be. I never did tell you in person, Lizzy, but I really am sorry for all the trouble I caused you."

"That's water under the bridge. There was a time that I couldn't wait for Kaleb White to be married, so you'd quit telling me what a wonderful catch he was." Elizabeth reached to squeeze her hand. "I'm thankful I got stuck in that cabin with him and not someone else. My life would be so empty without him."

"I knew all along you were made for each other. Kaleb needed someone with your spunk and delightful way of looking at life to make him smile. If you ask me, he was too stern for his own good."

"I couldn't agree more, but you're too kind to say what he does for me. He managed to settle me down just a tad, don't you think?"

"He has at that." Mrs. Grant stood and ushered Elizabeth into the back room. She had her sit at the small table, then disappeared for a few minutes. When she returned, she had a huge ham sandwich and a cup of tea. She placed it in front of Elizabeth with strict orders to relax and eat while waiting for her mother-in law to arrive.

❀ ❀ ❀

"Lizzy, we're heading over to your parents' house for the evening. Is there anything you need before we leave?"

"I'm fine, Mom. Kaleb should be here before long. I'll just take it easy while I wait.

"All right, Honey. See you tomorrow."

"Tell everyone I said hi!" Ruth nodded, and waved as she pulled away.

Elizabeth, though exhausted from the long bumpy ride, had a few things to do before she could take a nap. After indulging herself with a cool glass of water, she took Brutus for a short walk—or more accurately, he took her. She thought he was acting strange when she put him back in the house, but brushed care aside. Hanging the egg basket over her arm, she moved towards the barn, slipped inside the big door, shut it, and stopped to check on her horse. The way Lady carried on, you would have thought that Elizabeth had been away for months. Since this was nothing new, she gave her the attention she craved and offered her a cube of sugar, before moving down the row of stalls and doing the same for the other horses. They were coming to depend on her generosity as much as Lady. She tried to honor her husband's request that she not spoil them, but her overwhelming need to be fair had a tendency to cloud her judgment.

A strange growling sound coming from outside the chicken coop drew Elizabeth's attention away from her mission. With caution, she peaked out to see what creature was trying to raid the coop. Her father had said that it was rare for wolves to invade a farm, so more than likely this was a wild dog. She lingered a moment too long and he spotted her. Baring its teeth, a scraggly black beast with bright green eyes lunged towards her. She slammed the door behind her just in the nick of time, hearing a thud as the beast hit the closed portal. With a sense of urgency, she secured the other entrance. The last time this happened was shortly after she and Kaleb had been married, but then it was an entire pack. He made it clear that if the dogs ever came back, she should stay put. This was fine with her. In her present condition, she wouldn't be able to move quickly if the beast did find its way into the barn, so she climbed the ladder to the loft. For a time she sat perfectly still, listening.

At first, she thought Samuel might come to her rescue, but then she remembered Kaleb's family was gone. She would have to wait for her husband.

Exhausted, she made a bed of hay and lay down, covering herself in the mound. The hay offered no protection, but somehow it made her feel more secure. A shaft of light streaming through the small window was the last thing she saw before her weighted lids slid shut and she drifted into a sound sleep.

Kaleb could hear the snarling dog as he approached the farm. Stopping for his gun, a wave of panic passed through him. Elizabeth was not in the house. He went to the counter, but there was no note saying where she had gone, so that could only mean one of two things: she was at his parents, or possibly stuck in the barn.

Moving around the back side of the barn, he was able to take the wild dog by surprise. With the preditor eliminated, he continued to search for his wife. He didn't see her in the barn, so he ran over to his parents' house. No one was home. He didn't think she would have gone with them. They had an agreement, and she had never broken it. Moving back to their house, he did a little investigating. A package from town laying on their bed. *Where is she?* Kaleb, needing to bed Lightning down, checked the barn again. He found her egg basket—but not his wife!

"Elizabeth," he yelled in desperation as he neared the house again. "Why would you do this? We had a deal; you know how much I struggle with this!" Kaleb needed to get a handle on his raging emotions. After washing up, he poured a glass of water, plunked down on the wooden bench in front of their home, and began to pray. *Father, I need to trust you here. Forgive my irritation. Protect her. Show me what to do!* The longer he prayed, the calmer he became.

He had no idea how much time had elapsed when he heard the barn door squeal open. His eyes flew up, just in time to see his disheveled, hay-covered wife amble out. Grabbing at her stomach, she fell to her knees in agony. The glass went flying out of Kaleb's hand and his long strides covered the distance.

Kaleb waited for the pain to pass before asking what he already knew. "Liz, are you in labor?" Her nod was his undoing. "Oh, Honey, you can't be—there's no one here to help you. I'm sure it'll stop. Don't you think?"

She burst into laughter, but another pain stole it away. Her normally calm husband was in an obvious panic.

His thoughts rambled. *I can't do this! God, please, I beg you! Stop this until I can get help. I know you have a sense of humor, Lord, but trust me—I am not the man for this job!* His wife's tranquil tone brought him out of his thrashings.

"Kaleb, the pains are coming fast. Unless you intend to have this baby in the yard, you'd better help me into the house."

Kaleb lifted her easily into his arms just as another spasm racked her body. He rushed her into the house. Their child was coming, and Elizabeth would be counting on him to help her. He'd been around animals giving birth all his life, but he couldn't remember any of them ever being in this much pain. *Think, Kaleb, think! When the cows were in labor, what did you do? Nothing! You only watched. Same for the sows, sheep, and even the cats! Oh, heavens! This is getting me nowhere.* Besides, he was going to upset his wife if he didn't come to terms with what was about to happen. He asked her in the gentlest way. "Liz, do you have any idea what we're supposed to do?"

"No. If it's any comfort, neither did Adam and Eve. God will see us through; I know He will. He didn't bring us this far to abandon us now!" Elizabeth stared with compassion into her husband's befuddled eyes, claiming a kiss as he helped her prepare for the event that was about to take place, in spite of his apprehension.

The peace of the Lord settled over the room as husband and wife worked together as one to bring their precious baby into the world. Her contractions were coming fast and furious. One had no more subsided than another would come. When they became so close that she barely had time to rest, her breathless words tumbled out, "Kaleb, I need to push!"

Confused by her admission, he said the first thing that came to his mind: "Then maybe you should." As the contraction began to ease, she smacked him in the arm, bursting into laughter.

"What did I do to deserve that?"

"You made me ..."

"Liz! The baby's head—I see her."

The contraction eased, and Elizabeth fell back against the pillow—exhausted.

"Catch your breath."

She tried, but another contraction hit. Nothing could have prepared her for the astonishment that filled her husband's face, as she pushed with all she had within her. Their child was delivered; her relief was great. The joy on Kaleb's face was amazing.

As he lifted their newborn child in his oversized hands, he smiled, his eyes now brimming with love. "You were right, Liz. God has blessed us with a fine looking boy." Kaleb gazed in wonder at the slimy babe. "Look at him, Liz. He's got a head full of dark hair like Jesse."

Kaleb placed the squalling infant in his wife's arms, and kissed them both. "The hard parts over. What do we do now?"

Just then, they heard a knock on the door. Kaleb wiped the blood from his hands and went to answer it.

"Well, well, well, if it isn't two of my favorite mothers!"

"Kaleb," Jayne asked in a frenzied tone. "We were feeling rather unsettled. I hope you don't think we're being overly cautious. We just had to check on Lizzy. Is she all right?"

He was determined not to give away their little surprise.

"I think she is. We have a few questions about something. Maybe the two of you can help us out."

"Liz," he said as he led the women into the bedroom, "two of our favorite angels have arrived."

The mothers just stood in the entrance, stunned by the scene before them.

"We'd like to introduce you to the newest member of our family, Cameron Samuel White. And, by the way, would you mind telling us what to do next?"

Smiles erupted on their faces and eventually they found their tongues. Jayne asked, "Honey, when did you have him?"

"Just a few minutes ago. Isn't he adorable?"

The beaming grandmothers couldn't have agreed more. They had Elizabeth and their new grandson cleaned up and resting peacefully before Kaleb returned from the creek with more water. As Elizabeth expected, they wanted all the details before they went to get the rest of the family.

Kaleb lay on the bed beside his sleeping wife. When she awoke, and found him close, their attention went from their precious son, who was snuggled safely between them, to each other.

She couldn't help but smile when he tucked her stray wisps behind her ear. The devotion in his gaze—the tenderness of his touch—the curve of his mouth when he shared his heart, brought nothing but joy to hers.

Kaleb looked deeply into her eyes and said, "You've filled my life so much more than I could have ever imagined, Liz. I hope you know that I love you with all of my heart."

Elizabeth's soft blue eyes danced with happiness as she whispered the words he so longed to hear. "I love you too, Kaleb. Body and soul!"

"Liz," he asked, as a single tear touched his cheek. "How long have you known?"

A rosy glow kissed her face. "I was smitten with my brother's friend as a child. When my father insisted we marry, God was giving me the desire of my heart, I just didn't know it yet. My mother told me that loving someone was a choice. The Sunday we left their place, you confirmed her words and took it a step further. You said that my heart was a gift that only I could give. I felt as if you were telling me that the choice to love you belonged to me. In so doing, I no longer saw you as a man who was being forced on me. My love for you grew from that day forward."

"Are you saying that your love for me began with a simple decision?" The delighted beam that brightened her face eased his mind. Her softly-spoken words went straight to his yielding heart.

"Simple, Kaleb, yet so profound! Yes, My Husband, my love for you began with a decision—but it was a decision of the *heart*!"

As he leaned to caress the sweetness of her lips with his own, their thoughts were much the same: *although this marriage began with two caring hearts, our hearts are now interwoven as one!*

Epilogue

August 1830

ELIZABETH STOOD at the picture window gazing at her handsome husband, who was playing with their twenty-two month old son, Cameron, and their massive dog, Brutus. The dog must weigh as much as Kaleb now, but his gentle ways with their son were amazing. The minute they would stop romping, Brutus would lie down as if to call Cameron to his side. As yet, Cameron didn't know that Brutus was not his personal chair. Since the dog was most content when he knew exactly where Cameron was, they saw no need to tell Cameron otherwise.

Running her open hands along her protruding belly, she knew that her time was once again at hand. She could hardly wait. More than anything, she wanted this to be a little sister for Cameron. Elizabeth and her brother Jesse were so close growing up, how could she want anything less for her son? She had been telling Kaleb all along that this baby was a little girl. As always, he sought to guard her heart from disappointment. He would remind her that although God often gives us the desires of our hearts, we have to keep in mind that He sees the greater picture.

How well she knew this to be true. *Lord, you've shown me, over and over again, how much I would have missed without Kaleb in my life. The love and joy we share is immeasurable. Our son is such a blessing, and now this little one, who's running out of room, will greet us very soon. Who am I to presume upon Your design? Everything you've brought me through in life has brought me to this place of undeniable contentment. I could never be disappointed with Your will for my life. Although it often takes my stubborn heart time to accept it, Your way is always best in the long run. I trust you, Lord, implicitly. Continue to direct my path.*

"Kaleb," Elizabeth called as she stood in the frame of the door.

Glancing up, he smiled, scooped Cameron up and came to her side. "What can I do for you, My Sweet?"

As she returned his smile, another pain hit, and suddenly, no words were necessary. Kaleb helped her into their room.

She thought he seemed a bit frazzled as he grabbed Cameron's overnight bag. With their son arriving as fast as he did, they had a plan this time around.

He stood with Cameron in his arms and, for a moment, forgot himself, going back to another place in time. Piercing her with his dark amber eyes, his stern words did not have the effect he anticipated. "Don't even think about moving from that bed .... I'll be back in a minute!" When she merely stared in silent disbelief, he added, "Do you hear me, Young Lady?"

His last words were her undoing. She burst into uncontrollable laughter. The scowl he sent her way only added to her delight.

"What's so funny?"

She couldn't speak, but managed to shoo him away.

Kaleb must have run the whole way, because he was back before she could dry the tears from her outburst.

"Is everything all right, Kaleb?" It took him a minute to catch his breath.

"Yes. How far apart are the contractions?"

"I'm not sure; I've been laughing so hard, I couldn't see the clock."

His expression was unreadable.

"Kaleb, what has you so unsettled?"

"Forget that! I want to know what is so funny?"

"Oh, that!" She paused a tad too long.

"Yes, that! Are you going to tell me or not?"

"In a minute. Let this pass."

Elizabeth curled in a ball. Kaleb knew the pain was intense. He wouldn't have pressed her for the world, but he let her go on, thinking the conversation would get her mind off the pain.

"When we were stuck in the cabin, every time you went out the door, you'd remind me to stay put—just like you did a few minutes ago."

"And you found that funny?" He wasn't angry, although his tone *was* defensive.

"I found it hysterical. I couldn't imagine what you thought I'd do while you were gone. Kaleb, think about it—my ankle was broken. I couldn't exactly dance around the room."

"Oh," he said in a rather subdued tone that quickly turned

to childish laughter, "I suppose it *is* funny when you look at it that way."

"When we were first married, I didn't know what to expect when your temper would flair."

Another pain hit, passed, and Kaleb admitted, "I always hated myself for losing my temper. You have to admit: you pushed me to the limit at times. Especially the day I insisted we were going to see your family. I never understood how you managed to be petrified and combative at the same time."

"I never said my fears were rationale."

"Mine were ridiculous!" he confessed.

She could have said that she totally agreed, but her contractions were getting stronger by the minute, making it more difficult to talk. The next hour crept by. While he hated seeing her in so much discomfort, he knew she was about to deliver, when she suddenly said in a dull roar, "Kaleb, I've got to push!"

As another pain consumed her frame, he was spurred into action. Within minutes, he was holding his precious little Brenae Elizabeth, mesmerized by the delicate little wonder in his hands. The look he sent Elizabeth's way revealed his astonishment. "Liz, she's a mirror image of you."

A wave of apprehension struck him. "How can I ever be a good father to her?"

Confused, she assured him, "Kaleb, you'll be a wonderful father, just like you are with Cameron."

He fully expected this baby to be another son. A son he could handle, but a child who looked just like his wife was another story. His large finger touched her soft cheek. "She's such a frail little beauty."

Elizabeth smiled in the face of his quandary. "Kaleb, look at me."

He complied.

"If I remember correctly, you had no problems dealing with me as a child. Even as a young man, you were a wonderful presence in my life. Trust me when I tell you that little girls adore their fathers and seek to please them."

"I hope you're right." Kaleb sat down, kissed his infant daughter, then turned to his wife and offered more of the same. "I love you, Liz."

"I love you, too!"

The front door opened without a knock this time. The new grandmas bustled in to find the same scene they'd found almost two years prior, with one exception: their newest grandchild was a darling little *girl*.

Jayne was the first to speak. "Oh, Honey—she's like you all over again."

Elizabeth smiled. "If your mother was with us today, I'm sure she'd say it's like seeing you all over again."

"With Cameron having dark hair and blue eyes like Jesse, I might have to do a double take from time to time."

"Speaking of Jesse, where is that ornery brother of mine?" Elizabeth tried to hold back her tears, but gave up trying. Although Jesse had promised to stay until the baby was born, he would be leaving by the weekend. He earned his teaching certificate and had been offered a position in Frenchtown.

Elizabeth's thoughts went to her Heavenly Father as Kaleb and her two mothers took turns holding Brenae.

Thank you, Lord, for your blessings. My greatest fear has always been that I would somehow miss Your calling for my life. In opening my heart and yielding to all that You've given me, I've found that being a wife and mother is a big part of my calling. In choosing to love the man whom You so richly blessed me with, I've found contentment and a sense of belonging the likes of which I have never known.

The solitude I so desperately craved was not what I needed; however, it was a means to an end. Being lost in that storm and everything that followed was all part of Your plan, wasn't it, Lord? Your plan to bind me together with the man I adore.

Elizabeth's gaze fell on her husband as her reflections drifted to the words of a poem he had given her ....

As Ivy twines around a tree,
    and holds it in a close embrace.
So may we, Lord, both cleave to Thee,
    upheld and strengthened by Thy grace?

As partners of Thy grace of life,
    may we each other's burdens bear.
May mutual love exclude all strife,
    and kindness banish every care.

Thus blessed and happy may we live,
    and when we're called by death away,
The wreck of time may we survive
    and reign with Thee in endless days!

-Author unknown

He Loves Me!

The Michigan Chronicles

Donna's signature series, *The Michigan Chronicles*, is fiction at its best, with purpose.

As one reader tells us:

> *"Donna Rhine has a gift for writing stories that entertain and warm your heart, while teaching moral and Biblical principles. Her works may be fictional, but she has a real relationship with the Lord, as evidenced in every book she writes."*
>
> K. MacDonald

Book 1

A Decision of the Heart

He said her heart was a gift that only she could give ... *Could she?*

**Not just a moving story of faith rising above suffering, slander, and life's circumstances,
it's about a tender love that begins with a decision -
*A Decision of the Heart***

www.amazon.com/dp/0615455336
6x9 Paperback: 478 pages
Kindle Book

The Michigan Chronicles

Book 2

A Heart of Joy

When her impending loss plunges her into an uncertain future, her faith will be tested as never before ....

A moving saga of overcoming faith, it's also a heatwarming romance filled with adventure that ultimately leads to:
A Heart of Joy!

www.amazon.com/dp/0615466060
6x9 Paperback: 450 pages
Kindle Book

Book 3

A Heart Takes Flight

Will exposing the truth send her back to jail or into the arms of love?

A life changing story of God's abounding Grace and love's powerful influence - filled with intrigue, romance, and so much more ....

www.amazon.com/dp/0615486665
6x9 Paperback: 464 pages

The Michigan Chronicles

Book 4

A Heart Set Free

Her trials led to surrender. Could they also lead to her greatest blessings?

An an intriguing love story that evokes the heart's greatest passions, exposing the degradation of abuse in the light of God's Word — the power of God's redeeming love.

www.amazon.com/dp/0692021906
6x9 Paperback: 411 pages

Quick Note from Donna,

Thank you for all your continued support.

If this book has blessed you please let me know. Your comments and insights are both encouraging and enlightening. So often your input comes at a much needed time.

My hope and prayer is that my books have helped you get a little closer to the awsome God we serve.

My email: **donna@daisytales.com**

Other Works by Donna Rhine

In addition to Donna's popular series, **The Michigan Chronicles,** she has co-authored other books. Some of these titles include:

- **Still Dancing** - Gabriel Ford's autobiography shares the inspirational details of her life as a way of encouraging others yo move beyond their struggles and know that anything is possible.

- **Silent Tears, Loud Victory** - This heart wrenching story of one little girl's survival of abuse and her jourrney to become a woman of God. Edith Eddins reminds us that with God in our hearts, not only can we overcome horrific tragedy, we can forgive even the most deplorable sin and shine in the world as an example of His all-encompassing love.

You can find these and other works by Donna Rhine on Amazon.com by typing her name (Donna Rhine) in the search bar. Additional titles are in development, soon to be released.

Armoury House Publishing

Armoury House Publishing is dedicated to equipping of the saints through the printed word and other electronic media. Our mission is to draw all people one step closer in their personal relationship with Jesus Christ

Other Titles published by Armoury House Publishing:

Old Paths Series by John Charles Ryle

JC Ryle's conversational style of writing is easy to grasp and understand. Deep enough for the oldest of saints to find healthy portions of meat but lean enough to feed the new born Christian.

INSPIRATION of the Bible

How was the Bible written? Where did it come from ... Heaven? or of man? To what extent is God's word really God's Word? What do we mean when we say the Bible is inspired by God? How do the answers to these questions impact the way we live?

www.amazon.com/dp/1497476283
5x8 Paperback: 64 pages

OUR HOPE - The 5 Marks of a Good Hope

How do you distinguish a good hope from a mistaken hope that ultimately ends in a lie? Bishop Ryle gives us five characteristics of a good hope to follow.

www.amazon.com/dp/1499229798
5x8 Paperback: 48 pages

Old Paths Series (continued)

PERSEVERANCE

One of the most misunderstood topics of God's Word.

www.amazon.com/dp/1497590728
5x8 Paperback: 87 pages

KNOWING GOD THE HOLY GHOST

What place has God the Holy Ghost in your religion? What do you know of His office, His work, His indwelling, His fellowship, and His power?

www.amazon.com/dp/1499317018
5x8 Paperback: 76 pages

ALIVE OR DEAD?

By far one of JC Ryle's best talks. A topic deserving our full attention. What does God say?

www.amazon.com/dp/1497554136
5x8 Paperback: 54 pages

C.H. Spurgeon Works

PLAIN ADVISE FOR PLAIN PEOPLE

The wit and wisdom of one of the greatest men of the 19th century. Formerly published as "John Ploughman's Talk."

Spurgeon spans the denominational lines. His focus being that *"good wisdom is that which will turn out to be wise in the end; seek it, friends, and seek it at the hands of the wisest of all teachers, the Lord Jesus."*

John Ploughman

www.amazon.com/dp/1796309044
6x9 Paperback: 165 pages

These and other Armoury House Publishing books are available on Amazon.com and other on-line book distributors.

Thank you.

Armoury House Publishing
P.O. Box 60
Carleton, MI 48117   USA

No god is like you, O Lord.
No one can do what you do.

Psalm 86:8

GOD'S WORD Translation

www.ingramcontent.com/pod-product-compliance
Lightning Source LLC
Chambersburg PA
CBHW020825030726
47496CB00001B/96